THE BIG PARADE

THE BROADWAY LEGACIES SERIES

Geoffrey Block, Series Editor

Series Board

Tim Carter   Jeffrey Magee
Kara Gardner   Carol J. Oja
Kim Kowalke   Steve Swayne
Dominic McHugh

Stephen Banfield, Emeritus
Larry Starr, Emeritus

THE BIG PARADE

Meredith Willson's Musicals
from *The Music Man* to *1491*

DOMINIC MCHUGH

OXFORD
UNIVERSITY PRESS

OXFORD
UNIVERSITY PRESS

Oxford University Press is a department of the University of Oxford. It furthers
the University's objective of excellence in research, scholarship, and education
by publishing worldwide. Oxford is a registered trade mark of Oxford University
Press in the UK and certain other countries.

Published in the United States of America by Oxford University Press
198 Madison Avenue, New York, NY 10016, United States of America.

© Oxford University Press 2021

CIP data is on file at the Library of Congress.
ISBN 978-0-19-755473-9

DOI: 10.1093/oso/9780197554739.001.0001

3 5 7 9 8 6 4 2
Printed by Sheridan Books, Inc., United States of America

For Cliff Eisen

CONTENTS

• • •

FOREWORD

• • •

The last time I had the honor of writing a Foreword to a book by Dominic McHugh occurred when I introduced his indispensable and path-breaking examination of Alan Jay Lerner and Frederick Loewe's *My Fair Lady* (1956) entitled *Loverly: The Life and Times of "My Fair Lady."* Since *Loverly* appeared in 2012 as the fourth volume in Oxford's Broadway Legacies series, McHugh has more than fulfilled the implications of my reference in that Foreword to Mozart's reported reaction after he first met the sixteen-year-old Beethoven: "Someday he will give the world something to talk about."

Indeed, in the years since his youthful Broadway Legacies debut, Dominic has given us something to talk about. Soon after *Loverly*, he expanded his work on Lerner with richly annotated editions of Lerner's letters (Oxford University Press, 2014) followed by the complete Lerner lyrics (OUP 2018), the latter co-edited with Amy Asch. Other Oxford publications include *The Oxford Handbook of Musical Theatre Screen Adaptations* (2019) and *Adapting "The Wizard of Oz": Musical Versions from Baum to MGM and Beyond* (2019), the latter co-edited with Danielle Birkett. Among future books in the oven is an Oxford *Handbook* on original film musicals and the editorship of a planned new series, Oxford's Guides to Film Musicals. Stay tuned.

As *Show Boat*'s Cap'n Andy liked to say, "That was jest a sample." The above paragraph does not begin to tap the breadth and scope of Dominic's contributions to the field, but it's about time that as series editor of Oxford's Broadway Legacies I introduce the fine book you are about to read, no doubt with great pleasure: *The Big Parade: Meredith Willson's Musicals from "The Music Man" to "1491."* Not surprisingly, the book at hand will focus on *The Music Man* (1957), one of the most beloved musicals of all time. It was also the first musical by Willson (1902–1984), who authored its book and lyrics and composed its music at the advanced age of fifty-five, an age when most creators of musicals are gearing up to produce their final musical theater hurrah.

The Music Man, which arrived a little less than three months after *West Side Story*, initially overshadowed its predecessor, both at the box office and at the Tony Awards. In the years since these two shows made their debut, however, *West Side Story* has rained on Willson's parade when it comes to critical acclaim and historical verdict as a forward-looking musical. But if *The Music Man* seems to look backward, as is appropriate for a soundscape of rural America circa 1912 with its marches and barbershop quartets, it presents the past with impressive originality. Even Stephen Sondheim, *West Side Story*'s young lyricist, acknowledged *The Music Man*'s quality when he praised the catchy "rhythmic chatter" of "Rock Island" as "surely one of the most startling and galvanic openings ever devised," even the "forerunner of rap." Like *West Side Story*, but on its own original terms, *The Music Man* is a musical of considerable artistry and thematic insight with an excellent (and memorable) score.

In his pioneering scholarly study of this show based on extensive archival research, the first to seriously examine a Willson musical, McHugh vividly reveals how *The Music Man* came to be, what the show is about, and what it means. If *The Music Man* is purposefully old-fashioned, Willson's dramatic use of music remains cutting edge, perhaps most movingly when he gives the slick and fraudulent salesman Harold Hill and Marian (the Librarian) Paroo an ingenious variation of the same song to sing, albeit with different lyrics ("Seventy-Six Trombones" for Harold and "Goodnight, My Someone" for Marian), long before we, or they, realize the truth of their emotional as well as musical compatibility. The turning point for Marian occurs when she realizes that Hill's fantasy of a band helps her little brother Winthrop overcome his grief over his deceased father and the social isolation brought about by a speech impediment. Working together, the drama and the music persuasively demonstrate that Harold and Marian bring out the best in one another and that they are destined to be a good match.

McHugh's opening chapter sets the stage by looking at Willson's varied career before he was able to convert his roots in Mason City, Iowa, into the newly imagined River City, a town that's "got trouble" the Music Man plans to solve with a band. In real life, Willson attended Juilliard (then known as the Institute of Musical Art) before joining the John Philip Sousa band on the flute at the age of seventeen and the New York Philharmonic under Arturo Toscanini at twenty-three. Throughout the 1930s, Willson worked as the musical director for numerous live radio shows, including series broadcasts on national radio networks, composing occasional works in the process. In the 1940s, he composed the film scores for Charlie Chaplin's *The Great Dictator* (1940) and *The Little Foxes* (1941), based on Lillian Hellman's play, and received Oscar nominations for both scores. He also published two engrossing autobiographies prior to the premiere of *The Music Man* and a subsequent third volume recounting his experiences writing the show over a prolonged period. Readers of *The Big Parade* will learn in the first chapter how "each of these experiences contributed in some way to the technical or plot details of *The Music Man*."

In his second chapter, McHugh examines the creation of the show's book over the course of six years. In Chapter 3 he discusses the score and Willson's hard-won but ultimately successful efforts to allow "the songs to emanate naturally from the dialogue," a self-critical process that prompted Willson to discard most of the earlier versions of the songs. Chapter 4 explores the reception of *The Music Man* on Broadway and London stages and the merits and infelicities of its two film versions.

In the final three chapters McHugh tells us what we need to know about the lesser-known and less successful musicals that followed. *The Unsinkable Molly Brown* (1960), a fictional account of an actual person named Margaret Brown, whose adventures included surviving the 1912 sinking of the *Titanic*, was a modest Broadway success that ran for over a year. Four years later, MGM produced a financially successful musical film adaption of *Unsinkable* starring Debbie Reynolds, which unfortunately removed two-thirds of Willson's stage score.

Willson's *Here's Love* (1963), adapted from the popular 1947 Christmas movie *Miracle on 34th Street*, lasted only eight months on Broadway. In his discussion of Willson's third musical, McHugh shows how Willson exhibited several striking departures from its film source that remain of considerable interest. Willson's final musical *1491* (1969) centered on Christopher Columbus's preparations for his historic voyage. Despite its intriguing premise, however, the show closed prior to a Broadway run after disappointing brief runs in Los Angeles and San Francisco.

Willson's post–*Music Man* musicals do not enjoy the recognition and praise bestowed on their illustrious predecessor. How could they? Nevertheless, they most definitely merit our attention, which they receive in McHugh's chapters on these shows that offer a penetrating and balanced critique of what worked and what was less successful. In short, Dominic McHugh's *Big Parade* presents a rich, comprehensive, and insightful picture of the four fascinating musicals created by Meredith Willson, a significant and unjustly neglected musical theater practitioner who left an immensely important Broadway legacy.

Geoffrey Block
Series Editor, Broadway Legacies

ACKNOWLEDGMENTS

• • •

As with all my books, this project could not have happened without the remarkable support of my family. I am particularly indebted to my mother for copying much of the material on *The Music Man* during our first visit to Madison, Wisconsin, in 2008, to my father for his careful proofreading, and to my partner, Lawrence, for being there for me always.

The Broadway Legacies series is lucky to have two inspiring leaders, and I have been lucky to work with them both. At Oxford University Press, Norm Hirschy has been a cheerful and efficient guiding hand ever since I first proposed this project in 2009. Series Editor and leader of the field Geoffrey Block has been a constant source of support and encouragement since our first correspondence over a decade ago, and we have been close friends and colleagues since our historic first meeting when he did me the honor of being the keynote speaker at my first conference held in Sheffield in May 2014. I value his friendship more than anything but his close scrutiny of this manuscript is notable here: he made hundreds of comments on it and it's a lot better for it. I'm also grateful for the robust criticism of the two anonymous readers. Nevertheless, any remaining mistakes are all my responsibility. Thanks too to the rest of the team at Oxford, including production editor Melissa Yanuzzi, copyeditor Timothy DeWerff, and, before her retirement, Joellyn Ausanka.

Particular thanks are due to the archivists at the various depositaries where I conducted the archival research for this project. The supportive and knowledgeable Jane Gottlieb at the Juilliard School made many of the musical manuscripts available to me and I'm enormously indebted to Tom Camp of the Willson estate for facilitating all the necessary permissions, including from the music publishers, which has made finishing off the project much easier than it might have been. Thanks too to Richard Brewer for research assistance and to Gil McNaughton for providing me with materials from the Music Man Museum.

The bulk of the research for this book was conducted at The Great American Songbook Foundation's archives at Carmel, Indiana, whose founder Michael Feinstein has been a warm friend to me. His efforts have given me access to the materials I needed and I know nobody more freely generous than him. My first visit to Carmel introduced me to Lisa Lobdell, whose remarkable talents meant that I could access the newly acquired Willson papers within weeks of their arrival at the archive. Lisa has gone on to become a dear and supportive friend to me, and I really value and admire her energy and positivity. I'm also grateful to the rest of the team at the Songbook Foundation, including Chris Lewis and Renée La Schiazza, as well as the amazing team of volunteers, especially Marcia Jansen.

Thanks too to all my friends for their continued love and support.

Single moments in our lives can change the course of them forever, and for me, one of those times was taking an undergraduate course on the Broadway musical when I was a student at King's College London in 2004. I wrote an essay called "Firing the Broadway Canon: A Revaluation of *The Music Man*," and it became my first (albeit unpublished) contribution to Broadway scholarship. Thanks to the inspiring teaching of Professor Cliff Eisen on that course, and in particular his encouragement to see that musical theater studies had the potential to make a rewarding career, I ditched my plans to do a PhD on Verdi and did one under his direction on *My Fair Lady* instead. Since then, Cliff's mentoring, friendship, and general support have kept me going through many difficult times. I certainly wouldn't have become a professor at the age of thirty-five without him, and I'm delighted that we now do our research together. This book is dedicated to him.

THE BIG PARADE

INTRODUCTION

● ● ●

MEREDITH WILLSON'S *THE MUSIC MAN*

The period usually referred to as the Golden Age of the Broadway musical encompasses at least the 1940s and 1950s; for some writers it goes back to the premiere of *Show Boat* in 1927 and perhaps forward to *Fiddler on the Roof* in 1964. Whatever the terminal dates, surely most commentators would agree that it reached a particular peak from 1943 with the first Broadway collaboration of Richard Rodgers and Oscar Hammerstein II, the record-breaking *Oklahoma!*, through to the first performances of Leonard Bernstein, Stephen Sondheim, Arthur Laurents, and Jerome Robbins's *West Side Story* in September 1957.

Those two works are often perceived to be turning points. *Oklahoma!*'s triumphant run on Broadway was followed by further artistic and commercial successes for Rodgers and Hammerstein, including *Carousel* (1945), *South Pacific* (1949), and *The King and I* (1951), as well as others who followed in their footsteps, including the team of Alan Jay Lerner and Frederick Loewe (*Brigadoon*, *My Fair Lady*) and composer-lyricist Frank Loesser (*Guys and Dolls*). The period was characterized by musicals where the drama set the tone for everything else, and with it came a raising of the stakes in all departments, though the musical comedy roots of the Broadway show were still also normally in evidence. Choreographers such as Agnes de Mille and Jerome Robbins crossed from the ballet world to create distinctive dances that expanded the expressive possibilities of movement in Broadway musicals. Opera singers such as Ezio Pinza and Helen Traubel appeared alongside musical comedy actors like Mary Martin and Ethel Merman, while composers like Leonard Bernstein and Kurt Weill with a background in Western art music contributed to the same genre as those of limited traditional musical literacy (if stunning brilliance) such as Irving Berlin.

But accounts of the Golden Age usually see the unleashing of *West Side Story* on New York as the beginning of a new era. Though the composer and choreographer, Bernstein and Robbins, had worked on Broadway several times before, they were joined by a younger lyricist, Stephen Sondheim, and the playwright Arthur Laurents, and together they created a bold reworking of *Romeo and Juliet* set in contemporary Manhattan. Racial tensions and gang warfare on the streets provided a volatile backdrop for the forbidden love of Maria and Tony: a current story set in the environment of the theater in which it was first performed. *West Side Story* became Bernstein's most popular work and introduced Sondheim to Broadway with a bang, revealing the talent of the most influential writer for the

The Big Parade. Dominic McHugh, Oxford University Press. © Oxford University Press 2021.
DOI: 10.1093/oso/9780197554739.003.0001

musical theater after Rodgers and Hammerstein. No wonder the show is seen as the start of a new period.

In this context, where does Meredith Willson sit? As the composer, co-book writer, and lyricist of *The Music Man*, he ought to have an incontestable place in the history of the genre, for that show went on to become the third longest-running Broadway musical of the 1950s (after *My Fair Lady* and *The Sound of Music*): a blockbuster at a time when there was lots of competition from established writers. Numbers such as "Seventy-Six Trombones" and "Till There Was You" were heard everywhere, the last song even covered by The Beatles. It enjoyed rave reviews and won awards. So why is Willson's name so little known, his contribution so seldom celebrated?

One reason may be that *The Music Man* does not fit into traditional narratives of musical theater as a whole. It slightly postdates *West Side Story*—by just two months, but enough to lie beyond that crucial turning point—and the fact that it both outran Bernstein's work and beat it to many of the Tony Awards that season unsettles the way we like to think about that period of Broadway history. Indeed, other vastly successful musical comedies of the years immediately following *West Side*—including *Bye Bye Birdie* and two Pulitzer Prize winners, *Fiorello!* and *How to Succeed in Business without Really Trying*—have similarly been played down or overlooked in histories of Broadway because of their tone and nature. It is as if any work that resisted *West Side*'s pull does not count.

Willson's other problem was the shape of the rest of his career. He was Richard Rodgers's peer in terms of age, but his first show, *The Music Man*, appeared when Rodgers already had over three decades of Broadway and Hollywood musicals behind him. Willson was part of a generation that was coming to the end of its influence on Broadway, yet his debut work was appearing in the same few years as those of the next generation of writers such as Bock and Harnick, Herman, Strouse and Adams, Coleman, Kander and Ebb, and Sondheim. And unlike all of those writers, the rest of his musical theater catalogue was considerably less impactful—in fact, each of his remaining three shows was progressively less successful, both commercially and critically, than the last. Therefore, in his Broadway career he started at the top and gradually declined: no wonder he is a difficult figure to place in the broader picture.

This "in-between-ness" makes him an especially rich topic for study in the Broadway Legacies series, along with the fact that neither *The Music Man* nor Willson's career as a whole has been the subject of a major scholarly monograph before. To be sure, I was lucky to be able to start by reading two independently published biographies by serious journalists with an impressive knowledge of Willson and his times. Both John C. Skipper's *Meredith Willson: The Unsinkable Music Man* (2000) and Bill Oates's *Meredith Willson—America's Music Man* (2005) have a great deal to offer by way of introduction to Willson's life and career, and I could never hope to compete with their extensive knowledge of his family life in Iowa or his background in radio, for example. Nor could I match the depth of scholarly understanding of his orchestral works shown by Valerie A. Austin in her excellent dissertation on the subject, completed in 2008. Insightful shorter studies of aspects of the work, in chapters of monographs by Marian Wilson Kimber (2017) and Raymond Knapp (2006), were also formative for my understanding.

But this book has a different purpose. My intention was to reassess his four musicals within his career trajectory as a whole and in particular to think about how his debut hit paradoxically both facilitated and hindered his Broadway career. Following in the footsteps of other fine writers in the Broadway Legacies series, including Carol Oja (*Bernstein on Broadway*), Julianne Lindberg (*Pal Joey*), Todd Decker (*Show Boat*), and Jeffrey Magee (*Irving Berlin's American Musical Theater*), as well as earlier models by Geoffrey Block (*Richard Rodgers, Enchanted Evenings*), Stephen Banfield (*Sondheim's Broadway Musicals, Jerome Kern*), and Tim Carter (*Oklahoma! The Making of an American Musical*), I combine contextual and analytical approaches with archival research to present an entirely new take on Meredith Willson—one that acknowledges that some of his work is weaker but also examines new sources to show the challenges he faced behind the scenes.

Thanks to the support and guidance of Michael Feinstein, I was the first scholar to be granted access to Willson's papers and manuscripts, which were divided upon the death of his widow Rosemary between the archives at The Great American Songbook Foundation in Carmel, Indiana (curated by Lisa Lobdell), and the Juilliard School in New York (overseen by Jane Gottlieb). The Carmel collection is especially rich in revealing every aspect of his life and career, through documents ranging from letters to draft scripts and from piano-vocal scores to demo recordings. Together, these give a clear picture of his motivations and activities.

In Chapter 1, I give an overview of Willson's career before he hit Broadway at the age of fifty-five. The purpose of this is not to present a biography—the book makes no attempt to fulfill such a task—but rather to outline how, in my view, Willson's approach to writing *The Music Man* was paradigmatic. We are used to hearing how the show is autobiographical, as if it passively emanated from Willson's mere existence, but I contend instead that he actively, deliberately, and cleverly drew on ideas from his life and career. These include his experiences working as a radio arranger, presenter, and conductor; in advertising; as a film composer and musical director; as a writer of popular songs; as a symphonic composer; as a novelist and writer of two books of memoirs; and as a prominent organizer of music for the armed forces during the Second World War. Each of these experiences contributed in some way to the technical or plot details of *The Music Man*, but it is time to give Willson his due for drawing on them in a smart way, rather than continuing the myth that the show simply passed through him into the public sphere without his creativity and intellect.

Then in Chapter 2, I sift through hundreds of pages of draft outlines and scripts to show how difficult it was for Willson to create the musical's book. In the 1950s, Broadway's hits were almost always adaptations of existing sources, but Willson had the unusual challenge of writing an original: what was the show even going to be about? Practically every detail of the book changed from the first surviving draft in February 1954 to the Broadway opening in December 1957, and I give particular attention to Willson's dedication to a storyline about a disabled character that he was persuaded to drop after several years of trying to make the show about the issue of ableism—something on which he was well ahead of the curve.

Chapter 3 uses the rich resources of the Juilliard collection to examine how Willson structured, organized, and composed perhaps the show's greatest asset, its score. I examine Willson's comments about how he wanted the songs to emanate naturally from the dialogue rather than being "dragged" into and out of them. I also take a topical approach to consider different types of songs in the score and look at the sketches for "My White Knight" to show how Willson built up a complex monologue number for Marian Paroo and then dismantled it to create a conventional ballad. I also compare the first draft of the score with the final version and note that most of the songs were discarded along the way—a sign of Willson's sincere and intense self-criticism.

Following this, in Chapter 4 I look at the show's journey from its first previews in Philadelphia to Broadway and London, as well as its two screen versions. I note the challenges of keeping a hit going beyond opening night, as well as the sometimes unexpected stories of some of the people involved. For example, conductor Liza Redfield became the first woman to be the resident musical director of a Broadway musical during the run of *The Music Man*, a landmark that was widely celebrated in the press at the time.

The second half of the book deals with Willson's other three musicals. In Chapter 5, I look at how *The Unsinkable Molly Brown* suffered not only from some generic commonalities with Irving Berlin's *Annie Get Your Gun* but also from being judged in the shadow of *The Music Man*. Willson changed tack in his next show, *Here's Love*, by writing his first adaptation from an existing source, the classic movie *Miracle on 34th Street*; the show is examined in Chapter 6. Finally, in Chapter 7 I address Willson's ill-fated last musical, *1491*, using the wealth of documents in the Carmel collection to bring to life its five-year journey to the stage. *1491* received a critical drubbing and never reached Broadway—a sad end to Willson's twelve-year career in musical theater but not one that should lessen our perception of his unique contribution to Broadway through *The Music Man*.

1

SEEKING THE ROOTS OF
THE MUSIC MAN

● ● ●

MEREDITH WILLSON'S CULTURAL
ECLECTICISM

INTRODUCTION

That Meredith Willson's most successful Broadway musical *The Music Man* has
an autobiographical element scarcely needs to be argued. Many of the episodes,
characters, images, settings, and ideas in the show derive from Willson's childhood in Mason City, Iowa, as described in the first of his three autobiographies,
And There I Stood with My Piccolo (1948). Of note, as well as portraying a
largely idyllic family life, he painted his childhood experiences in the book in
aural terms:

> Sounds stay in your memory longer than anything else, it seems to me. The
> older I get, the clearer I can hear the sounds that were dimensions of the
> world during my first seven or eight years in it back in Mason City. Sounds like
> Mama scraping the burnt toast downstairs while you're hurrying into your
> "ironclad" stockings and your "underwaist"—that little harness affair with all
> the buttons on it. And the particular sound of your front door opening in the
> winter and the screen door slamming in summer, and Papa's derby hitting the
> newel post in the front hall, almost a dead heat with the six o'clock whistle you
> could hear all the way from the roundhouse, and "The Toreador Song" on the
> music box while you had to take your afternoon nap.[1]

He went on to describe "The street sounds" on a Sunday; the sound of his
mother playing "Jerusalem the Golden"; of his neighbor "shoveling off his walk
next door"; the sounds of the different lawn mowers along the street; the "happy
sounds" of "Mr. Hermanson's milk wagon" and the "gloomy sounds" of "Papa's
shaking down the ashes out of the grate down-cellar, reminding you that come
Saturday you have to struggle with them through the back-yard snowdrifts to
the ash pile."[2] By opening his book with these statements, Willson (shown in

The Big Parade. Dominic McHugh, Oxford University Press. © Oxford University Press 2021.
DOI: 10.1093/oso/9780197554739.003.0002

Fig. 1.1. Meredith Willson, ca. 1957. Credit: Photofest.

Fig. 1.1) portrays himself as experiencing life through noises, and it is easy to see how this soundscape became part of his depiction of River City in *The Music Man*. Music more specifically played a central part in his childhood, too, of course. He "hated to practice the piano"[3] and "missed more lessons than [he] took,"[4] but he dreamed of playing in John Philip Sousa's band and so took up the flute.[5] In one passage, he describes how he came upon his father and sister singing in parts, and he spontaneously joined in "on the baritone an octave higher."[6] This is one of many instances in both Willson's prose and stage works where "harmony" has a double meaning, but it also promotes a further connection between his own experience and that of the characters in *The Music Man* (specifically, the members of the school board whom Harold Hill magically transforms into an instant barbershop quartet).

Not only are the thematic parallels between his 1948 memoirs and *The Music Man* obvious, but Willson himself vigorously promoted the autobiographical aspect of the work, such as in an interview in *Time* magazine on December 30, 1957, just eleven days after the musical's opening, when he commented: "I didn't have to make anything up for *The Music Man*. I just had to remember."[7] His third autobiography, *But He Doesn't Know the Territory* (1959), provides his account of writing *The Music Man*, and again he repeatedly reinforces the connections between his life and this work.

Yet there is no doubt that there is more to the musical's development than meets the eye. For one thing, the show's protracted genesis—which, Willson readily admits in *Territory*, took five or six years—reflects the fact that it was not simply a case of remembering. For another, while Willson is rightly credited as composer, lyricist, and book writer of the show, he also had a co-book writer, Franklin Lacey, whose participation, while shadowy, unquestionably had an impact on the project's development and structure, as we shall see in Chapter 2. There are also anachronisms in the musical, such as Hill's reference in the song "Trouble" to *Captain Billy's Whiz Bang*, a magazine that only began circulation in 1919, seven years after the musical is set; obviously, this detail was not a memory from his childhood, or at least not an accurate one.

More important, though, while Willson is principally remembered today for writing *The Music Man*, his name and talent were firmly embedded in American culture before the show's Broadway premiere in 1957. Indeed, *The Music Man* is arguably best seen as a culmination of his activities up to that date, rather than as a debut. In particular, he was familiar from his work on the radio, not only as a conductor but also as a presenter. With the cultural shift to television in the 1950s, he made a reasonably successful transition to the new medium and widened his audience further. Alongside these appearances, he wrote a number of popular songs, such as "You and I" (1941) and "May the Good Lord Bless and Keep You" (1950), thus establishing his talent for writing words and music; and he wrote for Hollywood, including the score for Charlie Chaplin's historic first talking movie *The Great Dictator* (1940). As a composer of concert music, too, he had enjoyed a certain amount of success with two symphonies and several smaller pieces. His early career also brought him into contact with major figures in American music, most notably as a member of both John Philip Sousa's band and the New York Philharmonic during Arturo Toscanini's tenure (a remarkable cultural combination that would typify his career as a whole).

All these experiences were as important to the development of *The Music Man* as the more obvious connections to Willson's childhood in the Midwest, even if the composer himself was keener to emphasize his Mason City background than his other experiences and accomplishments.[8] Indeed, this chapter argues that his professional activities up to the early 1950s acted as a paradigm for the fabric of the show, ranging from plot points to musical ideas. Using a topical approach, the chapter outlines in turn Willson's childhood and education, his activities as a performer of band and symphonic music, a film composer, a writer of popular songs, a radio and television host, and a writer of fiction and memoirs, to set the scene for the discussion of the more "official" beginnings of *The Music Man* as a project in Chapter 2. This chapter particularly aims to demonstrate that while his previous activities had a profound effect on him, they also offered him opportunities and ideas that he could exploit to novel effect in his first musical, an imaginative approach that helps to explain the show's impact and quirky nature.

One strand of the literature on the Broadway musical has focused on how the genre was used by immigrant Jews to assimilate into North American society. Andrea Most, for example, has argued that Rodgers and Hammerstein, among others, chose to write about particular themes—such as the resolution of the long-running feud between the farmers and the cowmen in *Oklahoma!* (1943)— as metaphors for people of different ethnicities joining together in one larger community.[9] Furthermore, Charles Hamm's scholarship demonstrates the shift in Irving Berlin's early work from songs that focused on Jewish identity to those that focused on the American experience, reflecting his assimilation as a writer into a new country (Berlin was born in Russia but moved to North America as a child).[10] Berlin was one of many Jewish artists who changed their names, with other famous examples including George Gershwin, Fred Astaire, and Al Jolson; Betty Comden, Adolph Green, and Jule Styne satirized the trend in their song "Lila Tremaine" from *Fade Out–Fade In* (1964).[11] Roughly half a century after Berlin's first American songs, Bock and Harnick's *Fiddler on the Roof* (1964) turned back the clock and threw a spotlight on the experiences of some of these Jewish immigrants before they were forced to leave their original homes, a topic explored in a recent volume by Alisa Solomon.[12] These and other texts examine the works of Rodgers and Hammerstein, Lerner and Loewe, Kern, Gershwin, Berlin, and others as contributing to an exciting theatrical form that was dominated by Jews.

A well-known exception from this list (in addition to the rootedness of Broadway in Black musical culture) is often cited to prove the rule: Cole Porter, one of the most famous, prolific, and revered writers of the 1930–1960 period, who was born in Peru, Indiana. The relative lack of critical literature on Porter's work means that his relationship to the assimilation narrative of Broadway scholarship in general has not been explored extensively. But in the case of Willson, who was also a WASP born in the Midwest, it seems obvious that his three contributions to Broadway—in addition to *The Music Man*, he wrote *The Unsinkable Molly Brown* (1960, about the survival of the all-American Margaret Brown from the sinking of the *Titanic*) and *Here's Love* (1963, an adaptation of the Christmas movie *Miracle on 34th Street*)—constitute Americana. His fourth musical, *1491*, is less easily situated in this category, but its focus on Christopher Columbus's preparations for his voyage to discover the New World also provides an obvious connection to an important moment in North American history (albeit in a heroic portrayal of Columbus that was out of step with the civil rights movement, as we will see in Chapter 7).

The constructed atmosphere of these stories—most especially *The Music Man*—derives from Willson's description of his childhood in Mason City, Iowa, as noted at the start of this chapter. Yet in truth, all was not as harmonious in his upbringing as Willson sometimes implies. His father, John Willson (1866–1931), studied the law at Notre Dame, while his mother, Rosalie Reiniger (1858–1931), was a qualified teacher. Willson seems to have adored his mother, commenting in his second memoir *Eggs I Have Laid* (1955) that "Everything was Mama's doing. Mama had literally bottomless patience. She also had great wisdom where kids were concerned."[13] By comparison, he feared his father: "Mama was always a person, in addition to being a guy's mother. Too bad that a guy's father generally has to be a big granite institution instead of a person."[14] Of their three children who survived beyond childhood—it is suggested that there were another three, but no sources have emerged to prove or disprove this[15]—Meredith was the youngest. The eldest was a daughter known as Dixie, who was quite an accomplished and successful writer but clashed with Meredith later in life, to the extent that she even accused him of stealing the idea for *The Music Man* from her.[16] However, he maintained a strong bond with his older brother Cedric, as their surviving correspondence proves.[17]

None of Willson's books comments much on his parents' marriage, though it is conspicuous that they are rarely depicted doing things together. Nor does he mention their divorce. Yet as John C. Skipper's biography of Willson reveals, the end of their relationship was extremely bitter. Skipper reproduces a long scathing letter in which John Willson demands a divorce from Rosalie, indicating nothing short of loathing for his wife:

> In the past, you have accused me openly and insinuated that I was every thing mean and crooked. You have misjudged and twisted in crime every act of mine; therein I sought my own kind of companionship, You have never liked the same kind of people or entertainment that I enjoy. Your attitude has been one of bigotry [*sic*] and a determined obstinacy [*sic*] to make me go your way or destroy me. [. . .]
>
> You have always ignored my desire for personal contact and companionship, and your every word and act grates on my nerves until they have become raw and unstrung and are a menace to my health and usefulness [*sic*] in life. Life to me in your company has become simply a hell and not to be endured.[18]

Meredith cannot have been ignorant of these tensions. His father mentions in this document that although he had suffered through the marriage to try to maintain a stable family while the children were young, he was aware that they had become involved: "I regret that the children have had to listen too [*sic*] disagreeable and inharmonious conversations," he comments, "and have naturally acquired a querulous demeanor that will handicap them in life."[19] Decades later, Meredith briefly opened up about the negative side of his father's behavior,[20] but a 1929 letter from father to son, in the form of a poem, indicates that he had at least a passing sense of paternal pride:

> He was a little shaver but 20 years ago.
> He then began to play a flute and my how he did grow.
> He grew to be a fluteist [*sic*] before his pants were long
> and then, by jove, he started in and wrote a pretty song.
> He now is a conductor, but mightily with the wand.
> I think he's just as good as some that came across the "pond."

To Meredith R. Willson, my son, on the occasion of his debut as a conductor of the American Concert Symphony Orchestra of 70 at Seattle, Wash. for Adolph Linden on June 16, 1929. Jno. A. Willson[21]

Despite growing up against the background of his parents' strife, Willson's published recollections of Mason City are chocolate-box nostalgia. Several are of relevance to *The Music Man*. He recalls "all the exciting Wells Fargo Express boxes, like pecans from Uncle B.B., maple sugar from Sears Roebuck, the Flexible Flyer and the post-card projector and the flute from Chicago," laying the foundations for the list-song quality of the "Wells Fargo Wagon" number.[22] In another passage, he describes his old school building, an important setting in the musical: "that magnificent romantic symbol of worldliness and swaggering manhood, that so-phisticated gray stone two-story wonderland, the old original Mason City High School."[23] A further key section eventually provided the backdrop for the events of the second act of the musical: "The biggest event in any kid's life, of course, was the Paine's Fireworks on the last night of the county fair in September. We were always a little bored in the grandstand during the daytime on account of the sulky races, but for some reason Papa always wanted us to see them. Wholesome, I guess. There was, of course, the relief of the band music and the acrobats be-tween heats. And then the final glorious fireworks climax of 'The Last Days of Pompeii' (everybody back home said Pom-pee-eye)."[24]

The book also refers to the pool hall and billiards, which are the focus of the "Trouble" stirred up by Harold Hill;[25] to Beethoven's "Minuet in G," which is the piece that the band struggles through in the show's final scene;[26] the stubborn-ness of the Iowans;[27] the barbershop quartet;[28] the need for a music stand for a marching piccolo player;[29] the marbles that provide one of Hill's strategies to antagonize Marian in "Marian the Librarian";[30] and Willson even closes the last chapter with a comment about the sound of a steam engine that provides a tem-plate for the "Rock Island" opening number of the musical: "If I ever write an-other symphony, I'd like to take a crack at something that would include all the promises of the train whistle and engine shoofing."

That these images became part of *The Music Man* is far from a surprise: Willson was encouraged to write the musical on the basis of his achievement in *And There I Stood with My Piccolo*. On the other hand, it is impressive that he managed to use these elements in a fictional dramatic context without weighing down the show with tediously "researched" detail, even if the stylization and generally idyllic tone of *Piccolo* suggests that the memoir itself cannot be relied upon as a docu-mentary account of the composer's life.

MUSICAL EDUCATION AND LIFE AS A MUSICIAN

Willson's musical training started at an early age, but his talent inevitably led him quickly to outgrow the teachers available to him in Mason City. In her doctoral dissertation on Willson's orchestral works, Valerie A. Austin has explored how the composer picked up not only the piano at the age of six, but also the guitar and mandolin;[31] no wonder he eventually became so adept as a musical director of different genres.

Nonetheless, the flute was to become the instrument that established his career. Typically, Willson accounted for the choice of instrument in terms of whimsy: "Mama had always said, 'After you get so you can play the piano real nice, you must learn to play another instrument so you will stand out among the others [sic] boys when you go to school.' This sounded like a logical start toward Sousa's band, so Mama scraped up the money . . . and we sent away to the Chicago Mail Order House for a flute!"[32] (An alternative version of the story, on the back of a printed song sheet, runs: "He chose the flute because he had never seen one, and he was a very disappointed youngster when it arrived.")[33] Similarly, he explains that he "started to take lessons from a gentleman who actually played the cornet but who managed to stay one lesson ahead of me on the flute."[34] In the summer of 1918, he also enjoyed his first paid job outside of Mason City, when he was hired to play the flute and piccolo in a small band at the holiday resort at Lake Okoboji, roughly 100 miles west of his hometown.[35] For the last week of his tenure, he was asked to conduct the ensemble, anticipating a role that he would later adopt on a national scale.

As a young adult, Willson soon became a serious flute player of respectable professional standing. He left school in 1919, married the first of his three wives, his childhood sweetheart Peggy (they divorced in 1948), and moved to New York City, where his sister Dixie was already established as a writer. As Austin points out, although Willson often claimed the move was motivated solely by his desire to study under Georges Barrère (who was born in France but was the most influential flute player in America at the time), he later admitted he was mainly excited at the prospect of relocating to the big city.[36] Thanks to Barrère's intervention, Willson was able to get several small jobs playing in bands, cinemas, and pit orchestras (the least salubrious of which was in a burlesque house),[37] but of course his lessons with Barrère at the Damrosch Institute of Musical Art were his most impactful experiences in New York. While at the Institute, he also studied harmony and composition with Mortimer Wilson, Bernard Waganaar, and Henry Hadley.[38] The Institute became the Juilliard School of Music in 1946, and in 1990 the Meredith Willson Residence Hall was named in his honor thanks to a gift from his widow, his third wife Rosemary (who had been his secretary before their marriage in 1968).

A good example of where Willson sometimes becomes an unreliable narrator in his memoirs is when modesty overwhelms the facts. For instance, he makes light of the fact that he became first flautist of John Philip Sousa's band at the height of its fame, touring the country for three years. Equally, there is little explanation of the process whereby he became a member of the New York Philharmonic, yet this too is an indication of his comparative eminence, and certainly his ability, in his early twenties. Nevertheless, it is worth considering what these experiences really meant. In the case of Sousa's band, it allowed Willson to encounter one of America's most potent and familiar personalities at the height of his fame. "The March King," as he was known, was the composer of music that became—and has remained—emblematic of national identity, most especially

"The Stars and Stripes Forever," which was named the National March of America in a 1987 Act of Congress.[39] Sousa's march "Semper Fidelis" is closely associated with the United States Marine Corps, of which he was a member and later leader; the title is the Corps' motto. The enduring success of Sousa's marches (of which he wrote over 130) tends to overlook his general accomplishments as a composer; for example, he wrote fifteen operettas. Yet his association with the Marine Band gave his music a patriotic connotation that carried forward into the formation of his own band in the second half of 1892; the group continued for almost forty years, until his death in 1932, and remains the most influential band in the history of American music.

No wonder Willson had such reverence for Sousa—a name he memorably incorporated into the introductory speech leading into the refrain of "Seventy-Six Trombones" in *The Music Man*—and his time in the band is clearly worthy of more than a mere footnote in his biography. Willson describes two particular ways in which Sousa inspired him. First, he says that Sousa helped him to develop his understanding of orchestration, passing on his knowledge as a prolific arranger: "After I joined the band I used to sit on the train every day with a pocket score of the 'Nutcracker Suite' just to make an impression on anyone who happened to walk down the aisle. Actually, I had no idea how to read a score. Mr. Sousa suspected this, I'm sure, as I used to stay on one page entirely too long, but instead of asking me embarrassing questions he slid into my seat one day and started giving me little hints about orchestrating and how he got so he could read a score and all."[40] Willson's three years in the band—in which his brother Cedric also played the bassoon for two years before quitting music to study civil engineering in Kansas and New York[41]—introduced him to many of Sousa's well-respected arrangements of the warhorses of Western art music, including Dukas's *The Sorcerer's Apprentice*, and this paved the way for his decision to join the New York Philharmonic.[42]

Sousa's other great impact on Willson was the opportunity to experience the visceral thrill of being part of a large band under a great leader. Particularly memorable is Willson's description of the annual "grand super concert at Madison Square Garden" that closed each Sousa band season: "[I]t was a tradition among Sousa bandsmen, wherever they might be, to dig out their old Sousa uniforms and show up at that annual concert. We had at least four hundred men in the augmented band the first time I played at the Garden, and when we went down front for 'The Stars and Stripes Forever,' that was it. [. . .] [That] night there were forty trumpets blasting out the melody on one side, we piccolo players in the middle, thirty trombones playing the countermelody on the other side, and twenty drummers in the back with that rolling Sousa rhythm."[43] This is important not simply because Willson wrote a large band into *The Music Man* but, more so, because he recognized the *dramatic* quality that such an ensemble could have in the right kind of number: thus "Seventy-Six Trombones" represents Harold Hill's ultimate aspiration *and* articulates an important structural moment in the musical. (Hill's fantasy is actually played out in the spectacular finale under the closing titles of the movie adaptation, of course—something the Broadway version could not enact.) This is an example of how Willson's absorption of personal experience into *The Music Man* was the result of an active decision to use an idea in a different context rather than merely "passing through" him as a writer.

Eclecticism characterized Willson's entire career, as if he were always hungry for change, and his decision to move on from the Sousa band to the completely different atmosphere of the New York Philharmonic is representative of how he embraced music across the spectrum. When he joined the orchestra as flautist in the second half of 1924, the ensemble was in the middle of a period of change and expansion. It had merged with the National Symphony Orchestra (unrelated to the modern orchestra of the same name) in 1921, began making recordings in 1922, and merged with the New York Symphony Society in 1928.[44] At his first concerts with the orchestra, at Carnegie Hall on October 16 and 17, 1924, Willson is credited as "R. M. Willson"; he retained the initial from his first given name, Robert, for a number of years professionally. The conductor was Willem van Hoogstraten and the program for both concerts consisted of Weber's *Euryanthe* Overture and Respighi's recent *Sinfonia drammatica* in the first half, followed by Mozart's E-flat Symphony, K. 543, and Wagner's Prelude to Act I of *Die Meistersinger* in the second.[45]

Over the next five years, Willson played in dozens of concerts involving some of the most important names in the music business, as well as in a diverse repertoire. For example, he appeared in Igor Stravinsky's first appearances as a conductor in America, on January 8, 9, and 10, 1925. It was an all-Stravinsky program, featuring a wind arrangement of *Song of the Volga Boatmen*, the orchestral works *Fireworks* and *Scherzo Fantastique*, the symphonic poem *Le Chant du Rossignol*, and the *Firebird* and *Pulcinella* suites.[46] Two weeks later, Willson was in the orchestra for two concerts under Wilhelm Furtwängler that included another important Stravinsky work, *The Rite of Spring*,[47] and even played alongside the composer in the concerts of February 5 and 6, when Stravinsky appeared as piano soloist under Willem Mengelberg in his Concerto for Piano and Wind Orchestra.[48] He played in another concert in which Germaine Tailleferre—famously the only woman in the French group of composers known as Les Six—played her recently completed first piano concerto.[49] In the 1925–1926 season, Willson was promoted from third to second chair of the flute section (not their first chair soloist, as Bill Oates asserts),[50] with his first concert in the position including Bach's Second Suite, Strauss's *Don Juan*, and Brahms's Second Symphony.[51] Concerts under important conductors that season in which Willson appeared included two performances of Mahler's Second Symphony under Mengelberg (November 25 and 27, 1925)[52]; several programs led by Arturo Toscanini in January 1926, including the American premiere of Respighi's *Pines of Rome* (January 14);[53] and a performance of one of his favorite pieces, *The Sorcerer's Apprentice*, under Fritz Reiner (April 4, 1926).[54]

In later seasons, Willson played in other concerts involving major performers or significant premieres. Examples include performances with the great Danish-American tenor Lauritz Melchior in extracts from Wagner's *Siegfried* (November 28, 1926)[55] and the American premiere of Szymanowski's Third Symphony (December 16, 1926),[56] performances with the French composer Darius Milhaud featuring the world premiere of his Fantasy for Piano and Orchestra *Le Carnaval d'Aix* with the composer at the keyboard (December 9 and 10, 1926),[57] all-Beethoven concerts under Toscanini (February 1, 2, and 5, 1927),[58] concerts with the cellist Pablo Casals performing the Schumann Concerto under Furtwängler (February 10 and 11, 1927),[59] an all-Wagner program under Mengelberg (November 6, 1927),[60] the American premiere of Béla Bartók as a performer (he played the keyboard part in his own Rhapsody for Piano and Orchestra, Op. 1, December 22 and 23, 1927),[61] and unusual programs including the music of Honegger and Elgar under Toscanini in late January and February 1928.[62]

His final season began with the first performances of American composer Emerson Whithorne's symphonic poem *Fata Morgana* (October 11 and 12, 1928),[63] followed by other significant concerts such as the premiere of Respighi's Toccata for Piano and Orchestra (with the composer as soloist, November 28 and 30, 1928),[64] performances of Brahms's Second Piano Concerto with Vladimir Horowitz as soloist (December 6 and 7, 1928),[65] performances of Gershwin's Concerto in F with the composer at the keyboard (December 17, 1928),[66] and in concerts featuring the young Yehudi Menuhin performing Tchaikovsky's Violin Concerto (December 27 and 28, 1928).[67] He was also featured as flute soloist in a performance of Bach's B Minor Mass at Carnegie Hall under the baton of Albert Stoessel on April 21, 1927.[68] His tenure as a player came to an end at the close of the 1928–1929 season, but he made a return as the composer of a March that opened a concert on July 23, 1929, as part of the Philharmonic's regular open air series at City College's Lewisohn Stadium.[69]

This breathtaking gloss reveals that Willson was active as a professional musician at the highest level during a remarkable period of development and creativity for concert life in New York, performing in premieres and contemporary works with the participation of their composers while also encountering a wide variety of symphonic repertoire under the guidance of some of the world's finest conductors. Willson himself is responsible for underrepresenting the importance of these experiences in his development as a musician, partly because he tends to discuss only the most entertaining and amusing moments in his published memoirs, emphasizing rare moments of ineptitude rather than his general proficiency. Yet these years at the Philharmonic set the scene for his future career not only as a symphonic and film composer but also as an advocate for Western art music as a teacher and broadcaster. Arguably, these experiences of playing the latest avant-garde concert works also provided him with the tools to create the kind of complex harmonic language and forms that he would later develop and exploit in parts of *The Music Man*, most notably in "Marian the Librarian."

THE RADIO YEARS

Willson does not really explain why he left his position with the New York Philharmonic in 1929 to become a musical director for the Seattle radio station KJR, part of Adolph Linden's national American Broadcasting Company (ABC) network, but his enthusiasm is clear: "I was pretty excited about the whole thing," he exclaims.[70] Perhaps the general eclecticism of his career explains his decision to move on: he liked the opportunity to do something different. It must in particular have been appealing to have the chance to conduct a large orchestra with virtuoso players from New York, in the outdoor stadium at the University of Washington.[71] In the event, the venture was a financial disaster, partly due to the bad weather, but later in 1929 he got the opportunity to become concert director for KFRC in San Francisco; he looks rather severe in a profile shot as part of a Christmas message in the *Musical and Theatrical News* dated December 16, 1929, as if concerned to establish his seriousness (in contrast to the folksy persona he would later project).[72] Over the next year or so, Willson would work on programs such as *The Blue Monday Jamboree*, which he describes as "the big show in those days . . . a two-hour clambake every Monday night from eight to ten."[73] Each week of the program was devoted to a profession or industry and would feature a company of actors and orchestra, often performing a specially composed "radio musical" (perhaps his first professional exposure to the musical genre).

In 1930, he joined the rival NBC in San Francisco, the network that would become his professional home for much of the decade.[74] As musical director of the KGO and KPO stations, he appeared on shows such as *Captain Dobbsie's Ship of Joy* (1933), a corny program that featured a forgetful presenter whose real name was Hugh Barrett Dobbs;[75] *The Big Ten* (1934), a program in which Willson programmed the top ten most-played songs of the week according to *Variety* (Willson felt resentful when NBC purloined the idea for a different program called *Lucky Strike Hit Parade*, without crediting or reimbursing him);[76] and *Carefree Carnival* (from 1933), a long-running show in the style of a vaudeville, with regular spots for Willson and His Orchestra, comedians Tim Ryan and Irene Noblette, future TV star Pinky Lee, and host Ray Tollinger[77] (the May 12, 1935, episode can be heard online).[78] He also hosted his own show on NBC's Blue Network from April 22 to June 3, 1935, and again from June 16, 1936 to August 4, 1937.[79] In 1936, Willson moved to Hollywood to be on another NBC program, *The Maxwell House Show Boat*, a popular variety show that was supposedly broadcast from a real show boat but was actually recorded on the Warner Bros. lot.

This program was replaced in November 1937 with *Good News of 1938*, a co-production between NBC, Maxwell House, and MGM that would feature a cavalcade of the movie studio's greatest stars.[80] It was here that Willson became part of the Hollywood crowd, working with big names such as James Stewart, Robert Taylor, Dick Powell, Fanny Brice, Robert Young, Frank Morgan, Mickey Rooney, Alice Faye, and Mary Martin. On the first program alone, on November 4, 1937, there were nineteen stars, including Judy Garland, plus guests such as Louis B. Mayer and Jeanette MacDonald. Willson's input was drawn attention to from the start, as the program began with the announcer declaring: "Maxwell House Coffee presents Good News of 1938! Meredith Willson lights the fuse of the MGM Star Rocket! . . . Through the magic gates with Meredith Willson!"[81] Similarly, the closing speech of the first show mentioned him: "Now the finale! But first, a word about our talented conductor, Meredith Willson, a new member of our family here on the lot, who arranged all the music for this evening's entertainment, and who now leads the entire company in a fitting finale!" Another remarkable program, part of which is available on CD,[82] was devoted to a preview of the songs from *The Wizard of Oz*, two months before the movie's release; Judy Garland and most of the other cast members appeared and performed songs including "Over the Rainbow" (Walter Frisch discusses the broadcast in his landmark book on the song; see Fig. 1.2 for a rehearsal photograph).[83]

All of this experience stood Willson in good stead when in 1942 he became the musical director of the Armed Forces Radio Service, overseeing programs including *Command Performance*, their most prestigious show. This assignment allowed Willson to expand his network of star acquaintances while serving his country, and he describes with obvious pride a Dick Tracy–themed edition of the show (titled "Dick Tracy in B Flat") on February 15, 1945, in which a galaxy of Hollywood's best appeared, including Bing Crosby (Dick Tracy), Dinah Shore (Tess), Judy Garland (Snowflake), Bob Hope (Flat-top), Frank Morgan (Vitamin Flintheart), The Andrews Sisters (The Summer Sisters), Jimmy Durante (the Mole), and Frank Sinatra (Shaky)—the kind of cast normally reserved for a biopic like *Till the Clouds Roll By*, though during the war Hollywood also produced

Fig. 1.2. *The beloved songs from The Wizard of Oz were first heard on the radio show Good News ahead of the movie's premiere in 1939. Shown in rehearsal, clockwise from left: Bert Lahr, Ray Bolger, L. K. Sidney, E. Y. "Yip" Harburg, Meredith Willson, Harry Link, Harold Arlen, Judy Garland.*

patriotic movies featuring a galaxy of stars in cameo appearances (e.g., *Thank Your Lucky Stars*, 1943; *Hollywood Canteen*, 1944). Willson also describes how *Command Performance* presented the first-ever appearance of Crosby and Sinatra together, more than ten years before their celebrated turn in MGM's *High Society* (1956). The "Dick Tracy in B Flat" broadcast is available online and provides a small window into the extensive role played by Hollywood stars in entertaining the troops (Crosby, Hope, and Sinatra regularly appeared on the show).[84] This and many other episodes gave Willson the opportunity to start composing songs for dramatic contexts on a regular basis, and although the programs were usually spoofs, it was a useful training ground for his future Broadway career—further evidence that *And There I Stood with My Piccolo* was not the only reason Willson turned to musical theater.

He was appointed Major Meredith Willson for his service to the Armed Forces Radio. After the war, Willson continued his radio work, but with an important shift: he would now usually appear as a presenter or character in addition to his musical role, allowing him to develop more of a public persona; this would be a vital stepping stone toward *The Music Man*. The project that launched him was *The Burns and Allen Show*, starring George Burns and Gracie Allen. It was a long-running program that was first broadcast under that name in 1936, flipping several times between CBS and NBC before moving to television in 1950. NBC bought the show in 1945 and it went out on the airwaves on September 20, when Willson first appeared. That episode begins with Burns and Allen moving into a new house, signifying their move to a new radio station, and halfway through, Allen (whose character was written as a ditzy housewife) is introduced to their new neighbor, Willson:

> GRACIE: . . . Tell me more about yourself.
> MEREDITH: Well, I was born in Mason City, Iowa.
> GRACIE: Mason City, Iowa! Well, isn't it a small world.
> MEREDITH: You mean?
> GRACIE: Yes—I was born in San Francisco, California . . . right in the same country!
> MEREDITH: You don't say?

Allen then goes on to ask him what he does for a living and he replies:

> MEREDITH: I'm a musician. I play the flute.
> GRACIE: Oh, you poor man. . . . I should think you'd have taken up some better-paying instrument, like the clarinet.
> MEREDITH: But why should the clarinet be better paying than the flute?
> GRACIE: Oh, I don't know. It has so many more holes.
> MEREDITH: Gosh, I never thought of that.[85]

This dialogue not only establishes the function that Willson would play on the show (the butt of many of the jokes), it also initiates Willson's first opportunity to play a regular character on a long-running program. Specifically, he is playing a role called Meredith Willson, yet the dialogue self-evidently does not represent who he really is. Arguably, this established the persona he would expand in *And There I Stood with My Piccolo*, which in turn was the next stepping stone to *The Music Man*.

Willson had a few other important opportunities to appear on the radio. In the summer of 1946, he was invited to fill in for Burns and Allen when they went on holiday, then in the fall he started his own major show, *Sparkle Time*, on CBS. It ran from October 4, 1946 to March 28, 1947, changing its name to *The Ford Music Room* in 1948 following a change of sponsor; it continued until 1953. (The script for one of the later shows can be read on the Songbook Foundation's website.)[86] It mixed music with discussion, thus extending Willson's public profile, but it was more significant for bringing about "The Talking People." Willson thought that rather than having the show interrupted by commercials, they could be incorporated into the program by a small singing group (two women and three men) doing "some unison speaking . . . sort of Greek-chorus style." In *Piccolo*, Willson reproduces an example of a score that he wrote for The Talking People, revealing that the non-pitched rhythms of their speech were indicated in musical meter—an idea that he would reuse a decade later in both the opening "Rock Island" scene and the "Trouble" number from *The Music Man*.

Willson went on to appear on NBC's *The Big Show* with celebrated stage actress Tallulah Bankhead. Launched on November 5, 1950,[87] and running until April 20, 1952, it was an enormously popular program that attracted major stars of the kind he had encountered during the war—figures such as Ethel Merman, Jimmy Durante, Ginger Rogers, Groucho Marx, and Jane Powell appeared over its run (see Fig. 1.3 for a photograph of an episode with Merman). At the end of nearly each show, the guests would each sing a line of Willson's song "May the Good Lord Bless and Keep You,"[88] which became a popular hit in the ensuing years (it was also used by Kate Smith on her television show).[89] The show gave him new opportunities to work with both high-quality singers (the bass Ezio Pinza appeared in one episode) and prominent actors (whose limited singing abilities he often had to accommodate for the "May the Good Lord" finales). It also further developed the prominence of his public persona, because one of the running gags in the show was Bankhead's disdain for Willson's tales of Mason City. This began in the first episode, when Willson appeared about fifty minutes into the show to meet one of the guests, actor José Ferrer, who was there to promote his new film *Cyrano de Bergerac*. After greeting him, Willson comments:

> MEREDITH: Why, Mr. Ferrer, I certainly enjoyed that recitation you just spoke.
> JOSÉ [rolling the "r"]: Re-ci-tation?
> MEREDITH: Yeah, about the fellow with the big nose. It reminded me of a fellow back home. He had a big nose, too. Named Wally Parker.
> JOSÉ: A nose named Wally Parker?
> MEREDITH: Yes. No. His name was Wally Parker. Did you think I meant his nose was named Wally Parker? *His* name was Wally Parker! Ha, ha. How'd you like that, Miss Bankhead? He thought I meant his *nose* was named Wally Parker!
> TALLULAH: Meredith, dear boy, will you go on with your sordid little story?[90]

Fig. 1.3. Willson's contributions to The Big Show as musical director made him a household name in the 1950s. Here he is shown with Tallulah Bankhead and Ethel Merman. Credit: Photofest.

By this point, Mason City and its inhabitants had become one of the leitmotifs of Willson's career, and it seems no coincidence that during the run of *The Big Show*, which made a move to television in October 1952, he would start to think about writing *The Music Man*.

POPULAR SONGS

Willson's years working on commercial radio in the 1930s and for the Armed Forces Radio Service in the 1940s meant he was regularly called upon to produce popular songs at short notice. As already noted, he had enjoyed singing from childhood, and a few manuscripts in the Willson collection at Juilliard suggest he set some of his sister Dixie's lyrics to music, perhaps as a teenager or slightly later.[91] These little songs, each of which is only between eight and sixteen measures in length (i.e., half the length of the standard Tin Pan Alley and Broadway thirty-two-bar song), are inconsequential as pieces of music, but it is intriguing to note the potential for the collaboration between the brother and sister to have gone further. A separate group of manuscripts in the Juilliard collection shows that Dixie and Meredith later wrote a song called "The Moth" together. Both the autograph manuscript and a copyist's score survive, and the latter is in the same hand as his other popular songs from the mid-1940s and early 1950s, when his music was published by Plymouth Music Co.; perhaps he toyed with the idea of writing more extensively with Dixie. Again, "The Moth" is a simple children's song that deliberately eschews sophistication, showing that the composer knew how to serve his audience.

Another group of songs dates from the time of the Second World War and addresses a political purpose. Willson comments on some of these in *Piccolo*, describing how he wrote a song called "My Ten-Ton Baby and Me" for the Office of Defense Transportation, "Gangway, You Rats, Gangway" for the USO, "Yankee Doodle Girl" for the WAC, "Fire Up—Carry On to Victory!" for the Chemical Warfare Service, and "Hit the Leather" for the cavalry.[92] Though he probably hoped for the kind of success that Irving Berlin enjoyed with his patriotic musical *This Is the Army* (1942), Willson cheerfully catalogues the rejection (or rapid decline into obscurity) his list of specialty songs all met, well aware that they were written to serve a purpose—albeit a patriotic one that was hugely important to him—rather than break new ground. Nevertheless, each shows his ability as a songwriter in different ways. "Gangway," for instance, is (appropriately) a march in E flat major, but the second phrase moves boldly into F minor, and the piece features several chromatic chords.[93] By contrast, a wartime version of "Three Blind Mice" dating from 1942 unexpectedly reveals Willson engaging in political satire, with references to Hitler and Mussolini such as "While the pie-eyed piper of Berlin town / Pipes a tune for the Tokyo clown, / Benito's trousers come tumbling down."[94]

Nonetheless, Willson also created several bona fide hits before *The Music Man* took Broadway by storm in 1957. He had managed to get several songs published while establishing his radio career, including writing the lyrics for a quirky number called "My Cavalier," written in collaboration with composer Hugo Riesenfeld (in whose band he played in New York) in 1928, and in 1934 an angst-written piece about the plight of a steel worker called "The Song of Steel" appeared. But the turning point was the creation of "You and I," a simple love song written in 1941. Willson commented: "I wrote the words for this song as well as the music and it turned out to be the only song lyric in captivity that is just one sentence long."[95] The lyric of the refrain is indeed simple in this respect, but a slightly closer inspection of the entire song reveals a clever relationship between verse and refrain. In the verse, the lyric observes that "Poet and musician sing the same old tune / To the sweethearts that come and go," and entreats the listener to let his "intuition / Tell you little things the poet doesn't know." Thus the refrain's basic images, with its simple ending—"So to sweet romance, there is just one answer, / You And I"—are posited as an antithesis to the overelaboration of love poetry and love songs. The musical setting supports this position, with the first phrase underpinned by a circle of fifths and the vocal line set to an uncomplicated foxtrot rhythm.

However, Willson gives it just enough flavor to make the song distinctive: the second phrase employs contrary motion to reach the supertonic (G) minor chord on the words "birds in the trees," lightening into the major for the next words, "sing melodies." The fluency of the counterpoint is attractive, and Willson proves in this little piece that he already had the capacity to balance commercial appeal with musical ingenuity. "You and I" was widely covered by the popular singers of the day, including Bing Crosby and Frank Sinatra (neither of these versions contains the verse, though this was a typical practice at the time).[96] Later in 1941, Willson went on to create a complementary piece, "Two in Love," which his then-wife Peggy was quoted as saying was her favorite of the two.[97] Slightly more generic than its predecessor, the song still features some moments of chromatic interest in the midst of the driving foxtrot movement.

After the success of these two songs, it comes as no surprise that Willson increased his output in this sphere. In addition to the war-themed pieces mentioned earlier, he wrote "Iowa," which was introduced by Crosby on the radio show *Mail Call* in 1944.[98] But it was not until 1950 that Willson produced another major song, for NBC's *The Big Show*, as noted.[99] "May the Good Lord Bless and Keep You" was inspired by his mother's "farewell to her Sunday school class" at the church: "May the Good Lord Bless and keep you till we meet again."[100] In shape, the melody shares something with "Till There Was You"—which Willson also wrote around 1950, under the title "Till I Met You," long before it appeared in *The Music Man*—although "May the Good Lord" is far less sophisticated. The use of melodic sequence helped it to become memorable and therefore popular quickly, and no doubt assisted each week's guests on *The Big Show* to pick it up quickly for their ensemble rendition at the finale. Adding to the hymn-like quality of the lyric, Willson's musical setting frequently gravitates toward the subdominant, loosely but clearly referencing the traditional "Amen" cadence of Western religious music. Around the same time as "May the Good Lord," Willson also wrote "It's Beginning to Look a Lot Like Christmas," which was recorded to popular success by both Perry Como and Bing Crosby in 1951; Willson would later recycle it in his musical *Here's Love* (see Chapter 6).

Two other non-theatrical songs from Willson's pre-Broadway career are worthy of mention. Curiously, they were written within the same twelve-month period as "You and I" and "Two in Love," hinting at the composer's future fame in this area. In collaboration with Charlie Chaplin and Eddie De Lange, he composed "Falling Star" for *The Great Dictator* (a sketch for the melody of "You and I" is at the back of a folder of piano manuscript for themes for *The Great Dictator*, including the "Falling Star" motif, indicating the proximity of the works). The theme, which appears as the "Austerlich" underscoring in the movie, is in Willson's hand in the nineteen extant pages of holograph score for the film in his papers at Carmel, and several of the hallmarks of Willson's mature songwriting style are evident from the music, including an angular melodic shape followed by a rising scale, emphatic use of crotchet triplets, and unexpected chromatic harmonizations among a generally diatonic landscape. Since the song is not sung in the film but is based on a theme heard in the background, it seems likely that the words were written simply so that it could be published as a song (this was not uncommon at the time). For *The Little Foxes* he wrote "Never Feel Too Weary to Pray," an affecting spiritual that is heard four times in the film, as we will see later in this chapter. The lyric, which Willson wrote, refers to "Workin' in the cotton, forgotten."[101]

With the exception of the 1940–1941 period, when he wrote four prominent songs in succession, Willson's early songwriting activities (see Table 1.1) were part of his career as a kind of "portfolio" musician. Given that he was connected in the public consciousness (through his radio presence) with popular song, and had also written the music for two successful films, it is almost surprising that Willson did not make the leap to musicals sooner; in particular, the Hollywood musical might have been a suitable outlet for his approach to song in this period. But it is clear even from this brief analysis of a few of his pre–*Music Man* songs that these experiences of writing for radio, film, and the armed forces were useful for sharpening his tools for Broadway. Learning how to craft music and lyrics into a single unit helped to equip him to serve as both composer and lyricist for his musicals, making him one of the few figures to do so, and without having

Table 1.1. Selection of non-theatrical popular songs by Meredith Willson.

Title	Year of Copyright*
My Cavalier (with Hugo Riesenfeld)	1928
Show Us the Way, Blue Eagle	1933
The Song of Steel	1934
Falling Star (from *The Great Dictator*)	1941
Never Feel Too Weary to Pray (from *The Little Foxes*)	1942
You and I	1943
Two in Love	1946
Gangway, You Rats, Gangway	1947
Mind If I Tell You I Love You?	1949
Iowa	1950
I'd Like a Memory	1951
Gone to Chicago	1953
May the Good Lord Bless and Keep You	1953
And There I Stood with My Piccolo	1953
Till I Met You	1953
I See the Moon	1953
Iowa Fight Song	1953
Easter Time	1953
It's Beginning to Look a Lot Like Christmas	1953
Mother Darling	1953
Mason City, Go	1953

* In some cases, this postdates the year of first performance.

gained a reputation as an effective songwriter he would probably not have been encouraged to write his musical theater masterpiece.

CONCERT MUSIC

At the other end of the cultural spectrum, Willson also composed two symphonies. The first, titled *A Symphony of San Francisco*, was premiered by the San Francisco Symphony Orchestra under the baton of the composer on April 19, 1936, at the city's War Memorial Opera House. A newspaper article of the time, headed "His Score Won Race with Bridge," explained that "Meredith Willson's race with the San Francisco Bay Bridge ended with a victory for the brilliant young Musical Director of NBC's Western Division the other day. . . . Willson was collecting the themes of his symphony on paper while the engineers for the bridge were making their blue prints. While they were making a scale model of the construction he was setting down his preliminary piano sketch. During the months that followed, the NBC Musical Director watched the progress of the bridge while he worked in his office atop the twenty-second floor of NBC's San Francisco studios. Discovering an analogy between the two kinds of creation, he decided to try to finish his task before the bridge-builders finished theirs." He went on to say that the symphony "is an attempt to delineate in music the spiritual personality of San Francisco. . . . [In its final movement, it echoes] the harmonies wrought in steel and concrete across the waters of the San Francisco Bay."[102]

In her doctoral dissertation on Willson's symphonic works, Valerie A. Austin notes that the concert was "a special performance of the San Francisco Symphony Orchestra, a concert to mark the thirtieth anniversary of the great earthquake and subsequent fires, which had nearly leveled the city on April 18th, 1906."[103] The symphony is in late romantic style and written in four movements lasting a total of just over forty minutes, but there are some non-traditional quirks. In particular, Willson adds four saxophones to the instrumentation, in featured roles; for example, they play a stirring chorale theme in the first movement. The work is semi-programmatic; Austin reveals that the second movement "expresses the rebirth of a great city from smouldering ruins and ashes" following the earthquake.[104] It uses and develops a *passacaglia* theme in 4/8 time,[105] then the third and fourth movements run together without a break—the third a lyrical scherzo, the fourth a grand finale in cut common time. Overall, the work is a competent first piece in a large-scale form, with a heavy reliance on triplets and dotted figures that are at times tantalizingly similar to "Marian the Librarian," but as a piece of contemporary symphonic writing it is tame and insignificant; indeed, Willson's debut with the San Francisco Symphony as its youngest conductor to date seems as important an aspect of the occasion.

Austin notes that the work was performed again a year later with the same forces, on April 20, 1937,[106] but it has had little afterlife, other than a recording for the Naxos label by conductor William Stromberg and the Moscow Symphony

Orchestra, released in 2000. On that album it is coupled with Willson's Symphony No. 2 in E minor, *Missions of California*, a work that was premiered by Albert Coates and the Los Angeles Philharmonic on April 4, 1940. This is a slightly less accomplished work than his first symphony, perhaps because it has a similar overall approach and therefore feels less fresh. Again, it is a programmatic piece in four movements or "parts," each of which has a title: "Junipero Serra," honoring a Spanish Franciscan missionary of the same name (1713–1784), who lived in California; "San Juan Bautista," dedicated to the California mission of that name (St. John the Baptist, the "Mission of Music," as Austin points out); "San Juan Capistrano," focusing on the annual arrival and departure of the swallows to and from the San Juan Capistrano mission;[107] and finally "El Camino Real" ("The King's Highway"), which Austin explains is "the name of a series of roads, running along the California coast, which linked together twenty-one Spanish missions."[108]

Although the symphony as a whole is undistinguished, there are three features that Willson would later use in his musical theater works: he quotes Beethoven's "Ode to Joy" theme twice in the second movement, an example of "musical borrowing" that would become a feature of *The Music Man*; he writes a counterpoint to an existing theme given to him by the nuns at San Juan Capistrano, the prominent use of which would recur in several contrapuntal numbers in his Broadway career (e.g., "Pine Cones and Holly Berries" / "It's Beginning to Look a Lot Like Christmas" from *Here's Love*);[109] and in the final movement he uses a chiming motif to mirror the 150 bells that were at one time dotted along the road of El Camino Real, the same kind of imitation device that he would later exploit in songs such as "Seventy-Six Trombones." While neither of Willson's symphonies is significant in the development of the form, the fact that he was able to compose and orchestrate two long, relatively complex pieces of concert music demonstrates a level of musical sophistication and ability that is easy to overlook. Even more important, his musical compositions before *The Music Man* range in genre from the folk-like song "I See the Moon" to two full-length symphonies. This scope explains the mixture of high and low that he brought to his score for *The Music Man*.

WILLSON IN HOLLYWOOD

Although he played for various cinematic entertainments to make money, Willson's professionally significant introduction to the world of film came in 1923, when he encountered Lee De Forest (1873–1961), inventor of the Audion, an amplifying vacuum tube that later made radio detection possible. When Willson met him, De Forest was experimenting in sound film, a process called Phonofilm. In Willson's words, he was paid "to go with my flute to this man's studio every morning and eight o'clock and play scales. . . . I would play scales on my flute hour after hour while this man would record on film. The next day he would play it back and we would listen. There was so much surface noise and static scratching that you couldn't recognize the sound for a flute, but at least you knew you were hearing tones and the pitch was accurate. . . . [That] patient man panned out little grains of golden know-how, and after a few months the scales not only played back as clear as could be, but now you knew it was a flute."[110] John C. Skipper cites a column from the *Mason City Globe-Gazette*, dated November 21, 1923, in which Willson's exploits were reported back to his hometown: "The new success of the phono film on which Dr. Lee deForest, [*sic*] inventor of the audion tube, has been working during the past winter and which is now perfected, is due in part, according in a letter from deForest himself, to the assistance of Meredith Willson. . . . The new process is one by which music or voice is recorded on a motion picture film and which is reproduced when the film is run off. . . . Now that the experiments have been completed and the phono film is a practical reality, deForest expressed his deep appreciation of the former Mason City boy's help."[111] Willson himself notes that "everybody else but [de Forest] got rich on his genius."[112]

In 1929, Willson made the next step in film when he "scored some of the music"[113] for the early sound movie *Peacock Alley* (released in 1930) starring Mae Murray. Willson is not named in the opening credits so it is difficult to assess his contribution, since he may have been part of a team; perhaps he arranged Abner Silver and George Waggner's song "In Dreams You'll Still Belong to Me," which is heard several times, or one of the pieces of background music played diegetically through a radio in the second scene.[114] While working for the same film company, Tiffany-Stahl, he also scored what he describes as "a horrible thing called *The Lost Zeppelin* with Conway Tearle."[115] The film depicts romantic strife against the background of a doomed flight to the South Pole. Again, Willson's role is ambiguous, and Bill Oates complains that the movie "had no mood music to bridge scene changes: an actor entered a room, turned on the radio, and the music started. After a few lines of dialogue, like 'Shall I turn the radio off?' the music went silent until the next need arises."[116] In fact, the film's climactic scene does have non-diegetic musical underscoring, thus saving the effect for the dramatic moment where it might have the most expressive impact, but the predominance of music provided by onscreen cues (a fairly common device in that period of cinema, as Oates admits) is instructive in light of Willson's liberal mixture of diegetic and "book" songs in *The Music Man*.

While these experiences with early sound film certainly provide an intriguing additional context for understanding where Willson may be coming from with his musicals, they are considerably less impressive than the two major Hollywood films on which he served as musical director in the early 1940s. Willson reports that the famous actor-director Charlie Chaplin hired him for *The Great Dictator* (1940) as a result of having heard and admired his Second Symphony. According to Jim Buhler, Willson's contract was signed on July 24, 1940, and he was to act as "musical director, to write, compose, orchestrate, arrange, prepare, rehearse, direct and record, and to supervise the writing, composition, orchestration, arrangement, preparation, rehearsal, direction, recordation and dubbing of, the complete musical score, musical sound track [*sic*] and cue sheet."[117] The contract also stated that any music Willson wrote for the film automatically became Chaplin's property, and as musical director he was expected to act "in employing all musicians, composers, and other necessary personnel, and in securing musical material, all salaries of persons so employed." It was a six-week contract at

$833.33 per week[118] and, unlike most of the rest of the crew, Willson was allocated a solo slide in the opening titles of the film. The composer is unusually candid in his summary of Chaplin, as reported in *And There I Stood with My Piccolo*: "I can't say I see eye to eye with Mr. Chaplin on a lot of things, including his politics, and I think he is a very selfish and in many ways inconsiderate man, but I also think he is a great artist and I will certainly say that it was a real pleasure to watch him day after day and see him tick."[119] Whatever the relationship between the pair, the success of the film speaks for itself. Released in 1940, after the start of the Second World War but before America's formal involvement in it, the movie was a vehicle for Chaplin (as actor, director, writer, and producer) to parody and critique the behavior of Adolf Hitler and Benito Mussolini. Chaplin played the dual roles of the Jewish Barber and the dictator Adenoid Hynkel (an obvious allusion to the German Führer); the Barber lives in the tyranny of Hynkel, but toward the end of the film the two characters are mixed up due to their physical similarity and the Barber addresses the people in an extensive monologue, declaring that there is room for everyone in the world.

The movie's remarkable sense of style, which is entirely thanks to Chaplin's vision and artistry, is reflected in the unusual mixture of comedy, sincerity, mime, romance, political engagement, and sheer entertainment. Particularly notable is the role played by music, and Willson openly admits: "I got the screen credit for *The Great Dictator* music score, but the best parts of it were all Charlie's ideas, like using the *Lohengrin* 'Prelude' in the famous balloon-dance scene."[120] Table 1.2 shows the most important musical moments in the film—there are about forty-five, depending on how one chooses to interpret certain cues—and for the purposes of this volume, certain trends are noticeable. First, as Willson notes, the use of preexisting music as a quotation (a musical "borrowing") is essential to the film. While using classical music on the soundtrack is hardly unique to this movie, in *The Great Dictator* it is (unusually) no mere background effect or musical filler: all the quotations occur in important moments in the film's narrative. Two of them are heard when Hynkel plays snatches of Boccherini and Paderewski on the piano, zany vignettes that are illustrative of the dictator's eccentric behavior; he is also shown posing simultaneously for a portrait and a sculpture in two scenes that each last a matter of seconds.

The other two obvious examples of musical borrowings also happen to be arguably the most important and memorable scenes in the film. Their success is no coincidence, because they feature Chaplin miming to famous pieces of music, with no dialogue, thereby putting him back in the format of silent movie acting in which he had made his name (in fact, *The Great Dictator* was the first movie in which he was heard to speak). As it happens, the two scenes appear back to back in the film, almost halfway through, and with Chaplin first in one role, then the other. Rather than propelling the plot forward, the sequences together act as a kind of interlude (a little like an operatic *intermezzo*) to distill the main characters in a heightened form. The more technical of the two scenes is the Barber's. From the radio in his shop, we hear Brahms's Hungarian Rhapsody No. 5 being introduced, and the Barber proceeds to shave a customer, exactly timed to the

Table 1.2. Overview of musical cues in *The Great Dictator* (1940).

Time	Cue/Description
0.00.13–0:02:03	Opening titles: fanfare and string theme.
0.13:06–0:13:27	Spring in Tomainia: romantic violin theme.
0.14:11–0.15:06	Richly orchestrated dramatic music under a montage of newspaper headlines.
0.20.38–0:23:27	Marching band music after Hynkel's speech.
0.23:37–0.23:57	Violin theme to underscore Hynkel's plans to persecute the Jews.
0:25:15–0:25:25	Hannah appears: lyrical string theme.
0:25:40–0:25:49	Hannah wanders down the street: promenade music.
0:25:53–0:26:09	The stormtroopers are heard singing their anthem. Diegetic.
0:27:08–0:27:41	"Lamentation" theme as Hannah sits in shock after the storm troopers' attack.
0.28:20–0:29:43	Barber walks down the street. Surrying theme (strings/bassoon). Mime. Music turns eerie when Chaplin sees the cobwebs on the sink.
0:29:46–0.31:55	Outside the shop, the storm troopers are painting "JEW" on the windows: brass theme. Gestural/imitative music. Turns into a fairground waltz theme and then develops into a fuller waltz. Hannah smashes her frying pan on a soldier's head on the downbeat of the music.
0.33:13–0.34:07	Hannah tells Barber they should all fight back against Hynkel's men: romantic theme in the strings.
0.34:38–0.35:18	The stormtroopers arrive and catch Chaplin: chase music.
0.37:21–0.38:17	Hynkel's palace: marching band music.
0:39:05–0:39:23	Hynkel plays the piano: Boccherini's String Quintet in E, Minuet. Diegetic.
0:39:40–0:39:43	Bugle call. Diegetic.
0:39:54–0:40:07	Hynkel grabs his secretary: mysterious music.
0:43:58–0:44:48	In the barbershop, Jaeckel tells the Barber to "fix up the women" because the men are in concentration camps: klezmer music.
0:47:01–0:47:05	Hannah hums. Diegetic.
0:47:36–0:48:07	After the Barber has groomed her hair and face, Hannah looks at herself in the mirror: shimmering string theme.
0.48:27–0:49:15	The stormtroopers—now benevolent—help Hannah to pick up the potatoes she has dropped and they greet the Barber: the same theme is heard again.

Continued

Table 1.2. Continued

Time	Cue/Description
0:53:03–0:53:12	Hynkel skips across the room and climbs up the curtain: cartoon-like music, with string pizzicato and a "cuckoo" theme.
0:53:26–0:55-58	The globe scene: Hynkel contemplates the globe then bounces it around the room like a balloon. Wagner's Prelude to Act I of *Lohengrin*.
0:56:01–0:57:55	As Brahms's Hungarian Dance No. 5 is heard on the radio, the Barber shaves a customer in time to the music. Notably mimetic. Diegetic.
0.58:34–0:59:26	Jaeckel and Mann are playing chess: klezmer music.
1:02:39–1.03:34	Fade from Hynkel to the Barber, who walks down the avenue with Hannah: promenade music. Interrupted by Hynkel's speech through the speakers.
1:05:26–1:06:26	The troops are heard singing in the distance. Diegetic.
1:07:06–1:07:18	The singing resumes. Diegetic.
1:08:48–1:08:53	The singing resumes. Diegetic.
1:08:55–1:09:40	As Hannah and the Barber watch the building burn, the romantic string theme returns.
1:09:51–1:10.05	Hynkel plays the piano (Paderewski's *Humoresques de concert*, Menuet). Diegetic.
1:10:07–1:10:36	Back on the roof, Hannah and the Barber continue their conversation. Klezmer music.
1:13:18–1:17:06	The puddings are passed around in the basement. Mimetic. Minor key eerie music. No dialogue.
1:21:17–1:22:02	The Barber and Schultz try to make their escape: chase music.
1:22:43–1:23:37	Newspaper montage; Schultz and Barber in prison. Turbulent orchestral music with cymbal crashes segues to a minor-key martial theme.
1:23:37–1:25:26	Osterlich: the Jewish characters on the road; pastoral scene, with fields; Hannah writes a letter to the Barber in prison. Romantic theme ("Falling Star") interrupted by a fanfare.
1:29:47–1:30:33	At the train station, Napaloni arrives. Marching band music: diegetic.
1:32:49–1:33:37	Welcome to Napaloni by the public. Marching band music: diegetic.
1:35:12–1:35:14	Bugle call arrives the entrance of Napaloni.
1:39:18–1:39:47	Military display at the stadium: marching band music. Diegetic.

Table 1.2. *Continued*

Time	Cue/Description
1:41:01–1:44:14	Waltz music at the ball: diegetic.
1:48:25–1:48:58	The waltz music resumes: diegetic.
1:53:43–1:55:58	Montage of newspaper headlines: grand theme, followed by drumbeat.
1:56:01–1:56:33	Drum beat to accompany Barber (as Hynkel) climbing onto platform.
1:58:23–1:59:09	Return of the romantic theme as Chaplin climbs the steps to give his speech.
2:02:53–2:05:13	The return of the *Lohengrin* music as the Barber remembers Hannah, who is shown in the fields.

music (a process that Willson describes in *Piccolo*).[121] It is a master class in what would later be known as "Mickey Mousing": Chaplin creates a physical gesture for every musical gesture, responding sensitively to the changes in speed and melodic shape of the music. The scene is perhaps the most entertaining in the film, but the one before it is more directly important to the theme of the movie. Here, Hynkel contemplates a globe after Garbitsch, his Secretary of the Interior (a parody of Goebbels), has suggested he should take over the world. Set to a performance of part of the Prelude to Wagner's *Lohengrin*, Chaplin dances around the room with the globe, which turns out to be a balloon, and the ease with which he manipulates it (that is, until it bursts at the climax of the sequence) reflects the dictator's irrational belief that it will be easy to become dictator of the entire planet. The use of Wagner's music is unsettling on several levels, its richness compared to the rest of the movie's score standing out; the reference to Hitler's well-known preference for Wagner is chilling, made all the more so by the absurdly comic scene it plays out against.[122]

It would be a mistake to draw facile comparisons between *The Great Dictator* and *The Music Man*, especially since Willson's exact role in creating the music for the movie is unclear and he never commented on a connection between the two works. Yet it is curious to observe several aspects of *Dictator* that may have provided Willson with a blueprint for parts of *Music Man*. The coordination of physical actions and music (the "Mickey Mousing") is at the heart of why the "Rock Island" opening number to the show works so well, with its synchronization of steam, whistle, and engine noises, and for that matter the scene in *Dictator* in which Napaloni (a parody of Mussolini) arrives on a train that makes an awkward entrance into the station is not dissimilar in parts to what makes Willson's train scene in *The Music Man* so amusing. The composer's score for his show also features several instances of explicit musical quotation, most obviously Beethoven's Minuet in G, Christian Sinding's *Rustle of Spring*, and the patriotic song "Columbia, the Gem of the Ocean," to an extent that is uncommon for a Broadway musical. That *Dictator* and *Music Man* both make extensive use of marching bands is probably irrelevant, given the completely different contexts and political contexts, though it provides another link. Similarly, the use of a mixture of diegetic and non-diegetic music (respectively, music that happens as part of [diegetic] and outside [non-diegetic] the narrative of the film) is hardly unique to these works, but this mixture is vital to the success and sophistication of both projects. In summary, it is easy to believe Willson's open admiration for Chaplin's imagination and abilities led to his choosing to employ aspects of the great film maker's ideas in his own work, even if he did so flexibly and in ways that made them his own.

Willson's other major movie as musical director, *The Little Foxes* (1941), is also important and impressive but completely different in tone and style. Lillian Hellman's play of the same name had opened on Broadway on February 5, 1939, and was a triumph for its leading actress, Tallulah Bankhead. The story follows a Southern family in the early 1900s as they plot to acquire the inheritance of the dying Horace Giddens so that his wife Regina (played by Bankhead in the play) can contribute to her two brothers' scheme to open a cotton mill. The film version was produced by Samuel Goldwyn, with Bette Davis as Regina and direction by William Wyler, and Willson was called upon to write and oversee the music.[123] He is surprisingly dismissive of the project in *Piccolo*: "I didn't want to do the music for it. . . . [I]t was an interesting experience which, like the Army, I am glad to have behind me," he remarked.[124] Yet, rather like *The Great Dictator*, Willson's contribution to the film helps to create new contexts for understanding his later musical theater work.

Of particular note is the spiritual that Willson wrote for the movie, "Never Feel Too Weary to Pray." While *The Music Man* might reasonably be said to usualize whiteness rather than racial diversity, this song makes a significant impact on the way in which racial difference is made present in *The Little Foxes* to a degree that is not the case in the play. The Black characters in the film perform stereotypically marginal roles as servants or manual workers, but the addition of "Never Feel Too Weary" over the opening credits and end titles frames the movie with a musically potent reminder of how the (unseen) cotton mill at the heart of the protracted argument between the siblings relies on the labor of African Americans. Willson was proud of the song (he credits himself for using them over the end titles) and it certainly gives some representation (albeit, importantly, without agency) of Black characters who would otherwise have been silent in a movie that mostly revolves around the ruthless avarice of white businesspeople who exploit and depend on them. The piece is also briefly heard in the opening sequence of the action and at 0:55:39, when the journalist David—listening to the singing in the garden—remarks to the teenage Alexandra: "Well, the white people may have the pianos but the colored folks have got the voices." Alexandra looks startled at his admiration for Black people.

Elsewhere in the film there are moments of interest, too (see Table 1.3). It marks yet another occasion where a movie scored by Willson contains significant use of music within the narrative, not only in the two snatches of "Never

Table 1.3. Overview of musical cues in *The Little Foxes* (1941).

Time	Cue/Description
0:00:15–0:00:13	Opening Titles, featuring the song "Never Feel Too Weary to Pray."
0:01:14–0:01:57	The song continues under the narrative titles, which establish the setting of the film.
0:01:58–0:05:11	Establishing shots of the landscape of the film, with African Americans at work, one of whom briefly sings "Never Feel Too Weary" (diegetic). Alexandra and her maid Addie are seen in a horse and carriage, with generic "horse clopping" music underneath. The music develops through various themes to illustrate the action.
0:05:12–0:05:32	Inside the house, Aunt Birdie plays the piano (diegetic).
0:07:48–0:08:43	The men leave the table and there is a dissolve to David's house. A romantic theme alternates with pizzicato "walking music."
0:09:03–0:10:53	Mr. Venn exits his house; lyrical music plays until a dissolve to Regina in her garden, accompanied by a pastoral theme (solo violin + orchestra).
0:14:00–0:15:37	Alexandra and Birdie play a piano duet (diegetic).
0:28:03–0:30:10	Chord in the woodwind as the lights go out; dissolve to the next day, where Alex and Addie are in a horse and trap. Generic springtime music: strings and harp with woodwind comments. Scurrying music as the carriage draws off. A train bell is heard (diegetic) as the music fades.
0:31:02–0:32:21	Semi-comical string theme as David leaves the station. Perfect cadence in strings to end scene.
0:31:55–0:32:24	Regina lifts a photograph of Alexandra and a low string melody is heard; mysterious to reflect Regina's thoughts.
0:34:14–0:35:23	Diegetic music is heard (piano and violin) as Alexandra signs into the hotel.
0:36:01–0:38:35	A piano ascending scale as Alexandra runs off, into a more expansive theme in the strings, with fragmentary gestures to reflect her confusion.
0:38:57–0:39:27	Alexandra and David walk to her room; generic background music.
0:55:39–0:56:25	The African American workers are heard singing "Never Feel Too Weary To Pray" in the background (diegetic).
1:09:09–1:09:42	Birdie plays the piano (diegetic).
1:09:43–1:12:04	Orchestral music (generic pastoral theme in the strings) underscores scene with Horace in the garden.

Continued

Table 1.3. Continued

Time	Cue/Description
1:14:55–1:17:26	Birdie reveals she does not like her son or husband; anguished theme, thick string writing to end of scene.
1:33:30–1:34:54	Horace needs his medication and Regina does not help. Pedal note in the orchestra indicates Horace's strain as he attempts to climb the stairs, with harp glissandi and occasional comments from woodwind and cello. Music swells when Regina suddenly cries for help.
1:36:10–1:36:39	High strings underscore a religious tone as Alexandra approaches Dr. Sloan at her father's deathbed.
1:43:45–1:45:30	Regina, Alex and the doctor at Horace's deathbed: elegiac music plays in the background; there is silence as Horace breathes his last, followed by a sustained chord in the orchestra.
1:47:07–1:48:08	String tremolo when Regina informs the perpetrators that she intends to go to the judge and turn them in if they do not do as she demands. Music swells as Alexandra enters.
1:53:33–1:55:34	When Regina reaches the top of the stairs, organ music is heard as she is reminded of Horace's dead body in his bedroom; a string tremolo and general melodramatic music is heard when Regina sees David and Alexandra through the window. There are tears in her eyes.
1:55:34–1:56:05	End titles: "Never Feel Too Weary to Pray."

Feel Too Weary" that are heard within the body of the film but also in several other scenes. Near the start of the film, Alexandra is taught to play a piano duet by her Aunt Birdie—a tantalizing but coincidental foreshadowing of the piano lesson scene from *The Music Man* that at least shows that he had seen such a dramatic concept at work—and they later play the piece in the dinner scene. Birdie plays a solo later in the film, and when Alexandra goes to visit her sick father, diegetic music is played in the hotel foyer to create the atmosphere of a public space. As a whole, the film contains fewer cues than *The Great Dictator*, but it is frequently used expressively and there are even spots where there is a direct coordination between the score and the onscreen action. For example, during the scene depicting Horace's deathbed, the music pauses for a second so that his last breath can be heard audibly, acting almost as a musical sound, on the beat, before the score continues. There is a similar moment when Alexandra has boarded the train to visit her father and the music coordinates with her body and facial expressions to amplify her thoughts. Willson may not have wanted to draw

Fig. 1.4. *By the mid-1940s, Willson was an experienced figure in Hollywood. Here shown in 1946, seated from left: Franz Waxman, Dimitri Tiomkin, Meredith Willson, Bramwell Coles, Earl Lawrence, William Grant Still; standing, from left: Abe Meyer, Leith Stevens, William Broughton, Anthony Collins, Johnny Green, Miklos Rozsa. Credit: Photofest.*

attention to *The Little Foxes* in his memoir but it was obviously another opportunity for him to learn more about how music and drama can interact to interesting and powerful effect, and helped to establish him as a respected artist in Hollywood (as shown in Fig. 1.4, where he is seated among the finest Hollywood composers of the day).

WILLSON THE AUTHOR

Even before Willson hit Hollywood in the late 1920s, his sister Dixie had already been involved in the writing of four silent movies, including *The Age of Desire* (1923) and *Three-Ring Marriage* (1928), all of them now apparently lost. The films were adaptations of novels or short stories she had written and are just a handful of the several dozen prose works she published in her lifetime. She was especially fond of writing children's stories, such as the now out-of-copyright *Pinky Pup and the Empty Elephant* (1922), a digitized version of which can be freely viewed online.[125] Dixie also worked for Meredith for a time to suggest material for some of his radio shows, mostly consisting of jokes, limericks, and brief scenarios, thirteen folders of which have survived in Willson's papers at Carmel. One reads:

> We know a young lady named Lize
> Who's very resourceful and wise,
> She saves gallons of ink . . .
> And *how*, do you think?
> Why, just by not dotting her i's![126]

She would later threaten to make a legal claim on the concept of *The Music Man*, as we shall see.

Not to be outdone by Dixie's efforts as a writer, Willson added to his portfolio of professional activities by publishing several prose works before his first musical appeared on Broadway. The first, *What Every Young Musician Should Know: A Concise and Modern Volume Revealing the Inside of Radio Musical Technique*, was a pamphlet published in 1938 by Robbins Music Corporation. Willson's foreword to the publication sets out its aims:

> There are available so many fine textbooks relative to harmony, theory, counterpoint, composition, arranging, et al, that it would seem that any book of mine, embracing any of these subjects, would be (apologies to Ring Lardner) carrying coal to New Castle, Pennsylvania. However, the youthful American mind sometimes finds it difficult to absorb from a textbook the answers to certain practical problems of today's music, such as:
>
> How can you make a printed arrangement sound like a special? What are some simple rules for segueing from one chorus to another? With the modern instrumentation consisting so largely of brass, how can the strings be used most effectively to blend with saxophones, trumpets and trombones? How do you write a drum part? What are the signs used in a radio studio? What are the definitions of some of the new musical terms which have been born in the popular orchestras of the day?[127]

In forty-four concise but lively pages, Willson answers these and many other questions for the benefit of his imagined audience. It is difficult to know how many readers or how much influence the publication had, but it marks a step in the direction of influencing music education that Willson was later to pursue (and which he glamorizes in the figure of Marian Paroo).

His next book, *And There I Stood with My Piccolo*, was published in 1948, the year of his marriage to his second wife, opera singer Ralina "Rini" Zarova (who later recorded the score of *The Music Man* with Willson at the piano).[128] Upon its release, the book seems to have been warmly received; for instance, a column in the *Los Angeles Times* commented that it "is distinguished for the same charm, sincerity, and unpretentiousness that make his radio program such delightful and unique entertainment."[129] But John Webster Spargo in the *Chicago Daily Tribune* latched on to a perceptive point when it described the book as "a genially haphazard bundle of familiar essays. The familiar essay tends to reveal more about the writer than about the subjects discussed, and in this case the writer turns out to be unusually good company, always gently urbane and tolerant, never bitterly sarcastic. He knows and likes everybody who is anybody in music."[130] As Spargo astutely highlights, Willson's purpose in the book seems as much to be about projecting a public persona of geniality as it does to be about reliably recording his personal and professional reminiscences. The result has perhaps been that his accomplishments and sophistication have been underappreciated, influenced by his own largely whimsical and self-effacing accounts of his pre-Broadway work. This is further the case in the follow-up volume, the even more entertaining (but long out-of-print) *Eggs I Have Laid* (1955), where almost every page is filled with anecdotes of mishaps he has been responsible for. The reviewer in the *New York Times* noted that in the book, Willson "always seems to be working and commanding an audience,"[131] again revealing the self-conscious charm with which Willson writes about his experiences. Whatever one's attitude toward that, both books of memoirs represented the development of Willson's persona that would pave the way for his Broadway career—indeed, he mentions his plans for *The Music Man* in *Eggs*, which was published two years before the show's premiere.[132]

Willson also made a brief foray into the world of fiction with his only novel, *Who Did What to Fedalia?*, published in 1952. The plot, succinctly summarized by Gilbert Millstein in the *New York Times*, is disconcerting to say the least: "*Who Did What to Fedalia?* is a mildly baffling story about a young girl named Fedalia Parker. Inflamed by a private success on an autoharp and the belief of her plainly unbalanced father that she can sing, Fedalia leaves Fort Madison, Iowa, for New York and a career. She meets up with a collection of characters ranging from preposterous to incredible, including an uncle right out of Krafft-Ebing, who is finally carted off to the booby hatch; displays an innocence that is monstrous in its own right; discovers she can't sing, and gets back to Fort Madison, where, it is evident, she is going to marry a childhood sweetheart."[133]

Although the character of Fedalia has charm, the behavior of nearly every male character in the novel (which is set in the 1920s) is so predatory that the overall effect is creepy, which seems to be Willson's intention. It is easy to sympathize with Millstein's critical summary when he concluded his review: "The entire proceeding made at least one reader uncomfortable." Yet even here we can see explicit seeds of the development of *The Music Man*: not only did the novel give Willson the opportunity to experiment with structure and characterization for the first time, he also included words and phrases attached to the Iowan characters from the outer chapters of the novel that would be reused five years later in his Broadway hit, such as "Great Honk" and "Iowa stubbornness."[134] He even managed to weave in a discussion of his mentor Sousa's *Semper Fidelis*,[135] two passages about writing the lyrics to a song called "Ev'ry Day" (which almost matches the lyric of one of Willson's songs),[136] and a piano lesson.[137]

CONCLUSION: TOWARD BROADWAY

In several passages of *Who Did What to Fedalia?*, Willson has Fedalia or her father repeat her mother's favorite motto, promoting a single focus in life: "A division of interest is weakening."[138] But as we have seen in this chapter, Willson himself believed nothing of the sort. Far from pursuing one interest or profession to the highest level, he displayed an agility in moving between America's greatest band and symphony orchestra and from one important radio network to another, in composing popular and classical music, and in writing fictional, educational, and autobiographical prose works. We might accuse him of being, like Noël Coward, a jack of all trades and master of none, except that he was genuinely a virtuoso flautist, exceptional musical director, high skilled composer of film music, and popular writer. Although the advent of rock and roll eventually muted his ability to write in the popular vein, he had an eclectic range of abilities, a musical sophistication combined with the common touch, the ability to tell a story, and an increasing visibility in the media.

It is no wonder that the composer Frank Loesser, and Ernest Martin and Cy Feuer, producers of Loesser's hit musical *Guys and Dolls* (1950), all approached Willson with the idea that he should write a Broadway show combining his talents and experiences. The idea was commercial, but despite his many previous career moves, the forty-nine-year-old Willson was unsure whether this one would suit him. So it was that he sat down in 1951 to write a musical—"not, of course, to show these people that I could write a musical comedy but to show them I could not," he declared. "And for the next six years I was way out in front."[139]

2

FROM *THE SILVER TRIANGLE* TO *THE MUSIC MAN*

• • •

CREATING THE BOOK FOR
AN ORIGINAL MUSICAL

In the years following the opening of *The Music Man* on December 19, 1957, Meredith Willson provided several public accounts of how he wrote the show. These range from his book *But He Doesn't Know the Territory* (1959) to his album *And Then I Wrote The Music Man* (1959), as well as numerous interviews and a few self-authored articles. As we have seen, to an extent *And There I Stood with My Piccolo* (1948) provides a foundation for the musical's atmosphere and some of its content, and Willson's experience from his other professional activities helped to shape the piece too, though the show is obviously not simply a musical autobiography. A few other details about the evolution of *The Music Man* can be gleaned from his second memoir *Eggs I Have Laid* (1955), written when Willson thought he was on the brink of having the work produced, and articles in the *New York Times* (and other newspapers and entertainment periodicals) give brief glimpses into the show's slow progress.

Correspondence and other documents from producer Kermit Bloomgarden's papers at the Wisconsin Historical Society also provide insights into the development of the production, though these are mostly restricted to the seven months leading up to its premiere and are not extensive in quantity. Director Morton Da Costa's papers add certain other details, but correspondence on *The Music Man* is the one major gap in the Willson collection at Carmel, Indiana: it seems this portion of the sources was removed at a much earlier date, and is now lost or destroyed. Crucially too, the papers of producers Cy Feuer and Ernest Martin, who developed the musical with Willson for several years before abandoning it, are not currently available in a public archive. Therefore, it is difficult to document the month-by-month progress of the business side of the production.

On the other hand, there is a wealth of material on the development of the script, including early synopses and character studies. In particular, when the Carmel materials are combined with the various versions of the script in the Bloomgarden papers, it is possible to gain an unusually rich overview of Willson's

The Big Parade. Dominic McHugh, Oxford University Press. © Oxford University Press 2021.
DOI: 10.1093/oso/9780197554739.003.0003

evolving ideas and priorities as he developed the book. This chapter adopts a top-ical approach to explore major ideas in the draft and final scripts and synopses, which indicate the kind of show that Willson was trying to write as well as the problems he was facing; some of these problems were structural, because he had no experience of writing a large-scale dramatic work, and some of them involved characterization.

A key issue throughout these documents is the fact that *The Music Man* is an original, not an adaptation of an existing literary, theatrical, or filmic property, and therefore everything had to be invented from scratch. The chapter looks particu-larly at the initial ideas for the plot and elements of the story that were later aban-doned, and examines the evolution of major themes and characters. The chapter also briefly touches on the question of the possible influence of three other fig-ures on the script: Willson's sister Dixie, who contributed some initial ideas; Ernest [Ernie] Martin, who intended to co-produce the show before dropping it in January 1956; and Franklin Lacey, who is formally credited as a co-author on the book but the nature of whose input has long been unclear. Together with Chapter 3, which explores the score and musical sources, this chapter examines Willson's work on *The Music Man* before looking at its reception and performance history in Chapter 4.

SOURCES

Exactly when and how Willson came to start work on his first Broadway musical, which was initially called *The Silver Triangle*, is difficult to pin down. There is an absence of documentary insight due to a lack of correspondence in his papers on the period before the opening of *The Music Man* on Broadway, yet the seeds of the show had obviously been sown much earlier in ways he may not have realized at the time. As noted in Chapter 1, the most direct inspiration for the musical was his memoir *And There I Stood with My Piccolo* (1948), and both specific details and the broad landscape of his description of growing up in the Midwest had a direct impact on *The Music Man*. In addition, his earlier attempts at songwriting served as a kind of apprenticeship for writing the score, and the song "Till I Met You" (written and first recorded in 1950) even made it into the final score with a re-vised lyric ("Till There Was You"). Willson himself credits the combined success of *Piccolo* and his song "May the Good Lord Bless and Keep You" (1950) for giving him the confidence to embark on a musical, and also reports that his producer friends Cy Feuer and Ernie Martin approached him in 1951 about writing a musical in-spired by his memoir.[1] At around the same time, he describes how songwriter Frank Loesser, another friend from Willson's Hollywood days, also suggested he should write a musical. Feuer and Martin had come to prominence producing Loesser's *Where's Charley?* (1948) and *Guys and Dolls* (1950), so Willson's claim that these two suggestions were separate but simultaneous appears coincidental, but there are no sources to confirm or contextualize it.

What does seem convincing in his account is that he did nothing about the idea for roughly three years,[2] because he was busy on radio and television in this period, as well as publishing *Who Did What to Fedalia?* In 1953 he suddenly submitted over eighty compositions for copyright.[3] Not all of these were songs, but it is obvious that Willson was staking his claim on the back catalogue of musical numbers he had created for his radio work. In 1954 he added over a dozen more. Between these two sets of songs, it is clear that work on *The Music Man* was underway: "The Blue Ridge Mountains of North Carolina" (1953), "Mother Darlin'" (1953), "Blow" (1954), and "I Want to Go to Chicago" (1954) appear in several versions of the script; "The Wonderful Plan" (1954) was in the show until late 1957; and "Gary, Indiana" (1954) became one of the hits of the score. Oddly, most of the earliest script-related material in the Willson papers at Carmel dates from 1954 and 1955, including character outlines, several different synopses, and discarded script fragments, which may mean that Willson worked on the score before writing a full draft of the book. Perhaps this is why he struggled to make the show cohere.

The Carmel collection contains four complete draft scripts, the last of which is marked "c. Oct. 1956" in Willson's hand but the exact date of which is unclear. Similarly, the material from the Bloomgarden Papers starts with a script labeled in the finding aid "pre-June 1956" but the document itself is undated (most of the other typescripts have dates typed at the top of every page). There are a further seven versions of the script charting its development up to rehearsals in September 1957, but sadly Willson's working scripts from the pre-Broadway tryouts are lost. Nevertheless, this is an unusually fertile and illuminating body of sources, with a total of twelve complete scripts and various complementary documents charting the show's development as definitely starting from at least February 1954, with regular (often monthly) updates. The main materials are summarized in Table 2.1. The rest of this chapter mainly focuses on what these sources reveal about the evolution of the script and also reflects on what this tells us about the characterization, structure, and themes of the Broadway version of the show.

PROBLEMS OF FOCUS AND STRUCTURE: THE EARLIEST EXTANT DRAFT

While Feuer, Martin, and Loesser were right in thinking that Willson had the potential to write an effective musical, it was not enough simply to turn his anecdotes from *And There I Stood with My Piccolo* into a show. The situation of starting out as a musical theater book writer with a setting and atmosphere but no plot is perhaps less common than the reverse: because most of the big shows of the late 1940s and 1950s were adaptations of existing properties, the challenge was usually how to tell the story, not what story to tell. The long gestations of *West Side Story* and *My Fair Lady* (*The Music Man*'s direct rivals on Broadway) are

Table 2.1. Scripts, script fragments, synopses, and related archival material for *The Music Man*. (GASF = Meredith Willson Papers, Great American Songbook Foundation, Carmel, Indiana; WHS = Kermit Bloomgarden Papers, Wisconsin Historical Society; SF = Script Fragment; S = Script; SY = Synopsis)

Abbreviation	Date	Description
S1	February 2, 1954	Complete draft script, 120 pp. (GASF)
SY1	June 7, 1955	Synopsis (GASF)
SY2	June 15, 1955	Synopsis (GASF)
SF1	June 24, 1955	Fragments of script from both acts, 29 pp. (GASF)
SY3	June 25–30, 1955	Synopis (GASF)
SF2	July 5–7, 1955	Script fragments, Act 1, Scene 1 ("Gramma Bird" scene). 3 versions. (GASF)
SF3	July 11, 1955	Script fragment, "Bushkins," 4 pp. (GASF)
SY4	Undated, c. July 1955	Synopsis (GASF)
SY5	Undated, c. July 1955	One-page synopsis (GASF)
SY6	Undated, c. July 1955	Two-page synopsis (GASF)
SY7	Undated, c. July/ August 1955	Synopsis ("The Love Story of Harold and Marian, which we will call The Music Man") (GASF)
SY8	September 17, 1955	Synopsis fragments, Act 1, Scenes 1, 2, and 4. (GASF)
SF4	November 15, 1955	Script fragments, Act 1, Scene 2 ("Holy, Holy"). (GASF)
SF5	November 15–29, 1955	Script, Act 1 draft, 59 pp. (GASF)
S2	December 13, 1955	Script, complete, 93 pp, "Draft 3." (GASF)
SY9	December 20, 1955	Synopsis (GASF)
SF6	Pages variously dated January 10 and March 2, 27, 29, and 30, 1956.	Script fragments, Act 1, Scenes 1, 2, and 4 and Act 2, Scene 5, 22 pp. (GASF)
S3	April 2, 1956	Script, complete draft in three acts, 99 pp. (GASF)
SY10	April 13, 1956	Synopsis, two versions (one undated), 4 pp. + 4 pp. (GASF)

Table 2.1. Continued

Abbreviation	Date	Description
SY11	April 18, 1956	Synopsis, two versions, Act 2, 4pp + 4pp. (GASF)
SF7	May 26, 1956	Script fragment, pp. 12–26. (GASF)
S4	October 1956	Script (first four pages missing), labeled by Willson "Early Draft of Music Man, approx Oct '56," GASF, box 18, folder 8.
S5	pre-June 1956	Complete Script ("Original Script and Notes"), labeled pre-June 1956, 102 pp. + misc. inserts, WHS, box 28, folder 12.
S6	June 1956	Complete "First Mimeo Script," June 1956, 102pp + 3 pp. corrections dated April 5, 1957, WHS, box 28, folder 13.
S7	November 27, 1956	Complete script, "FM Rev." (WHS)
	December 9, 1956–October 4, 1957	Script with multiple inserts ("Assembled Version"), WHS. [Contains scenes from different versions but no new material other than the lyrics to Shinn's version of "Trouble," dated December 9, 1956.]
S8	January 19, 1957	Revised Master Script, 119 pp. (WHS)
S9	April 5, 1957	Complete Script, 108 pp. (WHS)
S10	July 17, 1957	Complete Script, 108 pp. (WHS)
S11	September 10, 1957	Complete Script, 119 pp. (WHS)
S12	September 23, 1957	Complete Script, 110 pp. (WHS)

good examples: *Romeo and Juliet* and *Pygmalion* were at the heart of those shows from the very beginning and the challenge was how to carve them up, reframe them, and create song moments. In Willson's case, he had ideas for characters and songs from early in the process, but did not know what to do with many of them for several years. This is well illustrated by a brief examination of the earliest surviving script, from February 1954 (S1), which is the focus of this section of the chapter.

Superficially, there are various familiar aspects to S1. Many of the character names would make it through to Broadway: Harold Hill, Marion [*sic*; she becomes Marian in later versions], Mrs. Paroo, Marcellus Washburn, Eulaly [*sic*; she becomes Eulalie] Mackecknie, Zaneeta, George, and Tommy. But the devil is in the details, and of these, only Hill's name and "profession" went unchanged. Here, Marian is Marion Maddy, niece of George and Eulaly Mackecknie Breen, who own the Mercantile Emporium (grocery store); George is not the Mayor in this version, though he is the chairman of the school board and the most influential citizen of River City (which remained the show's setting in all versions), and Zaneeta is not their daughter but their neighbor's. Zaneeta also has a younger sister, Gracie.

Crucially, Marion is unrelated to Mrs. Paroo, who is the school janitor here, and her son, Jim, is a wheelchair user; there is no lisping character called Winthrop (or otherwise). Marcellus is married (to Nettie) and is the town photographer, rather than a worker at the livery stable; he is not Hill's former or current accomplice and he has particular status in the town, acting as Chair of the Entertainment Committee at the Fourth of July celebrations and leading the community in several ensemble scenes. Tommy is still a troublesome youth but his surname is Britt rather than Djilas and his father, Earl Britt, is the Editor of the *River City Gazette* and a member of the school board. Of several unfamiliar characters, the most important is Gramma Bird, proprietress of the thread store and a key ally to Hill in various permutations of the script through the next three years.

In place of the iconic "Rock Island" opening on a railroad train, the first scene of S1 takes place in River City and it establishes both the date—the Fourth of July—and Tommy's delinquency. He and a friend, Barney Hughes, are trying to set off firecrackers on a front porch, and their conversation is underscored by two phonograph records of patriotic songs (the record player is unseen, inside the house): "American Patrol," which is playing as the curtain rises, and "Stars and Stripes Forever," which "accidentally syncs" with the boys' conversation. Willson indicates these moments in the script with punctuation marks, as the opening line illustrates: "BARNEY: Hey, Tom, the punk won't burn --- * --- * (sound of blowing)." Thus although the scene is unfamiliar, Willson had already decided to start the show with rhythmic dialogue (a device that reached fruition in the "Rock Island" train scene in the Broadway version).

More obviously familiar is the second scene of S1. Every draft of the book has a scene depicting the Fourth of July celebrations at the school hall/gymnasium; this would ultimately become Act 1, Scene 4, in the Broadway script. In S1, the scene is incredibly long—at nineteen pages, the longest in the show—and Willson's lack of experience is apparent in the absence of focus and structure. He crams nine musical numbers into the scene, six of which are diegetic songs that form part of the festivities and are simply for display or pageantry rather than dramatic impetus. Indeed, it seems extraordinary that several minutes are devoted to a prolonged general introduction to the secondary characters in the form of the Independence Day "exercises," yet Harold Hill's arrival in the town has taken place at some point in the preceding days, unseen by the audience.

It is announced that the school board has previously decided to give permission for the boys' band, so he has already made his pitch and won, against George Breen's wishes as chairman of the school board. Hill is now, at last, introduced to the community as a whole and attempts to lead a group singalong of the traditional, nationalistic song "True-Hearted, Whole-Hearted" before charming them with "Gary, Indiana." He then sits (there is no "Trouble" or "Seventy-Six Trombones") and there is further "filler" material as Marcellus takes a group photograph and Eulaly leads a rendition of "America, My Country 'Tis of Thee." Hill forms a barbershop quartet from the school board—a vignette that takes place later in the Broadway version of the book—and when the hall has cleared, Harold and Marion are left alone. Although they have not previously met, Harold proceeds to woo a surprisingly jovial Marion, bursting within seconds into a love song:

> (*Everybody gradually leaves the stage as Harold helps Marion Maddy erase black-board. We do not hear their conversation until they are alone.*)
> HAROLD: I want to thank you very much, Miss Maddy. You were wonder-fully helpful.
> (*She is a little surprised at herself as she says:*)
> MARIAN: I enjoyed myself. I heard orchestra music, too, as you said! And it couldn't have been from my memory because I never heard music like that before!
> HAROLD! Why, Miss Maddy! (*He gestures*) Strings, please . . . thank you. What happened to the harp? . . . thank you. (*He sings to hidden accompaniment:*)
> There were bells on the hill but I never heard them ringing [etc.][4]

With the benefit of hindsight, we can marvel at the double misstep Willson takes here. There is immediately no tension between Marion and Hill, because she seems enthralled by his charisma rather than skeptical of it, and "Till I Met You" is heard early in the show, rather than being reserved as the eleven o'clock number (i.e., the last major new song in the show). Marion does not sing it at all in S1, and instead the scene continues with a contrived discussion about Chicago, where Hill purports to have lived. He makes a derogatory comment about Breen and then learns that Marion is Breen's niece, whereupon he departs apologeti-cally (though she seems mildly irritated at the comment rather than completely annoyed). Alone, Marion sings "I Want to Go to Chicago," indicating she has bought into the fantasy of the great city that Hill has outlined to her.

In summary, while Willson has succeeded in devising the broad idea of a scene at the school hall involving members of the community in Independence Day exercises, most of the details fall flat; and the opportunity both to have Hill con-trive the need for a boys' band as the antidote to the town's perceived delinquent youth and to establish Marion as too perceptive to be susceptible to Hill's charms is completely lost. The scene is long, too filled with songs that do not propel the plot forward, and dissipates the impact of the two principal characters on their first appearance. There is no notable exposition of the plot.

By contrast, the next scene establishes the most impactful strand of the story in S1. We meet Mrs. Paroo, the janitor, in her "small, dark, humble quarters" in the basement of the high school. Willson describes her vividly: her "stringy hair and flushed face testify to the demands of unending work. She is dressed in 'home-made' attire made in the fashion of men's trousers." George Breen arrives as chair of the school board to let her know that her duties will now include cleaning up after the band rehearsals. He critiques her appearance, using gendered language to degrade her: "[I]t's disappointing to me to learn that you don't even dress like a God-fearing woman here in the home. . . . [W]hen you wear this wanton costume during your janitor work you are frequently seen in the halls, constituting a shocking lack of respect for the women in this town" (1-3-26).

He then discovers Jim Paroo (hidden away), "a grown boy . . . rocking slightly in a shabby wheel-chair," and when Mrs. Paroo explains that Jim is her son, Breen declares the following in an abrupt close to the scene: "An imbecile son all these years. These kind of creatures belong in the asylum, Mrs. Paroo" (1-3-27). In the space of just over three pages, Willson creates an emotionally charged tableau of a working woman, living in fear and squalor to protect her disabled son, and her patron, who viciously resolves to punish Jim for his difference. Ironically, the scene lands too powerfully and would be at the heart of Willson's struggles with the book for the next three years as the disability plot proved a distraction from Hill's activities and relationship with Marion.

Similarly, Scene 4 seems disconnected with what comes before, as well as much longer than the material merits. At the thread store, Hill and Gramma Bird discuss how Tommy Britt has reformed because he is finding the band engaging; Hill explains that he has given Tommy the challenge of inventing a music holder for a marching piccolo player, an idea that Willson wrote about in *And There I Stood with My Piccolo* and used in every draft of the script.

Later in the scene, Tommy enters and shows Hill his initial attempt at creating the contraption and Hill gives him feedback. Tommy sings the school song "River City" to the tune of "On Wisconsin," the fight song of the Wisconsin Badgers at the University of Wisconsin–Madison and the official state song of Wisconsin (the music is by William T. Purdy). Gramma Bird tells Hill that she pities the town's youth for having to sing such a poor song (it does not rhyme or scan when the name is changed to River City) and Harold suggests that she should write a new one, with music by a yet-to-be-chosen member of the town. They could sell the song to other four-syllable towns in Iowa, potentially making a fortune in comparison to the debt she is incurring as an "untalented" store owner: the "everyone has a hidden talent but not everyone is talented in the way they want to be" theme comes from *Who Did What to Fedalia?* and appears in various drafts. Among these drawn-out discussions, the scene's most important function is for Hill to discover that Marion is the town's librarian—a seven-page scene for a purpose that could have been quickly covered when Hill met Marion in Scene 2.

Scene 5 is likewise protracted. Hill walks down the street, "almost doing a Pied Piper, with assorted boys and girls in his wake" (1-5-36), and greets Mrs. Britt on her porch. "She is a little 'Suth'n'-spoken, high-class North Carolina lady," a contrivance to allow Willson to include his song "The Blue Ridge Mountains Are in North Car'lina." The number starts when Willson pretends he has created a successful band in Mrs. Britt's home state and feigns nostalgia for the Blue Ridge Mountains, but one of the children corrects him: "In our joggraphy [sic] class the Blue Ridge Mountains are in Virginia, Professor Hill" (1-5-36). A vamp plays under the dialogue and Hill contradicts the child by singing the number, which has the same music as the more familiar song "The Wells Fargo Wagon" (which does not exist in this version). Mr. Bushkins, a German neighbor of the Britts, wanders in and tells Mrs. Britt that Tommy has been making fun of his accent. Tommy has explained to him why his mispronunciation of certain words is amusing and advised Bushkins to listen to himself; he did and was highly amused. This gives rise to a moral song, "Too Soon Old and Too Late Smart," about how the old can learn from the young. Bushkins makes no further appearance in the show and the song does nothing to explain or enhance the plot, so it is another unhelpful prolongation.

The dialogue resumes as Harold reveals to Mrs. Britt that Tommy is in love with Zaneeta, and we learn that Hill is an orphan; Mrs. Britt "adopts" him, and as he is leaving, he bumps into Marion. Hill apologizes for insulting her uncle, and there follows a love scene, heavily embellished with distractions. As they are talking, seven-year-old Gracie Graham comes in crying because one of her roller-skate straps has broken. Hill fixes it using Marion's hairpins, and as she removes them to give them to him, her hair falls. The school board barbershop quartet then enters and interrupts with the song "Mind If I Tell You I Love You?" as well as a discussion about harmony and scansion. They go inside the house and continue the song in the background as Hill tells Marion how beautiful she is, and they kiss.

As if this were not saccharine enough, Willson continues with a discussion between Hill and Marion about what they would do if someone caught them and they agree to "rehearse" being interrupted while kissing. By coincidence, Breen arrives and takes Marion indoors. There is further discussion and song from the school board, then Tommy and Zaneeta appear, discussing Tommy's piccolo music holder. They sing the duet "You Don't Have to Kiss Me Goodnight," and only after that does the scene come to a close with Harold (who has been hidden throughout the latter part of the scene) and Tommy singing goodnight. As with Scene 2, there are too many building blocks in this scene and not enough purpose. The Hill-Marion relationship is especially inert, with Marion remaining passive and Hill apparently sincere in his attentions.

In Scene 6, Harold visits Mrs. Paroo and meets Jim for the first time. Once again, the Mrs. Paroo character is emotively drawn—a widow, a working woman, a tirelessly committed mother to a disabled son—and much of the scene plays well, with a serious discussion about Jim's condition and how he could be integrated into the town by joining the band (Hill promises to get him a triangle, which will be easier to play). However, the relationship between scene and song causes a schism, as there is a page of dialogue about Mrs. Paroo's Irish heritage to provide a (weak) context for the song "Mother Darlin'." The scene gets back on track when Hill's background as an orphan is also discussed (like Mrs. Britt, she offers to "adopt" him), giving him some depth of character, and when left alone with Jim, he promises to help him to learn the triangle and comforts him through the song "The Wonderful Plan."

The penultimate scene of the act takes place a few minutes later upstairs in the school assembly room, where Breen interrogates Hill in front of the school board about his plans for the band (the boys have not yet played a note). Breen is interrupted by the barbershop quartet—a gag that interrupts the scene rather than providing genuine comedy—and Harold manages to deter him by telling him about Gramma Bird's plan to write a new school song and her need for a composer; he suggests Breen's wife and Breen is delighted.

Attention is then turned to Mrs. Paroo, and Breen refers to "a demented creature" (i.e., Jim; 1-7-65) whom she has been hiding in the cellar. Hill tries to defend Jim but Breen announces that the boy has been secretly taken to the asylum during the meeting. Mrs. Paroo shows the board a Valentine's Day card in which Jim has punched holes to create the shape of a heart, as evidence of his cognition, but Breen is uninterested and the scene ends. Mrs. Paroo rushes out and in the final scene (which is set ten minutes later) she stands on the street as a windstorm is beginning, singing the number "Blow" in which she entreats the winds to "bring him back to me" (1-8-70). By having this as the final gesture of Act 1, Willson unfortunately underlines Mrs. Paroo as the show's most vivid character and main protagonist.

There was a long way to go before this became what we know today as *The Music Man*, and the second act of S1 is similarly full of conflicting messages and unmotivated topics. For example, the first scene (which is in two parts) opens with Eulaly berating Marion for wearing makeup, leading into the song "Don't Put Bananas on Bananas." The episode's real function, which emerges in the dialogue following the song, is to inform the audience that the Breens are going away to Des Moines for a week to select new rolls for the school pianola. The second half of the scene takes place in the library, where a version of the familiar "Marian the Librarian" scene takes place. However, Marion's resistance is weak and she merely complains, "I cannot permit you to kiss me in the public library," implying that she does not mind being kissed by him in general. He then asks for a book called *Casper Hauser* about a boy with a wooden horse who is rejected by society but is shown to have great talent; Hill wants the book for Jim. Again, the Jim Paroo plotline is much stronger than the Hill/Marion one.

Similarly, the next scene takes place in the Paroo quarters, where Oliver Hix (one of the school board members) has restored Jim to his mother's care. Hix leaves, and while Mrs. Paroo cleans up around his chair, the voice of Jim is heard singing "his own soft ballad rendition" of "Mother Darlin'." (This was to be done via a recording, as Jim is unable to speak.) Hill and Marion enter with the triangle for Jim and Hill tells him the story of Casper Hausen, which comes to life in ballet form. Marion becomes more engaged by Jim's story and entreats Harold to put him in the band, but Hill is unusually open about his lack of confidence in the likelihood of the boys being able to play (he admits it's impossible). Again, a scene involving Jim and Mrs. Paroo is heavily emotional and Hill and Marion seem like secondary characters merely commenting on it.

Set three nights later, the next scene reveals Marion and Hill secretly taking Jim to the school hall to try to teach him the triangle while Hill plays C. R. Howell's *The Rustic Dance* (1888) on the pianola (the same piece would later be used in the familiar piano lesson scene from the final version of the show). They discover that Jim has been making holes in a piano roll and resolve to send it to the manufacturer to get turned into a functioning roll to see whether Jim has revealed a secret musical talent. The action quickly continues to Scene 4, several days later, where Harold visits Gramma Bird with copies of her song lyrics. Reference is made to the income from the song, then Eulaly bursts in to announce that she has composed the music for the school song ("River City, Go"), a performance of which ends the scene. Once again, a secondary character dominates rather than Hill or Marion.

Scene 5 then follows, and the plot scarcely advances: there is further discussion between Tommy and Hill about the piccolo music holder (by now a tedious topic), Hill mentions that the piano roll will arrive on Saturday, and he sings the love song "I'd Like a Memory" to a young girl, Gracie Graham, who is trying to run a lemonade stall on the street. These are charmingly drawn vignettes but the scene is mostly redundant. The plot stabilizes in Scene 6, when Harold and Marion try out Jim's piano roll and are disappointed to discover that it doesn't seem to make sense. Hill resolves to teach Jim the triangle, then Breen bursts in and announces that Harold is a fraud; as in the Broadway version of the show, he has claimed to have been a graduate of the Gary Conservatory in '05 but George has discovered that the town itself was only built a year later. According to the script, "Marion is thunderstruck" but when Breen threatens to drive Hill out of town, she objects. She also refuses to help him force Mrs. Paroo to sign Jim's commitment papers for the asylum.

The next morning is Sunday, and Scene 7 depicts Mrs. Paroo and Jim overhearing the religious service going on in the assembly hall upstairs (it has been moved there because the plumbing at the Methodist church has broken—another contrivance). Mrs. Paroo prays but there is no action. Scene 8 shows the River City streetscape, where the boys are seen through the windows trying on their band uniforms, and there is no dialogue.

This gives way to the final scene of the show; by this point, there is little tension or momentum. It takes place in the assembly hall—rather like in the Broadway version—and Breen tries unsuccessfully to force the band to play. Hill admits he is a fake, but he asks that Jim not be punished on his account—he is a far more contrite character than the Harold of the Broadway version and does not attempt to run away. Breen has Jim wheeled in with his triangle, which he drops, then Marion interrupts. She announces that she has a new piano roll that Jim has created; when it is played, it turns out to be the melody of "River City, Go," which Eulaly claims to have written. Unexpectedly, Eulaly admits that she heard it at the Playola Company in Des Moines and later remembered it but thought she had written it herself. Breen then turns the situation around by crediting his wife with the discovery of "this fine song" and himself with giving Jim the "chance to appear here today" (2-9-35). He then tries to blame Hill for everything and challenges the townsfolk to stand if they have "learned anything about music from Professor Harold Hill." In turn, they all do, with the exception of Breen and Jim. "Finally," notes the script, "Jim makes it with no help from anyone." This leads without further comment or dialogue to the arrival of the band, which plays Beethoven's Minuet in G (as it does in the Broadway version).

But the story does not end there. Members of the school board commend Hill for bringing harmony to the town, and one of them reveals that Hill has spent his own money on the band, using funds made in his cut from the sales of Gramma Bird's song. Following a pause, Breen asks whether he can become a member of the barbershop quartet ("Oliver, is there such a thing as a quartette with five men in it?" [2-9-37]) and after Hill promises to reform, Marion rises and sings a reprise of "Till I Met You."

Reflecting on all of this, we can see the bones of *The Music Man* in places, and the style and atmosphere of the show are vivid, but there is not a great deal at stake. In Broadway terms, the potential of the romance plot between the leads is entirely missed because Marion falls into Harold's arms within seconds of first talking to him, while the disability plot is overwhelmingly emotive and overrides all other elements. Harold's fraudulence is played down—we do not see the band's rehearsals so we only hear secondary reports of their lack of activity—and Breen is an obnoxiously vicious antagonist who seems much more of an outsider to the otherwise placid community than does Hill. Other secondary characters are given extensive stage time without reason.

No wonder that although Feuer and Martin were enthusiastic when Willson auditioned the first version for them in (according to *Territory*)[5] June 1954, they felt "the story had to be rebuilt from the ground up" and that "all the people in it had to be reshaped—their dimensions emphasized with respect to themselves as well as to each other."[6] Willson also reports that the producers felt it was "a play with music" and that Martin declared: "Feuer and Martin don't produce 'plays with music'—we produce musical comedies."[7] With this in mind, the rest of this chapter examines the process by which Willson enacted this transformation from a play with music into *The Music Man*.

THE DISABILITY PLOT

In *Territory*, Willson is open about his personal investment in the show's disability plot, as well as about how this made it difficult to create the book: "When you have a twelve-year-old character with a brilliant mind locked up in a body with no muscular control to where everyone takes for granted he's crazy, as people did in 1912 (and still do, far too many of them), you have an awful time keeping such a boy from not only stealing his scenes, as Cy [Feuer] warned, but from stealing the whole show. I even tried one draft where the audience never saw him on stage at all." He also notes that as he worked on the script, the love story "was getting stronger, a lot stronger, but you'd never notice it with that wheel-chair kid in the show. I wasn't quitting on him, but I was kind of miserable."[8] Reading the eight available drafts of the script in which the character appears, it seems obvious that the storyline does not fit—or, to look at it differently, that it needed to be more explicitly the main plot of the show if it were to be included at all, rather than a subplot.

Nevertheless, it is worth considering the level of daring involved in trying to write a musical about disability on Broadway in the 1950s. Six decades later, *Dear Evan Hansen* (2016) has proved popular in many quarters for its portrayal of a character battling with a chronic condition (anxiety depression), but at the time of writing *The Music Man* Willson was grappling with a society for which disability was often taboo or a point of embarrassment. Intellectual disability, for example, was frequently referred to in derogatory terms and people of disability could be badly treated or exploited. In one famous case that came to the attention of the national media in 1993, Clemens E. Benda, clinical director at the Fernald School in Waltham, Massachusetts, and MIT Professor of Nutrition Robert S. Harris performed research on seventy-four children at the Fernald Institution, which had opened in 1848 under the denigrating name of the Experimental School for Teaching and Training Idiotic Children.

The first study occurred in 1946, when seventeen children were exposed to radioactive iron, and the second between 1950 and 1953, when a further fifty-seven were fed calcium radioisotopes orally or intravenously over seventeen experiments. The experiments were incentivized for the children by telling them they were joining a "science club" that would entitle them to receive "a quart of milk daily . . . [be] taken to a baseball game, to the beach and to some outside dinners." The letters sent to their parents requesting permission for them to participate indicated that they were to benefit from a therapeutic process, but this was untrue: they were non-consensual subjects of radiation experiments.[9]

At the same time, in the early 1950s a charity (the National Association for Retarded Children or NARC; it was renamed The Arc of the United States in 1992) was set up by parents of intellectually disabled children and initial attempts were being made to create national barrier-free standards, particularly as a result of the large number of physically disabled veterans following the Second World War. The fight for disability rights had just begun.

In this context, to put a story about a disabled teenager on the popular stage cannot have been easy or, for that matter, a serious commercial prospect, regardless of Willson's claim that Feuer and Martin "ate it up—loved it, in fact."[10] His insistence on pursuing it, therefore, found him in a perhaps unexpectedly liberal stance, hinting that his politics were not as conservative and his attitudes not as parochial as people might assume *The Music Man* implies. (He also co-founded the Big Brothers of Greater Los Angeles charity in 1955 to help vulnerable children, another sign of his commitment.)

On the other hand, the motivation behind the project was more admirable than its execution. If Willson researched the topic, there is no obvious evidence of such investigations, and this is reflected in some of the unfortunate ideas that are projected in several of the script drafts. We have already seen a couple in S1: in particular, the idea that Hill is capable of "inspiring" Jim to stand (unaided) in the final scene implies that overcoming disability is simply a question of will-power on the part of the disabled person. The business with the pianola rolls is also far-fetched: quite reasonably, Willson's idea is that Jim has heightened musical abilities to compensate for his physical struggles, but the notion that this should manifest itself by making holes in a piano roll in a pattern that would actually play a recognizable melody is almost certainly impossible and therefore undermines the positive intention behind it. There are some good ideas, however, including the concept that even if Jim cannot literally speak, the musical theater form can be used to show that he has an inner voice when we hear him sing "Mother Darlin'" in his head.

The next document of Willson's evolving thoughts on the depiction of Jim is a collection of script fragments from June 24, 1955 (SF1). In this version, Marion has become Marian Malthouse, the school principal, who is fighting with the town to be allowed to have Jim (still no relation) attend school and receive an education. The other children and their parents do not like the idea and Jim is openly reviled by the mayor's wife, here called Vitel Shinn, who refuses to allow her daughter Zaneeta to take part in a tableau at the July 4th exercises with "that feeble minded Paroo boy." Marian is Jim's champion: in Act 1, Scene 3, she goes to consult with the town's notary public, Oliver Hix, to ascertain her legal position, and Willson even adds a confrontational duet for them about it ("Clarification"). The scene is significant in that although Jim's education is under discussion, the subject of the episode is really Marian's authority in her classroom and therefore her power. The only other mention of Jim in Act 1 of SF1 is when Gracie comes on with her broken roller-skate strap: this time, she has broken it because she has run away supposedly scared from seeing Jim through the window of his basement home.

But neither Jim nor Mrs. Paroo appears in the first act (which is now only four scenes long). They enter together for the first time in Act 2, Scene 2, the "Marian the Librarian" scene. After the song, the library clears and Mrs. Paroo wheels Jim in for Marian to read to. She has been doing this for some time, recognizing his need for intellectual stimulation. She also sings to him ("The Wonderful Plan"). Scenes 3 and 4 are missing, so it is impossible to know whether Willson intended further development of this storyline, but the subject of Jim does not come up again until Scene 6 (the final scene), when Marcellus Washburn announces that 379 signatures have been collected in a petition to ban Jim from the school. Hill appears, admits his guilt, and then proceeds to demonstrate Jim's abilities by singing Beethoven's Minuet in G while Jim plays the triangle on the first beat of every bar, thus highlighting the town's misconception of him. There is no suggestion, however, that Jim should join the band, which would allow him to achieve integration, respect, and acceptance. Overall, this version shows Willson's realization that the plot could not be dominated by Jim's story, but the addition of the witch hunt–style petition unfortunately renders the plot even more sinister.

No doubt recognizing this was not working, Willson tried new variations on the theme in the November 1955 new draft of Act 1 (SF6) and the December complete draft (S2). Jim Paroo is now called Jerry Barkus and Marian is once more the librarian; Jerry has a father but no mother. Marian has been leaving books for Jerry to read and it is explicit that he has read them for himself—indeed, in SF6 (but not S2) Mr. Barkus comments that Jerry has been through every book in the library "two or three times" (1-1-8A). This represents an important shift in establishing from the start that Jim has significant intellectual ability and interest. Another addition to the plot is that Hill arrives and sells Mr. Barkus a triangle for Jerry without bothering to meet him; he interrupts Barkus's attempts to tell him about Jerry's disability and signs him up to the band without discussion. No further mention of Jerry is made until the closing lines of Act 1 (Scene 8), in which Hill's fraudulence has been uncovered. As he attempts to make his getaway, Marian reveals that Jerry has a special reason for valuing the band (she explicitly reveals his disability in SF6 and makes a veiled reference to it in S2, showing that Willson could not decide whether to leave the audience in suspense about Jerry's "secret" or not). Although Jerry hardly appears in the act, this cliffhanger reinforces his thematic presence and importance. In S2, Jerry finally appears in the first scene of Act 2, in which he discusses Harold with Marian: communication is not a problem for him in this version. He reappears at the end of the show (Scene 5) and, as before, successfully plays the triangle in time to Hill's sung rendition of the Minuet in G.

By now, the Jim/Jerry character was becoming both marginalized and compromised; the nature of his disability was getting simplified and he appeared only in two scenes. In late March 1956, Willson revisited the character again, this time redrafting the scene in which Hill sells Barkus the triangle by having Barkus tell Hill that Jerry is "a paralyzed boy, doesn't move but a little on his right side . . . he doesn't walk, even stand up" (SF7). Rather than impacting on the depiction of Jerry, though, this tweak merely makes Hill more sympathetic: instantly, he shows an attitude of inclusion when hearing of Jerry's condition, and rebukes Mr. Barkus for trying to talk him out of involving him ("Don't keep putting up blocks in the road"). Another draft of the scene (also part of SF7), dated March 28, has a younger Jerry (ten years old) whose father has created a pulley-rope so that Jerry can pull himself up through the trap door in the floor of the assembly hall. Barkus refers to his social anxiety ("the older he gets the more bashful he gets to be in front of people" [1-1-18A]), and this now seems to be his main problem; in this version, he can still read and talk. He even becomes Marian's confidante in yet another version of this scene in an undated synopsis (probably from April 13, 1956, as it is filed with another similar synopsis of that date, SF8), when Marian opens her heart to Jerry in the song "Goodnight, My Someone" and explains she longs to meet someone to fall in love with.

Willson remained determined to make the character work. S4-7, dating from around May/June 1956 to January 1957, contain similar versions of the disability plot. In all four drafts, as in the Broadway version, Marian is now Mrs. Paroo's daughter and Jim is now her younger brother (he is called Terry in S5 and S6). Willson regresses to a scenario similar to S1, where Jim/Terry is being hidden and nobody knows of his existence until Act 1, Scene 7, when he first appears. He is again unable to speak and in S4, S7, and S8, the pianola roll plot has returned. The story is made even more melodramatic by two revelations: that Marian lives separately from her mother and brother in order to distract from Jim's presence (it's easier to keep him hidden under the school) and that the family has been run out of several other towns because of prejudice against Jim.

As in S1, Shinn decides the boy must be institutionalized. Hill leaps to Jim's/ Terry's defense and in the patter number "Ridiculous" (delivered over the music to "Marian the Librarian" in S4 and S8) he persuades Shinn that the holes Jim/ Terry has made in the piano roll may be a sign of musical ability; they agree to have it sent off to be processed at the factory and Shinn leaves. Willson also adds the detail that Jim/Terry had an accident at birth, which is the cause of his disability (see S4: 1-7-49). In the second act, Jim/Terry is given the triangle but no lessons. His story is completely unresolved in S4 (he disappears), but in S5 and S6 he plays the Minuet in G on the triangle with the rest of the band in the final scene, focusing the plot on his acceptance by the town (the pianola roll strand is completely removed in these two versions); S7 and S8 focus instead on the revelation that the holes he has made in the pianola roll mark out the melody of the school song "River City, Go!"

By April 1957, Willson had finally let go of the Jim/Jerry/Terry character, around six years after first thinking of the project and only months prior to the show's Broadway opening. For some time, friends and colleagues had been telling him this would be necessary. A notable example is documented in a letter of December 17, 1955, from playwrights Jerome Lawrence and Robert E. Lee to Willson, who had evidently asked them for help or comments. The second paragraph of the letter notes: "Meredith, the *easy* solution is to dump Jim Paroo; the result can be a bright and probably highly successful show. But I cannot help sensing that this whole work was *born* around Jim Paroo—who is really the 'prime-mover-unmoved.' Following this easy course might conceivably reduce a major work to the dimension of mere entertainment."[11]

This remarkably insightful statement sums up Willson's dilemma candidly: the disability strand of the story had the potential to elevate the show to the level of the socially conscious librettos of (for example) the Rodgers and Hammerstein musicals, which provided the benchmark for artistic achievement on Broadway in the 1940s and 1950s. Not for nothing had Feuer and Martin—commercially minded producers of musical comedies and in some ways the antithesis of Rodgers and Hammerstein—warned Willson from the start that Jim would "steal every scene" and must be "prune[d] down."[12] Willson reports that Martin had spent considerable time and effort between 1954 and 1955 trying to help him "lick the book,"[13] but an announcement in the *New York Times* on February 10, 1956, revealed that Martin and Feuer had decided to "table" the project;[14] Willson says they did not tell him in person.[15]

Only a fortnight later, he received a message from another producer, Kermit Bloomgarden: "I UNDERSTAND YOU ARE MAKING SOME CHANGES TO YOUR PLANS FOR THE MUSIC MAN. I'D LIKE VERY MUCH TO GO INTO THE POSSIBILITY WITH YOU. WOULD IT BE POSSIBLE FOR ME TO SEE A COPY OF THE BOOK."[16] Although he never became a household name, Kermit Bloomgarden (1904–1976) was responsible for producing some of the most important plays of the twentieth century, including Arthur Miller's *Death of a Salesman* (1949), *The Crucible* (1953), and *A View from the Bridge* (1955); the stage adaptation of *The Diary of Anne Frank* (1955); Lillian Hellman's *Toys in the Attic* (1960); and Peter Shaffer's *Equus* (1973).

His forays into musical theater were somewhat less distinguished, with Howard Dietz and Arthur Schwartz's short-lived *The Gay Life* (113 performances, 1961), Manos Hadjikadis and Joe Darion's slightly more successful (but hardly enduring) *Illya Darling* (320 performances, 1967), and two all-out flops that each ran nine performances, namely Sol Berkowitz and James Lipton's *Nowhere to Go but Up* (1962) and Stephen Sondheim's *Anyone Can Whistle* (1964).

Nevertheless, when Bloomgarden sent the above message, he was about to bring Frank Loesser's ambitious *The Most Happy Fella* (1956) to Broadway (it opened in May). Bloomgarden seems to have pounced quickly on the *Music Man* project once Feuer and Martin had withdrawn: news of his possible adoption of the production met the ears of the Hollywood producer, Jesse L. Lasky, who wrote to Bloomgarden on February 29 to inform him that he had a stake in the material. "I recently entered into a partnership with Meredith Willson for the production of THE MUSIC MAN as a motion picture," he informed Bloomgarden, going on to explain that he had been working with Willson on the script and planned to take the work to a major film studio by the end of March.[17] This chronology challenges the sequence of events outlined by Willson in *Territory*, where he suggests that in December 1956 he approached Bloomgarden, who invited him to come and audition the show, agreed to produce it, and then arranged to meet up again in January 1957 about it. It is clear, instead, that Bloomgarden was already interested in the production, almost a year earlier than Willson claims. On the other hand, a brief memo on June 4 from one of Bloomgarden's assistants asks whether "anything further [was] ever done" on *The Music Man*, but no reply is documented, suggesting that this early interest was abandoned (perhaps because of Lasky's rights in the piece).

It was not until the following year that more was heard in the press about the show's development. On January 13, 1957, the *New York Times* announced that Bloomgarden—who was humorously described as "a producer with a somewhat unorthodox desire to know what he will be doing months before he's doing it"—had "chosen his first item for production in the fall." He was quoted as saying the material was "delightful," while Willson added that the show was "a combination of the Pied Piper and Johnny Appleseed with a dash of Jimmy Valentine set to music."[18] This announcement neatly coincides with the last script in which Jim Paroo appears (S8, 19 January 1957). Willson admits in *Territory* that Bloomgarden knew from the start that the character "had to go, but he also knew the way to lose him was not to give me an ultimatum about it—he knew that just digging the subplot out of there would leave a pretty raw hole. Also he understood my strong feeling about [Jim Paroo] and how important I felt it was to the play. So he never told me for sure we had to lose the kid, preferring to let me find out for myself."[19] In fact, one of Bloomgarden's staff, a script reader of some kind, had commented strongly on the problem in a report from early 1957:

> Working backward from Harold and Marion, one sees the need for Harold Hill to relate to someone in River City in terms of his real self—unknown to the rest of the characters until the rest of the play. And this brings us to the boy.

One feels that Meredith's instincts are right in that there must be someone to whom Harold can give real courage, not just big talk. And it needs to be someone weaker than Harold, and serious rather than comic. This is more important than the boy himself, though it being a child & someone related to Marion in some way is logical and natural. But, as physical disability in a child is impossible to view in any terms but pity and sentiment, the problem is to find some other form of disability besides physical.[20]

Willson credits his co-book writer Franklin Lacey, who came on to the show around May 1956, for providing the solution to the problem exactly along these lines: to replace Jim with Winthrop, a young boy with a lisp who introduced "The Wells Fargo Wagon" in drafts from S4 onward. The two characters had both appeared in drafts S4–S8 but they were now combined and Winthrop became Marian's brother with a social anxiety condition. In this way, Willson could retain the theme of accepting difference without the problematic aspects of the direction he had been taking with Jim's character; thus the disability plot was retained in function but without its ambitious roots and dominating narrative presence.

ROMANCE AND FRAUDULENCE: DEFINING AND REFINING HAROLD HILL AND MARIAN PAROO

With all of these deliberations about the presence and function of Jim Paroo, it is no wonder that it took Willson some time to make sense of the characters of Harold Hill and Marian Paroo. We have already seen that in S1, the relationship between Hill and Marion is incidental: there is no trajectory to it and they mostly seem like placid citizens who are out to do good for Jim. There is no sense, even, that Hill has been a conman in other towns: his fake credentials are revealed but the River City project appears to be a one-off. And apart from a short outburst when Breen tries to rope her into helping him to institutionalize Jim, Marion is frustratingly passive. Hill's pursuit of her seems mild and sincere— because there is no disclosure of a history of him wooing the piano teacher in each town, this again seems specific to Marion and genuine—and as he has no shill (i.e., Marcellus in the Broadway version), there are no conversations early on during which Hill discusses the truth. Indeed, his open doubts about his ability to lead the band in time for the concert suggest that he is more honest here. This section of the chapter considers how Willson went about strengthening the characterizations and storylines of both Marian and Hill, as well as creating their turbulent romance.

By the end of June 1955 (SF1), Marian has already become significantly stronger as a character. She is now intellectually independent, not only insisting that Jim be allowed to receive an education but going to the trouble of proving her position legally. She is much more of a victim of the town's stubbornness than she is in the Broadway version: the Mayor and his wife are working against her on the subject of Jim's education, so Marian's tenacity is all the more impressive. Her first conversation with Hill is more nuanced and does not include a love song, but the second scene adds a peculiar new scenario as Harold and Marian are (unwittingly) staying at the same boarding house. This brings them together in the same space rather awkwardly, so that they converse too easily.

For example, in Scene 4 they talk about putting Jim in the band and are clearly at one in their ambitions for him, dissipating the sense of moral disconnect that helps to structure much of their relationship in the Broadway version. In Act 2, Marian has a major sequence where we witness her reading and singing to Jim, and she now leads the singing of "Till I Met You" as a duet with Harold in the final scene. This gives her stage time as a principal (rather than supporting) character, yet the overall focus is still not right.[21]

Willson had begun to realize that Marian must have a more important role, but he seems to have struggled to create the nuances of her character without resorting to gender stereotypes. He started to invent other ways of giving her depth. For example, in SF5 (a script fragment from November 15, 1955) we see Marian praying during a church service, a device that allowed Willson to reveal her inner thoughts (specifically, and curiously, about the universality of faith across different religions).

More interestingly, in SF6 (November 1955) and S2 (December 1955) Marian and Hill bond over their discovery that they are both orphans. They discuss their experiences (which were similar) of growing up in an orphanage and Gramma Bird asks them to make popcorn together, thereby giving a domestic and romantic setting to this intimate conversation. (In one cute line, Hill has never made popcorn before and asks, "Where's the pop-corner?" to which Marian replies, "Corn-popper" SF6 [1-2-12/13].) That they are destined to be together is therefore clearly communicated but without the abruptness of Hill's advances in S1.

Willson also starts to move away from the disability plot in these late 1955 versions by introducing a new point of adversity. Marian is once more the public librarian, and she has been promised $165 for new books (a considerable amount in 1913, when the show is set). When Hill arrives and proposes his boys' band idea to the town, the council decides to spend the money on band uniforms instead of books for the library. Marian's legal confrontation (Act 1, Scene 5, of SF6/S2) now becomes about the written evidence she has that the money has been promised to her. But in the next scene Marian becomes less angry because she has seen the children's enchanted reaction to the band instruments, which arrive on the Wells Fargo Wagon. She tells Hill of her disappointment about the books and he immediately offers to hold the band's first concert to aid the book fund, thus helping to raise the needed money. He also sings "Till I Met You" to her and they kiss; seductively, he encourages her, "[T]rust your imagination—it won't betray you, I promise" (SF6: 1-6-45). She sings a refrain of the song and the scene ends with them embracing.

Although it would not be retained for Broadway, this scene finds Willson significantly closer to the combination of ideas that would make *The Music Man* successful. For example, the moment when Marian sees the children's reaction to the instruments (albeit without the specific effect on Winthrop) became the climax of Act 1 of the show on Broadway: she is shifting her values to prioritize heart over head. Perhaps even more crucially, Hill is now making love to Marian as part of his ruse. He promises her the earth (or at least the money for the books) just to win her heart, knowing full well that he cannot teach the band to play. The power of their personalities has started to emerge and Willson has strengthened the key ingredient that will sustain the tension in their relationship, namely that Hill is a fake (which Marian knows by the end of Act 1) and for a portion of the show does not love (or realize he loves) Marian.

Willson is still tantalized by how this idea might interact with the disability plot in the final scene of Act 1 in the two December 1955 versions, as noted earlier in this chapter: Hill's true identity is revealed and in SF6 Marian tells him about Jerry's disability (which Harold does not previously know about in this version) and the boy's particular need for music in his life, which causes Hill to drop the valise he has been hurriedly packing with the intention of fleeing town; in S2 Marian refers less explicitly to Jerry's condition and Harold leaves.

But Act 2 (which exists in S2 only) features a milder Hill from the start. Scene 2 contains the revelation that Harold is in love with Marian (he admits it openly at this early point) and he returns to town to save the book fund. Next, the "Marian the Librarian" scene plays roughly as it does on Broadway but it is sincere in this version (it is placed much earlier in the Broadway version, in which Harold is only pretending to pursue Marian seriously). Hill also makes an attempt to actually teach the boys their instruments, developing an idea from the June 1955 draft (SF1) in which Gramma Bird secretly decides to instruct the boys in the Minuet in G to save Harold's bacon.

Willson seems to have been aware of the question of plausibility regarding exactly how the boys manage to come out at the end and play the piece (however poorly); this goes unresolved in the Broadway version, of course, and is either a fantasy or the result of the boys secretly working out how to play their instruments for themselves. But here in S2, Hill genuinely tries to teach them, and in the final scene, after the band's performance, Grover Hawks of the William K. Burns detective agency arrives to announce that he has been searching for Hill for two years because all the previous towns he has visited want to establish a Harold Hill Day in his honor to thank him for transforming their communities.

Sometime during April or May of 1956, Willson started to collaborate with another writer, Franklin Lacey (1917–1988),[22] on the book of the show. While his credentials as a capable songwriter were impeccable, Willson was obviously having difficulty in making his ideas for the book hang together and needed help. For example, from SF3 (July 1955) onward, Willson (still working alone) incorporated an opening scene set on a train, in which Hill's scheme is exposed. In all the versions from 1955, this is conveyed through a discussion with a Mr. August Bushkins, instrument manufacturer, who variously persuades Hill to start the boys' band racket (SF3 and SY7, in which Hill has until recently been a hardware clerk in Garnet, South Dakota) or tries to persuade him to end the business after a six-year run together (SY8). Hill's callousness and shallowness is therefore explicit to the audience from the beginning, which makes the conclusion of

S2—that Hill is such a hero he deserves to have a day named in his honor, as just previously mentioned—unconvincing.

His promiscuity is especially distasteful: in SF3 (July 11), for example, he comments: "Fifty different girls in fifty different towns! That's my self-imposed goal—consecutively, of course—forty-nine so far, without a miss" (SF3, p. 5). This conversation continued to be used throughout the other 1955 versions, but it is noticeable that when Lacey's name appears on a script for the first time, just a few months later (S4, c. May 1956), a version of the familiar Rock Island railway scene has appeared, in which a group of traveling salesmen are instead discussing Hill's reputation. This means that we have a sense that he is a rogue but he does not come out with any predatory remarks himself. All the remaining scripts open with different versions of this basic scenario, and it seems likely that it was one of Lacey's key innovations. Indeed, the scene became so integral that in S4 and S8 (drafts from 1956) Willson and/or Lacey add a reprise toward the end of the show as the conclusion of a "River City Panorama" number, in which orchestral reprises of all the main songs are heard as Hill walks around town, before the voices of the salesmen are heard discussing how he never actually forms a band. This was cut early in 1957.

It was not all straightforward, though: it took some months for the new Willson-Lacey team to address the complexity of portraying Hill. His repulsively predatory nature toward women, for example, had been explicit in the November and December 1955 scripts, such as in a scene where he woos the townswomen Alma Barrett (who is otherwise of no significance to the plot) in the song "It's You" simply to fill time while the school board makes their decision about whether to allow the band scheme to go ahead (Act 1, Scene 4, in SF6 and S2). The Lacey versions drop this kind of behavior (i.e., making love to every woman in sight) and introduce the first of two "walking" scenes (Act 1, Scene 3; there is another one in Scene 6 in the Broadway script) in which Hill follows Marian around town, but from S4 to S8 (up to and including the January 1957 version) the moment is made more uncomfortable by Hill deciding to sing "The Sadder-but-Wiser Girl" to Marian's face; no wonder she slaps him.

By S9 (April 1957) it has been moved so that it would now be addressed to Marcellus, while the revised "walking" scene would play without a song, thus providing a swifter transition to the next scene (the second instance of the "walking" number was also added at this point, i.e., to S9). Even the Broadway version, of course, retains the uneasy aspect of Hill following Marian around without permission, though Willson's condemnation of it is made clear by Marian's repeated and forthright rebuttal of Harold's advances, ending with her slamming the door in his face (Scene 3) or running into the library (Scene 6). He is no match for her and her discomfort is clearly depicted.

The addition of "Trouble" to the score during the early months of 1956 also helped Willson and Lacey to revise the school gymnasium scene into a more effective state. Curiously, the very first surviving draft (S1) of this scene from 1954 contains the notice: "The added Fourth of July exercises in this scene and descriptions thereof were written in collaboration with Dixie Willson" (1-2-4). Willson's sister would remain bitter about the lack of recognition she received for her input into the book, writing a long letter to the *Mason City Globe-Gazette* in August 1954 to outline her participation in the early stages (Valerie Austin's doctoral dissertation contains the letter and the reply).[23] Another series of extensive letters from 1959 (now housed in the Carmel collection) reiterated these claims,[24] and it appears that Willson paid her regular royalties between at least 1958 and 1960, thus acknowledging that she had had some input into his hit show.[25] But the element for which she is credited in S1—which may have been her *only* input—suggests that her help was also a hindrance, because until the Lacey drafts of 1956 (S4 onwards) the school scene was too focused on the general atmosphere of the Fourth of July and had no dramatic impetus.

It is true that "Seventy-Six Trombones" had been added by Willson to the scene from SF1 (June 1955) but putting "Trouble" into the mix instantly changed the tone. Rather than the band proposal being just one of a series of town announcements, it is now the answer to Mayor Shinn's rabble-rousing: the Mayor sings "Trouble" in S4-S8 and Hill responds with "Ya Got No Trouble" before segueing into "Seventy-Six Trombones" (the solution to the problem). The scene was now no longer about the Fourth of July but instead depicted Hill's ability to "spellbind" the towns-people. It improved further from S9 (April 1957) onward, when a new scene was added (the familiar Act 1, Scene 2) to introduce the stubborn Iowans; here, Hill is now the one who invents the "Trouble," thus making the civil unrest caused by the pool table imaginary and therefore gentler. The scene also helps Willson gently parody the insularity of small-town America, as well as amplifying Hill's charisma—an essential quality for making the entire plot convincing.

The final aspect of the romance and fraudulence plots that had to be resolved was the major point of their interaction, namely Marian's reaction upon learning that Hill is a fake and her decision about how to act upon that information. We have already seen that that happens well into Act 2 of the first draft (S1) and that although Marion [*sic*] is "thunderstruck" by the news, it does not appear significantly to modify her attitude toward Hill. Willson credits Ernie Martin with recognizing that Hill needs to be identified as a fraud early on: " 'Look,' he says, 'you got the favorite character of all audiences—a lovable rogue. How can that terrific asset be going for you unless you tell the audience he's a phony right at the start?' Of course he was right and I started over."[26]

But Marian's attitude toward the subject is a different matter. In the Broadway version, there are two pivotal moments related to this topic that contribute significantly to Marian's characterization and the depiction of her romance with Harold. The first is Act 1, Scene 11 (the "Wells Fargo Wagon" scene), in which Marian has researched and found evidence of Hill's lies, then conceals that evidence from the Mayor when she sees how thrilled Winthrop is after receiving his cornet. This is a good example of how powerful Marian is in the Broadway show: she has the intelligence to see through Harold in the first place, the skill to know where to look for the proof of his lies, and the perception to see that there is also good in him. In contrast to her passiveness in S1, where she is too gullible to be wise to Hill's tales and too weak to do anything about them, in the Broadway version she has agency.

The other important scene is where she uses her sexuality to prevent Charlie Cowell, a salesman who is out for Harold's head, from catching his train on time (Act 2, Scene 3, of the Broadway version). Again, her agency is striking: apart from Harold and Marcellus she remains the only person in town who knows the truth *and* she has repeatedly been shown to be sexually conservative, yet she makes an active decision to assert her sexuality in order to protect Harold. She continues to see the good he has done for the town even though he represents the antithesis of many of her values (she is rational, he is a fantasist; she is intellectual, he is intuitive). In the final scene, her faith in him is presented as the catalyst for the boys' performance—the ultimate in contrived Broadway happy endings—and it is arguably set up in this scene in which she attempts to mute Cowell's threat to Harold's presence in the town (though according to the script she is "stunned" at Cowell's suggestion that Hill has a girl in "every county in Illinois").

Both of these key scenes took months to create. As late as S7 (November 1956) and S8 (January 1957), Marian only learns from Cowell in the middle of Act 2 that Hill is a fake (she does not find out for herself); her response is to tell Harold to give himself up (she does not try to impede Cowell). Lacey and Willson created a new distraction in Act 1, Scene 10, of S9 and S10 (April and July 1957): the Mayor receives a letter revealing that Hill has invented his credentials, but as he is about to read it out his daughter Gracie interrupts to announce the arrival of the band instruments. The subject is put on hold until Act 2, Scene 4, when Cowell shows Marian proof of the situation, and she tearfully confronts Harold with it. In all the 1957 scripts, Marian makes an effort to defend Hill in the final scene and she tries to prevent Cowell's interference, but her independent discovery of Harold's invented educational background must have been added at some point during rehearsals (or the tryouts) because it is not in any of the draft scripts (the last of which, S12, is dated two weeks before rehearsals began on October 9). Yet it is perhaps the most important element of all: only Marian is smart enough to prove that Hill is lying.

FRAGMENTS OF SMALL-TOWN AMERICA

In a note published in the script of *The Music Man*, Willson wrote:

Dear Director:

THE MUSIC MAN was intended to be a Valentine and not a caricature. Please do not let the actors—particularly Zaneeta, Mayor Shinn and Mrs. Shinn, who takes herself quite seriously—mug or reach for comedy effect. The Del Sarte [*sic*] ladies also should be natural and sincere, never raucous, shrewish or comic per se. The humor of this piece depends upon its technical faithfulness to the real small-town Iowans of 1912 who certainly did not think they were funny at all.

Faithfully,
MEREDITH WILLSON

In part, this is just another example of Willson promoting the "researched" or "remembered" nature of the show, as discussed in Chapter 1. As such, it should be approached with caution, but it is an interesting statement on style, implying that the humor should be played straight. Equally, while Willson obviously loves the small town, it is also integral to the show that the parochial attitudes one can find there need to be challenged. Not for nothing did he add the song "Iowa Stubborn" to the score at some point in 1957, making it clear that the "River Citizians" do not generally have open minds. Although River City is connected to the wider world through the railway, the latter's main purpose seems to be to deliver goods; one can hardly imagine most of the characters in *The Music Man* leaving to go somewhere else, hence their excitement when the Wells Fargo Wagon arrives. The small-town figure leaving the Midwest to visit the big city is a theme of both Willson's (real) *And There I Stood with My Piccolo* and (fictional) *Who Did What to Fedalia?*, and it is clear that he valued the opportunity to experience the wider world. Marian's speech in the final scene ("Well I should think there ought to be some of you who could forget our everlasting Iowa stubborn chip-on-the-shoulder arrogance long enough to remember River City before Harold Hill arrived") is a call to attention, reminding the community that sometimes outside influences are positive. Mayor Shinn's statement that "[if] there are those, as I have heard, who are melting tar and collecting feathers, I will not say them nay!" is equally a reminder that there is a dark side to this show, lurking beneath its charming surface.

Both the charm and the darkness are essential to its success and we have already seen how difficult it was from the beginning to achieve a balance between the two. Because the story is an original there was no natural structure to follow and for at least two years of the book's genesis it seemed like a jumble of interesting ideas that mostly did not cohere. This chapter has addressed numerous examples already, most especially the serious disability plotline that was not only emotive because of the situation of Jim Paroo but also featured a particularly nasty iteration of the George Breen/Shinn character. Willson played around for some time with practically all the main figures in the town before reaching the familiar configuration from the Broadway version. For example, George Breen the chair of the school board (S1) becomes Mayor George Shinn (SF1), still provocative and vicious; he remains so in all versions up to and including S8, after which Jim disappears as a character and Shinn softens somewhat.

Nevertheless, there are versions in which Willson presents him as gentler in some scenes. For example, in SF1, Shinn is part of the barbershop quartet with Marcellus Washburn, Oliver Hix, and Chief Lock quite early in the story. This means that he is depicted singing love songs with the quartet and also seems more of a team member than in S1, where he tends to act on his own. At the other extreme, two synopses from 7 (SY1) and June 15, 1955 (SY2), make him much more psychological and more central to the plot. Here, he is called George Knott, owner of the town's Emporium (formerly the Corner Store). He is the father of two daughters, Maida and Marian. The former has died before the show begins; after running off with a piano teacher called Homer Paroo, she died giving birth to Jim. Homer is also dead, and George keeps Jim hidden due to his disability. Therefore, George uses his position as head of the school board and various other civic positions to ban music in River City because he blames Homer—the piano teacher—for the death of his daughter. This creates a need for Harold Hill in the town but it also frames George as the main protagonist, quite different from the blustery, relatively harmless, secondary figure depicted in the Broadway show (and particularly through Paul Ford's performance in the movie).

We have also seen that Eulalie Mackecknie Shinn went through various permutations before the Broadway version. The drafts in which she has secretly stolen Jim Paroo's melody to pass off as the school song (e.g., S1 and S2—the idea was retained throughout 1954 and 1955) turn her into exactly the kind of caricaturish figure Willson admonished directors to avoid in his introduction to the script. He seemed to feel she was an important cornerstone of the community, though, and in one synopsis from April 13, 1956, Willson begins the story with her: "Eulalie Mackecknie Shinn runs River City, Iowa. From her late father, old Truthful Mackecknie, she inherited, not only a few representative mortgages, but also his 'sticky' fingers. The mortgages, plus the Mackecknie Grocery helped to put her husband George Shinn into the Mayor's chair and her 'sticky' fingers helped to keep him there. Nothing by way of public funds ever gets by the City Council, of whom Eulalie is prime intimidator, unless some part of it is divertible to the Shinns." As with Shinn, Willson is overreaching here, trying to make Eulalie into a rounded character but instead overcomplicating her—and by Broadway, she had been considerably toned down, expressing outrage at Marian's "dirty books" of love poetry but not significantly getting in anyone's way (see Fig. 2.1).[27]

Fig. 2.1. A scene from the original Broadway production of The Music Man *starring Robert Preston. Credit: Photofest.*

To balance both the George-Eulalie and Marian-Harold relationships, Willson added a third couple from a different generation: the teenagers Tommy and Zaneeta. This pairing was weak, leading to the excision of their only number, "You Don't Have to Kiss Me Goodnight," during the out-of-town tryouts; Ethan Mordden notes that this cut made them become "little more than part of the Merry Villager body count."[28] Yet Willson had seen some version of them as integral to the show during its entire development, starting from S1 when the opening scene showed Tommy trying to set off firecrackers. Indeed, Tommy is a vital conduit between Hill and the boys in all versions: he is their leader, deputizing for Hill in his absence. Tommy also represents the delinquency that is used as the premise for the creation of the band, and his reformation is enacted partly through his musical activities and partly through his burgeoning love for Zaneeta. Significantly, Tommy's surname changed from Britt to Djilas between S8 (January 1957) and S9 (April 1957), indicating that his family has immigrated from Europe at some point in its past. This is an example of River City being less socially homogenized than it might first appear.

Intriguingly, a draft of Act 1 written during November 1955 (SF5) contains roughly a page of conversation between Marian, Harold, and Gramma Bird in which Willson expands on this idea. Marian tells the other two about going to Powder Street, an area across the creek where the immigrants in the community live, to sell them tickets to the band concert (this is the version where Harold promises that the proceeds from the concert can pay for the book fund). Marian reports that "They were so nice to me" and admits, "I'm so ashamed I've never been over to Powder Street, never even asked those people to come to the Library" (1-9-B). Harold counters that there were "two killings last month over there, and Doc Swale sewed up forty-three knife cuts in a Power Street Polack last week," but Marian says, "I don't care, we just don't give them a chance. . . . Harold, there's a French-Canadian family over there. They came here all the way from Cambrodia, three hundred miles north of Saskatoon. And there's Montenegrans and Lithuanians and Bulgarians" (1-9-C). With this discussion, suddenly ethnicity was an explicit topic of the musical, ironically taking it into territory that would be the main theme of *The Music Man*'s chief competition of the 1957–1958 season, *West Side Story*. Within a couple of weeks this dialogue had been cut (i.e., by S2), but we can see that Willson was at least partly conscious of the overwhelming whiteness of River City and that in the Djilas family there was at least some representation of the immigrant experience (albeit a crude, stereotyped one).

Two other important characters moved in and out of various drafts of the script. Just as Jim and Winthrop were combined into one character, characteristics of Gramma Bird and Marcellus Washburn were merged together into the figure of Marcellus; elements of Gramma Bird also moved over to Mrs. Paroo's character and parts of Marcellus come from August Bushkins. In S1, one of the reasons why Harold seems weak is that there is little opportunity for him to openly discuss the deviousness that makes his character entertaining in the

Broadway version. This led to the addition of Bushkins (the instrument maker) over the summer of 1955 (SY2–SY8 and SF3).

In most of these versions, it is explained that in each town, Harold sells the instruments and uniforms to the people, flees, and Bushkins (who has been hiding just outside the town for weeks) arrives, pretends to be shocked by his partner's fraudulence, and buys back the unused instruments and uniforms for a fraction of the cost, thereby making a regular profit. Marcellus also exists in all these versions, alternating as the sheriff, the town photographer, the head of the entertainment committee, or a combination of all three, and from S4 (c. May 1956) he sings "Shipoopi" at the top of Act 2, but he only becomes Hill's accomplice from S9 (April 1957) onward. (It is perhaps no coincidence that this is the first script that reflects Kermit Bloomgarden's formal input and perhaps Franklin Lacey's too.) The new Harold-Marcellus partnership then becomes a narrative device to show the audience what's really going on, right down to the revelation that Harold's real name is Gregory (something that adds to his aura and mystique: we never actually learn who he is).

As well as Bushkins, Willson also explored the possibility of having Gramma Bird as Harold's confidante in various versions from June 1955 (SY2, SY3, SF1). She sees through him within minutes of meeting him and reveals that she too is a fraud: she makes money as the town piano teacher but is actually using the pianola to demonstrate points and can neither play nor read music. This element was removed by the late 1955 versions, in which she becomes more of a matchmaker (such as in the popcorn scene discussed above). In S2 (December 1955) she has a slightly bigger role again, this time recognizing that Eulalie Shinn is trying to hide something (the pianola roll that proves she has not written the new school song) and threatening to expose her as a means of silencing her efforts to expose Jim. And as late as S7 (November 1956), Gramma Bird is the one who stands up in the final scene to defend Hill as a "ray of sunshine" (2-10-2). But by S9, that strand of her persona has been transferred to Mrs. Paroo (who exists in nearly all versions) while Marcellus has become Harold's accomplice, and—no longer having a function—she disappears.

CONCLUSION: THE CHALLENGE OF WRITING AN ORIGINAL

It is highly unusual that Meredith Willson wrote the book, music, and lyrics for *The Music Man*. Stephen Sondheim's only completed attempt at that configuration of responsibilities, *Climb High* (1953), has never been produced, and although several British figures—including Lionel Bart, Noël Coward, and Sandy Wilson—were solely responsibility for the writing of various of their musicals, only one other major golden-age American figure adopted this model: Willson's friend and sometime mentor Frank Loesser (who wrote *The Most Happy Fella*, which was also produced by Bloomgarden, on his own).[29] Leaving aside the much earlier output of George M. Cohan (also a composer-lyricist-librettist, but one who operated in quite a different production system), this makes *The Music Man* by far the most successful American musical before *Hamilton* (2015) in which the book, music, and lyrics were all contributed by the same person (which is not to dismiss the input of Franklin Lacey or Willson's orchestrators). This achievement is all the more impressive given the particular challenge of writing this musical: an original story without a literary or cinematic background, albeit one with resonances of the Pied Piper, Jimmy Valentine (a reformed criminal in O. Henry's short story "A Retrieved Reformation" from 1903), and Johnny Appleseed (the pioneer nurseryman), three influences that Willson frequently acknowledged.

This chapter has revealed that the main difficulty in putting *The Music Man* on the stage was not the typical one of production issues such as finding a producer or financial backing but rather of getting the book right. It is true that the production team and cast had to be hired and of course the success of these decisions should not be taken for granted; yet first Feuer and Martin and then Bloomgarden were keen to produce the show, which meant that the kind of business and logistical problems that plagued the production of *My Fair Lady*, for example, were not as pressing for Willson as they were for Lerner and Loewe.[30] Instead, as Shakespeare's Hamlet observes, the play's the thing, especially by the 1950s when the book for a Broadway musical was expected to consist of more than a contrived series of excuses for song and dance.

3

COMPOSING THE SCORE FOR
A MUSICAL ABOUT MUSIC

• • •

INTRODUCTION: THE NATURE OF SONG IN
THE MUSIC MAN

When he set out to write the show, Meredith Willson had strong feelings about the role of music in *The Music Man*. We saw in Chapter 2 that the plot shifted significantly from the earliest surviving draft (S1, February 1954) to the opening night (BV, December 1957), but common to all versions was the positive use of music by a musically illiterate fraudster to transform a repressive community. This meant that music had a narrative role in the show as a theme of the plot, with various characters singing or playing music as part of the story. Yet Willson also had an aesthetic vision for the musical that was not merely a reflection of the book of this specific show. He commented in *But He Doesn't Know the Territory*:

> I had developed an abiding conviction through the years that in a musical comedy the musical numbers ought to grow out of the dialogue without interruption or jerkiness. . . . [T]he song ought to materialize out of the dialogue, and I didn't care how many unjustified musicians there were doing the accompanying in the orchestra pit so long as the audience wasn't *pushed* into song—and then *dragged* out again into dialogue. And *pushed* and *dragged* all evening long. "In fact I'm dying to make the whole show like one song lyric," I says [to Ernie Martin], "dialogue and all. All in one piece."[1]

He went on further to explain how this approach was the subject of a disagreement with Ernie Martin (who was to have produced the show with Cy Feuer before eventually withdrawing; see Chapter 2). For example, Martin was concerned that Willson wanted to "write the dang dialogue like a song, with rhymes," and this could make the show seem like a poem, but Willson rebutted him: "I said just the opposite—write the dang *songs* as dialogue. *Without* rhymes. People don't talk in rhyme. I want to have an underlying unsuspected rhythm underneath the dialogue when I'm ready for a song, like a cable running underneath Powell

The Big Parade. Dominic McHugh, Oxford University Press. © Oxford University Press 2021.
DOI: 10.1093/oso/9780197554739.003.0004

Street—then I can hook on to it any time I wish without the audience realizing it." He continued: "I . . . think there's a way of making rhythmic dialogue get you unsuspectingly into song, in fact serve as either dialogue or song. The rhythm could make it perfectly acceptable song whenever you want to reveal that rhythm, and the fact that there's no rhyme makes it perfectly acceptable dialogue in the meantime."[2]

What's particularly interesting about these statements is that Willson seems to be talking about the same kind of motivation that led to what Rodgers and Hammerstein called the "integrated musical," but with quite a different aesthetic vision. Willson was not just talking about developing a dramatic relationship between a song and its context (which is the idea at the heart of the integrated musical) but more specifically a musical one too. He states an interest in particularly engaging with the process of segueing into and out of song and talks of having an overall sense of rhythm whereby textual material could be song, dialogue, or both. This helps to account for various of the numbers in the score, such as "Rock Island" and "Trouble," where a sense of song creeps in without its necessarily being articulated through attention-grabbing or disruptive introductory music. By writing the songs and book in a particular way, he proposed that the score and book could be at one rather than at odds with one another (or even one serving the other).

Nevertheless, he also envisaged using diegetic numbers to make music fit within the world of the show too. This was the case from the earliest draft of the score, shown in Table 3.1, right through to the Broadway version, shown in Table 3.2. Examples include "American Patrol" and "Stars and Stripes" in 3.1, pre-existing numbers with music not by Willson that would be played through a phonograph, and the traditional song "Columbia, Gem of the Ocean" in both 3.1 and 3.2. In these examples, Willson appears to be appealing to the idea of authenticity—however strained—by populating the landscape of the show with music that people in a Midwestern town might have heard in 1912.

Other borrowings include church music ("Love Divine," "Doxology," "Holy, Holy"), Albert Parlow's *Anvil Polka* (which is used for two cut numbers in which a character [Gramma Bird or Marian] delivers a rhythmic patter in time to it), patriotic songs ("True-Hearted," "America, My Country"), and dance music (C. R. Howell's *Rustle of Spring*). On top of this, there are numbers where the characters are playing or singing music as part of the story, including "Gary, Indiana," "You Never Miss the Water," and the piano lesson. The last of these is an especially good example of how diegetic music is used to facilitate non-diegetic song: Amaryllis's "real" piano lesson is heard, then as Marian and Mrs. Paroo argue in time and tune to it, the orchestra subtly joins in and the song is suddenly taking place on a parallel diegetic plane to the onstage music (the piano exercises). (Scott Miller claims it is "hard to tell whether the music is diegetic or not," but it seems clear that it is both.)[3] Such an approach to song is quite at odds with Willson's dismissive attitude toward the function of diegetic music expressed in *Territory* (see his earlier mention of "unjustified musicians in the pit").

Table 3.1. Synopsis of musical numbers for *The Music Man*, February 2, 1954 version. Note that Marian's name was spelled differently in this version (see Chapter 2). Sources: S1, GASF; *The Silver Triangle*, vocal score, Juilliard.

Act 1		Act 2	
Scene 1: A street outside of River City High School. The morning of July 4th, 1913.	"American Patrol" (Phonograph) "Stars and Stripes Forever" (Phonograph)	Scene 1: a) Exterior of River City Public Library. Several weeks later. b) Interior of River City Public Library. A half hour later.	a) "Don't Put Bananas on Bananas" (Eulaly Mackecknie Breen) b) "Marion the Librarian" (Harold and Marion)
Scene 2: River City High School Assembly Room. That night.	"Columbia The Gem of the Ocean" (Townspeople) a. "You Never Miss the Water Till the Well Runs Dry" (Eulaly Mackecknie Breen) b. "The Rustic Dance" (Eulaly Mackecknie Breen) "True-Hearted, Whole-Hearted" (Harold) "Washington Post March" (offstage band) "Gary, Indiana" (Harold and Townspeople) "America" (Townspeople) "Till I Met You" (Harold) "I Want to Go to Chicago" (Marion)	Scene 2: Mrs. Paroo's Quarters. The next night.	"Mother Darlin'" (reprise) (Jim Paroo) Caspar Hauser Ballet
Scene 3: Mrs. Paroo's Quarters. Later that night.	[No numbers]	Scene 3: River City High School Assembly Room. Three nights later.	Rustic Dance (player-piano)

Continued

Table 3.1. Continued

Act 1		Act 2	
Scene 4: Gramma Bird's Thread Store. Just after supper, two weeks later.	[No numbers]	Scene 4: Gramma Bird's Thread Store.	"River City, Go!" (Eulaly, Gramma, Harold, Band and Chorus)
Scene 5: A street in River City. The same evening.	"The Blue Ridge Mountains are in North Carolina" (Harold, Kids, and Mrs. Britt) "Too Soon Old" (Mr. Bushkins) "Mind If I Tell You I Love You" (Quartet) "Sweet and Low" (Quartet) "You Don't Have to Kiss Me Goodnight" (Tommy and Zaneeta)	Scene 5: A street in River City. That afternoon.	"Gary, Indiana" (reprise) and "River City, Go" (reprise) (Harold and Kids) "I'd Like a Memory" (Harold and Grade)
Scene 6: Mrs. Paroo's Quarters. A few minutes later.	"Mother Darlin'" (Harold and Mrs. Paroo) "The Wonderful Plan" (Harold)	Scene 6: Mrs. Paroo's Quarters. The following Saturday afternoon.	[No numbers]
Scene 7: River City High School Assembly Room. A few minutes later.	"In the Evening by the Moonlight" (Quartet) "River City, Go" (without music) (Harold)	Scene 7: The same. The following morning: Sunday.	"Love Divine" (Townspeople) "Doxology: Praise God from Whom All Blessings Flow" (Townspeople)

Table 3.1. Continued

Act 1		Act 2	
Scene 8: A street outside of River City High School. Ten minutes later.	"Blow" (Mrs. Paroo)	Scene 8: A street in River City. That night.	"River City, Go!" (reprise) (Background Band)
		Scene 9: River City High School Assembly Room. The following afternoon— Monday, September 8th.	"River City, Go" (reprise) (Everybody) "Minuet in G" (River City Boys' Band) "Till I Met You" (reprise) (Harold and Marion)

This chapter examines Willson's score for *The Music Man* by considering different types of musical number. A brief comparison of Tables 3.1 and 3.2 reveals that only six of the numbers outlined in the original score actually made it to Broadway and that two of these were not by Willson (the traditional "Columbia, Gem of the Ocean" and Beethoven's "Minuet in G"). Only the latter two stayed in roughly the same position in the Broadway version; the rest were significantly reworked or reframed. Furthermore, Table 3.3 reveals a list of the surviving songs and other musical numbers—including traditional songs and the "Minuet in G"—that Willson wrote or considered using in *The Music Man* at one time or another. Ignoring these pre-existing numbers and songs that bear a close relationship to one another, Willson wrote almost sixty songs for the score, two-thirds of which were discarded along the road. Many of these songs will be examined during the course of this chapter, which also uses various of the sources listed in Table 3.3 to shed new light on Willson's remarkably inventive, creative score for his Broadway triumph.

CREATIVE PROCESSES

In 2012, the estate of Meredith Willson donated most of his music manuscripts to the library at the Juilliard School of Music in New York, where Willson himself had studied as a teenager. There are over 630 entries in the library's catalogue, covering his major compositions and numerous lesser and unused works, including various songs that were cut from *The Music Man*. However, the sketch material for the show is not exceptionally complete. In some cases, this may be

Table 3.2. Synopsis of musical numbers for *The Music Man*, Broadway version.
Source: published piano-vocal score.

Act 1		Act 2	
	Overture (Orchestra)		Entr'acte (Orchestra)
Scene 1: A Railway Coach. Morning, July 4th, 1912	Train Opening (Orchestra) Rock Island (Charlie Cowell and Salesmen)	Scene 1: Madison Gymnasium. The following Tuesday evening.	"Eulalie's Ballet" (Orchestra and Stage Player-Piano) "It's You" (Olin, Oliver, Ewart, Jacey, Eulalie, Maud, Ethel, Alma, and Mrs. Squires) "Shipoopi" (Marcellus, Marold, Marian, Tommy, Zaneeta, and Kids) "Shipoopi (Playoff)" (Orchestra) "Pick-a-Little, Talk-a-Little" (reprise) (Eulalie, Maud, Ethel, Alma, Mrs. Squires, and Ladies)
Scene 2: River City, Iowa, Center of Town. Immediately following.	"Iowa Stubborn" (Townspeople) "Trouble" (Harold and Townspeople) "Trouble (Playoff)" (Townspeople)	Scene 2: The Hotel Porch. The following Wednesday evening.	"Lida Rose/Will I Ever Tell You?" (Olin, Oliver, Ewart, Jacey, Marian)
Scene 3: A Street. Immediately following.	"Walking Music" (Orchestra)	Scene 3: The Paroos' Porch. Immediately following.	"Gary, Indiana" (Winthrop) "Lida Rose (Reprise)" (Olin, Oliver, Ewart, Jacey)

Table 3.2. *Continued*

Act 1		Act 2	
Scene 4: The Paroo House. That evening.	"Piano Lesson/ If You Don't Mind My Saying So" (Marian, Mrs. Paroo, and Amaryllis) "Goodnight, My Someone" (Marian and Amaryllis)	Scene 4: The Footbridge. Fifteen minutes later.	"It's You (Ballet)" (Townspeople, Boys, and Girls) "Till There Was You" (Marian and Harold)
Scene 5: Madison Gymnasium. Thirty minutes later.	"Columbia, Gem of the Ocean" (Eulalie and Townspeople) "Trouble (Reprise)" (Harold) "Seventy-Six Trombones" (Harold, Boys, and Girls) "Seventy-Six Trombones (Playoff)" (Orchestra) "Sincere" (Olin, Oliver, Ewart, Jacey)	Scene 5: A Street. Immediately following.	"Goodnight, My Someone/ Seventy-Six Trombones (Double Reprise)" (Marian and Harold)
Scene 6: Exterior of Madison Library. Immediately following.	"Walking Music (Reprise)" (Orchestra) "The Sadder but Wiser Girl" (Harold and Marcellus) "Pick-a-Little, Talk-a-Little/Goodnight Ladies" (Eulalie, Maud, Ethel, Alma, Mrs. Squires, Ladies of River City, Olin, Oliver, Ewart, Jacey)	Scene 6: Madison Park. A few minutes later.	"Ice Cream Sociable" (Orchestra and Stage Player-Piano) "Chase Music" (Orchestra) "Till There Was You (Reprise)" (Harold)

Continued

Table 3.2. Continued

Act 1		Act 2	
Scene 7: Interior of Madison Library. Immediately following.	"Marian the Librarian" (Harold and Dancers) "1st Seventy-Six Trombones (Crossover) (Orchestra)	Scene 7: River City High School Assembly Room. Immediately following.	"Minuet in G" (Stage Band and Orchestra) "Finale" (Orchestra) "Curtain Call Music" (Orchestra) "Exit Music" (Orchestra)
Scene 8: A Street. The following Saturday noon.	"2nd Seventy-Six Trombones (Crossover) (Orchestra)		
Scene 9: An Impressive Doorway. Immediately following.	"3rd Seventy-Six Trombones (Crossover) (Orchestra)		
Scene 10: The Paroos' Porch. That evening.	"My White Knight" (Marian)		
Scene 11: Center of Town. Noon the following Saturday.	"The Wells Fargo Wagon" (Winthrop and Townspeople) "Finale—Act One" (Orchestra)		

because he wrote the lyrics first and then improvised at the piano; an example is "Trouble," Hill's patter song, where sorting out the words almost certainly came before the rhythmic accompaniment. In other cases, there was nothing much to be worked out: there may be no holograph sketch for "Goodnight, My Someone," for example, because the melody is based on that of "Seventy-Six Trombones." Nevertheless, there are several numbers for which some sense of Willson's working processes can be gleaned from the holograph manuscripts.

It is unsurprising that "Marian the Librarian" is one of these, because it is the most chromatic and in respects the most complicated song in the score. Two pages of sketches show a curious evolution for the refrain. Fig. 3.1a shows that the opening vamp was sketched in one measure and was then to be repeated in mm. 2–4 but mm. 3–4 have then been crossed out. Harold's opening "Marian . . . Madam Librarian" ensues up to "What can I . . . ," then the soft-shoe music that follows

Table 3.3. List of sources for musical numbers for *The Music Man*.

Title	Versions in Which It Appears	Sources
America, My Country 'Tis of Thee	S1; SY7	No music; existing [traditional] piece. JST indicates where it would be played.
American Patrol	S1	Phonograph record of existing [traditional] music: no score. JST indicates where it would be played.
Anvil Polka	S1; S2; SF2; SF5; S6	Performed to pre-existing music. Dance only in SF2. JST indicates where it would be played but contains no music.
Being in Love	Movie only.	Movie soundtrack; lyric drafts, Juilliard (W181)
Blessings	S4; S6; S8-S10	Holograph score and typed lyric sheet, Juilliard (W078)
Blow	S1	JST; GASF also has several copies of a different finale with a stanza of new lyrics for a reprise of this song (part of a medley reprise-finale); holograph sketches and copyist's score, Juilliard (W079); holograph score and sketches, Juilliard (W110)
The Blue Ridge Mountains are in No'th Car'lina	S1	JST; holograph score and sketches, Juilliard (W079)
Casper Hauser Ballet	S1	JST indicates where it would be played but contains no score. [Probably never composed.]

Continued

Table 3.3. Continued

Title	Versions in Which It Appears	Sources
Clarification/Legitimate Rights of Procrastination	SF1; two versions bound with SY8; SF5; SF5; S2; S3	SF1 has lyrics only, spoken in time to "American Patrol"; GASF also has several alternate lyrics, including one with Hix/Marian, another with Hix/Shinn
Columbia, Gem of the Ocean	S1; S4-12; BV	PVS
Don't Put Bananas on Bananas	S1; SF1; SY3	JST; lyric sheet with annotations, holograph sketches, copyist score with annotations, Juilliard (W079)
Doxology	S1	JST indicates the position but does not include the score.
Een-teen	Not found in any dated script.	Copyist's score, Juilliard (W227); holograph sketch and score, Juilliard (W078)
Eulalie's Ballet	S9; S10; S12; BV	PVS; adaptation of Sinding's *Rustle of Spring*
Fireworks	Not found in any dated script.	Juilliard (W228)
Gary, Indiana	S1; S2; SY1; SY7; SF5; SF6; S3; S4; S6–S8; S11; S12; BV	JST (two identical instances); PVS; OCR
A Girl Should Never Give Her Lips until She Hears "I Love You"	SY11	No lyrics or music found.
Goodnight, My Someone	SF6; S3–S12; BV	PVS; OCR; holograph score and typed lyric sheet, Juilliard (W078)
Goodnight, My Someone/ Seventy-Six Trombones (double reprise)	S12	PVS; OCR

Table 3.3. Continued

Title	Versions in Which It Appears	Sources
Hepzibah	SF2	SF2 has lyrics only (music not found); GASF includes five script fragments including the lyric.
Holy, Holy	SF5	Lyrics only; music not found
Ice Cream Sociable	BV	PVS; adaptation of Sinding's *Rustle of Spring*
I Found a Horse-Shoe	SF7; S3-S12	Lyrics in SF7; holograph sketch, Juilliard (W078)
I'd Like a Memory	S1	JST (melody line only)
In the Evening by the Moonlight	S1	JST indicates where it would be played but contains no score.
Iowa Stubborn	S6; S9–S12; BV	PVS; S6 has a version with different lyrics for the salesmen and a solo reprise in the final scene for Harold; OCR
I-o-wuh (The Iowa Indian Song)	S3–S8; S11	Copyist score, Juilliard (W686)
It's You	SF2; SF5; S2; S9–S12; BV	PVS; GASF includes lyrics for version with Harold and another version for Tommy and Zaneeta; OCR
I Want to Go to Chicago	S1; SF1; SF5; S2	JST; holograph sketches, Juilliard (W079)
Just Becuz	Not found in any dated script.	Script fragment with lyric at GASF; holograph sketch, Juilliard (W079)
Lida Rose/Will I Ever Tell You?	S12; BV	Holograph score and annotated copyist's scores, solo version, Juilliard (W266); holograph score (including counterpoint), Juilliard (W145); PVS; OCR

Continued

Table 3.3. Continued

Title	Versions in Which It Appears	Sources
Love Divine	S1	JST indicates the position but does not include the score.
Marian the Librarian	S1; SF1; SY1; SY2; SY7; S2–S12; BV	JST indicates the position but does not include the score; holograph score, Juilliard (W078); holograph fair copy score, Juilliard (W267); annotated lyric sheet, Juilliard (W079); holograph sketch, Juilliard (W267); PVS; OCR
Mind If I Tell You I Love You	S1; SF1; SF5; S2; SY11; S3–S10	JST
Minuet in G	SF1; SY2; SY3; SY7; SY9; S2; BV	PVS
Mother Darlin'	S1; S4-S8;	JST (Irish Reel and Ballad Versions); holograph score, Juilliard (W079)
My Baby (I've Already Started In to Try to Figure Out a Way to Go to Work to Try to Get You)	Listed in S12 but crossed out.	Lyric only: GASF.
My White Knight (solo version)	S6; S9–S12; BV	PVS; OCR; annotated lyric sheets, holograph and copyist scores of extended soliloquy version, Juilliard (W232); four sections of extended version, holograph score, Juilliard (W267)

Table 3.3. Continued

Title	Versions in Which It Appears	Sources
My White Knight/The Sadder but Wiser Girl (duet version)	S4; S6; S8–S10	Copyist score, Juilliard (W233); holograph fair copy and annotated typed lyric sheet (duet); holograph sketches (two versions of the "White Knight" parts only), Juilliard (W078)
Piano Lesson/If You Don't Mind My Saying So	S9–S12; BV	Holograph sketches (score and lyrics), Juilliard (W267); PVS; OCR
Pick-a-Little, Talk-a-Little/ Goodnight Ladies	S6; S9–S12; BV	PVS; S6 includes a version with a counterpoint in which three male townspeople complain about Hill; OCR
Rasmussen's Law	S6; S11	Copyist's scores, Juilliard (W303)
Ridiculous	S4; S8	Patter speech set to the music of "Marian the Librarian"; CDR
River City, Go!	S1; S2; SF1; SY1; SY2; SY3; SY5; SY7; SY9; SF5; S4; S7; S8	JST (one version has no score but notes: "tap routine unaccompanied"; the three second-act versions have a score); "Mason City, Go" version, holograph sketch and copyist score, Juilliard (W079)
Rock Island	S4–S12; BV	PVS; OCR; holograph sketches and copyist score (dated August– September 1957), Juilliard (W305); holograph fair copy with piano accompaniment, Juilliard (W078)

Continued

Table 3.3. Continued

Title	Versions in Which It Appears	Sources
Rustic Dance	S1	Existing piece by C. R. Howell. JST indicates the position but does not include the score; PVS.
The Sadder but Wiser Girl	S4–S11; BV	PVS; OCR; holograph sketch, Juilliard (W306); holograph melodic sketch, annotated typed lyric sheet, and holograph fair copy with extra lyrics, Juilliard (W078); additional lyrics, GASF
Seventy-Six Trombones	SF1; SF5; SY8; S2; SF6; S3–12; BV	JST; PVS; alternate two-strain version and encores with antique instruments, lyric only (GASF); holograph sketch with unfamiliar counterpoint and holograph score, Juilliard (W079); lyric sheets, Juilliard (W308); OCR
Shipoopi	SF5; SF6; S2; SY11; S3–S12; BV	JST; PVS; GASF includes lyrics for versions for Harold and Bushkins; S6 includes version for Eulalie, Tommy, and Zaneeta; holograph sketch and holograph score, Juilliard (W079); holograph sketch (six measures), Juilliard (W008); OCR
Sincere	BV ["Ice Cream" section is in SY7]	Juilliard (W310); PVS; OCR

Table 3.3. Continued

Title	Versions in Which It Appears	Sources
The Skirt Dance	SF5; SF6; S2	Referenced in script; music not found
Stars and Stripes Forever	S1	Phonograph record of existing music: no score. JST indicates where it would be played.
Sweet and Low	S1; S6; S7; S9	JST indicates where it would be played but contains no score. Presumably the same as "Will I Ever Tell You?" but without "Lida Rose."
The Think System	Not found in any dated script.	Holograph score, GASF
This Is It	SF2	SF2 has lyrics only; score material, Juilliard (W686); GASF includes lyrics for another version for Harold.
Till I Met You	S1; SF5; S2; SY11; S3; S4; S7	JST
Till There Was You	S10–S12; BV	PVS; OCR. See also "Till I Met You."
Tomorrow	S9–S12	Holograph score, Juilliard (W331)
Too Soon Old	S1	JST; holograph score, Juilliard (W079)
Trouble	S4–S12; BV	Holograph fair copy, Juilliard (W078); PVS; OCR
True-Hearted, Whole-Hearted	S1	JST (two identical versions).
Walking Music	S4–S12; BV	PVS
Washington Post	S1	No music; existing piece. JST indicates where it would be played.

Continued

Table 3.3. Continued

Title	Versions in Which It Appears	Sources
The Wells Fargo Wagon	SF1; SY8; SF5; S2; S4–S12; BV	JST (extra lyrics unfamiliar from BV); holograph score, Juilliard (W079); PVS; OCR
The Wonderful Plan	S1; SF1; SY2; SY7; S2–S10	JST (notes: "After a sermon by Mark Hague"); holograph sketch, Juilliard (W110)
You Don't Have to Kiss Me Goodnight	S1; SF5; SF6; S2; S6; S7; S9; S12	Lyric sketch, holograph sketches, and alternative version, Juilliard (W079); holograph sketch (alternative) and holograph fair copy, Juilliard (W342); sketch, Juilliard (W008)
You Never Miss the Water Till the Well Runs Dry	S1	JST (includes Schottische section that matches the "Piano Lesson" cross-hand piece from the Broadway version.)

JST = copyist's bound score of *The Silver Triangle*, Juilliard (WillsonBxB06f02)
PVS = Published vocal score
BV = Broadway version
OCR = Original Cast Recording
CDR = Composer's Demo Recording
Codes starting with W indicate the Juilliard catalogue entry

in the Broadway version of the song appears on an alternative page (Fig. 3.1b). Many of the lyrics have been laid out on the music (both pages) and a few extra ones have been sketched (presumably as they came to Willson) at the bottom of 3.1b. This suggests (but does not prove) an unusual relationship between music and lyrics whereby they were developed in tandem: the music does not seem like a straightforward retrospective setting of the lyric (not least because the lyrics at the bottom of the page are obviously new ideas) but the structure is so particular that he obviously had several sections in mind. Fig. 3.1c also shows some interaction between the development of words and music: the lyric has been changed in red pen in various places and some chords have been sketched in pencil against the words to the bridge passage.

(a)

Fig. 3.1a. "Marian the Librarian," sketch 1.

Further, it is possible that the material in 3.1b was written before that for 3.1a because the fourth system of 3.1b contains a very rough sketch with chord names for the bridge passage ("In the moonlight"); this section is written out with considerably more detail on 3.1a. Also, the third system of 3.1b consists of unfamiliar music with no lyric, again suggesting that this is an early idea that was superseded by the final version of the bridge on 3.1a. Another striking feature of 3.1a is the metronome marking at the top left-hand corner, suggesting Willson

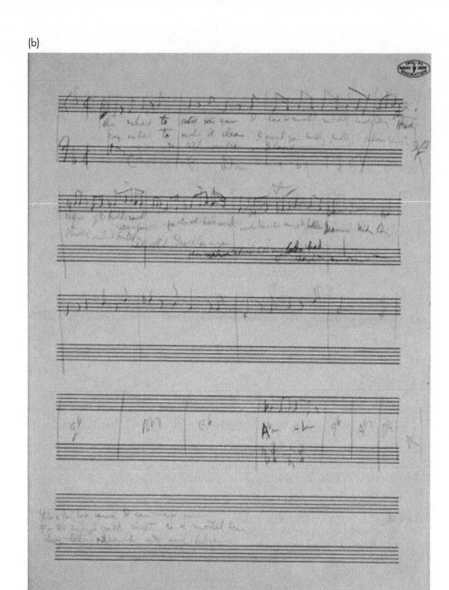

Fig. 3.1b. "Marian the Librarian," sketch 2.

had a clear sense of how the piece should be performed. His manuscripts do not tend to indicate metronome markings, so this may also be a reflection of the hypnotic,[4] metronomic quality of the opening vamp of the song.

Despite the use of a soft-shoe rhythm, "Marian the Librarian" may be the closest that Willson comes to Western classical music in his songs for the show. There may be no deliberate allusion but there are some broad noticeable similarities between the number and that of Dukas's *The Sorcerer's Apprentice*, one of Willson's favorite pieces and one of the few he mentions by name in *And There*

(c)

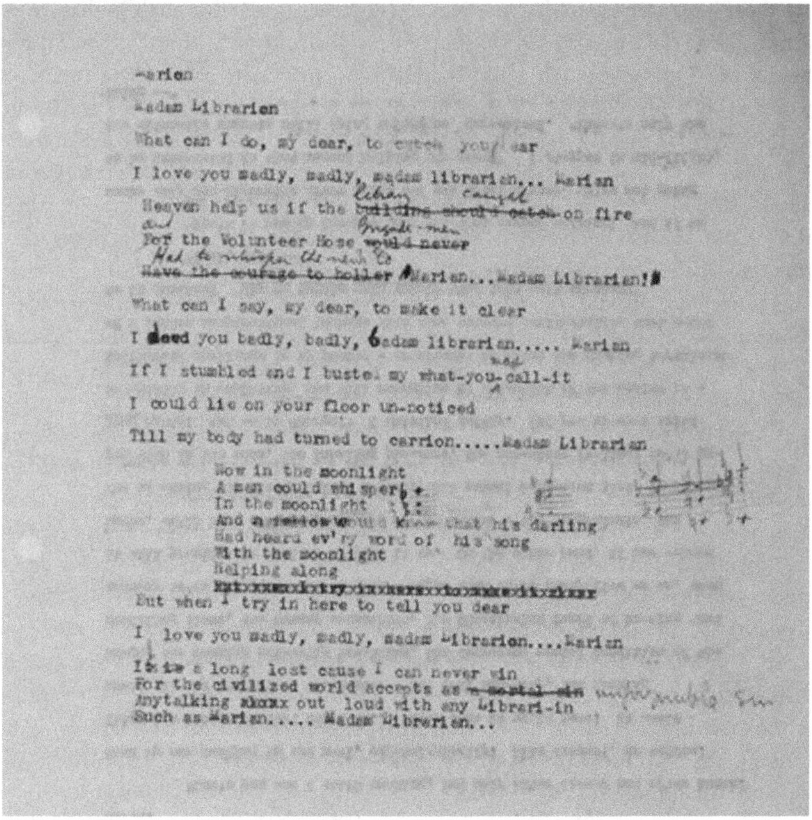

Fig. 3.1c. "Marian the Librarian," lyric sheet.

I Stood with My Piccolo.[5] Musically, both feature a chromatic ostinato figure played by the bassoon, prominent use of triplet figures, a mixture of long sustained chromatic chords (e.g., the D minor 6 on "Marian") and fast-moving rhythms, and a hypnotic quality caused by repetition and harmonic tension. The abruptness of the last four chords of both pieces is similar too, and they even have the same notes in the bass. While the structure of the *Apprentice* is obviously more complex (and the piece is much longer), there is even a broad similarity between the overall story being depicted by both pieces: a feeling of stability is followed by a sense of chaos before control returns.

These similarities are so broad that there is no doubt that they are not meant to be noticed, if they exist at all. Yet Willson believed that more should be done to make classical music more accessible. At the time of writing *The Music Man*, he was presenting a radio program devoted to concert music (*How to Listen to Longhair Music*), and he wrote an article for *Variety* titled "Selling Long-Hair" in which he declared: "Europe has always sneered at America's lack of appreciation for long-hair music. This gulf of contempt has been tacitly presented at every council table of nations, has inspired basic mistrust, has impeded world progress, has cluttered international understanding, and continues to be thoroughly effective in perpetuating the barriers political, religious, lingual and racial. Even the most rose-bespectacled optimist must admit there is some justification for this attitude so wouldn't you think some patriotic soul would turn around and go to work and begin to start to try to dispense a little long-hair propaganda here in our beloved land?"[6]

Evidently Willson saw himself as such a figure, and the way he mixes complexity with accessibility in *The Music Man* could be seen as an extension of that. In addition to the unusual harmonic language of "Marian the Librarian," the plot's ultimate goal is the boys' performance of Beethoven's "Minuet in G" in the final scene. This piece has a presence through much of the show and therefore gives presence to art music (acknowledging, of course, that it is heard at its most banal because of the boys' lack of skill). Musical literacy and ability is part of this theme: a significant aspect of Harold Hill's shame is that he cannot read or play music.

Complexity of a different kind is heard in other parts of the score too. Willson reported that "Bob Fosse, the famous choreographer, turned down *The Music Man* on the grounds that the score all sounded alike to him,"[7] a reference to the fact that a number of the songs in the show were written to be performed in counterpoint and therefore had identical or complementary harmonies. An obvious example that made it into the Broadway text is "Lida Rose" and "Will I Ever Tell You?" (Sweet and Low), which the barbershop quartet and Marian perform together in Act 2. Another is "My White Knight" and "The Sadder but Wiser Girl": these were written to be performed together in counterpoint as part of the footbridge scene at the end of Act 1 from S4 to S10, that is, in versions from June 1956 to July 1957. (The number can be heard on Erich Kunzel's 1991 studio recording of the score with the Cincinnati Pops Orchestra.)

In these drafts of the script we have already heard Harold and Marian singing about their ideal partners earlier in the act, and in the duet version we suddenly discover that they—the songs and the characters who sing them—fit together. This resonance is sadly missing in the Broadway version of the show, but it has an equivalent in the double reprise of "Goodnight, My Someone" and "Seventy-Six Trombones," this time positioned two scenes before the end of Act 2, when we discover that these two songs have almost the same melody but in different time signatures (and with different rhythms). Although contrapuntal numbers had appeared in Broadway musical comedies before—"You're Just in Love" from Irving Berlin's *Call Me Madam* (1950) comes to mind—the employment of the device for psychological dramatic reasons is highly unusual. It is at once (musically) complex and (dramatically) easy to understand, satisfying Willson's vision for making sophisticated music comprehensible to all.

PATTER SONGS

Probably the most distinctive and admired aspect of the score is the use of patter songs to depict Hill and the other salesmen's spiel. It is this subgenre that allows

Willson to get the closest to the seamless transition between song and dialogue discussed earlier, especially in the numbers where there is little or no pitch in the vocal delivery, namely, "Trouble" and "Rock Island," as well as much of "The Sadder but Wiser Girl." Again, Willson draws attention to this in *But He Doesn't Know the Territory*:

> One day, in my constant preoccupation with cudgeling the brain for authentic recall, I got down a lot of stuff about the evils of the pool hall and some similar social scourges of 1912. This grew into a diatribe of some length and in reading it over I realized I had at last actually applied my lyric writer's ear to a hunk of dialogue without consciously intending to do so. Well. In fact the whole pool-hall speech would pass the standards of a good honest lyric, I thought, it having a fine rhythmic feel to it. Its words fell trippingly off the tongue without consonant bumping into consonant and without any embarrassing nonsustainable syllables showing up at the ends. And it didn't rhyme! So I started to work out an accompaniment—*not a tune, an accompaniment*.[8]

One of Willson's drafts for the lyric is reproduced in Fig. 3.2. It is already quite advanced but there are various signs of Willson working out how to make the song work rhythmically, especially the longest line (starting "J'ever try 'n'"), which he has chopped into several shorter lines with horizontal strokes. Some rhythmic beats are indicated by the word "slam" while important words to be emphasized in performance are underlined.

While Willson's account of the number draws attention to how it satisfies his personal aesthetic of how to make songs seem like dialogue, it is also obvious that this type of delivery is largely specific to Hill (and in one case the other salesmen) in *The Music Man*. The casting of the two main characters in the show is deliberately polarized musically: in the original production Hill was played by a charismatic actor, Robert Preston, while Marian was played by a legit soprano, Barbara Cook. Hill's numbers tend to emphasize the sense of "selling" that happens through the long lists of "Trouble," "Seventy-Six Trombones," and "The Sadder but Wiser Girl." The first two of these songs share a common format whereby Hill excites the townspeople and they repeat his words, showing they are buying into his pitch. However, there is a significant melody in "Trombones," while there are only occasional moments in "Trouble" where Hill sings with any kind of tone—and if the original Broadway cast album is anything to go by, the pitches written in the published score are not necessarily prescriptive or a reflection of what might have been performed on Broadway. Especially noticeable in this regard is the phrase "Plymouth Rock, and the Golden Rule," which is written as a descending scale in the score (from four bars before rehearsal mark K in the published score) but performed as an ascending scale by Preston on the album.

"Trombones" is also an example of musical mimesis, where Willson uses devices in the score to give an illusion of reality: the orchestration of the number, particularly the non-sung passages, uses the brass section—especially the trombones—to support Hill's message. Although the townspeople cannot literally hear the

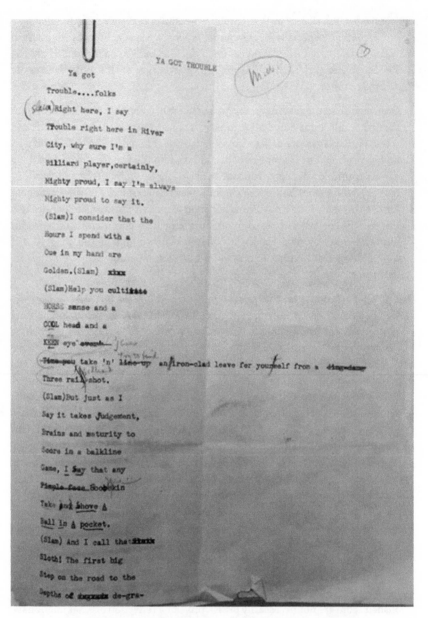

Fig. 3.2. "Trouble," typed lyric sheet with holograph annotations.

orchestra, the effect on the audience in the theater is to show that Hill's powers of persuasion are so potent that the characters believe they *can* actually hear the instruments whose names he is reeling off.

Willson was greatly enamored of the song and experimented with two other versions. One involves two encores with new lyrics describing antique instruments; he reproduces the words in *Territory*.[9] The other version—which

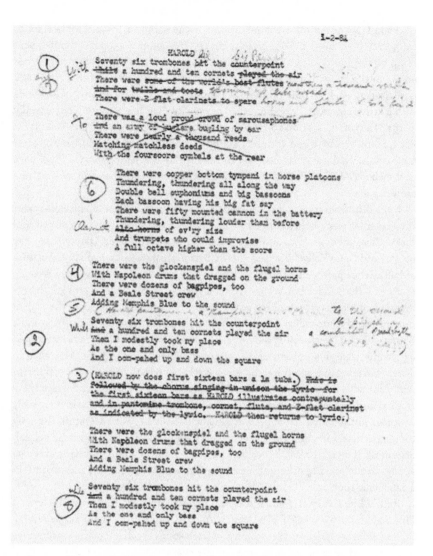

Fig. 3.3. *"Seventy-Six Trombones," typed lyric sheet showing amendment of original version to create (almost) the familiar Broadway version.*

was actually the original draft—uses a different structure whereby the music for the first four lines (the A section) is heard twice in a row, the second time with new lyrics, before the B section ("There were copper-bottom timpani . . ."). Fig. 3.3 shows a typed lyric sheet of the original longer version, with Willson's annotations to indicate how he intended to change and move lines around to create something closer to the more succinct version that was performed on Broadway. Nevertheless, he had not yet decided to cut the section marked 4 (i.e., the stanza starting "There were the glockenspiel and the flugel horns"), which was also repeated later in the song as the penultimate stanza.

Aside from these different renditions of the song, in S2 (a complete script from December 1955) Willson tried to make "Trombones" a flexible number that could be used as a kind of Leitmotif in the form of mini-reprises at two other points in the show. For example, at the end of the first scene of this script Hill is advised to seek accommodation at Gramma Bird's house and the scene ends with a little reprise of "Trombones" to new lyrics: "On the wings of your friendly words / I am off to Gramma Bird's / Just a block the other side of Main." Similarly, Act 2, Scene 2, was to end with Hill asking Oliver Hix to keep his scheme a secret for a few more days, once more set to the melody of "Trombones": "You'll have nothin' but GOOD NEWS now / If you keep me out'a the Hoose-gow / Until the uniforms arrive."

None of the actors who were considered for the role of Harold Hill were major singers: they were either known primarily as actors, like Robert Preston and Jackie Gleason, or as song-and-dance men, such as Dan Dailey, Danny Kaye, Ray Bolger, and Gene Kelly.[10] The last four names perhaps help to explain the nature of Hill's other patter-like songs, which tend to take the form of vaudeville-style routines. "The Sadder but Wiser Girl" is a good example. Like "Trouble," the orchestra begins softly with a few notes under the dialogue to obscure the transition into song, but unlike "Trouble" there are frequent rhymes in the lyric and a strong sense of "performing a number"; in the movie version, this is intensified by having Amaryllis present as an onscreen audience for Hill and Marcellus to deliver the song to, something that does not happen in the Broadway version. (In fact, Amaryllis is such an inappropriate audience for the song, and the staging emphasizes performance over content to such an extent, that the lyric is arguably undercut in the movie version.) The vaudevillian quality is written into the song too, particularly in the (thrice) repeated rising cadential figures in the section beginning "I snarl, I hiss"; repetition makes the music more emphatic and also alludes to the practice of repeating steps (or moving in the opposite direction) in a vaudeville routine.

Rather like Henry Higgins's "A Hymn to Him" from My Fair Lady, the lyric of "The Sadder but Wiser Girl" is an opportunity to laugh at the character delivering it. The offensive lyrics and sentiments of both songs are deliberately extreme: we are supposed to read them as signs of the characters' ingrained bias and need to develop, not of their lyricists' bigotry. In drafts of The Music Man from S4–S8 (June 1956–January 1957), Hill delivers "Sadder" to Marian and she slaps him at the end, arguably on behalf of the audience. (The slap is moved in S9–S12 to the end of "Marian the Librarian," another example of Willson clearly rejecting Harold's sentiments; in the Broadway version, the slap is still directed at Hill but Marian misses and accidentally hits Tommy instead.) By S9, "Sadder" is now sung to Marcellus, who joins in at the end, and the joke is that Harold's complacency (expressed in the lyric) about categorically not wanting to develop commitment to or respect for a woman is about to be shown up as he falls for Marian. In truth, he does not know himself at all.

As with "Trombones," Willson originally wrote much more material for the song, including a refrain with sentiments such as "I prefer the disillusioned face

/ And the heart that remains in place."[11] For a while, he also experimented with a song called "Rasmussen's Law," which extends some of the ideas of "Sadder" but is far less catchy. In S11, the plan was to give the song to Marcellus with responses from the barbershop quartet. But with sentiments such as "If she's a girl of easy virtue treat her like a maiden undefiled" and "If she's a princess treat her like a hussy / If she's a hussy treat her like a prude" set to a drawn-out "slow drag" tempo, the number has no charm or humor and it is easy to see why it was dropped. The fact it was not given to Harold despite being in "his" musical style must also have been a consideration; the same probably goes for the misogynistic "Don't Put Bananas on Bananas," an unattractive patter number for Eulalie in early versions in which she admonishes Marion (S1) or her friend Alma Barrett (SF1) for wearing makeup.[12]

One other vaudevillian song that did make it into the show was "Gary, Indiana," although the way it is used is quite different from the original intention. In all the draft scripts in which it appears (from S1 onward), the song is delivered by Harold. It does not appear at all in the final pre-rehearsal draft (S12) and is also not used in S9 and S10. This may seem surprising given the importance given to the number in all the early versions: in S1 and S2 it is placed in the opening scene as part of Harold's introduction to the town and was the vehicle used to captivate the townspeople before "Trouble" had been written. In S11 it is employed by Harold to distract the angry parents who are hounding him about why the instruments have not arrived, and it immediately precedes "The Wells Fargo Wagon" (which fully satisfies their complaints, of course).

But as the show reached its final version during 1957, it must have become apparent that Hill had too many songs, hence it only appears in one of the last four drafts. Willson does not mention the song in *Territory* and it is unclear how it came to be given to Winthrop, though it seems like a natural expansion of his character following his integration with Jim Paroo's character from S9 onward (see Chapter 2) and it makes sense that he would be given a second chance to sing after his prominent role in "The Wells Fargo Wagon." Nevertheless, the song truly belongs to Harold because it is in his musical style and it is obvious that he has invented it in order to develop the myth of his musical education at the Gary Conservatory. The lyric just about remains credible because Winthrop prefaces the song by explaining that Harold has taught it to him, but one can see why the decision was made in the movie version to give its first iteration to Hill, with a reprise for Winthrop, Marian, and Mrs. Paroo.

Although Hill is a one-off, he is also one of many dozens of traveling salesmen who toured North America in the period during which the show is set, so it makes sense that their common language is established in the opening number of the show. "Rock Island" underwent two major adjustments before it reached its familiar Broadway version. Fig. 3.4a reveals Willson's sketches for the melodic material that is heard in the brief "Train Opening" number in the published (Broadway) score but which was originally intended to be played underneath the salesmen's patter during "Rock Island." Fig. 3.4b shows an example of the opening

(a)

Fig. 3.4a. "Rock Island," holograph sketches.

of this version as well as an indication of the other major change made to the number during the tryouts: until late in the day, the curtain went up with the song—and the conversation—already in progress. Willson realized during the previews in Philadelphia that the audience was not engaging with what was going on onstage (because it was not very obvious) and also struggled to hear the words clearly. This led to the cutting of the orchestral part entirely, thus emphasizing the words, and then the decision to open the show with brief dialogue before showing the train gradually setting off, the latter impression depicted by the sound of the men's conversation increasing in speed.

It was a daring move to dispense with the orchestra in a song, especially one placed in the first scene, where musical comedies traditionally had upbeat, loud, lively accompaniments, and it is a sign of Willson's ingenuity that he saw how such an unconventional idea could work, despite having rehearsed and performed it with orchestra for some time. The result was, as Stephen Sondheim has observed, "one of the most brilliant numbers ever written, and the first time anybody had attempted to make music out of speech in the American theatre."[13]

Fig. 3.4b. "Rock Island," copyist's score, 1.

MARIAN'S SOLILOQUY

Willson's ambitions for the score of *The Music Man* meant that by the time the show reached rehearsal, most of the numbers had something quirky or unusual about them. The amount of time he spent writing the music was considerable and even the few sketches examined so far in this chapter draw attention to a high level of detail, editing, and self-criticism, for example in the decision to remove the orchestra from "Rock Island." But an even more striking instance of a drastic change to a number is Marian's "My White Knight." The first time it appears in a script (S4), it is in the duet version in which Harold enters after one refrain to sing "The Sadder but Wiser Girl" in counterpoint with it. But in S6, then from S9 right through rehearsals and into the tryouts, Willson wanted to develop the song into an extended solo soliloquy, providing Marian with a distinctive number—and stage time—to counterbalance Harold's "Trouble."[14] By the time Willson was writing The Music Man, the extended soliloquy had become an important song form on Broadway thanks to the impact of Billy Bigelow's soliloquy from Rodgers and Hammerstein's Carousel (1945). Two numbers from the same team's The King and I (1951), "Shall I Tell You What I Think of You?" and "A Puzzlement," and "I've Grown Accustomed to Her Face" from Lerner and Loewe's My Fair Lady (1956), provided further examples of this natural development of the way song could be used on Broadway at a time when the genre was increasingly leaning toward musical complexity equivalent to an operatic form. With Willson's desire to provide a marriage of song and drama in his score, it is understandable that he wanted to express Marian's inner thoughts in the form of a sophisticated number made up of contrasting sections that match her vivid and emphatic ideas.

Nonetheless, as Willson admits in Territory, this idea caused a diversion in his process because he started out with a ballad, spent months trying to turn it into a semi-operatic soliloquy, and ended up with a ballad. Much of this effort is reflected in the extensive archival sources for the song (see Fig. 3.5a for a draft of the lyric). Figs. 3.5b and 3.5c show part of the musical development of the first version (i.e., the one that was used in the duet), the melody of which would eventually be transferred to the familiar Broadway version. These music examples prove how much work Willson did on it. A particular sticking point was mm. 3–4: on 3.5b, he has added extra notes in these bars to replace one long note (a whole note tied to a quarter note) with eleven (two triplets and a quintuplet) to allow more words. That "new" eleven-note version is represented in 3.5c, but he has written an alternative for mm. 3–4 immediately above it. Fig. 3.5c also shows that mm. 10–12 have been worked on, too, in an attempt to get them right.

It has been rumored in print on several occasions that Frank Loesser—a good friend of Willson's as well as the associate producer (through his company Frank Productions) and publisher of The Music Man—was the ghostwriter of "My White Knight."[15] Yet from even these two sketches, it is difficult to believe that anyone other than Willson was making decisions about the melody, note by note. His authorship of the extended soliloquy version is similarly promoted by the extensive sources in the Juilliard collection. The lyric for it is shown in Fig. 3.5a, with numerous annotations in both pencil and red ink showing some of the layers of creativity. It is almost Verdian in scope, an exhaustive list in which Marian reflects on the qualities she does and does not want from her life partner. The musical setting, which can be heard in full on Barbara Cook's Carnegie Hall album (1975), is mainly built around a polka theme, beginning with the words "All I want

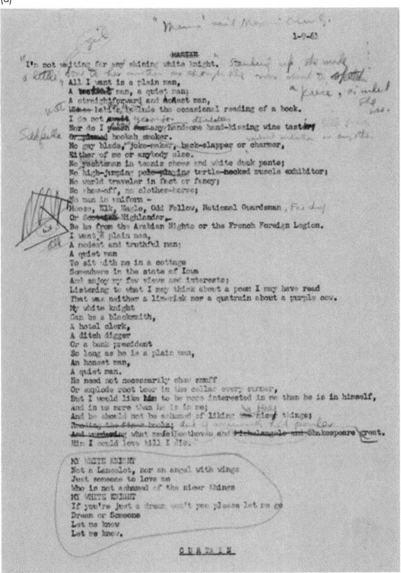

Fig. 3.5a. "My White Knight," typed lyric sheet of soliloquy version, with holograph annotations (red ink).

is a plain man." It is breathless and contains lots of short, fast notes (not unlike a more melodic version of "The Sadder but Wiser Girl"), but certain words are emphasized musically, such as a long high G flat on "await," stereotypical open fifths on "Arabian Nights," and a long high A sharp on "[more interested in] me."

(b)

Fig. 3.5b. "My White Knight," holograph sketch of duet version (refrain 1 only), with holograph annotations in red ink.

That none of this came easily is obvious from the sources. Even after he had composed the duet version (which contains the bones of the crucial melody), Willson continued to experiment in the soliloquy version with the "My White Knight" melody: the top two systems of Fig. 3.5d reveal a rising chromatic setting of "My white knight can be blacksmith, well-digger, banker, president, milkman, hobo, clerk or king." Similarly, the numerous crossings-out on Figs. 3.5e and 3.5f indicate the incremental development of the song, with various options explored, refined, and rejected. Nevertheless, the solution to making the song work is hinted at on the lyric sheet in Fig. 3.5a, where Willson has drawn a red box around the last stanza, which would take him back to the ballad form.

Fig. 3.5c. "My White Knight," holograph melodic sketch, duet version (both refrains).

He explains in *Territory* that the number had to be simplified during the tryouts if it was to stay in the show: "Finally, on Friday of the next-to-closing week, I got it through my thick head that, what with The Train, Iowa-Stubborn, Trouble, the Piano Exercise Song, Seventy-Six, and Pickalittle, we had enough specialties a'ready. By the time you get to Marian's big song late in the first act you better at least let her start with the feeling of a by-God ballad. With a sad and reluctant pencil I deleted two 'inevitable' pages of my favorite song, and rerouted the rest. When the moment came that night Barbara

(d)

Fig. 3.5d. "My White Knight," holograph melodic sketch.

[Cook] soared into the ballad chorus first. The audience was with her all the way."[16] Making the song into a simple statement of longing for someone who will respect and love her finally helped it to land with the audience, as well as providing a useful extra ballad for the score, which is generally rather light on such material.

Fig. 3.5e. "My White Knight," soliloquy version, holograph sketch, first page.

For the movie version of *The Music Man*, Willson reused the interlude section ("All I want is a plain man") of "White Knight" in the middle of a new song, "Being in Love." It is common for movie adaptations of stage musicals to replace or add a number—for example, "Fated to Be Mated" (*Silk Stockings*), "Adelaide" (*Guys and Dolls*), "Something Good" (*The Sound of Music*), "Just Leave Everything to Me" (*Hello, Dolly!*)—but it is unusual to retain part of a discarded song in a new

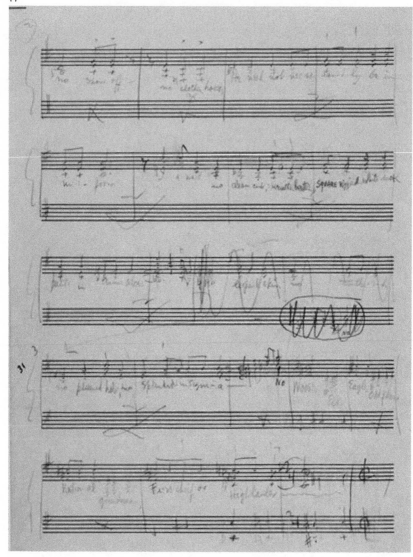

Fig. 3.5f. "My White Knight," soliloquy version, holograph sketch, second page.

song.[17] Willson kept every draft of the lyric for "Being in Love" in his archive, with alternates including:

December 27, 1960, version:
    Being in love is a very favorite dream of mine
    Being in love makes the ordinary sparkle and shine
    In love, your sparrow's like an eagle

Your beggar-man like a king
Rusty gates play symphonies
And tone-deaf people can sing
[etc.]
January 20, 1961, version:
Being in love is a custom I approve—hands down
I've been in love more than anybody else in this town
You remember the motorman on the street car
Well, I worshipped his every clang, clang
[etc.]
Undated versions:
Being in love doesn't guarantee the words "I do"
I've been in love more than anyone and that includes you
[etc.]
Being in love doesn't always mean a dream come true
Being in love doesn't guarantee that famous "I do"
[etc.]

Although everyone will have their preferred song (perhaps influenced by whether they heard "My White Knight" or "Being in Love" first), and many may feel that "Being in Love" is inferior, it is undeniable that Willson worked hard to make it work as a new expression of Marian's feelings for the movie version. An important shift between the songs is that "Being in Love" adds the idea that the movie Marian has been in love before and therefore speaks from experience, while the Broadway Marian is mostly fantasizing about a "white knight" based on ideas she has read in books (though she rejects many of the literary clichés). Indeed, in the movie Marian specifically says (in a new line of dialogue) that she is *not* "waiting for a knight in shining white armor to come riding up the street" and in "Being in Love" she confesses: "I've been in love more than anybody else has, I guess." This makes the Marian of the movie more knowing and less innocent—and therefore, arguably a stronger foil for Hill. As she declares to her mother, love is not enough anymore: "Somehow, / Me deep in love's only half of what I'm longing for now."

BALLADS AND CHARACTER SONGS

While the unusual nature of the *Music Man* score was an enormous asset to it in the theater, commercially it posed more of a challenge. As both associate producer and publisher of the score, Frank Loesser (and his company Frank Productions) oversaw the exploitation of the score in the form of sheet music and recordings. A member of his staff, Herb Eiseman, wrote to Kermit Bloomgarden (the lead producer) on October 2, 1957, as rehearsals were about to begin, to lay out their plans. On November 8, they intended to release "It's You," "Seventy-Six Trombones," "Till There Was You," and "Lida Rose," followed on December 13 by "Goodnight, My Someone," "Iowa Stubborn," "Gary, Indiana," and "Marian the

Librarian." Eiseman noted that it was "impossible for us, at this time, to set release dates" for other songs such as "Trouble" and "Rock Island" because "they fall
into the special material area. By special material I mean, not an obvious popular
song for the single record market."[18] One can see their problem and might argue
that "Iowa Stubborn" also belongs in this category. The songs are mostly so specific to their dramatic contexts—and so far from being generic—that many of
them do not easily lend themselves to being covered by popular crooners such as
Doris Day[19] or Tony Bennett. Indeed, it is striking to read in a letter of October
21, 1957, that Frank Loesser was willing to allow Jule Styne to use four songs from
his own musical *Guys and Dolls* on popular singer Eddie Fisher's television show
of October 29 if he would agree to have Fisher "fully" perform "Goodnight, My
Someone" and "Lida Rose" on the program of December 12. Loesser adds: "You
agree to present these with [a] prominent announcement to the effect that they
are by Meredith Willson from the forthcoming Broadway musical production
'THE MUSIC MAN.'"[20]

Loesser realized the importance of getting the songs heard by a general audience and apart from "Seventy-Six Trombones," the show's ballads were the best
chance they had of doing that. As noted earlier, however, the score contains little
in this area—just three clear ballads, all of them sung by Marian: "My White
Knight," which was rather operatic for popular coverage even in its final version,
"Goodnight, My Someone," which is perhaps a little simple and does not lend itself to a commercial arrangement, and "Till There Was You." Of these, the last had
by far the best chance of release, as it proved in 1963 when it was recorded in an
up-tempo version by The Beatles on their second studio album *With the Beatles*
(their only Broadway cover). It was also covered by Peggy Lee in 1960 and by Vic
Damone in 1964, but surprisingly it was not recorded by many of the biggest pop
stars of the day. On the other hand, it had already been heard several times before the show opened on Broadway. Willson wrote it in 1950 under the title "Till
I Met You" (which is how it appears in scripts up to and including S8; it does not
appear in S9 and returns as "Till There Was You" in S10) and it was recorded by
Eileen Wilson in 1950 and performed on television by Fran Warren in 1951 (the
latter on *The Big Show*).

In the Broadway version of *The Music Man* it holds the eleven o'clock slot—the
last important new number before the end of the show—and it lands with visceral power in this position, as if the whole piece is leading up to Marian's emphatic musical declaration of love in it, so it is perhaps surprising to realize that
Willson pulled it out of his trunk years after it was written. The harmonies, which
shift in unusual directions throughout the refrain, certainly seem ready-made for
the rest of the score.

"Goodnight, My Someone" also has a sense of being ready-made: it was
created as a waltz version of "Seventy-Six Trombones," a definite afterthought,
though it works beautifully in the scene. It follows on from the "Piano Lesson"
number, which—as noted earlier in this chapter—features Marian and Mrs.
Paroo singing in harmony to Amaryllis's piano exercises. "Goodnight" similarly
starts with Amaryllis playing her "cross-hands piece" as part of the story (diegetic

music), and soon after Marian starts singing the melody (non-diegetic music) the orchestra seamlessly joins in (non-diegetic music). This is another example of the subtle transitions between different modes of performance thanks to Willson's use of music in and beyond the story.

He wrote one other conventional ballad for the score, a song called "I'd Like a Memory" that was to be sung by Harold to the young girl Gracie Graham in the earliest surviving script (S1). It is an attractive number that can be heard in Willson's demo recording on the CD release of the original London cast album, but it is obvious from scanning the song lists of all the drafts of the show that Willson quickly decided that Hill would not be played by the kind of performer who would sing ballads well; and more specifically, there was also no good reason to direct such a romantic song to a child (the effect is clumsy rather than creepy).

The other songs of this type that were written for the show do not quite qualify as ballads because they are too upbeat or border in some other sense with the genre of character songs, which is why the latter are also considered in this section. Of especial note is "The Wonderful Plan," which was a major song for Harold (or in one version, S3, Marian) to sing to Jim/Winthrop in the second act. Indeed, it was more specifically designed to be the eleven o'clock number before "Till There Was You" was moved to take its place from S11 onward, another reminder that Jim/Winthrop was the focus of the plot for a very long time during the show's genesis. The song is derived from "a sermon by Mark Hague," according to the copies of the score at Juilliard, and it expands on the idea that the world is the result of a grand design:

> Did the universe start as an accident,
> A little dust in a circular breeze
> Giving ultimate birth to the earth in an accident-
> al otherwise meaningless sneeze?
> Pretty big accident, wouldn't you say?
> You don't believe it happened that way?
> But if you are not part of an accident,
> You must be part of a world that began
> As a wonderful part of a wonderful, wonderful plan.

Harold is trying to convince Jim/Winthrop that although his day-to-day existence is difficult because of his disability, he has to look for the meaning in his own life. Musically, the setting relies heavily on slightly bouncy dotted rhythms but because of the "moderate walking tempo," it has more of the feeling of a ballad. The song had a curious evolution: after it was cut from *The Music Man*, Willson tried it out in his second and third musicals, cut it again each time, and it was finally performed in front of an audience in his last completed show, *1491*. Evidently Willson was very proud of it.

A little similar in tone was "Tomorrow," another song cut from the show late in the score's evolution (during the tryouts, in fact); it was reused in *The Unsinkable Molly Brown* and then cut again. The focus of this lyric is for Harold to tell Marian to "dispose" of her problems by using "tomorrow" as a receptacle for them,

"Leaving you only sunshine / Day after wonderful day." It puts into song the memorable sentiment that Hill speaks to Marian when persuading her to meet him at the footbridge in the Broadway version: "Pile up enough tomorrows and you'll find you've collected nothing but a lot of empty yesterdays. I don't know about you but I'd like to make today worth remembering" (Act 2, Scene 3). Unlike "The Wonderful Plan," the lyric for "Tomorrow" is a little upset by Willson's musical setting, which is in the style of a tango and contains a lot of repeated notes; this tends to sound a little like recitative delivered over a tango accompaniment, giving the impression of insincerity or pastiche, but Willson persevered with it into the Philadelphia tryouts, clearly believing it to have merit. Certainly its *carpe diem* message sits well with the character of Hill.

One of the most problematic aspects of *The Music Man* from a revival point of view is that most of the solo numbers are delivered by either Hill or Marian, with one each for Winthrop ("Gary, Indiana"), Eulalie ("Columbia, Gem of the Ocean," admittedly a brief appearance), and Marcellus ("Shipoopi"), leaving the others with little musical definition and Marian and Hill with a lot to carry. Willson made two attempts to lighten their load by adding songs for Tommy and Zaneeta, the young lovers (which would be a conventional structural move in a musical). The first, "You Don't Have to Kiss Me Goodnight," appeared in the first (S1) and last (S12) drafts, as well as many in between: Willson obviously considered it to be a good song and finally dispensed with it only in the Philadelphia tryouts. It is in two parts: Tommy sings the refrain in ballad style ("You don't have to kiss me goodnight, my dear, / If that's how you want it to be"), then Zaneeta responds with a more lively version ("No, no, now wait, now please, I'd / Like you to kiss me goodnight, my dear, / If that's how you'd like it to be").

There is a holograph fair copy of the song at Juilliard in which the number is a quartet, with Marian and Harold singing the song "straight" and the young lovers singing it to a jazz version, but all the other sources show it as a duet for Tommy and Zaneeta. In reference to the earlier discussion, this song is more akin to the typical Broadway pop ballads of the 1950s, with its stepwise melodic movement and more generic lyric, so it would probably have been a useful commercial tool for the show had it not been cut. In contrast, Tommy's "Fireworks" (Fig. 3.6) is another of Willson's quirky tunes, with lots of chromatic notes and a jazzy rhythm depicting the "fireworks" that went off in his heart when Zaneeta kissed him. One of the copies of the score refers to it as being "from the motion picture" of the show, so it is possible that it was specially written for the movie version. It is highly charming and quite a loss to the score; it could easily be added in revival as an experiment.

It was noted in Chapter 2 that Mrs. Paroo had a considerably bigger role in the original conception of the show, leading to her solo scene at the end of Act 1 in which she stands on the street and sings the number "Blow." Her son Jim has secretly been taken to the asylum without her knowledge and she entreats the winds of morning and evening to "blow him back to me." It is perhaps the most peculiar number written for the score, with limited lyrical content: mainly, she repeats the word "blow" over and over. Willson appears to have intended to write

Fig. 3.6. "Fireworks," cut from The Music Man.

a musical evocation of the wind as a climactic gesture to close the first act, and Fig. 3.7 gives a good impression of how this might have worked, with demonic chromatic motion at a loud dynamic. However, it is extreme, does not fit in with the other colors of the score as it developed, and was designed for a scene that was dropped, so it is unsurprising that it disappeared after S1. Similarly, "Too Soon Old" became redundant as Willson tightened the story and made the show into more of a musical comedy and less of a play with songs. It was written in the style of a jaunty gavotte, a little like another vaudeville number, but (as we saw in Chapter 2) it was allotted to Mr. Bushkins, a peripheral character whose barely existent storyline was dropped; with the character went the song.

Willson gives a rather misleading account in *Territory* of how he came to write "Blessings." He claims that the Main Street scene (Act 1, Scene 2) was not working well in the tryout performances, so he "disappeared" for two days and wrote "Blessings," which he describes as "a one-in-a-bar waltz opening."[21] He even describes how, "being eager to hear it," he returned with it to the theater; he says that it "proved to everybody's satisfaction that the song [he] already had, 'Iowa Stubborn,' was a very good opening," leading him to "file" the "two-day-old upstart" "without a backward glance."[22] In fact, the song appears in scripts S4, S8, S9, and S10, which means it dates from at least May 1956. Fig. 3.8 shows the opening of the number, which is, as Willson says, a waltz. In S4 and S8, Marian and Mrs. Paroo sing the song to Jim Paroo to give him a sort of "count your blessings" sentiment to cheer him up: he is under threat from Mayor Shinn. The song changes context and focus in S9: it is now part of a general song involving the community (but particularly the Djilas family) when they are singing of their determination

Fig. 3.7. "Blow," excerpt from copyist's score.

to prove Shinn wrong about the band. Without question, it was not written in two days during the Philadelphia previews.

Nevertheless, Willson does seem to have made an unexpected last-minute experiment, for which music manuscripts survive but no script. As we can see from Fig. 3.9, he decided to rewrite "Blessings" in a minor key and turn it into "The Think System," a song in which Shinn confronts the town with Hill's ruse in the second act. For some months, Willson had been trying to give the Mayor the opportunity to sing, most notably in a possible reprise of "Trouble" (in which Hill is now the

Fig. 3.8. "Blessings," excerpt.

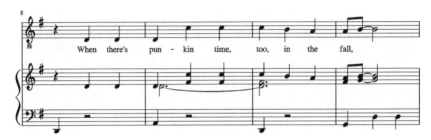

Fig. 3.9. "The Think System," excerpt.

subject of the song); this was long after the composer had abandoned the version in which the Mayor sings the original iteration of the song and Hill sings "Ya
got no trouble" (this disappears after S8, i.e. January 1957). "The Think System"
was another attempt at that, and the mock-serious minor-key waltz is frequently

interrupted as Shinn stumbles over his words and gets various metaphors mixed. But as with Tommy and Zaneeta, Shinn was not destined to sing solos in *The Music Man*, because aside from the main lovers, in a musical about a community the community as a whole must be given opportunities to sing as a group, not as individuals.

BARBERSHOP SONGS AND ENSEMBLES

Recognizing that it was important for the community to have the opportunity to sing together, Willson included the song "Shipoopi" in all versions of the script from SF6/S2 (November/December 1955) onward.[23] It provides a major choreographic moment, employing the Virginia reel (a folk dance popular in America in the nineteenth century) and giving Harold and Marian their only opportunity to dance together in the show. Lyric-wise, the song's use of words such as "hussy" to describe a woman, and its general description of a man trying to "get" a woman, is problematic to many audiences and perhaps seemed so for Willson too, for he adjusted the number to address its framing several times. However, he seemed keen on the word "Shipoopi," which he appears to have coined himself, and in one early synopsis (SY8, September 1955) had the instrument manufacturer Mr. Buskins tell Harold that he was keen to end their boys' band ruse because he wanted to "settle down with some nice Shipoopi." Along similar lines, an undated script fragment in the Willson collection at Carmel has Hill sing the song to Bushkins to explain what a Shipoopi is.

But in all other sources where the word appears in dialogue, it is immediately before a large group performance of the song is heard. Context seems important for the song and this took some time to get right. For example, a bizarre version in S6 has the song open Act 2 with Eulalie singing the first verse to the Ladies' Auxiliary Committee (which includes Marian). Tommy's "gang" appears upstage in time to sing the refrain and Tommy leads the rest of the song. Also incongruous is the version in S2: Zaneeta reports that she heard Marcellus "tell Papa the Professor was wasting his time because Miss Marian was a Shipoopi" (1-8-64A). Marian is present in the scene and she asks her what this means. Marcellus responds by leading the town in singing the song.

It was only in September 1957 (S10), not long before rehearsals were to begin, that the script for this scene started to resemble the Broadway version, when the kids request that Marcellus sing "The Shipoopi" (2-1-2). This suddenly frames the song as a "known" dance number, explicitly diegetic, which helps to distance the characters (and the audience) from the idea that they are openly singing about Marian. Of course, on a different level it is obvious that the lyric reflects Harold's pursuit of Marian—and on a subtler level, this idea is a joke because he is about to fall in love with her. Thus the uproarious, seemingly gratuitous number serves quite a powerful dramatic purpose. Still, it may have been preferable for Willson to stick with the original lyric, in which Hill sings "The girl you can't forget" rather than "The girl who's hard to get," possibly a useful alternative for future revivals.

Another group of songs brings the community to life through the barbershop quartet made up of the once-bickering members of the school board. It was noted in Chapter 1 that Willson was a keen barbershop singer himself from childhood, and this aspect of the score is truly autobiographical. The "ice cream" vignette that opens the song "Sincere" encapsulates in a few chords both the positive and negative aspects of Hill's behavior: he uses music as a trick to distract people from his lies but also to bring together a fractured community. Both in "Sincere" and "It's You," the quartet's singing—again diegetic—is especially powerful because they are performing love songs; interestingly, "It's You" was sung by Tommy and Zaneeta in the last four drafts of the script (S9–S12) and by Hill in others (Sf2, SF6, and S2), which shows just how romantic the song was intended to be. In those versions, the quartet instead sang a number called "I Found a Horseshoe," and in S4–S8 this was combined with "Mind If I Tell You I Love You?" Again, these are in romantic mode, helping to compensate for the score's general lack of ballads. Even more entertaining and vivid are "Lida Rose/Will I Ever Tell You?" and "Pick-a-Little/Goodnight, Ladies," when the quartet sings in counterpoint with Marian and the Ladies' ensemble, respectively. The second of these is especially effective, with the men joining in with the women to show that although they are singing different melodies, they fit together as one community. Willson was fond of "Goodnight, Ladies," and had used it in one of his "Talking People" radio advertisements (the transcription can be heard in the Carmel collection).

Yet the most affecting ensemble number depicting the community is clearly "The Wells Fargo Wagon," in which the people both individually and collectively sing of their aspirations. Although they are generally closed to the outside world, it is also exciting when they are touched by it. Gracie Shinn immediately realizes, "It could be the band instruments!" but the citizens of River City take turns in hoping for things of their own. It is particularly emotive when Winthrop sings the penultimate verse on his own, finding a voice in public for the first time thanks to the newfound confidence given to him by Hill. It is a suitably rousing number for the final scene of a fairly long first act (eleven scenes), but the music derives from a discarded song with a weak lyric: "Oh, yes, the Blue Ridge Mountains are in No'th Car'lina, lina, / That's where my heart belongs." This corresponds to the scene in S1 outlined in Chapter 2, in which Hill has an argument about geography with some of the children. The transformation into "Wells Fargo" is another example of Willson's insightfulness in learning how to craft and recraft his show with dramatic structure in mind, as opposed to the "play with songs" style of S1 in which the "Blue Ridge Mountains" version belongs.

Despite Willson's story in *Territory* about trying to replace "Iowa Stubborn" with "Blessings," there is no doubt that "Stubborn" is a terrific number with which to introduce the town. Arguably it is even better in the film, when Harold is greeted in surly voice by several individuals who inform him in a musical phrase, "You are in I-o-way." This leads to a smooth segue into the refrain that exists in the Broadway version too: "Oh, there's nothin' halfway about the Iowa way to treat you, when we treat you, which we may not do at all." Unlike "Blessings," "Iowa Stubborn" immediately establishes the provincial atmosphere that Hill is going to be up against and whatever Willson claims about the show being a valentine to the rural American community, this number also hints at the need for transformation. On the other hand, the close harmonies in which the chorus sings during the *a cappella* section ("But we'll give you our shirt . . .") hint at the kind of unity that already exists in the community at its best, and which Hill will exploit as he brings the school board—and later the whole town—together in song.

CONCLUSION

Chapter 1 explored the diverse career and musical experiences that Willson enjoyed earlier in his life and it is clear that this eclecticism served the score for *The Music Man* well. We have seen how his advanced musical literacy allowed him to develop complex scores in detail, such as in the extensive sketches for "Marian the Librarian," while on the other hand his ability to write commercial ballads—honed during the 1930s and 1940s when writing for radio—helped him to realize that "My White Knight" needed to be reshaped in form, as well as recognizing the value of pulling "Till I Met You" out of the trunk and, with only a slight change of wording, turning it into a hit. His use of patter songs to satisfy his views on the relationship between song and dialogue in musicals and his employment of barbershop singing also enriched the range of styles and moods in the score. Getting these disparate elements finely balanced was as difficult as it was to refine the book—but after roughly four years of adding, cutting, and editing dozens of songs, *The Music Man* was finally ready for Broadway.

4

MARCHING STILL RIGHT TODAY

• • •

THE MUSIC MAN FROM PHILADELPHIA TO BROADWAY AND BEYOND

Roughly six years after first deciding to write a musical, Meredith Willson's Iowa stubbornness paid off when the curtain went up on the world premiere of *The Music Man* at the Shubert Theatre, Philadelphia, on November 18, 1957. It was an unqualified success from the very start: the *Philadelphia Inquirer* called it a "happy premier," the *Daily Times* said it was "an American 'My Fair Lady,'" and *Variety* described it as "a grand musical with all the indications of a hit."[1] The advance box office had already been large two months earlier: an article in the *New York World-Telegram and Sun* on September 7 revealed that the Broadway production had taken "close to $500,000" a whole month before rehearsals had even begun; another article reported that after the reviews appeared, $13,000 was taken at the Philadelphia box office for the remainder of the four-week tryout. Several critics compared it to *My Fair Lady*, Lerner and Loewe's hit of the 1955–1956 season, not only because of the high quality of the show but also because of the audience re-action: the review in *Variety* specifically reported that it "got the most tumultuous final curtain, not only this season, but back to 'My Fair Lady.'"

Although the amount of documentation available in his papers related to the run-up to the opening of the show is limited, it is obvious that Kermit Bloomgarden's oversight of the production was incredibly efficient. Once he had bought the rights to produce *The Music Man*, it took him just over half a year to bring it to the stage—far less time-consuming than Willson's struggles with the book and score had been up to that point, as we saw in Chapters 2 and 3. The documents reveal that Bloomgarden signed an agreement with Willson on March 29, 1957, outlining various provisions including the payment of Willson's expenses during rehearsals.[2] The director, Morton Da Costa, had also overseen the successful Broadway musical *Plain and Fancy* (1955) and the play *Auntie Mame* (1956) and was therefore a safe pair of hands; Onna White had choreographed some revivals but was less experienced and therefore a little more of a risk. By early July, much of the production's finances had been raised: Anne Gordon of Bloomgarden's office reported to one prospective backer

The Big Parade. Dominic McHugh, Oxford University Press. © Oxford University Press 2021.
DOI: 10.1093/oso/9780197554739.003.0005

that "The financing on this production is moving ahead very quickly and if your group is interested in participating I would like to suggest that you let us know as soon as possible."[3]

A further document located in the Bloomgarden papers reveals the estimated production costs. Overall, *The Music Man* was budgeted at $300,000 (roughly $60,000 less than *My Fair Lady* had cost in March 1956), with the most expensive items being painting and building ($50,000), execution of costumes ($35,000), orchestration and copying ($25,000), and advertising (a group of costs totaling $14,500). It is interesting to put this into the context of the costs of the senior personnel on the show: the estimates show that the set designer, costume designer, and director would each be paid $5,000, the producer $1,750, and the choreographer $3,000.[4] Barbara Cook's contract to play Marian Paroo was signed on August 5 and shows that she would be paid $600 per week for the first thirty weeks of the New York run and $750 up to the end of the 1957–1958 season; from September 1, 1958, she was entitled to be paid $850 per week when the gross box office receipts exceeded $50,000 per week.[5] Robert Preston's contract to play Harold Hill was inevitably more complicated and more favorable: while Cook had appeared in a number of Broadway shows including *Plain and Fancy* (another Bloomgarden production) and *Candide*, Preston was a popular name from twelve years of Hollywood films and eight previous roles in New York City and was therefore the main box office draw.

His contract entitled him to $1,500 per week plus 5 percent of the box office receipts between $40,000 and $50,000; if the show made more than that amount, he was entitled to a further sum of 2.5 percent of the box office (up to and including $60,000). From November 25, 1958, he would be paid the same standard fee plus 7.5 percent of the box office between $40,000 and $50,000 and an additional 5 percent for box office income over $50,000. He was also entitled to $75 per week for a dresser and to have his name billed immediately below the title of the play on a line of its own (and no smaller than 60 percent of the size of the title of the play). That his name was not above the title shows that he was not a star of the magnitude of Rex Harrison in *My Fair Lady* or Ethel Merman in *Gypsy*. A separate agreement covers the cast album, for which Preston would be paid $2,250 per day, a significant amount for someone who was not known as a recording artist.[6] In contrast, members of the ensemble were paid $100 per week during the Broadway run, with David Burns earning $500 for playing Shinn, Larry Douglas earning $300 as Preston's understudy (plus $100 per performance if he had to go on for him), Pert Kelton $400 for Mrs. Paroo, Eddie Hodges $225 as Winthrop, and Danny Carroll $150 per week as Tommy.[7] Broadway is an expensive business, which is why Bloomgarden's effectiveness in generating a large advance box office income—$500,000 against the $300,000 production costs, more than three months before the Broadway opening—was both impressive and essential to its success.

As noted in Chapter 3, several songs were modified or cut during the Philadelphia tryout, most significantly including the removal of the orchestra from "Rock Island" and the deletion of numbers such as "Tomorrow" and "River City, Plunge" (a version of the school song "River City, Go"). Before it moved to New York, Henry T. Murdock of the *Philadelphia Inquirer* returned to review *The Music Man* again after many of the changes had been made, publishing a second appraisal on December 8 that concluded: "Although we couldn't find very much to fault at the premiere beyond the too-generous length of all musical-comedy tryouts, the current production is faster, sharper." He added that "we will be very much surprised—and very much disappointed—if it doesn't score" at its New York debut.

BROADWAY

On December 19, when *The Music Man* finally opened at Broadway's Majestic Theatre, the front page of the *New York Times* was a reminder that America was still actively engaged in the Cold War. Three columns reported on different aspects of important NATO talks that had just concluded in Paris. One revealed that diplomatic exchanges were to begin with the Soviet Union to clarify the positions of East and West on disarmament prior to possible formal talks; heads of government in NATO were "firmly opposed to any long, wearying discussion with the Soviet Union" but there was "a common acceptance of the need for approaching [them] on disarmament."[8]

Despite this talk of disarmament, another column addressed the United States' attempts to equip the West German army with intermediate-range ballistic missiles and nuclear warheads and the political issues (in West Germany) that were complicating this possibility.[9] A third column revealed a division between Europe and the States on the approach to be taken on the Soviet Union: a "formula of 'arm and negotiate' reconciled the United States' preoccupation with the military strengthening of the alliance and the Europeans' desire that the West should concurrently show its willingness to seek peace."[10] Of note, the United States "had obtained its major objective—agreement that missiles in Europe were necessary to its defense."

Elsewhere on the front page, a further article described the successful firing of a new Atlas intercontinental ballistic missile from Cape Canaveral the previous night.[11] Thus *The Music Man* opened under the shadow of continued potential conflict—and despite the show's unquestionable mood of nostalgic Americana, it would not be true to say that it merely provided escapism from the political tensions in the wider world (though it did this too). As has been discussed in Chapters 2 and 3, both Marian and Harold are outsiders who open the eyes of the small-town Americans to external influences and in the process unify a community that has long been fractured into different factions (for example, the bickering members of the school board). While the musical may appear reactionary and conservative on the surface, it unequivocally condemns most of these elements, such as the Mayor with his call for tar and feathers and Mrs. Shinn with her attempts to censor love poetry (Marian's "dirty books").

Nevertheless, the unanimous rave reviews that the show received upon its New York opening ignored the current political situation and focused their admiration on the craft with which it had been executed. For example, Frank Aston in the *New York World-Telegram and Sun* declared it to be "a knockout, right from the first blare in the Majestic's orchestra pit," concluding that "it deserves to run at least a decade."[12] Of particular relevance to this book, most of the critics focused specifically on Willson's brilliance and not just the star performances (writers do not always get the spotlight in musical theater reviews). In the *New York Journal-American*, Jim O'Connor made the following striking assessment: "What I observed especially about 'The Music Man' is the unusual manner in which composer Meredith Willson uses the entire large cast as an orchestra. Each actor and actress plays his or her singing or speaking part like an instrument in a melodious whole." John Chapman of the *Daily News* not only called it "one of the few great musical comedies of the past 26 years," comparing it favorably to *Guys and Dolls* and the Gershwins' *Of Thee I Sing*, but he specifically appreciated its authorship: "A remarkable thing about 'The Music Man' is that it is the product of one man . . . Meredith Willson." Walter Kerr in the *Herald Tribune* similarly called him "triple-threat man Willson." Earl Hall, the major journalist from Willson's hometown paper the *Mason City Globe-Gazette*, was not exaggerating when he noticed that—unusually—"If anything, New York's critics were more unreserved in their praise of the Willson opus than Philadelphia's had been during the play's 'dry run' there last month."

This warm critical reaction had the hoped-for effect on the box office. Jim O'Connor's article reported on December 21 that the show had got "100 percent rave notices from all drama critics in yesterday's papers" and went on to describe the impact: "Despite the rain, the line of ticket seekers started queuing up yesterday morning, and when treasurer Irving Morrison opened the window, there were 112 customers waiting for him. By early afternoon, the line stretched all the way up 44th St to Shubert Alley. Last night, six additional mail order clerks were put on the job by producer Kermit Bloomgarden to handle the deluge of ticket orders." Several articles particularly noted the reaction of individual audience members to the show, underlining how strongly and personally people were engaging with it: a Mrs. Alice Kaplowitz of the Bronx made the interesting comment that "The original story made 'The Music Man' a really different musical," while Richard P. Cooke's review for the *Wall Street Journal* reported, "A lady seated on my left remarked as the boys and girls were whooping it up in the town gymnasium: 'I haven't wanted to go to a (stage) party so much since Rosalinda,'" a reference to the hit 1942 English-language adaptation of *Die Fledermaus* that had an extended run on Broadway. As Walter Kerr noted of *The Music Man*'s score at the end of his review: "The beat is catching: the audience was applauding in rhythm as last night's curtain came down. I think you'll have a splendid time."

Within the next few weeks, Willson became a prominent figure in the press. On December 21, *Cue* magazine ran a profile of him titled "Iowa's Music Man: New Musical by Meredith Willson of Mason City May be Hawkeye State's Answer to 'Oklahoma!'" John Chapman wrote another profile in the *Sunday News* on January 12, 1958, headed "The Corn Belt's Noel Coward." It began:

Broadway is as provincial a neighborhood as, say, Mason City, Iowa, and it thinks that people it has not heard about simply do not exist. So this little hick town which lies along a short segment of the world's most famous cowpath was struck all of a heap when a Mason City fella named Meredith Willson came up with a musical smash, "The Music Man," which will rival for endurance such works as "Oklahoma!" and "My Fair Lady."

Several other facts have flabbergasted show people. For one thing, this man who has burst upon the neon neighborhood like a pinwheel is 55 years old, and finding a new career at such an age is better than Rip Van Winkle did. For another thing, Willson did the whole show himself, music, lyrics and book— but he does credit a young Californian, Franklin Lacey, with an assist on the storyline.[13]

Willson's public profile expanded exponentially almost overnight.

There was other important business for him to attend to, as well. On December 29, 1957, the original Broadway cast album was recorded by Capitol Records. As was conventional, the album does not entirely reflect the numbers as they were performed in the show but instead features some changes, partly to enhance the home listening experience and partly because of time constraints. For example, the Overture is shortened so that we only hear "Seventy-Six Trombones," in an extended version for the album; "Till There Was You," "The Wells Fargo Wagon," and "Will I Ever Tell You?" are cut from the number. In the barbershop songs, the solo introductions (where one singer begins before the rest join in) are all replaced by fully harmonized versions throughout. A new introduction is added for "Iowa Stubborn" to cut the music that accompanies the departure of the train from the stage and extend the one-and-a-half measure lead-in to the song (as seen in the vocal score) into a more conventional three-and-a-half measure introduction. In the same number, the dialogue involving Mayor Shinn and Alma in the fermata one measure before figure C in the published score is cut; the plural "thermometers" is changed to "thermometer" for the album, possibly to avoid a sibilant sound on the "s" coming across as harsh on the album; and the Farmer's Wife sings her line as a solo rather than as a duet with the Farmer. Similar tweaks are made to most numbers.

Not all the dialogue is removed from the score, however: unlike the cast albums made by Columbia, whose producer Goddard Lieberson liked to cut the talking from songs on cast albums, Capitol was willing to include spoken dialogue cues to songs such as "Trouble" and "Piano Lesson," as well as much of the internal dialogue in "Pick-a-Little." A newly conceived "Finale" track combines Marian and Harold's double reprise of "Goodnight, My Someone" and "Seventy-Six Trombones," continuing straight into a choral rendition of "Seventy-Six" that does not occur at that point in the show. Occasionally, the album suffers slightly from a reverberant acoustic that causes an intrusive echo when the salesmen are performing "Rock Island" *a cappella* and during the early part of "Trouble," when there is little orchestral accompaniment to Hill's lines (so one becomes more aware of the acoustic of the space in which the recording was made). In a couple of places (including the end of "Trouble") it is noticeable that Robert Preston struggles to sustain longer notes, but otherwise his performance—and the album in general—is wonderfully fresh, and a theatrical, spontaneous-sounding document of the show.

According to the booklet accompanying the CD release of the album it debuted on the Billboard charts on February 24, 1958, held the number 1 spot for twelve weeks, and charted for a total of 245 weeks.[14] *The Music Man* also triumphed at the awards ceremonies: it won the New York Critics Award for Best Musical, the Outer Circle Award, and Tony Awards for Best Musical, Best Actor (Preston), Best Actress in a Featured Role (Cook), Best Actor in a Featured Role (Burns), and Best Conductor and Musical Director (Herbert Greene).

No wonder the show set in for a hugely successful run of 1,375 performances. Robert Preston stayed in the show for over two years, describing it in a note to Bloomgarden as "the happiest engagement of my career."[15] In an interview in October 1959, he explained his continued enjoyment of and freshness in the role: "I can't fall down, because the audience response is always so enthusiastic. How can you help being stimulated when you play to full houses, and when the

Fig. 4.1. *Robert Preston and Barbara Cook during the "Marian the Librarian" scene of* The Music Man *on Broadway, 1957. Credit: Photofest.*

applause at the end of the show never fails to be the same rhythmic handclapping we got on opening night? Seventeen hundred people handclapping to 'Seventy-Six Trombones' every performance is enough to keep you going indefinitely."[16] He left on January 9, 1960, and was replaced first by Eddie Albert (January 11–June 1) and then Bert Parks (June 27, 1960–April 15, 1961, when it closed); Preston briefly returned to the role from June 13–25, 1960, to fill in the time before Parks was available.[17] Morton Da Costa regularly held auditions for possible replacements for all the roles as and when necessary. For example, a letter of April 12, 1958, shows that he had auditioned Marni Nixon, best remembered as the ghost singing voice of Deborah Kerr in *The King and I*, Natalie Wood in *West Side Story*, and Audrey Hepburn in *My Fair Lady*, and commented that while she was "a highly trained singer and not an impossible type for Marian," Da Costa "would imagine her acting rather inexpert."[18]

The show also broke new ground at the matinee performance on July 4, 1960, when Liza Redfield became the show's musical director, replacing Herbert Greene. Willson's involvement in this decision is unclear, but there is tangible evidence of his strongly negative feelings about Ben Steinberg's conducting of the show as Greene's assistant ("I don't think I will ever forgive him. I can never forget the sight of his vacant smiling face while conducting a pit full of ugly out-of-tune, over-balanced noises with complete unconcern")[19] so we can reasonably assume that he approved of her appointment. The significance of this moment was that Redfield was the first woman to become a full-time musical director of a Broadway musical. She was profiled in both the *New York Times* and *Time* and both articles were full of sexist remarks and questions.

For instance, Louis Calta of the *Times* asked her what she would be wearing ("a simple black dress with long sleeves"), inquired as to her age ("Let's say I'm old enough to do the job well"), and pondered whether one should call a female maestro a "maestra" ("'Well,' she replied, 'if you want to be grammatical, I guess you should").[20] *Time*'s article similarly noted: "With striking Titian-red hair, plus face and figure to match, Liza Redfield has the looks for anything except what she is: Broadway's first fulltime female conductor."[21] On July 17, 1960, she was a guest on the popular television show *What's My Line?* and when her occupation was announced to the audience, they let out a collective gasp before applauding enthusiastically; one of the panelists, Bennett Cerf, noted that the audience was also "visibly impressed."[22] Later, one of the other panelists, Dorothy Kilgallen, asked, "Are you one of the strippers in *Gypsy*?" and the panel was ultimately unable to guess what she did for a living, a sign of how unusual her appointment was—in other words, unthinkable as a profession for a woman at that time.

BEYOND BROADWAY

The Music Man also started its journey beyond New York, beginning with a national tour of America on August 18, 1958, with Forrest Tucker (Hill) and

Joan Weldon (Marian) in the lead roles. It played the Philharmonic in Los Angeles until September 30, then moved to other cities including San Francisco, Dallas, Denver, Omaha, Des Moines, Kansas City, and an extended run in Chicago (February 1959–March 1960).[23] It later played St. Louis, Cincinnati, and Washington, DC, and was in general a hit across America. But inevitably Bloomgarden also saw *The Music Man* as having the potential to enjoy a place on the world stage, even if the all-American content and style of the piece may not automatically sit well in other cultures. The first international production took place in Australia, when producer Garnet H. Carroll brought a new production to Melbourne's Princess Theatre on March 5, 1960, where it ran until July 30; the director was John Fearnley, who had earlier served as Rodgers and Hammerstein's casting director. Later in the year, it moved to Sydney's Tivoli Theatre, where it ran from December 13 to February 4, 1961.

Even more important to Bloomgarden and Willson was the British production. As early as October 1958, they were hoping to be able to take Robert Preston to appear at the Theatre Royal, Drury Lane, in a recreation of the Broadway staging, but *My Fair Lady* was set in for a long run at that theater. As for the alternatives, Bloomgarden commented: "The danger of most of the theatres in London for a show like MUSIC MAN is that they're either too large or too small. They will probably offer us the Coliseum which I think is much too big. Perhaps they might have other ideas but in any event, I don't believe we should do it until Bob is through in New York. Certainly [Laurence] Olivier is a good idea, and I can think of nobody better, but I think we then get down to the problem of how long he would stay with the show."[24] Willson was also keen on the idea of Sam Wanamaker playing Hill in London, and the actor commented, "I think it is delightful and I am prepared to have a crack at trying to do it."[25] British veteran Max Bygraves was also mentioned as a strong possibility;[26] Broadway favorite Alfred Drake was named too,[27] and the longlist even included Gene Kelly, Peter Ustinov, Donald O'Connor, Gordon MacRae, and Paul Newman.[28]

In the event, Hollywood veteran Van Johnson was cast in the role and the production was staged at the Adelphi Theatre rather than on Drury Lane (there was a tryout period at the Bristol Hippodrome too). Harold Fielding, the most important producer of musicals in Britain at the time, oversaw the production, which involved a faithful recreation of the sets, costumes, direction, and orchestrations of the American production. Patricia Lambert, a young British actress who had appeared in the short-lived London production of *Once upon a Mattress*, was cast as Marian, with a young Denis Waterman—later to become a major television and stage actor in Britain—as Winthrop. The show was reasonably successful upon its opening on March 16, 1961, but it quickly folded after Johnson left on February 17, 1962 (he was replaced by his understudy, the British actor Gordon Boyd).[29]

Just as Willson remained highly involved in the Broadway production, regularly giving the cast and crew notes (some of which are extant in the Bloomgarden papers at Wisconsin),[30] he periodically offered comments on the London production. Soon after the opening, he wrote to Harold Fielding on March 21, 1961, to convey some concerns, including, "Beg Van not to make that crying face in the last scene when he conducts the little band. He is desperate and he is scared but the great Harold Hill is never a crybaby."[31] He visited the production again on October 18 and created four pages of typed notes on the performances, beginning with his familiar direction: "The people in this play are real, not review caricatures. The attitude must be completely sincere and played to each other, not to the audience review style." He tells Mrs. Shinn, "Please don't scream in 'Columbia,'" and remarks of Lambert and Johnson, "Please adore each other in Shipoopi and forget the audience." Of particular interest is his commentary to the musical director, Gareth Davies:

> Tempos on the whole good, except for 76 in the overture, which must be a march not a gallop. In the gymnasium 76, the orchestra is late after "On the Same Historic Day." The orchestra must pile in instantly without the drum beat continuing on solo for a measure or two. The two "Trouble" responses after "Swell" and "So's Your Old Man" should be taken out. [Added in ink:] Orch. Way to [*sic*] loud for vocals and under dialogue.[32]

As ever, Willson was meticulous in obtaining the desired effect, and his extensive experience as a conductor and musical director meant that he knew exactly how to describe what he needed. He does not seem to have overseen any other productions of the show—though it is possible he was involved in some capacity with the 1965 New York City Center revival starring Bert Parks, a limited engagement that ran for fifteen performances—but the show was by now a confirmed hit on stages the world over. There was just one thing left to address: the film adaptation.

THE MUSIC MAN ON THE BIG SCREEN AND THE SMALL SCREEN

On May 29, 1959, Willson wrote to his agent Julius Lefkowitz: "He who does not note the falling leaf can also overlook the fact that the winter is not far behind. For the first time since 'Music Man' opened we missed capacity two weeks in a row. A very small leaf, true, but a leaf nonetheless. I would appreciate it if the time table could be moved up a little with respect to readying a draft of the movie deal on paper."[33] Willson saw that the time was right to sell the film rights before the show was seen to be in decline. Two weeks earlier, Kermit Bloomgarden had bowed out of co-producing the potential film version after being made to feel he did not have a meaningful contribution to make compared to Da Costa and Willson (he had never produced a movie before); he also noted that he did not really want to spend eight months in Hollywood, away from his roots and family.[34] With Bloomgarden out of the picture, perhaps Willson felt it was the perfect time to pounce.

Another letter from September 8 reveals that Willson had been in talks with Ross Hunter, who had just produced the Doris Day movie *Pillow Talk* for

Universal-International. Hunter was interested in bringing *The Music Man* to Universal with Day as Marian and Preston repeating his stage role as Hill.[35] Reference was also made to "waiting for Cary Grant's terms" (Grant is well known to have been a possible choice for the role of Hill), but Willson had a firm "hope of working out a Preston deal." It was proposed that the movie rights be sold for "a million against ten"—whereby Willson, Bloomgarden, Da Costa, and Lacey would (as a group) get an advance of $1 million and then start earning 10 percent royalties once the distributor's gross exceeded $10 million—and Bloomgarden agreed on September 10.[36] Ann Stein of the William Morris Agency sent a letter to the rights holders on September 18 to indicate that they agreed on these terms and also confirmed that Warner Bros. would first be offered the property.[37] The formal terms were presented to Warner Bros. on December 8 and accepted on December 15.[38]

Morton Da Costa was hired to direct the movie, following his well-received work on the stage show; he also acted as producer, allowing him overall control of the content and style of the film. Correspondence between Da Costa and Willson from 1960 (in the Carmel collection) illustrates some of the discussions that were going on behind the scenes. For example, on May 26 Da Costa assured Willson that "Bob Preston is practically set [to play Harold Hill]. Haven't bored you with details but have consistently refused to give them second choices. Anyway, they've now made the decision and they're happy with it."[39] He also informed Willson that he was going to insist on screen testing Barbara Cook and that Onna White was "pretty well set too" to restage her choreography for the show. Da Costa "would agree to Doris Day but not Marty Melcher in any official capacity," a reference to Day's husband, and also named several members of the Broadway and touring companies of *The Music Man* whom he would like to screen test for the film, including Pert Kelton (Mrs. Paroo) and Harry Hickox (Charlie Cowell), both of whom went on memorably to play their roles.[40] However, the bulk of the letter is spent discussing the idea of proposing that the State of Iowa should build "an entire little town of circa 1912 to our design where we would shoot locations." He hoped Iowa would pay for the construction of the town and afterward they could use it as a visitor attraction. "As far as we are concerned," explained Da Costa, "this would save the picture a lot of money, give us authenticity and a lot of exploitation."[41]

Quite why building a fake town in Iowa would make the picture significantly more "authentic" than building an equally fake one in Hollywood is unclear from Da Costa's message, but Willson responded enthusiastically to this idea—and indeed to most of the director's message—on May 31, noting that he was "ecstatic about Bob [Preston]" and he encouraged Da Costa to think of casting Paul Ford (who had taken over as Mayor Shinn on Broadway on June 1, 1959) in the movie.[42] Willson drafted a letter to Governor Loveless of Iowa on June 3 and sent it to Da Costa for approval. The director gave him seven suggestions of details to add—including "Time is of the essence as shooting will probably begin around April 1, 1961"—and Willson sent it on June 6, signing himself "Colonel Meredith Willson, Aide to the Governor."[43] Presumably the plan was turned down as impractical or too expensive; the exact reasons are not documented in Willson's papers.

In July 1960, Willson met with a possible screenwriter for the movie, Marion Hargrove, who was a prolific writer of fiction and for television and film. Other names were proposed on August 1 by the William Morris Agency but Hargrove was hired for the job.[44] There was also regular back-and-forth about casting for the film. For example, on July 11 Da Costa suggested Shirley Jones, Shirley MacLaine, and Mitzi Gaynor for Marian, Hermione Gingold for Eulalie, Stubby Kaye for Marcellus, and Fred Clark for the Mayor.[45] A note headed "Steve Trilling" (of Warner Bros.) further mentions Jack Oakie for Marcellus and Eva Marie Saint as Marian, reiterates enthusiasm to test Barbara Cook and Shirley MacLaine, and says Gingold as Eulalie is a "staggeringly good idea."[46] In the end, Jones was cast as Marian, with Gingold as Eulalie, Paul Ford as Mayor Shinn, the Buffalo Bills singing and acting as the school board, Buddy Hackett as Marcellus, and a young Ron Howard as Winthrop.

Shooting began on April 3, 1961, on the Warner Bros. lot and completed on July 10, either ten or twenty-two days ahead of schedule (at a saving of $10,000 per day), depending on the source.[47] Obviously, Da Costa ran the production effectively. There were regular updates in the press regarding the progress of the film: for instance, on July 30 the Los Angeles Times revealed that it had taken seven weeks of rehearsal and five weeks of filming to shoot the three big dance numbers in the movie, "Marian the Librarian," "Shipoopi," and "Seventy-Six Trombones."[48] Another article, in the New York Times, showed that for the film's "Seventy-Six Trombones" finale the studio hired 143 schoolboys to simulate the band, even though the fifty-five-person studio orchestra heard on the soundtrack contained only twelve trombones and eight cornets. "The consensus in the Warner Brothers music department," the article explained, "is that electronics can be used to magnify the ensemble to whatever size desired. Quality was the crucial factor in electing to have the high school bandsmen carry but not play the instruments, lent by the obliging Elkhart people of Indiana. The boys were chosen on their skill as marchers, rather than musicians."[49] Another challenge during filming was that Shirley Jones discovered that she had become pregnant, as she reveals in the documentary accompanying the DVD release of the movie, therefore requiring some adaptation of her costumes and choreography.[50]

Jack Warner, head of the studio, planned an elaborate two-day festival in Willson's hometown of Mason City to mark the release of the movie on June 19 and 20, 1962, to include a Music Man Marching Band Competition involving thirty-two different bands and a national press premiere screening of the movie. The festival involved around 100,000 people and was covered widely in the national media, separately to reviews of the film itself. Robert Preston, Shirley Jones, Ron Howard, and Willson were all present, and approximately 175 journalists attended to cover the event. Hedda Hopper, for example, wrote an extensive article about it that was published in both the Washington Times and Chicago Daily Tribune.[51] "It was 11 p.m. before the world premiere of 'Music Man' got underway at the theatre," she reported. "But it went beautifully. At the finish when they played '76 Trombones,' the roof literally fell in . . . A perfect climax for a perfect day."

The Music Man opened at the Hollywood Paramount on July 25 and at Radio City Music Hall on August 23. The pressure for the film to deliver a satisfying adaptation of this, the third longest-running Broadway show of the 1950s, was high, but Bosley Crowther began his review in the *New York Times* by assuring readers that "all who were sadly disappointed they never got to see 'The Music Man' with Robert Preston in the top role during its lengthy run on Broadway . . . are going to miss nothing of its quality and character in the film."[52] He continued: "If anything, the munificence of the big, booming, sentimental show that established an international standard of seventy-six trombones for a first-class band has been enhanced and expanded in the huge Technirama color film," referring to the sharp-image widescreen technology that Warner Bros. had employed. Similarly raving about the movie, Philip K. Scheuer of the *Los Angeles Times* admitted that he had not particularly enjoyed the show on the stage but that "Now all is forgiven. The picture goes right on clickety-clacketying its way into our hearts after it leaves the River City roadbed, up to and through the grand finale. . . . This music man [sic] will make millions and, what is more important, make music for millions."[53]

Several of the major reviewers specifically mentioned their admiration for Da Costa's approach to adapting a stage fantasy into a musical for the screen. Crowther's insightful assessment gets to the heart of the movie's unusual but intelligent style:

[The] lush amalgam of the many elements of successful American show business that Mr. Willson brought together on the stage, has been preserved and appropriately made rounder and richer through the magnitude of film.

It is noticeable that Mr. Da Costa has not tried to endow the show with a quality of graphic realism in moving it onto the screen. Wisely, he has avoided an attempt to kid anyone into thinking that this is a reproduction of anything that might have happened—or any place.

His town is as obvious a stage set—only more so—as it was on the stage. His adventure in emotional excitation could only happen within a theatre. The scheme is set in the opening number, when a full cut-away of a railway coach encloses a chorus of traveling salesman doing the "Rock Island" number the same as on the stage. And thenceforth, in the cleanness of the street scenes, the shininess of the sets, the formality of the choral groupings, the farcicalness of the characters, it is clear that Mr. Da Costa is putting this forth as a "show."[54]

A week later, Crowther wrote an additional article that focused entirely on the film's "Terms of Unreality," as he called it, explaining why he thought Da Costa's aesthetic was successful:

In making his decision not to try to use the motion picture for a pictorial illusion of reality in "The Music Man," Mr. Da Costa was wise, by our reckoning, because he rightly recognized the essential artificiality of the story and the treatment of it that he had to do. To set the ebullient Robert Preston, whom he also brought over from the stage to play the agreeably exaggerated role of the music man, right down in the middle of a real-life, dusty Iowa town, with genuine country around it and distant horizons, and then have him walk along the sidewalk and burst into musical-comedy song, with townsfolk choraling around him, might have been just a wee bit too absurd.[55]

Similarly, a reviewer for *Variety* praised Da Costa's efforts: "Somehow, and this is no minor achievement, he has captured a quality that has been notoriously elusive over the years for the makers of film musicals—the robust, spontaneous air of theatrical make-believe within the natural settings and wide-open dimensions of the screen. It is a happy marriage of two art forms."[56]

Thus while it might be tempting to dismiss the fantasy style of the movie against the more conspicuously realistic settings of the *West Side Story* movie released a year earlier, the film of *The Music Man* was regarded as artistically satisfying, perhaps even ingenious, by leading critics at the time. It is also true that the film is not simply a transposition of the Broadway production onto a movie set. The screenplay offers a genuine opening-up of the show's book to enable much more extensive use of street scenes, such as in the new material leading into "Iowa Stubborn." The medium of film allows the camera to take Hill directly from the train into the middle of River City, gradually meeting and talking to several individuals before the song builds into an ensemble number. Similarly, the use of the camera during "Trouble" is particularly effective, swirling around in a circular motion from behind and above as Hill gets the townsfolk to start a Mexican wave as he infects them with his manufactured concerns.

In the opening to "Goodnight, My Someone," Da Costa tries another interesting camera position as we see Amaryllis playing the piano keyboard as if the camera is inside the piano rather than from her side or behind her. Most of the rest of the song is shot in close-up from outside the house, with the window framing Shirley Jones's performance using exactly the same kind of technique that Vincente Minnelli memorably uses to frame Judy Garland's performance of "Have Yourself a Merry Little Christmas" from *Meet Me in St Louis* (1944). And in "Marian the Librarian," the music begins even more subtly and tentatively than in the Broadway version (emphasizing the possible allusion to *The Sorcerer's Apprentice* with its now fragmented introductory phrases), while the camera work and staging both emphasize a 360-degree approach that is especially effective during the hypnotic section of the dance break when Marian dances backwards in a circle, discarding her spectacles as she surrenders to Hill's captivating chaos. In short, the movie is cinematic while preserving the fantastical atmosphere of the stage, an updated version perhaps of the 1930s style of Hollywood musical where song and dance were not conceived as being anathema to the realism of the camera.

Four decades later, Craig Zadan and Neil Meron—veteran producers of film and television musicals—brought a new version of *The Music Man* to the small screen. Adapted by Sally Robinson, the production featured seasoned musical theater performers Matthew Broderick and Kristin Chenoweth as Hill and Marian, with Victor Garber as Shinn and Debra Monk as Mrs. Paroo. Zadan and

Meron had previously enjoyed success in Disney's *Wonderful World of Disney* series with their popular new versions of Rodgers and Hammerstein's *Cinderella* (with Whitney Houston and Whoopi Goldberg, 1997) and *Annie* (with Kathy Bates and Victor Garber, 1999), and *The Music Man* was planned to be the next installment in their series, premiering on February 16, 2003. In itself, the date was a problem from which the production could not recover: the *New York Times*'s review was headed "Bad Timing!" and went on to explain, "It is an unfortunate weekend for ABC to be showing its new movie version of 'The Music Man.' After all, movie musicals almost never get any attention. . . . But this week everybody is talking about movie musicals. Or at least they're talking about one. That, of course, would be 'Chicago,' whose 13 Oscar nominations announced on Tuesday belie the conventional wisdom that moviemakers can neither do justice to stage musicals nor suitably adapt them to their own medium."[57] The screen version of Kander and Ebb's *Chicago*—also produced by Zadan and Meron, curiously—was still enjoying enormous success several weeks after its release, and the less glossy *Music Man* could do little to compete.

Naturally, there are some interesting and commendable aspects to the new version. The adaptation adds some subtle new ideas while combining features of both the Broadway and Hollywood versions. For example, most of the score is left intact in the broadest sense, but the arrangements are new. "My White Knight" is used from the Broadway score (i.e., rather than "Being in Love" from the 1962 film), but it begins with the "All I want is a plain man" interlude section rather than the beginning of the refrain; this is ironic because Willson's original draft version of this song also begins with that passage (see Chapter 3). An example of an idea taken from the film is the moment when Hill looks over the footbridge into the water and fantasizes that he is going to conduct the band, though the Disney version emphasizes Hill's uncertainty more. Some of the dialogue is tweaked or embellished too: to soften the potentially misogynistic portrayal of Mrs. Shinn and her friends, they are given new dialogue in which Marian is commended for her piano playing to accompany their dance performance. The production also begins to reflect contemporary values in employing a multiracial cast, but actors of color are not given any of the principal roles and are sometimes problematically marginalized, such as the Black pianist who accompanies Hill and Marcellus in "The Sadder but Wiser Girl" but who has no lines or substantial identity. There is no equivalent of, for example, Queen Latifah's casting as Mama Morton in the contemporaneous *Chicago* movie.

Zadan commented of the *Music Man* television production: "Our take was to make it real without losing the comedy. Matthew [Broderick] finds comedy in everything. Instead of coming to town as a tornado, he's a mischievous, impish con artist who is making it up as he goes along. And it's the first version where you really believe these two are falling in love."[58] Unfortunately, the reviews tended to disagree. For example, the *New York Times* commented: "There is, as a matter of fact, a great deal of fun to be had with this material—as anyone who saw Susan Stroman's splashy, raucous and colorful recent stage revival on Broadway knows. . . . But the direction here, by Jeff Bleckner, is stifling; his camera is a jittery one, in the manner of a film school auteur, and the movie is full of un-necessary quick cuts that seem out of synch with the story, as if MTV had been invented a century or so earlier than it was."[59]

Also damning was Edward Guthmann's review in the *San Francisco Gate*, headed "Unassertive lead weakens musical." He wrote: "Broderick, for all his boyish cheer and aura of goodwill, isn't very good in the three-hour 'The Music Man' revival. . . . [He] is cute, wide-eyed, a bit squishy and about as dynamic and intimidating as Winnie the Pooh. His singing is adequate, his dancing heavy and forced."[60] Whatever the strengths and novelties of the project, and regardless of Kristin Chenoweth's stellar performance as Marian, *The Music Man* had come up against the problem of competing with Preston's matchless portrayal of Harold Hill as preserved in the 1962 film.

THE MUSIC MAN IN REVIVAL

Success in revival productions is one of the main signs of a musical's robustness and longevity, and the repeated returns of shows such as *Oklahoma!* (1943), *Guys and Dolls* (1950), *The King and I* (1951), *My Fair Lady* (1956), *West Side Story* (1957), *Gypsy* (1959), *Hello, Dolly!* (1964), and *Fiddler on the Roof* (1964) to Broadway since their original substantial runs has been key to their continued cultural presence and impact.[61] By contrast, as of this writing, *The Music Man* has only enjoyed one successful Broadway revival in the six decades since its premiere. Leaving aside the two-week limited run at City Center with Bert Parks in 1965 (part of a regular season of short runs of popular musicals), it took the show almost twenty years to come back to New York, in a touring production starring Dick Van Dyke. Again, it played City Center, opening for eight previews from May 29, 1980, and playing twenty-one performances from June 5, closing on June 22. It was originally sup-posed to run for twelve weeks.[62]

Despite having one of Broadway's top director-choreographers in Michael Kidd and a Hollywood and television favourite in Van Dyke, the production had little impact right from its pre-Broadway opening in Los Angeles. A review of the latter by Dan Sullivan was direct: "The revival at the Pantages [Theatre] is coarse."[63] Of the star, Sullivan remarked: "Van Dyke presents a country bumpkin in a city slicker's suit, and you can see why River City would take to that combi-nation. He's one of them. . . . The singing is OK, but we noticed a certain wool-liness in 'Trouble' . . . What he doesn't do very well is relate to the rest of the cast, possibly for fear of losing the audience. 'Trouble,' again, is Dick Van Dyke doing a number in front of a folksy chorus, not a con-man charming the boots off the good parents of River City." The review was also critical of the designs: "Peter Wolf's settings leave us to imagine too much. They're flimsy and canvasy looking."

In a promotional interview for the production, Van Dyke—"himself the son of a small-town salesman"—remarked that his view of Hill was "a little more pro-vincial than some of the city slickers who have played him in the past. The way

I play him, he's just a little bit—but not too much—smarter than the people he's trying to fool."[64] This was at the heart of Walter Kerr's damning review of the production when it reached New York. Citing the scene where Hill confesses to Winthrop that he is "a dirty rotten crook," Kerr wrote: "And right then and there we know—if we didn't know earlier—exactly what's been subtly wrong with this 'Music Man' from the beginning. Mr. Van Dyke *isn't* a dirty rotten crook. He's not even a natty gentleman crook. He's not a crook at all. He's a nimble performer, and an attractive one. . . . But he's a straight shooter, honest from the word go, virtue spilling out of every pocket, innocence written all over him where sly graffiti should be. He's simply—and only—nice. And that hurts."[65]

Similar problems dogged the show's next appearance in New York for another limited run, this time at the City Opera in 1988. In the *New York Times*, Stephen Holden complained: "The director Arthur Masella's inability to resolve basic logistical problems in a coherent manner is compounded by the serious miscasting of the usually capable [Bob] Gunton. . . . Although Harold is a creature who survives on gutsy charm, Mr. Gunton's portrayal is anything but endearing. On the contrary, his performance is almost sinister in its tight-lipped tension—he barely cracks a smile." Holden also remarked that the revival was let down by "its grandly spacious staging, leisurely pace and overly formal performances."[66] Opening in previews on February 26, the production closed after six weeks on April 10 and was never revived by the company.

During the 1980s, the show appeared in regional productions, such as a summer stock revival with Broadway star Jim Dale in Dallas and St. Louis in 1984 and another in 1988 with dances by the show's original choreographer Onna White. It also appeared in London at the Regent's Park Open Air Theatre from July 25 to September 4, 1995, in a production starring classical and screen actor Brian Cox and musical theater actress Liz Robertson. It was generally well received, with Cox being described as "wonderfully dicey" (*The Observer*) and Robertson as "utterly charming" (*The Sunday Times*) and "exactly right" (*Observer*),[67] and the same year Jim Dale recorded the show for a special BBC broadcast on Radio 2.

But the first major revival of *The Music Man* was not staged until April 27, 2000, over forty-two years after its Broadway debut. A year before her record-breaking direction for the original production of *The Producers* (2001), director-choreographer Susan Stroman brought a new staging of *The Music Man* to the Neil Simon Theatre—its first production at a Broadway theater since the original. Mirroring the casting of Robert Preston, Stroman selected television and film actor Craig Bierko to play Hill, followed later in the run by television star Eric McCormack (*Will and Grace*) and popular stage and screen actor Robert Sean Leonard (*House*). As with the original production, Marian was played by a Broadway veteran, Rebecca Luker.

Stroman's approach was sympathetic to the original rather than revolutionary. In an interview not long before the opening, she talked about the show in terms that could almost have come out of Willson's own mouth: "'The Music Man' is about the rhythm of the pitch of the traveling salesman," she said, "and then about the language of the people of Iowa."[68] However, she was conscious that aspects of the show had the potential to trouble audiences and said that "taking Willson at his word" was a way to ward off what the journalist writing the article called "the cringe factor" of the show: "I've done a lot of research on Mason City and on Iowa," she commented, and "each ensemble member has been provided with a history and a connection to another ensemble member." She added that the town "is treated like a real town." Through this detailed approach, Stroman aimed to harness the show's strengths in a fresh way that did not conflict with the nature of the material. Ben Brantley's review in the *New York Times* was critical of her direction of the book, which he described as "sleepy," but he also commented, "What Ms. Stroman gets right, she gets wonderfully right, and that goes back to the idea of what the Gershwins called 'fascinatin' rhythm.' . . . This 'Music Man' may be disappointingly earthbound for at least half of its nearly three hours, but it still has more helium than any of the other self-described family entertainments on Broadway."[69]

CONCLUSION

Stroman's production proved that *The Music Man* still had relevance both in its message and substance to entertain and move twenty-first-century audiences. The show has appeared in occasional short runs since that last Broadway revival, including a 2008 production at the Chichester Festival in the UK, and a concert production at the Kennedy Center in Washington, DC, in February 2019 marked probably the first major performances in the States to star a Black actor, Norm Lewis, as Harold Hill.[70] There was also an all–African American concert production starring Isaiah Johnson and Stephanie Umoh at the New Jersey Performing Arts Center and the Two River Theater in Red Bank, in 2014.[71] The show has also proved its ability to relate to international audiences, for example in a successful production in Beijing in 1987 that was covered by the *New York Times*.[72] As American musical theater becomes more globalized, it has been essential for the classics to adapt through racially diverse casting and by considering how to frame and reframe their messages for today's audiences, displaced from the context of the original Broadway productions.

Such casting and productions may also start to address the problem that *The Music Man* has for some time suffered from comparison to *West Side Story*, which originally opened on Broadway just under three months before *The Music Man* on September 26, 1957. Voters on the Tony Awards committee were clear that *The Music Man* was the "Outstanding Musical" of the season (along with four other awards), while *West Side* won just two Tonys, for design and choreography. As we have seen in this chapter, reviews of *Music Man* were uniformly glowing and compared it to the greatest and most enduring musicals of all time, while those for *West Side* were significantly mixed. Brooks Atkinson of the *New York Times* wrote a rave for *West Side*, calling the show "an organic work of art," but the *New York World-Telegram and Sun* referred to it as being "as exciting (and sordid) as a subway mugging with music."[73] *West Side* ran only 732 performances—three months short of two years—while *Music Man* continued for 1,375 performances, three years and four months. Yet with the release of the movie versions of the two musicals, the reverse happened: *West Side* was a cinematic phenomenon upon its release in 1961, winning ten Academy Awards, while *The Music Man* was a more modest success, if also positively received and profitable.

Both in journalistic and in scholarly debates, these two musicals have evolved into a binarism, pitted against one another as if they were designed to be considered in tandem. Brantley's review of the Stroman revival of *Music Man* even included the comment: "[F]inger-wagging hindsight tends to make 'West Side Story' the breakthrough upstart, with 'The Music Man' as a comforting throwback." Brantley is clear in not ascribing to this negative view of what he calls Willson's "doozy of a debut,"[74] but his comment neatly confirms an attitude of resentment from which Willson's show has suffered. This is, of course, ironic, because both *Music Man* and *West Side* took many years to write and could have been given their premieres at several points during the 1950s, both in different forms and with different competition. *West Side* might at one time have had lyrics by Betty Comden and Adolph Green, who wrote the lyrics to Bernstein's previous musicals *On the Town* (1944) and *Wonderful Town* (1953), thereby lacking the vital contribution of Stephen Sondheim to the score, and it could have opened in 1956, making its direct competitor *My Fair Lady* (1956), the longest-running musical of the decade. In either scenario, its run could have been briefer or longer, but it would also have removed the temporal connection with *The Music Man*. Equally, the latter show might have reached the stage at any point in the previous few seasons, potentially without the input of Franklin Lacey and Kermit Bloomgarden that helped to push it toward its successful end; it too may have suffered from comparison to *My Fair Lady* had it opened a year earlier, or it might have done even better in the 1958–1959 season when the competition was more limited (the Best Musical Tony Award was given to *Redhead*, a now forgotten work).

These arguments are, of course, irrelevant in terms of what actually happened, but the juxtaposition of *The Music Man*'s opening with that of *West Side Story* is important to understanding its reception history. It is especially tangible in terms of its scholarly reception, where the two shows have been explicitly formulated as being related to one another. For example, both Carol Oja and Warren Hoffman have written essays comparing them through the lens of race, with Oja remarking that they "yield an odd sort of couple—wildly mis-matched yet interconnected nonetheless."[75] More specifically, she says that "*West Side Story* dug its heels into the gritty pavement of the here-and-now, confronting gang violence and racial prejudice against Puerto Rican immigrants as they negotiated the urban jungle. *The Music Man*, meanwhile, spun a gauze of nostalgia, traveling back to the imagined simplicity of the early twentieth century to evoke an America of racial purity and grass-roots values."[76] She concludes by remarking that fifty years on, the tensions between different social codes "continue to resound" and remarks that *West Side* and *Music Man* are "like the 'Red States' and the 'Blue States,' with all the notions of divided social values and unresolved identity conflicts that they represent."[77] Hoffman, on the other hand, condemns *The Music Man* for "turn[ing] so fiercely away from the topic of race when it was a subject that was extremely present in New York and elsewhere around the country."[78] For him, there is a clear hierarchy whereby *West Side* is a greater work because it depicted one of the biggest social challenges of the day while *The Music Man* ignored it; Oja is more balanced in understanding both works as illustrative of America at the time, as well as sharing themes such as the prickly attitudes of closed communities to outsiders.

Nobody would disagree that there is an obvious difference in the depiction of race in the two shows, though we saw in Chapter 2 that Willson did attempt a draft that incorporated greater representation of immigrants, as well as defining Tommy Djilas as coming from a family of immigrants in the final version of the show. It is also of note that *West Side* began as a modern version of *Romeo and Juliet* (i.e., the updating of a classic text was its starting point, not racial tensions) and the creatives were willing to compromise on what the modern equivalent of the Montagues and Capulets would be; for some time, it was to be about sparring Jews and Catholics during the Easter-Passover celebrations.[79] Further, *West Side*'s depiction of the Puerto Rican community was written entirely from a white perspective, and could be said in its way to reinforce whiteness just as much as *The Music Man* does. Yet the comparisons between the shows persist, almost in fury—or perhaps embarrassment—that *West Side Story* was commercially and critically far less successful than *The Music Man* at its Broadway debut.

A particularly insightful aspect of Oja's discussion of the works is that there is plenty of overlap between them. There are others that she does not mention, and of especial relevance to this book are the aspects that have an impact on Willson's status—for not only have the musicals been seen as positing socially and politically polarized positions, they have also been read as departing from aesthetically different positions too. Here, it may be more useful to consider the opposite. It is striking that both Bernstein and Willson came from a background in art music, both were broadcasters, both wrote film music, both were capable of writing both words and music, both wrote symphonic music, both were conductors, and both incorporated vernacular musical styles into the scores for their shows. They both even had a strong connection to the New York Philharmonic, and while nobody would pretend that Willson came near Bernstein's towering position in classical music (or in the Philharmonic specifically), it is also important to understand that they were coming from the same place on many issues and that they were both culturally eclectic (to refer back to Chapter 1) in general.

And if *The Music Man* may seem like an anomaly in histories of the Broadway musical, that should never be because *West Side Story*—a *sui generis* work—is perceived as the beginning of a new era in which commercially and critical musical comedies such as *The Music Man*, *The Sound of Music* (1959), *How to Succeed in Business without Really Trying* (1961), and *Hello, Dolly!* (1964) are not worthy of scholarly attention. In truth, *The Music Man* was a reminder that the musical comedy was an important, creative, and viable commercial form on Broadway whose inventiveness (e.g., the "Rock Island" scene) was in some ways fresher than the persistence and dominance of ballet forms in *West Side Story* (the show's choreographer Jerome Robbins had already used them extensively in *On the Town* [1944], after all).

In 1958, when Willson could probably not have imagined that *West Side* would overtake *The Music Man* in terms of legacy, he started to think of his next project and came up with an idea that was generally not thought to work in musicals: a sequel. (The Gershwins' *Let 'Em Eat Cake*, a sequel to their hit *Of Thee I Sing*, was a flop in 1933.) To be true, it was not a direct sequel of *The Music Man* in either characters or setting, but it was titled either *The Son of the Music Man* or (in one case) *The Son of the Son of the Music Man, or Harold Hill III*; in either version, a direct allusion was being made to the earlier show. There are six draft synopses in the Carmel collection, dating between July 23 (just two days after *The Music Man* and Willson appeared on the front cover of *Time* magazine)[80] and September 25, 1958. A further copy of the September 25 version lies in the Kermit Bloomgarden papers, along with a four-page response from Betty Hart, a member of Bloomgarden's script-reading staff who became close to Willson during the production of *The Music Man*. There are a few differences between the July versions, which are three pages long and general, and the September ones, which are between ten and twelve pages long and give a scene-by-scene breakdown. But the main theme of the synopses remains consistent: Willson's preoccupation with bringing "long-hair" music to the masses, as discussed in Chapter 3.

The premise of the show is that Harold Hill (called Cleve Browning in the July versions) is a concert pianist who falls in love with Bill Gaynor (Natalie Gaynor in the July versions; she has been called Bill because her father wanted a boy), the daughter of a successful music publisher, Emanuel Gaynor of the Gaynor Music Corporation. Much of the action takes place in the Bill Brillding, a joking reference to the Brill Building on Broadway in New York, an office block where many of the biggest popular music hits of the 1950s and 1960s were written; naturally, the fictional version has been named the Bill Brillding in Bill Gaynor's honor.

Emanuel hates classical music—a lawsuit over Offenbach's "Barcarolle" from *The Tales of Hoffmann* bankrupted his father—and has brought up Bill to do the same, so when Harold falls in love with Bill there is an immediate conflict. In a parallel plot, Bill is engaged to Dick Janis, who pretends to have been trying to persuade Gaynor's rival, Jerry Golden of Golden Music, to help Gaynor by recording his songs, since Gaynor is struggling financially; it later emerges that Dick is actually paying Golden not to record Gaynor's songs in the hopes that that he, Dick, will be able to take over the Gaynor company through his relationship with Bill.

Recognizing the need for Gaynor to have a hit *and* to be converted to classical music, Harold quickly provides three excellent tunes and in a scene with Bill the two of them soon write the lyrics. Harold tells Gaynor he may publish the songs if he provides him with the funds to book the New York Philharmonic to play a concert with him at the helm as conductor. Bill and Emanuel, as well as all their staff, are obliged to attend. Reluctantly, Gaynor agrees. The final scene of the show features Harold conducting the Philharmonic onstage in a performance of Brahms's Fourth Symphony while the Gaynors recognize that the melodies for the three songs all derive from themes in the symphony. Cards (whose content is projected onto the back wall of the stage) are passed to Bill to inform her that the music is all in the public domain so they don't need to worry about rights and also tell her that Dick has been paying Jerry not to record Gaynor's music. Bill runs to the stage and kisses Harold as the curtain comes down.

On July 21, Willson wrote to Betty Hart and commented, "Am holding off on [sending] the outline of 'SON OF THE MUSIC MAN' till I get some kind of synopsis of scenes which I think should be completed before we really can tell what we've got or haven't got."[81] He continued to work on the synopsis over the summer and on October 20 Hart responded to the September 25 version, praising its focus on concert music but also querying whether the use of Brahms's music would appeal to all audiences. She also asked questions such as "Is Harold Hill III advocating that we appreciate good music for its own sake, or that pop songs be made from classic themes?" and wondered, "if, in terms of character, as well as issues, the tail doesn't wag the dog in the present structure of the story. Harold Hill III is an established celebrity and a creative artist. The combination gives him a tremendous power to influence. I can't help feeling he is more of a force than any publisher ever could be. But we have the focus of the story on the Bill Brillding with HH III coming into it, rather than the focus on HH III and his exploits, with the Bill Brillding coming into them."[82]

In the latter comment we can hear echoes of the problems with the early versions of *The Music Man*, especially S1 (see Chapter 2) in which Harold and Marian seemed secondary to Jim Paroo and his mother. There are some interesting ideas in Willson's synopsis and once more he had created an original plot in which music was at the heart of the story, in theory making songs sit naturally within it. The mixture of high and low culture was a subject dear to his heart and was something he had advocated throughout his career to date; and the idea of making popular songs out of classical music was a new direction for him (notwithstanding the suggested derivation of "Marian the Librarian" from *The Sorcerer's Apprentice*, as discussed in Chapter 3). Equally, it was a logical move because of the popularity of the musicals of Robert Wright and George Forrest, other songwriters signed to Frank Loesser's publishing company, who often used classical music as the starting point for songs (most notably *Kismet*, 1953, based on themes by nineteenth-century Russian composer Alexander Borodin).

Yet the idea seems not to have been pursued any further, whether because Willson lost interest, felt he could not resolve the problems Hart outlined, was busy with writing his book *But He Doesn't Know the Territory* (which was published in 1959), or because he decided instead to write the score for *The Unsinkable Molly Brown*, a project that already had a producer, book writer, and director and that instinctively appealed to his taste for Americana.

5

AFTER *THE MUSIC MAN*

• • •

THE UNSINKABLE MOLLY BROWN IN THE SHADOW OF A HIT

From Chicago, where he had been checking on the touring company of *The Music Man*, Morton Da Costa sent a telegram to Meredith Willson on May 24, 1959: "SHOW HERE IS EXCELLENT. HAD LUNCH [WITH] DORE SCHARY[.] HE IS ON WAY TO HOLLYWOOD[.] SUGGESTED HE SEND YOU SCRIPT (UNSINKABLE MRS BROWN)[.] HE LOVED IDEA AND WILL PHONE YOU"[1] Thanks to the preservation of this telegram, we know exactly when and how Willson came to be involved in his second Broadway musical, *The Unsinkable Molly Brown*: through the director of *The Music Man*. Just four days later, Willson replied to Da Costa, seriously intrigued by the project:

> Dear Tec,
> Many thanks for your wire. I have read the manuscript and like it very much in the main. In fact I had a meeting with Dore and the author [Richard Morris] yesterday and told them I was very taken with it. I felt the drabness, scenically, in the first act—shanties, the saloon, etc.—could be overcome by a mammoth cyclorama-effect portrayal of the Rocky Mountain empire, Pike's Peak and stuff, then doing the shanty and saloon locales with mostly props. I thought there was a cliché scene or two, notably the party when nobody came. I am confident, however, that a much more interesting snobbing [*sic*] of Molly could be accomplished than that old thing. I would give Dore an OK right now if there was a chance of you directing it after "Saratoga [Trunk]."[2] Dore indicated his possible availability to direct if everyone else thought that was desirable. I am a great admirer of Dore's but I have no way of evaluating his ability to direct a musical comedy. I promised Dore an answer within a week. At this point I have a pretty good feeling that I will do it.[3]

One week later, Willson's enthusiasm for the project had grown to the point where he had not only informally committed himself to doing it but also announced it to the press. On June 4, Sam Zolotow wrote an article in the *New York Times*, headed

The Big Parade. Dominic McHugh, Oxford University Press. © Oxford University Press 2021.
DOI: 10.1093/oso/9780197554739.003.0006

"WILLSON WORKING ON SECOND EFFORT," in which he said that "Although contracts have not been signed, everything points to 'The Unsinkable Mrs. Brown' as Mr. Willson's second Broadway attempt. But not on as extensive a scale as 'The Music Man.' In this instance, he will be responsible only for the music and lyrics."[4]

Since writing the book of *The Music Man* had been the most time-consuming and difficult challenge in bringing that show to the stage (as we saw in Chapter 2), it makes sense that Willson was enticed by the prospect of having somebody else write the script for *Molly Brown*. His attraction to the material was instinctive and rapid, as we can see not only from the above correspondence but also from a further comment in Zolotow's article: "Asked how he came to select 'The Unsinkable Mrs. Brown,' Mr. Willson recalled the advice imparted to him by Richard Rodgers. It was simply this: To tackle things that sparked his enthusiasm. With that in mind, Mr. Willson said he must have evaluated eighty stories since the opening of 'The Music Man.' "[5]

It says a lot, then, that *Molly Brown* appealed to him, though his archives do not seem to reveal what most of the other seventy-nine stories might have been.[6] He was at least the second choice of composer for the show—Irving Berlin was later revealed to have been the original choice[7]—but the sustained success of *The Music Man* made him an obvious final selection.

When Willson met him, Richard Morris, who created the book of the show, had written a few screenplays earlier in the 1950s, namely *Finders Keepers* (1952), *Ma and Pa Kettle at the Fair* (1952), and *Take Me to Town* (1953). However, his main experience was in television. Programs for which he wrote include *Kings Row* (1955), *Private Secretary* (1956), and *Encounter* (1959), and he was principally known for being a senior writer on the popular *Loretta Young Show* from 1956 onward.

The *Unsinkable Mrs. Brown* musical (as it was called until April 1960)[8] was mentioned in the press as early as April 1958. It was described as a co-production between the Theatre Guild (of *Oklahoma!* fame) and Dore Schary, an enormously successful producer, director, and writer whose career at MGM included a stretch as President before he was fired in November 1956.[9] He subsequently wrote and co-produced (with the Theatre Guild) the hit play *Sunrise at Campobello* (1958) on Broadway and *Molly Brown* was a follow-up project for the Guild-Schary team. At this point, Vincent J. Donehue was named as the director of *Mrs. Brown*, following on from his Tony Award–winning direction of *Campobello*, but he withdrew at some point in the ensuing months, perhaps when he became the director of Rodgers and Hammerstein's final show *The Sound of Music* (which opened on November 16, 1959).

No composer or lyricist had been found at the time of the April 1958 article being written, but it was obvious from the description that Morris had already made significant progress on the book. This is confirmed by the fact that one of three drafts of the script in the Willson papers at Carmel is dated August 7, 1958. It is titled "Revised Copy 'B,'" which indicates there was a previous version. Although much work was done on the book after Willson joined the project in June 1959, it is clear from the August 1958 draft that Morris had already created a functioning structure that would only change in one significant respect, as well as much of the dialogue that was ultimately performed on Broadway. He had also indicated where many of the songs would come and had even suggested titles for some of them, including "Belly Up to the Bar, Boys" and "I'll Never Say No to You, Mol," which was adopted by Willson without the word "Mol[ly]" in the Broadway score.

Given the opportunity to work with major names such as Schary and the Theatre Guild, and starting with the basis of a workable book that he did not have to write, it is no wonder that Willson jumped at the chance. As we will see in this chapter, it gave him the opportunity to return to devices he had used in *The Music Man*, ranging from barbershop songs to numbers with counterpoint, while the subject as a whole was a natural extension of his engagement with Americana in his musicals. The show was a success on Broadway upon its opening in 1960 and even more so in its 1964 movie version with Debbie Reynolds, but the collaboration with Schary proved unhappy and *The Music Man* loomed large in its reception.

AN AMERICAN LEGEND

Two of the three typescripts for *Molly Brown* in the Carmel collection are subtitled "An American Legend," a term that provides a useful point of departure for understanding what the show is about. From one perspective, it is a musical biography of the real-life Margaret Brown (1867–1932), who rose from humble beginnings to marry a gold miner, J. J. Brown (1854–1922), and later survived the sinking of the *Titanic* in 1912. Yet it is obvious even from Morris's August 1958 draft that he understood that the musical must not be an academic history lesson or biography but rather an entertainment. Although several scenes were chopped and changed over the following two years, one has to admire the fact that Morris's basic plan for the show, including the placement of the intermission and therefore the division of the material over the two acts, survived the tempestuous waters of bringing a musical to Broadway just as Brown herself survived the sinking of the ship. That is perhaps because he recognized that genre is more important than truth when it comes to writing a musical comedy, and he rearranged the bones of certain episodes of Brown's life to make a self-contained and lively narrative focusing on familiar Cinderella and Wild West tropes.

When the show opened in Philadelphia on Monday, September 26, 1960, the book was presented in the form of a flashback, with the opening and closing scenes set on the lifeboat where Molly has found relief from the sinking ship. In a prologue before the Overture of this version, she takes charge of the lifeboat, commandeers an oar, and announces that she is "unsinkable" because she was born in a cyclone and has weathered many other storms.

The rest of the show in its pre-Broadway form goes on to recount her life story from her own perspective, therefore, and when the flashback concludes just before the end, one of the passengers asks: "Do you mean to tell us, Mrs. Brown, that all that's true?" She answers: "Well, I was born in Hannibal, Missouri. The rest is colored up a bit. But hell, just sittin' in this rowboat ya gotta make things interestin.'"[10] This framing device underlines the idea that the show has presented a heavily fictionalized version of the truth, allowing the audience to join in with it as fun and not feel that it is to be taken too seriously.

Morris's August 1958 libretto (L1) presents a total of nineteen scenes, including the lifeboat opening and finale, versus twenty-five in the published script based on the Broadway version (L4). Two interim drafts (L2 and L3), undated but with distinctly different material, each have nineteen scenes; all four libretti can be found in the Carmel collections.[11] The scene structures and musical synopses are reproduced in Table 5.1.

L1 proceeds from the lifeboat opening (Scene 1) to the exterior of Molly's parents' shack on the day she was born (Scene 2), a rather silly vignette in which the baby Molly is whipped from her father's arms by a cyclone; this is dropped in all later versions (Willson has firmly written "Out" on his copy).

A scene at the Tobin shack follows, set fifteen years later, and this appears in all versions: it becomes Scene 2 in L2 and L3 and is the opening scene of L4. Two of Molly's brothers are wrestling with her and she refuses to surrender, declaring in L2-4, "I ain't down yet." This is the first of various moments where Molly broadly resembles the main protagonist of *Annie Get Your Gun*, Irving Berlin's 1946 musical about the crack shot Annie Oakley, and to a lesser extent the movie musical *Calamity Jane* (1953): two popular musicals about women who prove their prowess in physically fighting against men, in both cases displaying generic "tomboy" characteristics in both dress and attitude.[12]

Related to this, in the first two drafts of *Molly Brown*, Molly's gender identity is the main topic of this scene: she pronounces "I don't wanna be no girl" and later clarifies, "[Out] there poor lads can become rich lads. That's why I gotta be a boy, pa. . . . [It] ain't the money I love, pa. It's the no-havin' it I hate" (L1 and L2). By L3 and in the Broadway version, the emphasis of the scene moves to the departure of Molly's brothers to go and seek their fortune. The scene continues in L3 as Molly's father tells her to get married and she replies, "If he's gonna crawl in next to me, he's gonna have to be the richest Irish-Catholic next to the Pope." This marks a significant change in Molly's characterization, from feeling frustrated at the limitations enforced on her by gender to seeing her fortune as being obtainable through marriage; essentially, Morris's change makes Molly conform to 1950s gender roles. Act 1, Scene 2, of L4 acts as an appendix to Scene 1 and depicts Molly's decision to follow her brothers in leaving home to seek her fortune; the dialogue about her need to get married is lifted almost verbatim from the previous scene in L3.

All four versions then feature a scene at the Saddle Rock Saloon in Leadville (Scene 4 in L1; Scene 3 in L2-4). Gender is again a major topic, this time in all versions: Molly responds to a sign saying "BOY WANTED" and is told by the owner that the saloon is "no place for a young girl," adding after looking at her hard, "You are a girl?" Molly responds, "I can make any man 'round abouts look like the sissies they is" and she is given the job. From there, the scene evolves

Table 5.1. Synopsis and song lists for four versions of the libretto of *The Unsinkable Molly Brown*.

	L1: August 1958 Libretto	L2: Undated Interim Draft	L3: Further Undated Interim Draft	L4: Published Libretto (Broadway Version)
Act 1: Scene 1	A lifeboat in the mid-Atlantic. 2:30 A.M. April 15, 1912.	A lifeboat in the mid-Atlantic. Shortly after 2:30 A.M. April 15, 1912. Musical number: Overture at end of scene.	A lifeboat in the mid-Atlantic. Shortly after 2:30 A.M. April 15, 1912.	The exterior of the Tobin shack, Hannibal, Missouri. The turn of the century. Songs: "I Ain't Down Yet" (Molly and her Brothers); "Belly Up to the Bar, Boys" (unaccompanied) (Shamus, Molly, and her brothers).
Scene 2	Exterior of the Tobin shack, Hannibal, Missouri. The day Molly was born.	Exterior of the Tobin shack, Hannibal, Missouri. Years earlier. Songs: "I Ain't Down Yet" (Molly); "The Wonderful Plan" (Shamus).	Exterior of the Tobin shack, Hannibal, Missouri. Years earlier. Songs: "I Ain't Down Yet" (Molly and Brothers); "A Wonderful Plan" (Molly and Shamas).	The road by the Tobin shack. Sunup the next morning. Song: "I Ain't Down Yet" (Reprise) (Molly).
Scene 3	The Tobin shack. Fifteen years later. Suggested song title: "High On the Hog."	The Saddle Rock saloon in Leadville, Colorado. Two weeks later. Song: "Belly Up the Bar, Boys" (Molly).	The Saddle Rock saloon in Leadville, Colorado. Two weeks later. Song: "Belly Up to the Bar Boys" (Molly and the Miners).	The Saddle Rock Saloon, Leadville, Colorado. Late at night, weeks later. Song: "Belly Up to the Bar Boys" (Molly, Christmas, and the Miners).
Scene 4	The Saddle Rock saloon in Leadville. Midmorning, a week later. Suggested song title: "Belly Up to the Bar, Boys."	A clearing in the mountains. Immediately following. Song: "Colorado, I'm Yours" (Johnny).	A clearing in the mountains. Immediately following. Song: "Colorado, My Home" (Johnny).	Exterior of the Saddle Rock Saloon. Sunday night, three weeks later. Song: "I've A'ready Started In" (Johnny, Christmas, Charlie, Burt, and Gittar).

Scene 5	Outside the Leadville Catholic church, Sunday morning three weeks later.	The woods near the Leadville Catholic Church. Sunday morning, three weeks later.	Exterior of the Saddle Rock Saloon. Sunday night, one week later. Song: "I've Already Started In" (Johnny and his friends).	Johnny's log cabin. A month later. Songs: "I'll Never Say No" (Johnny); "My Own Brass Bed" (Molly).
Scene 6	Johnny's log cabin. A bit later. Suggested song title: "I'll Never Say No to You, Mol" (Johnny) with counterpoint, "The Hell Ya Says" (Molly).	Johnny's log cabin. A month later. Songs: "I'll Never Say No" (Johnny) and "Big Brass Bed" (Molly) in counterpoint; reprise at end of scene.	Johnny's log cabin. A month later. Songs: "I'll Never Say No" (Johnny); "My Own Brass Bed" (Molly).	On the road to Johnny's cabin. Three weeks later.
Scene 7	The same. Two weeks later. Suggested song: "Belly Up to the Bar, Boys" (reprise).	Johnny's log cabin. A week after the wedding.	Johnny's log cabin. Three weeks later.	Johnny's cabin. A minute later.
Scene 8	The same. A week later.	The boardwalk in front of the Saddle Rock. The next afternoon. (The lights dim during the scene to show the passing of a few weeks.) Suggested song title: "Paper Five Cents with a Reading Ten" (Ensemble). Song: "The Beautiful People of Denver" (Molly).	The boardwalk in front of the Saddle Rock. The next few weeks. Songs: "Don't Take My Word for It, Neighbor" and "With a Readin', Ten" (Medicine Man, Newspaper boys and chorus); "The Beautiful People of Denver" (Molly and the Leadville Citizens).	Pennsylvania Avenue, Denver. An evening, six months later. Song: "The Denver Police" (Three Policemen).

Continued

Table 5.1. Continued

	L1: August 1958 Libretto	**L2:** Undated Interim Draft	**L3:** Further Undated Interim Draft	**L4:** Published Libretto (Broadway Version)
Scene 9	The boardwalk in front of the Saddle Rock. (The lights dim during the scene to show the passing of a few weeks.) Suggested song title: "Paper Five Cents with a Reading Ten."	The terrace of Mrs. McGlone's Denver mansion. An evening a year later. Song and musical item: "Are You Sure?" (Molly and Guests); "The Minute Waltz" (played by Professor Gardella).	The terrace of Mrs. McGlone's Denver mansion. An evening six months later. Song and musical item: "Are You Sure?" (Molly, Monsignor Ryan and guests); "The Minute Waltz" (played by Professor Gardella).	The terrace of Mrs. McGlone's Denver mansion. Immediately following. Songs: "Beautiful People Of Denver" (Molly); "Are You Sure?" (Molly and Guests).
Scene 10	The terrace of Mrs. McGlone's Denver mansion. An evening a year later.	The red parlor of the Browns' Denver home. A month later. Song: "I'll Never Say No" (Molly).	The red parlor of the Browns' Denver home. A month later. Songs: double reprise of Songs: "I'll Never Say No" and "My Own Brass Bed" (Johnny and Molly).	Pennsylvania Avenue. Immediately Following.
Scene 11	The red parlor of the Browns' Denver home. A month later. Suggested song: "I'll Never Say No to You" (reprise).			Mrs. McGlone's morning room. Later that week. The red parlor of the Browns' Denver mansion. The evening of the housewarming. Song: "I Ain't Down Yet (reprise) (Molly and Johnny).

Act 2: **Scene 1**	The Browns' Paris salon. A spring afternoon years later.	The Browns' Paris salon. A spring afternoon years later. Song: "The Grand Tour" (Molly). Musical item: "The Minute Waltz" (Molly).	The Browns' Paris Salon. A spring afternoon, years later. Songs: "Happy Birthday, Mrs. J. J. Brown" (Princess DeLong and her friends).	The Browns' Paris Salon. A spring afternoon, years later. Songs: "Happy Birthday, Mrs. J. J. Brown" (Princess DeLong, Prince DeLong, and the International Set); "Bon Jour" (Molly, Prince DeLong, and the International Set); "If I Knew" (Johnny).
Scene 2	The red parlor of the Browns' Denver home. A month later. [End of scene notes: "A GOOD SPOT FOR A SONG FOR JOHNNY."]	A Paris street. Immediately following. "Colorado, I'm Yours" (Johnny).	The red parlor of the Browns' Denver mansion. An evening a month later. Song and musical item: "The Ambassadors' Polka" (Molly and the Ambassadors); "The Minute Waltz" (Molly).	The upper hallway of the Browns' Denver mansion. An evening months later. Song: "Chick-a Pen" (Molly and Johnny).
Scene 3	The same. That evening.	The red parlor of the Browns' Denver home. An evening a month later. Song; untitled (Molly greets each Ambassador in song). Musical item: "The Minute Waltz."	The Browns' rose garden. Immediately following. "If I Knew" (Johnny's friends and Princess DeLong's friends).	The red parlor. Eight o'clock that evening.

Continued

Table 5.1. Continued

	L1: August 1958 Libretto	L2: Undated Interim Draft	L3: Further Undated Interim Draft	L4: Published Libretto (Broadway Version)
Scene 4	The morning room. The next morning.	The morning room. The next morning.	Molly's bath. The next morning. "One Day at a Time" (Molly).	Pennsylvania Avenue. Immediately following.
Scene 5	Monte Carlo. A terrace restaurant off the Casino. An evening in March 1912.	Exterior of the Brown house. Later that week. Song: "I Ain't Down Yet" with "reprises of other musical numbers" (Molly)	Monte Carlo. A restaurant off the Casino. Early spring 1912. "Dolce Far Niente" (Molly and Prince DeLong).	The red parlor. The next morning.
Scene 6	The red parlor. A few weeks later.	Monte Carlo. A terrace restaurant off the Casino. An evening in March 1912. Musical number: "The Tango" (Molly and the Prince dance).	The red parlor. A few weeks later.	The street in front of the Saddle Rock Saloon. An evening, months later. Songs: "Keep A-Hoppin'" (Johnny and his Leadville Friends); "Leadville Johnny Brown (Soliloquy)" (Johnny).
Scene 7	The Browns' Paris salon. Two weeks later. Suggested song: "I'll Never Say No To You, Mol" with Molly's counterpoint (reprise).	The red parlor. A few weeks later. Music under scene: "I'll Never Say No."	A street in Paris. An afternoon in April. Song: "Fourth of July" (A Boy and Molly).	Outside a club at Monte Carlo. Years later. Early spring 1912.

Scene 8	The lifeboat in the mid-Atlantic. Suggested song: "Belly Up to the Bar, Boys" (reprise).	The Browns' Paris salon. Two weeks later. Music under scene: "I'll Never Say No."	The Browns' Paris Salon. The next day.	A club off the Casino at Monte Carlo. Immediately following. Songs: "Up Where the People Are" (Monte Carlo Guests); "Dolce Far Niente"; and "I May Never Fall in Love with You" (Prince DeLong and Molly).
Scene 9	The mid-Atlantic. Songs: "Belly Up to the Bar, Boys" (Molly); "Colorado, I'm Yours" (Molly and Johnny).	The mid-Atlantic. Songs: "Belly Up to the Bar, Boys" (Molly); "Colorado, My Home" (Johnny and Molly).	Outside the club at Monte Carlo. A moment later. Song: "Dolce Far Niente" (reprise) (Prince DeLong).	
Scene 10				The mid-Atlantic. Shortly after 2:30 A.M., April 15, 1912.
Scene 11				Upper hallway of the Browns' Denver mansion. Late April.
Scene 12				An aspen grove in the Rockies.
Scene 13				The Rockies. Song: "I Ain't Down Yet" (Finale) (Johnny, Molly, and Leadville Friends).

considerably between the versions. In L1 and L2, the scene is completed by Molly leading a rendition of "Belly Up to the Bar, Boys" and then going to the boarding room upstairs, where she is surprised to discover Johnny Brown ("a handsome bull of an Irishman") underneath one of the blankets, "all six-foot-four of him encased in well-worn, red underwear." He throws his arms around her and pulls her onto the cot, starting a fight, and then carries her downstairs. She refuses to give in, bites his leg, and then he declares his intention to marry her, much to her horror. As he starts to walk back up the stairs, "like a flash, she grabs a gun out of one of the miners' holster and fires at Johnny. He is standing on the stairs with his back upstage. We see the flap on the back of his longjohns drop." The miners are all watching, "bug-eyes and open-mouthed."

In this moment, we can see on the one hand a thoroughly dislikeable version of Johnny and on the other further echoes of Annie Oakley and Calamity Jane. No wonder that by the time the show reached Broadway, the scene removed both the gun and the predatory sequence in the bedroom. Instead, in a concept that was obviously Willson's idea, Molly gets the bar job by pretending she can play the piano, then we see her trying out different notes; a blackout follows to indicate that she stays up all night learning how to play the instrument, and the following day Molly is now seen leading "Belly Up," miraculously accompanying herself with (admittedly simple) chords on the piano. Willson liked the idea of showing music as being accessible to all and the scene's emphasis on Molly's innate musicality makes her the spiritual sister of Harold Hill.

In the Broadway version (L4), Johnny and Molly still fight but his teasing of her is much more mild, and he does not propose marriage until the next scene (Scene 4), set three weeks later. It is a Sunday morning and Molly has been to church; Johnny makes a serious attempt to woo her and says that he wants to make her happy but she rebukes him ("I ain't settlin' for happiness"), saying she wants "decent bed and board" for herself and her father. Johnny and his friends prevent her from entering the saloon by performing a wooing song for her ("I've A'ready Started In") and she pretends to be impressed but unexpectedly screams for the Sheriff at the end, closing the scene.

Earlier versions (L2 and L3) have an extra scene before this exchange, showing Johnny in the mountains, singing the number "Colorado, I'm Yours" (a later version of this, titled "Colorado, My Home," was cut in Philadelphia but reinstated for the movie adaptation and most revivals), and L1 and L2 set the Sunday morning discussion scene outside the church, revealing that Johnny has been attending Mass to please Molly (her Catholic faith is a major theme in several scenes). In essentials, though, the script remained the same in all versions in this stretch of the show, concluding in the next scene (Scene 5 of L4) with Johnny winning Molly's hand by showing her the new log cabin he has built for her. She initially resists but is tempted when she sees the big brass bed he has bought and capitulates when he reveals that he has included a bedroom for her father to come and live with them. This is an especially powerful moment in Molly's trajectory: materialism is at the heart of her aspiration so the bed is a serious lure, but her father's comfort—and in particular, her realization that Johnny recognizes the importance of her father to her—tips the balance and she immediately falls into Johnny's arms.

Morris's concept for the final scene of the act was clear from the start, but getting there required a lot of fiddling around with the intervening scenes. Johnny disappears for a week after the wedding and the drafts deal with this in different stages; the difficulty seems to have been to avoid making the change from the happiness of Molly's acceptance of Johnny at the end of one scene to his abandonment of her at the start of the next too abrupt, with both episodes played against the same scenery. The solution for Broadway (L4) was to add a short scene (Scene 6) played in front of a drop depicting the road to Johnny's cabin, in which Christmas Morgan[13] (the owner of the Saddle Rock saloon) has a brief discussion with two women of Leadville to establish that a week has gone by. This avoids having two consecutive scenes in the same setting and the cinematic flow it provides may reflect the Hollywood influence of the show's producer-director Schary (though Morris was an experienced screenwriter too, of course). Scene 7 then depicts Christmas discovering Molly in her misery, followed by Johnny's return with $300,000, which he has made by striking a silver mine.

This introduces a thematic connection to Lerner and Loewe's Gold Rush musical *Paint Your Wagon* (1951), but unlike Lerner's heavy treatment of how gold is the undoing of the miners, Morris's book takes a frivolous view. Molly hides the money in the stove, thinking it will be safe there, but Johnny unwittingly lights it and the money is instantly burned and lost. Cheerfully, he announces, "I'm going out right now an' talk to the silver again" and the next we know, in the Broadway version (L4) Molly and Johnny have moved to the city of Denver and built a house. L4 drops a scene that appears in L1–3 before the move to Denver in which Johnny's successful second strike is revealed, as well as his plans to build a property there; arguably, cutting the scene made the narrative less clear.

The concluding sequence of the act finds the warm but primitive manners of Molly being rejected by middle-class Denver society. Mrs. McGlone is the self-appointed leader of the community and Scene 8 (L4) shows a group of policeman singing about how she has paid them to "keep an eye on her party" at her mansion, highlighting her patronage. There is a quick segue to the longer Scene 9, the party itself. Molly and Johnny arrive without an invitation, intending to introduce themselves to their new neighbors rather than gate crash, and although Molly proves a hit with the local priest by collecting money for a new church from the guests, Mrs. McGlone pretends there is no room at the table for them and rudely makes them leave rather than inviting them to stay for dinner.

Outside on the street (Scene 10), Molly resolves to emulate the Denver people's "dignity" and learn how to be more refined in her behavior, not recognizing that she and Johnny have been snubbed. In Scene 11 Mrs. McGlone thwarts the Browns' attempts to hold a party for their new neighbors by telling the latter not to attend, and in Scene 12, when Molly and Johnny realize that nobody is coming, Molly persuades Johnny to take the Monsignor's advice for them to travel to Europe and become more cultured; Johnny prefers to return to Leadville but he gives in to her ambitions.

These last three scenes of Act 1 transform the theme of the show. Initially, it is about Molly's aspirations for financial security as a teenager, with an emphasis on escaping poverty; from Scene 9, it is now about class. This shift is powerful from a dramatic point of view: the departure for Europe presents an effective cliffhanger going into the intermission; Molly's ruthless persuasion of Johnny presents a counterbalance to his aggressive pursuit of her hand in marriage earlier in the act; and the change in her priorities, from the genuine to the pretentious, creates a new tension that will not be resolved until the end. Gradually, through Act 2 she loses both her values and her connection with Johnny.

In a striking similarity to the plot of Lerner and Loewe's *Camelot*, which opened on Broadway a month after *Molly Brown*, the second act presents a slow moral decline, whereby the main couple of the musical grow apart and the female lead (Molly/Guenevere) falls for another man (Prince DeLong/Lancelot). The second act of *Molly Brown* is somewhat more fun than that of *Camelot* and there is a conventional musical comedy denouement in Willson's show that does not occur in Lerner and Loewe's, but both works are follow-ups to major hits (*The Music Man* and *My Fair Lady*) and both get a little caught up with seriousness and conflict. Neither was even half as successful as its predecessor in their respective writers' canons.

In broad outline, the second act of *Molly Brown* in its Broadway version (L4) presents Molly and Johnny in Paris (Scene 1), where they have become friends with European royalty (including the Prince DeLong) and aristocracy; upon their return to America the Browns decide to show their friends off to the snobs of Denver at a party (Scenes 2–4); Molly is upset when a reporter in Denver writes an article about her uncouth behavior, leading to her decision to leave Johnny and return to Europe (Scene 5); months later, Johnny is seen at the Saddle Rock, mourning Molly's absence (Scene 6); the Prince pursues Molly and proposes marriage, which she ultimately rejects, deciding to return to Johnny on the next sailing of the *Titanic* (Scenes 7–9); Molly is seen in the lifeboat after the sinking of the ship (Scene 10); and she is reunited with Johnny, whereupon she agrees to go and live with him in his home state of Colorado (Scenes 11–13). The general plan of the act was mostly in place from L1–3, but crucially L1 concludes with Molly in the lifeboat and L2 and L3 dissolve without delay from the lifeboat straight to the tableau of Molly and Johnny in the mountains together (i.e., without dialogue in between).

Even a glance at Table 5.1 shows that L4 is considerably expanded compared to L1–3 and it is arguably drawn out too long. Indeed, L1 presents a much more concise structure dramaturgically and in particular L4's addition of Scenes 6 (which mainly exists to give Johnny more stage time and another song) and 11 (Molly's arrival in Denver) seems to contribute little to the show's momentum. Plus, the decision to remove the flashback device created an overall change in tone, away from the feeling of myth or legend and toward an episodic saga of the *Show Boat* (1927) or even *Allegro* (1947) variety—two musicals, interestingly, whose books (by Oscar Hammerstein II) were notoriously difficult to fix and have been changed for later productions. Rather than Molly telling her own story in her own words, the finished work adopts the tone of a more serious or elevated saga in the second act, as a result of the changes made between L3 and L4 in Philadelphia, and this perhaps helps to explain why the show is not fully coherent or satisfying.

That is not to say that the second act is in any sense a failure. There are, of course, numerous effective moments and Morris's final version of the book continues to address meaningful themes, engagingly portrayed. For example, Molly remains a formidable protagonist and even while there is a clear sense of her having lost her way by trying to transcend her social background for the wrong reasons, her dedication to her task is forceful. She learns how to communicate in ten languages, representing a more multicultural perspective than might be expected from the Wild West setting of Act 1, and Morris prevents her from seeming too shallow by having her remark in the second act, "I'll admit all this studyin' started as a cloak to wear on Pennsylvania Avenue, but once I got to know a little I knew what I hankered all my life was to know a lot. Hell, I'm just a hawg for knowledge." She also learns how to play the piano properly and in Act 2, Scene 3 (L4), she performs Chopin's "Minute Waltz" for the company, expanding her character by introducing a sincere interest in the topics of art music and high culture generally; in place of her gun, education becomes her silver bullet.

There are also a couple of well-drawn but troubling emotional peaks. The first is the end of Act 2, Scene 5, when Molly declares she is going "home" to Europe, even if Johnny refuses to come with her. She says (to her father Shamus), "I'll leave ya and go live wherever I damn please. . . . Ya only live this life once and I ain't wastin' it here. It's gonna be beautiful. At least, it is for me and if he don't want it the way I want it, to hell with him. . . . Yes and to hell with the Church." Shamus responds by slapping her "forcefully across the face." The gesture represents in microcosm the patriarchal world in which Molly exists: she has been punished by her father, not only for threatening to leave Johnny but also for blasphemy against her family's religion.

This violence is all the more shocking because Molly's main priority in the first half of Act 1 is to raise her father out of poverty; she marries Johnny while hardly knowing him primarily because he is willing to put a roof over Shamus's head. Johnny does not actively participate in the moment of violence between father and daughter but by failing to intervene, he implies some kind of acquiescence. This double rejection by her two closest relatives, in addition to the claustrophobia of her life in Denver, sets up Molly's need to flee to Europe effectively, even though it is very uncomfortable to watch.[14]

The other peak is in Scene 8, when Molly is in a restaurant in Monte Carlo. She is a changed person and tries to escape her life by assuming a new, colder personality. She allows Prince DeLong to woo her and she parades around the restaurant with her cape behind her, pretending to be a princess and forcing the other diners to bow to her. One of the guests is a much older Mrs. McGlone, who happens to be visiting Monte Carlo. Molly cruelly forces her to bow down to her, taking vengeance for treating her badly when she first arrived in Denver (see Fig. 5.1). She taunts her with: "Up, up, come on out, sweetie, this here's my domain. . . . (*Her voice turning hard . . . demanding*) Up and over, honey . . . down, girl, a thousand

Fig. 5.1. In Monte Carlo, Molly Brown makes Mrs. McGlone bow to her. Credit: Photofest.

bucks and all the doctor bills if your nose hits the floor." But Molly suddenly realizes she has been nasty. The moment is powerfully written by Morris:

> *Molly smells her final victory. Mrs. McGlone sees the revenge in Molly's face. Too late to turn back, Mrs. McGlone has to follow through. She starts to curtsy. Seeing the older woman's embarrassment suddenly sours Molly's frivolity. It all becomes so unimportant. Molly swoops down to Mrs. McGlone and lifts her to her feet. The music breaks off.*

Molly helps Mrs. McGlone to her feet and looks after her before bolting for the door. Having crossed a line by adopting sadistic behavior that is antithetical to her innate humanity, she is brought up short and decides to return to her former life and to Johnny, via a brief trip on the *Titanic*. Moments such as this are beautifully written and raise the show above the everyday. Yet the scenes added in Philadelphia make this plot resolution more problematic because they include dialogue in which Johnny demands that he and Molly live in his cabin in Colorado rather than in their Denver house; in L4 Johnny controls Molly's destiny whereas the dissolve from the lifeboat to the mountains in L1–3 emphasizes Molly's agency in getting what she wants (Johnny). Again traditional gender roles come into play, with the wife following the path chosen by her husband, and again the parallels with *Annie Get Your Gun*, in which the independent and dominant Annie similarly submits in order to preserve Frank's fragile masculinity, are too easy to draw.

WILLSON'S SECOND BROADWAY SCORE

If the pressure was high for Richard Morris to find success with his first book for a Broadway musical, for Meredith Willson to match or outdo his score for *The Music Man* was almost impossible. He was certainly enthusiastic: prior to October 22, 1959, he told a reporter he had already written five songs for the show (he does not name them), just five or so months after first reading the script.[15] He finished the bulk of the score by early February 1960 according to a further newspaper preview, in which it was reported: "After the fantastic success of 'The Music Man,' Willson was besieged with scripts, books, ideas and plots people wanted him to musicalize. . . . [He] exercised a great deal of restraint. He is a man who recognizes his own ability and limitations, and he knew if he did a second musical comedy it would have to be acceptable to his own unique talents."[16] Evidently, he was aware of the problem of writing the next work after a hit.

Trying to lay the ground for another success, he participated extensively in publicity for the show, months ahead of the November premiere on Broadway. For example, in May 1960 he appeared in a charity concert called *An Evening with Meredith Willson* in aid of the Denver Society for Crippled Children (further evidence of his commitment to this issue, following on from his attempts to write a disabled child as a character in *The Music Man* as we saw in Chapter 2), and the *Los Angeles Times* reported: "Meredith and Rini Willson slept in 'the Unsinkable Molly Brown's' suite at the Brown Palace in Denver while appearing there for the Crippled Children's Society."[17]

But as the show went into full company rehearsals from August 24, Willson started to be more open in his bigger concern about the show: "Whether the overall result is good, bad or indifferent, someone—several someones probably—is bound to comment that I am repeating myself," he admitted.

> There will be some numbers in the new show that, I suppose, will result in comparison with the "Trouble" song and the music-less but rhythmic "Rock Island" of "The Music Man." . . . I don't claim to have invented anything. After all, if you look long and hard enough you can find an "ancestor" for almost anything that seems to be "original." But I do claim, in all modesty, that there are some things in "The Music Man" that no one else has been doing. Now these things were successful in that show and they were not just "stunts." They are part of my style as a songwriter. They represent the way I think when I compose and write lyrics. So, why shouldn't I use them again? When you find something that is effective, you just don't throw it away.

He elaborated on a technical aspect of this too: "I like to compose music to words that represent the rhythm of speech. . . . There is a naturalness and lack of artificiality in such a style that is simply part of me. I don't mean to disparage other styles—in fact, I'll rhyme as well as the next one when the occasion calls for it—but I hope there is no penalty for continuing with something that comes naturally to me and that I feel is effective."[18]

If Willson seems a little sheepish about the comparisons between his new and previous scores in these comments, it may possibly reflect the fact that he attempted to recycle a few numbers that had been written for or considered for use in *The Music Man* (though it is important to remember that *Music Man* also contains "trunk songs," including "Till There Was You," so this was not a new approach for Willson). Of the songs that made it to *Molly Brown*'s Broadway score, "I've A'ready Started In" and "If I Knew" were both originally intended for use in *The Music Man*; two other cut songs from *Music Man*, "The Wonderful Plan" and "Tomorrow," were also tried in *Molly Brown* at some point (a summary of the songs written for and used in the musical, as well as their sources, is provided in Table 5.2).

There are other overlaps too. In *The Music Man* the lead male character is written for an actor (Harold Hill/Robert Preston) who either croons or delivers patter numbers and a legit soprano (Marian Paroo/Barbara Cook) who carries the ballads; in *Molly Brown* the pattern is reversed, with the male character (Johnny Brown/Harve Presnell) requiring a baritone who can sing the ballads while Molly (Tammy Grimes) has the patter numbers, with her other songs lying in her chest voice. Having two characters of such polarized vocal types allows Willson to create equivalent contrast and range in his score, but it also represents a repetition of approach from *The Music Man*, albeit with reversed genders; it is also the same vocal model as *Annie Get Your Gun* and *Calamity Jane*.

As Willson hints, there are also a few numbers that use similar musical gestures or strategies to *The Music Man*. Like Harold Hill, Molly is introduced in a number that reinforces the composer's lyric-led approach, "I Ain't Down Yet." The importance of the lyrics to Willson's conception can be gleaned from a source in the Carmel collection, on which he has sketched the words and worked out the rhythm on a piece of blank paper rather than on more traditional music manuscript paper; the mechanics of this creative process almost seem like a gesture to say that this is *not* music but heightened speech (see Fig. 5.2). In the Broadway version of the song as shown in the published piano-vocal score, there are twenty-six and a half measures of music before the orchestra first enters, yet Molly's interaction with her brothers in those twenty-six measures is written out in rhythm, providing a neat segue from speech to song: exactly the same strategy used to get from dialogue into Hill's "Trouble."[19]

In some ways, "I Ain't Down" is more extreme: the vocal section without orchestra is longer, and Molly is suddenly required to sing out fully in chest voice (starting at the refrain "I'm goan' to learn to read and write," which starts another forty-five measures after the orchestra's entrance). The vocal line demands that she sing an E flat at the top of the treble stave, and on the original cast album

Table 5.2. List of songs associated with *The Unsinkable Molly Brown.*

Song Title	Sources and Comments
Main songs included in the Broadway show:	
I Ain't Down Yet	Appears in PVS. GASF sources: copyist score marked "Final Revision" and dated November 11, 1959; copyist score for Finale Act 1 duet version for Molly/Johnny (marked "one town down") with holograph annotations and an added counterpoint for Johnny; holograph rhythmic sketch; holograph trio/piano-vocal arrangement; holograph lyric sketches and piano-vocal sketches for initial version titled "Tuckered."
Belly Up to the Bar, Boys	Appears in PVS. GASF sources: holograph piano-vocal score; typed lyric sheet dated November 27, 1959, with holograph annotations. Juilliard source: copyist's piano-vocal score (five copies).
I've A'ready Started In	Originally written for *The Music Man.* Appears in PVS. GASF sources: holograph piano-vocal scores (three versions, one titled "My Baby"); copyist's piano-vocal score. Juilliard sources: copyist's piano-vocal score; typed lyric sheet dated December 8, 1959, with holograph annotations.
I'll Never Say No	Appears in PVS. GASF sources: holograph piano-vocal score for "extension" section; copyist score for duet version with "Brass Bed"; holograph sketch/fragment. Juilliard sources: holograph piano-vocal score; copyist's piano-vocal score.
My Big Brass Bed	Appears in PVS. GASF sources: holograph piano-vocal score; copyist scores for solo version and duet version with "I'll Never Say No"; typed lyric sheet dated December 16, 1959 ("The Big Brass Bed"), with holograph annotations. Juilliard sources: copyist's piano-vocal scores (two versions), titled "The Big Brass Bed"; typed lyric sheet with holograph annotations (originally dated December 17, 1959, marked "correct as of 25 October 1960").
The Denver Police	Appears in PVS. Also known as "I Got a Dollar from Mrs. McGlone." GASF source: holograph piano-vocal score. Juilliard: copyist's piano-vocal score.
Beautiful People of Denver	Appears in PVS. GASF sources: copyist's piano-vocal score dated October 3, 1960; copyist's piano-vocal score, "Device and Trickery" version sung by Doc Myerbeer. Juilliard sources: holograph piano-vocal score; holograph lyric sheets.

Continued

Table 5.2. Continued

Song Title	Sources and Comments
Are You Sure?	Appears in PVS. GASF sources: holograph piano-vocal score and sketches; copyist's piano-vocal score (two versions). Juilliard sources: copyist's vocal scores (three versions).
Happy Birthday, Mrs. J. J. Brown	Appears in PVS. Juilliard sources: copyist's vocal scores (two versions).
Bon Jour	Appears in PVS. GASF sources: copyist score marked "36" with holograph annotations; holograph piano-vocal score. Juilliard sources: two holograph piano-vocal scores; two copyist's piano-vocal scores.
If I Knew	Appears in PVS. GASF sources: holograph piano-vocal scores, two versions; holograph piano-vocal for cut reprise titled "Then I'd Know"; holograph barbershop quartet arrangement for The Buffalo Bills, originally written for *The Music Man*.
Chick-a-Pen	Appears in PVS. GASF sources: holograph piano-vocal score of brief reprise/bridge into Act 2 Denver party scene with vocal for Molly. Juilliard sources: holograph piano-vocal score; copyist's piano-vocal score.
Keep-a-Hoppin'	Appears in PVS. GASF sources: holograph piano-vocal score titled "Hop-a-long Peter"; holograph piano-vocal score for "new intro"' holograph piano score for "After Radio Barrell," underscoring based on this melody, marked "New 15A: Replaced old 15A Robber Music I, II, III) with this."
Leadville Johnny Brown (Soliloquy)	Appears in PVS. GASF source: holograph piano-vocal score. Juilliard source: copyist's score for earlier version (trunk song?) titled "I Could Never Say 'Good-Bye' to You Again."
Up Where the People Are (instrumental)	Appears in PVS.
Dolce Far Niente	Appears in PVS. GASF source: holograph piano-vocal score, including Molly's counterpoint. Juilliard sources: holograph piano-vocal score; typed lyric sheet dated October 28, 1960, with holograph annotations.

Songs added to the film:

Colorado, My Home	Originally written for the Broadway show; appears in PVS. GASF sources: five holograph piano-vocal scores plus reprise. Juilliard sources: holograph piano-vocal score; holograph piano-vocal score for "Reprise Finale" version; typed lyric sheet with holograph annotations, dated October 17, 1960.

Table 5.2. Continued

Song Title	Sources and Comments
He's My Friend	Juilliard sources: holograph piano-vocal score; copyist's piano-vocal scores (two copies); published song sheet (piano-vocal).

Songs written for or intended for use in the show or film but cut:

Song Title	Sources and Comments
The Wonderful Plan	Originally written for *The Music Man*. GASF source: copyist's piano-vocal scores for solo (Shamus) and duet (Shamus/Molly) *Molly Brown* versions of song (see also Chapter 3 for sources for the *Music Man* version).
Tomorrow	Originally written for *The Music Man*. Juilliard sources: piano-vocal holographs, two versions (one a duet); copyist's score for Prince DeLong's tango version.
One Day at a Time	GASF sources: holograph piano-vocal score and holograph sketch; copyist's piano-vocal score for Molly's version, two copies (one dated August 16, 1960, the other undated) with holograph annotations; typed lyric sheet dated January 22, 1960, with holograph annotations; copyist's piano-vocal score for Johnny's reprise.
Another Big Strike/ Extra—Extra	GASF source: copyist's piano-vocal score with holograph annotations; alternative copyist's score headed "Extra-Extra (New)" dated October 24, 1960; alternative titled "Read the Label on the Bottle/Get Away Boys, You Bother Me," copyist's piano-vocal score with extensive holograph amendments.
The Ambassador's Polka	Also titled "Bon Jour" but partly different to the song from the published score. GASF source: holograph piano-vocal scores (two versions); copyist's piano-vocal score.
Dignity	Written for the film. Juilliard sources: holograph piano-vocal score; copyist's piano-vocal score.

PVS: Published vocal score (Frank Music Corp. and Meredith Willson Music/Hal Leonard: New York, 1962). GASF: Great American Songbook Foundation, Carmel, Indiana; Willson papers. Juilliard: Juilliard School of Music, New York; Willson manuscripts.

Grimes audibly struggles with the high tessitura, but the fact that this causes her to abandon pitch and become declamatory is turned into an expressive gesture that represents the character's boisterousness. Later in the song, the brothers sing in counterpoint to Molly's main melody—another favorite Willson device, but here used earlier in the score than in *The Music Man*. The use of a martial style at the heart of the number is also brought forward compared to *The Music Man*, in which it is not used (apart from in the Overture) until "Seventy-Six Trombones." In sum, we can see that Willson is reusing various ideas from the *Music Man* score but in different combination and with the added layer of Molly's fuller vocal delivery.

Another number that feels strongly linked to *The Music Man* is "Beautiful People of Denver," Molly's song of introduction when she arrives at Mrs. McGlone's house in Act 1, Scene 9, to meet her new neighbors. As with most of Molly's songs, it reinforces her as the star of the show by framing her as charismatic, something she has strongly in common with Harold Hill. In this number, the melodic and rhythmic resemblance to "Seventy-Six Trombones" is noticeable: it is another march in 6/8 time with similar triplet-plus-dotted-quarter-note figurations. Both numbers use the assertiveness of the all-American military march (with its personal associations for Willson of John Philip Sousa) to promote a façade, in Hill's case to pretend that he is capable of creating a boys' band and in Molly's to pretend she is at home among the middle-class social structures of Denver (one stanza reads: "We dined out—musta been half past eight / Et catfish off of a silver plate / Soup to nuts—even a bowl of fruit / What you call 'Table de hoot.'"). For these reasons, Willson's compositional choice is convincing in terms of musical semiotics/gesture—what could be more appropriate and meaningful for such "American" characters than to address the respective on-stage communities of these musicals than through an American-style march?—but at the local level of melodic figures, the similarity to the hit from *The Music Man* is distracting (see Fig. 5.3).

Another similarity between the two scores is that for the second musical in a row, Willson wrote songs for the two romantic leads that were designed to be heard first separately and later in counterpoint to reflect that the characters who sing them have been metaphorically "in tune," "in synch," or "singing the same song all along"—but in both shows, the revelatory "combined" version was cut before the show reached Broadway. In the case of *The Music Man*, this was the never-heard duet version of "My White Knight" with "The Sadder but Wiser Girl," while in *Molly Brown*, Molly's "My Brass Bed" (in which she sings of the romantic appeal of the brass bed Johnny has bought to persuade her to accept him as her husband) was written to be sung in counterpoint to Johnny's song of constancy, "I'll Never Say No." In some of the Philadelphia tryouts (when script L3 was used), this duet reprise of "Brass Bed" and "Never Say No" was heard at the conclusion of Act 1 to reveal the connection between the songs and reinforce the underlying strength of the Browns' relationship, but it was replaced by a brief duet version of "I Ain't Down Yet" with a new counterpoint figure for Johnny.[20] There are no obvious sources to confirm why this replacement was made—perhaps "Ain't Down" was seen as a more impactful finale than the romantic ballad style of the "Never Say No"/"Brass Bed" duet—but it is striking that Willson has fallen back on an old music-dramatic device (albeit one that was not fully realized in *Music Man*) rather than inventing a new one.

Fig. 5.2. Lyric and rhythmic sketch for "I Ain't Down Yet," GASF.

Fig. 5.3. Excerpt from "Beautiful People of Denver."

This, in a way, was the fate of *Molly Brown* no matter what he wrote, as Willson admitted in the interview cited earlier. *The Music Man* was so fresh, unusual, and distinctive that it was scarcely possible for *Molly Brown* to hit the same heights of originality. Still, Willson's score is never less than entertaining. For example, another of Molly's charisma numbers, "Are You Sure?," is in a Southern Gospel Revival style: Molly wants to persuade Mrs. McGlone's guests to donate money to the new church building project so she invokes a religious musical style to underline her rhetoric.

Rather like the Iowans in "Trouble" (which also has gospel elements that are culturally at odds with the white characters), the people of Denver are carried away by the energy of Molly's performance and start to repeat part of her message: the kinetic dimension of song is used to transform (indeed, reverse) an opinion. The gospel rhythms and vocal arrangements make this an even more spectacular number than "Trouble," with use of canon (where the chorus repeat Molly's tune with staggered entries, for example starting a measure after her) and an especially powerful final section in which the chorus sings, "Think children, think children, think when you pray, children" for eight measures in syncopated rhythm (two dotted quarter notes followed by a quarter note) in dramatic minor and diminished chords. The number's strong Broadway antecedent in "That Great Come-and-Get-It Day" from *Finian's Rainbow* (1947), in which the multiracial ensemble includes Black characters (though the songwriters were white), underlines the problem of Willson's decision to appropriate gospel music for white characters here, but in musical and theatrical impact the number is certainly lively and powerful.

The chorus features centrally elsewhere in the score too. The opening number of Act 2, "Happy Birthday, Mrs. J. J. Brown," begins with Molly's Parisian friends offering her a greeting set to a gavotte, signifying their elevated social status; this segues into a fast cakewalk section in two, where the Prince initiates the main dramatic arc of the second act by announcing his admiration for Molly ("She looks right at you with her big, blue eyes"); and the friends re-enter with an ironic grand march version of "Belly Up to the Bar, Boys," the drinking song that Molly leads in the Saddle Rock Saloon in Act 1. This broadly tripartite structure allows Willson to move fluently from one dramatic theme to another, again in a fashion that seems to go beyond techniques in *The Music Man*.

Of course, even when aspects of songs appear familiar, Willson often finds ways to make them fresh. In "Bon Jour" Molly responds to her Paris friends' compliments about her determination to learn as many languages as possible by saying that if everyone else is going to learn English so that they can communicate with her, she should do the same for them. In the song, the Prince names different nationalities and Molly responds with the appropriate greeting in each language. The music is a generic up-tempo Broadway cakewalk style (again derived from Black musical culture) in cut common time, with numerous sequences and cadential figures to mark the interactive nature of the number: it is more like dialogue with lively underscoring than a song, an impression confirmed by the vocally free performance on the original cast album. But the main feature of the song is the multilingual lyric, with Molly reeling off the various greetings in an almost vaudevillian manner, emphasized by the cakewalk accompaniment.

As noted earlier, Johnny's music mainly reflects the casting of the character as a skilled baritone. This is seen consistently in "I'll Never Say No," "Leadville Johnny Brown" (the Soliloquy), "If I Knew," and "Colorado, My Home," a song that was heard in the tryouts, cut for Broadway, then reinstated for the movie (1964) and included in the published vocal score (1962). The exception to the group is the trunk song "I've A'ready Started In," which was conceived as a barbershop number for *The Music Man* and recycled for Johnny's declaration of love to Molly in Act 1, Scene 4.

The barbershop feel is retained for the *Molly Brown* version: Willson marks his holograph score "barbershop rubato," and although most of the song is a solo, the words "this morning" are harmonized in four-part barbershop harmony, providing yet another link to the *Music Man* score. On the other hand, the number is accompanied onstage by the character named Gittar on the guitar, implying it is a diegetic number that the characters can actually "hear"; this is underlined by its improvisatory mood, with numerous off-beat pauses and a generally fragmented melodic structure. Johnny does not yet know how to relate to Molly and resorts to a series of awkward predatory clichés (the connotations of which Willson was no doubt aware) exemplified by the opening phrase, "I've a'ready started in to try to figure out exactly how to go about to get you." Having had her path barred and being told by Johnny that he wants to "get" her, Molly quite understandably yells for the Sheriff and the men run off, yet it is clearly set up as a comical song that intends to show that a group of miners is no match for Molly Brown; the fun is at Johnny's expense, not Molly's.

Johnny's other numbers frame his masculinity by showcasing the power of his voice, though their static nature tends to draw attention to his high levels of vanity and lack of agency, especially compared to Molly. Willson strikes a clever balance between these themes in "Colorado, My Home," one of two quasi-operatic *scenas* in the mold of Marian Paroo's "My White Knight" (from *The Music Man*). Whereas Marian sings about the qualities of her ideal man, Johnny allies himself with the Rocky Mountains and sings about how the fact that they cause his voice to echo "gives a man confidence." Another line states: "When a man depends on all this elevation, / He will never go away." Willson creates a clever effect in the song, where he has the off-stage chorus sing the words "sweet home . . . sweet home" as an echo of Johnny's phrase, "home sweet home."

Johnny is at one with nature and he identifies strongly with what he perceives as the masculinity of the Rio Grande, which is Willson's way of poking fun at his superficiality. The character lists the things that make Colorado his home: "A sky full of Rockies for my roof up there, / A great golden meadow for my rockin' chair." An earlier draft (represented on one of the holographs from the Carmel collection) has an even more ridiculous image: "A fine-tempered woman and my grizzly bear." The self-consciously operatic style of the music, with use of declamatory triplet quarter notes and an over-the-top climax to the song, completes the depiction of Johnny, pre-marriage, as a well-meaning but self-absorbed and vain man of the mountains, obsessed with the landscape as a reflection of his voice and masculinity.[21]

In "I'll Never Say No to You," Johnny somewhat reverses this emphasis, obsessing instead over Molly, though the return of cliché language ("I'll weep if you want me sad") sustains the impression of a certain vacuity to his personality. The same could be said of "If I Knew," Johnny's second-act ballad in which he sings of "what makes [Molly] so wonderful," resorting again to familiar romantic tropes: "If I knew what the nightingale sings in her song; / If I knew why the meadow is sweet all day long . . . / At last I'd know the secret of you." Yet in both numbers, the musical setting is so beautiful that Willson is able to give Johnny more sincerity than his words might imply, an excellent example of music conveying an inner psychological "truth" that the verbal text obscures. "If I Knew" has a particularly rich harmonization of the angular melody (itself conveying mystery), with frequent use of enigmatic-sounding dominant seventh chords; the harmony of the song is unsettled in general, a powerful gesture that indicates Johnny's determination to persevere with Molly despite the growing strain in their relationship (the number comes in the first scene of Act 2 when he has grown tired of Europe and she still loves it).

Johnny's most operatic number of all is the impressively complex "Leadville Johnny Brown," subtitled "Soliloquy" in a clear reference to Billy Bigelow's solo from the first act of Rodgers and Hammerstein's *Carousel* (1945). Johnny's is not nearly as long but the harmonies are again vividly unsettled; see, for example, the climbing melody as the bass line descends by step in the top system of Fig. 5.4, followed by the chromatic progress of the melody from rehearsal mark H. (Note that Willson's holograph score sets the word "when" at the end of this excerpt on a high A, which would have pushed the voice much higher.)

It is a fascinating number that segues out of the deliberately banal ensemble song "Keep-a-Hoppin'" (a borrowing and adaptation by Willson of the nineteenth-century blackface minstrel song "Kemo Kimo" without the racist verse, itself derived from the much older British folk song "Frog Went a-Courtin'")[22] via twenty-four measures of (mostly) spoken rhythm. Once the Soliloquy itself begins, it is almost daringly lacking in conventional melody or any feeling of song, instead setting Johnny's overwrought words into drawn-out phrases that move around with no sense of resolution or arrival. And although some air of cliché is still present in the lyric for this song ("I could easy [sic] take that heart and tear it free"), Johnny's sense of profound loss at his separation from Molly in the previous scene has finally given him the ability to express himself more sincerely; the move away both from four-square phrases and a general flavor of the musically conventional is a potent metaphor for his state of mind.

"Keep-a-Hoppin'" is not Willson's only musical borrowing in *Molly Brown* (another prominent device from the *Music Man* score repeated here, of course). His more "classical" side comes through this time in several performances of Chopin's "Minute Waltz," the first by a concert pianist in Act 1 and the others by Molly herself in Act 2. Indeed, when she finally masters the piece, her triumphant performance is so important that it practically takes the place of a song. A curiosity

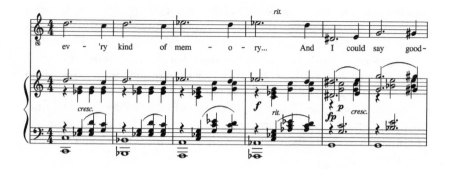

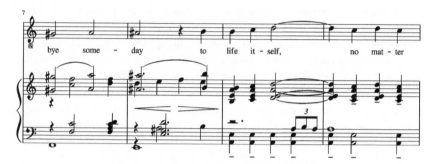

Fig. 5.4. *Excerpt from "Leadville Johnny Brown."*

of the second act is that Molly has little to sing after "Bon Jour" in the opening scene, and no solos at all: she merely joins Johnny in "Chick-a-Pen" and sings a brief response to the Prince's "Dolce Far Niente." Neither of these is an impactful moment musically or vocally and Molly's role in each duet is secondary to that of the man.

"Chick-a-Pen" puts into musical form an argument between Johnny and Molly that starts when she is angry with him for inviting his friends from Leadville to the party for the European set on their visit to Denver. Molly refuses to get dressed for the party until he sends them away and he responds with the number, which is a slow soft-shoe shuffle. This helps to control the mood of the scene, so that the argument is not too angry: Johnny teases Molly with mock-violent words ("Chick-a-pen, goan' to have to whop you right on top-a your head"), she responds in kind ("Chick-a-pen, goan' to have to give your smeller a hell of a tweak"), and he adds a third refrain. At the end of each refrain, the soft-shoe tease is abandoned and each character shifts into a slower, straight tempo with an image of affection that expresses his or her true feelings: Johnny sings, "Or hold your lily-white hand instead" and Molly has "Or stroke that leathery he-man cheek!"

The song is interrupted near the end of the third refrain when Johnny suddenly presents Molly with a new wedding ring (they were married using the band of a cigar and he has commissioned an identical design made out of jewels). He ends the song with "Chick-a-pen, goan' to somehow reach your heart," confirming his domination of the number. Molly is also secondary to Prince DeLong in "Dolce Far Niente," a stunning slow waltz and perhaps the most tender song of Willson's output. Arguably, the insincere Prince does not deserve such beautiful music—he is trying to seduce Molly for financial reasons—but she herself makes this point in her response to the Prince: "Music and love always go hand in hand; / Both make me feel so grand till the band ain't playing." Indeed, her articulation of her realization in song of the Prince's motives seems to provide the impetus for her decision to return to America and to Johnny. Once she has said goodbye, the Prince sings a reprise of the number, a complete refrain, thereby confirming it as "his" song.

The absence of a big solo for Molly in Act 2 was caused by the cutting of "One Day at a Time," a galvanizing song in a "moderately fast 4" in which Molly sings of her resolve to move forward by returning to Europe where she was happy. The song is present in L3 but was cut during rehearsals, apparently because of Tammy Grimes's limited vocal stamina: "We agree we should discuss replacing 'One Day at a Time.' Whatever she does she shouldn't throw it away like she is now doing," wrote Willson and Morris to director Dore Schary on September 1, 1960, after a run-through.[23] The number has a bolero flavor with repeated triplets, though it is in duple meter (a bolero is in three). Its emphatic nature would have given Molly's character a lift in the generally negative tone of the second act, as well as providing her with a powerful moment of self-expression to counterbalance Johnny's Soliloquy.

Most of the other excisions to the score were less significant: "The Ambassador's Polka" recycled material from "Fireworks" (cut from *The Music Man*) with new patter writing for Molly that was very similar to (and replaced by) "Bon Jour"; "Extra! Extra!" (also known as "Another Big Strike" and "Read the Label on the Bottle") was part of the long Act 1, Scene 8, in which Johnny's second strike was revealed (the scene was important but the song merely embellished it); the duet "Tomorrow" (arranged as a comical tango) was replaced by the far superior "Dolce Far Niente"; and the excision of "The Wonderful Plan," in which Shamus sings to Molly early in the show about God's conception of the universe, did not affect the story or character development. But the cutting of "One Day at a Time" did, as did the decision to turn another song for Molly, "Up Where the Joke's Goin' On," into a dance-only number (i.e., with no singing); it became "Up Where the People Are" and another vocal showcase was lost. The fact that the book tends to take precedence over the score in Act 2, with fewer big songs, may present another explanation of why the show as a whole never quite became a long-running smash hit.

PRODUCTION AND RECEPTION

As Willson neared the end of his composition of the bulk of the score in February 1960, serious consideration was being given to the cast and production team. By this point, it had been proposed that Dore Schary might direct the show as well as produce it, but Willson wrote him an impassioned letter on January 13, 1960, to reiterate his clear preference to be reunited with the director of *The Music Man*:

Dear Dore:

As you know I played the score for Tec Da Costa when we were in New York. He was not only genuinely excited over it that day but it has come to me from various other sources that he is telling everyone else the same thing. I know that you approached Tec several times to direct our show. Because of his excitement over our project this might be the propitious time to approach him again. I certainly don't have to tell you, Dore, that I have complete faith in you as one of the world's great triple-threat men [director-producer-writer]. I mention Tec to you, however, for several reasons. First of all I am disturbed to learn that you will be producing "[Sunrise at] Campobello" March to July. I know that you can work all day on one project and all night on another but I don't have your metabolism or vitality. Come nightfall I'm through for the day. I am completely convinced to the last fiber and belief of my anatomy and being that "Mrs. Brown" is a blockbuster. During the comparable period preceding the "Music Man" rehearsals (March through July) Tec and I were working together some part of every day. I can't do that kind of tense work at night. Also, aren't the casting problems exacting to the point of requiring frequent New York auditions during the pre-rehearsal months? I know Tec's editorial, choreographic, dramatic and organizational abilities in the musical-comedy theatre as well as I know my own name and I believe that with the combination of Dore Schary producing and Tec Da Costa directing we would have the kind of insurance this project should afford to carry. In fact, I am convinced it would be historic.[24]

Schary's response does not survive in the Willson papers but whether or not he approached Da Costa again, the outcome was that the producer would indeed take over as director (this was clear in all newspaper articles from March onward).

While these negotiations were happening, Willson also took an active role with Richard Morris in approaching actresses to play Molly Brown. Indeed, Willson and Morris did a series of pre-auditions with several of them, before a more formal audition that would include Schary (who was on the West Coast) in the third week of February. For instance, Willson went to great lengths to send the score and his own recording of "I Ain't Down Yet" to the actress and comedian Kaye Ballard, whose previous Broadway credits included *Top Banana* (1951) and *The Golden Apple* (1954).[25] He also wrote to Schary on January 29: "Dick and I saw Lisa Kirk do 'Ain't Down Yet.' She has quite a remarkable conception of it and manages to belt it out in the original key. What she would do with one of the ballads is something else again but I do think it would be worthwhile for all of us to take a look at her on a stage."[26] Kirk's credits included originating the larger-than-life role of Lois/Bianca in *Kiss Me, Kate* (1948), so she was a natural choice for Molly. Willson was also in correspondence about the show with Shelley Winters, who was best known for her numerous Hollywood appearances but also appeared as Ado Annie as a replacement late in the run of *Oklahoma!* (1943).[27]

While Willson and Morris were deliberating on all these possibilities they also searched for someone to play Johnny Brown, including an obvious choice, John Raitt. Best remembered for portraying Billy Bigelow in the original Broadway production of *Carousel* (1945), Raitt was a formidable baritone and his other credits included originating the male lead in *The Pajama Game* on Broadway (1954) and on film (1957). Yet on February 3, Willson made it clear to Schary that he had found his preferred choice:

Dear Dore:
God willing I think I have found Johnny Brown. He is Harve Presnell. He is six foot four, a blond giant of a man. He is twenty-five years old—looks thirty. He has already had a distinguished opera career having sung all over the world with the big companies. I saw him yesterday morning and had him sing. His voice is unbelievably spectacular. I asked him to come back late yesterday afternoon to meet Dick [Morris]. He bowled us both over.

The two big questions, of course, were can he act and can he sing like a human being with words instead of with opera broad A's and umlauts the way so many of them do. Then it came out: the guy is a cowboy! Raised in Nevada, he bulldogged steers and broke broncs for a living while learning to sing, even working in professional rodeos bulldogging and roping for the prize money. As he told us about it his dialect began to betray him here and there, quite a number of "fergits" starting to filter into his speech.[28]

On this issue Willson would have his way and Presnell was cast as Johnny.[29] There are no surviving documents to reveal the details of Tammy Grimes's hiring but on March 10 the composer sent her a telegram: "WE ARE SO DELIGHTED DEAR MRS. BROWN THAT I WROTE YOU A NEW SONG. LOVE ALSO FROM RINI, MEREDITH."[30] Two days earlier, the *New York Times* had announced that she had been offered and accepted the part.[31] Grimes was just twenty-six years old at the time and was by no means a star: she had been an understudy in the play *Bus Stop* (1955) and played the lead in Noël Coward's *Look after Lulu!* (1959) but had yet to play a role in a major Broadway musical. Although she would go on to win a Tony Award for Best Featured Actress in a Musical (she was not eligible for the Best Actress award because she did not have star billing), Willson and the rest of the team had considerable trouble with her before and after the show opened on Broadway. For example, The Theatre Guild wrote with concern to Willson on July 6 upon discovering that Grimes had not yet had any vocal lessons for the show or begun to learn the score. Willson commented: "It is tragic that she has wasted all this time when she could have taken advantage of [musical director] Herb Greene's unique talents. It will be rather desperate if she doesn't at least have a nodding acquaintance with her numbers by the time we get back to New York [for rehearsals]."[32]

Meanwhile, the fact that Willson, Morris, and Schary were not together most of the time leading up to the rehearsals in August 1960[33] became a problem as the composer had anticipated, and it is clear from the correspondence from Willson to the others that he had strong opinions about changes that should be made to the book and score. For example, he wrote at length on April 8 to argue that a reprise of "I Ain't Down Yet" be used as the first-act finale rather than the "I'll Never Say No/Brass Bed" duet reprise, as well as to make suggestions about the staging of "One Day at a Time" and to argue that Johnny should perhaps be the one to slap Molly's face in Act 2 (to make him less sympathetic and "let her defend herself").[34]

Even more revealing are three sets of notes on three run-throughs of the entire show in the first two weeks of September. One of these is undated and reflects Willson's personal view of a performance, starting with frustrations about Tammy Grimes: "(a) Can't hear her. (b) Talks too fast. (c) Continually up-stages herself. (d) Has too many facial and arm movements at the same time. (e) Continually hunches her shoulders. (This is most disappointing in the 2nd Act of the play when she is supposed to be a different person . . .) (f) Tammy must not be afraid of her high notes. She certainly can sing, as evidenced in 'Brass Bed' but in 'Dolce Far Niente,' she leaves the audience on the edge of their seats wondering whether or not she is going to make the next note."[35] After further criticisms of Grimes, Willson gives a blow-by-blow assessment of the show, calling the lifeboat prologue "too long," complaining that the staging of "Ain't Down Yet" is "hyster-ical" and "too animated," wearily stating that a scene change vignette involving a bear "is not funny at any time in any place," and ruthlessly stating that other songs need "complete re-staging" or "just do not work." He could not be clearer that he disliked what Schary had done: of "Bon Jour" he writes, "I think the two-beat tempo is absolutely wrong and the staging abominable," for example.

Another set of notes is written "From Meredith and Dick to Dore" and dated September 1, relating to a specific run-through. This created a clear division be-tween writers and director, and their six-page report reflects on both the per-formance and the preservation of the text (Schary appears to have made some cuts in rehearsal without telling them). "Virtually all of the comments made here relate to the 'magic' we have planned and hope for but which was not in the run-through," they comment. They go on to explain the psychology of var-ious scenes; for example, they critique the staging of the lifeboat prologue by pointing out that "There are too many men and not enough chaos and confusion to justify Molly taking over leadership of the boat. . . . Male passenger must be hysterical, endangering other passengers, to justify Molly pulling her gun." (Here again, the parallels with *Annie Get Your Gun* come to the surface.) Elsewhere in the show, they highlight "important interjections that have not been assigned as yet," remark that "Tammy has been consistently throwing away key lines," and complain about changes made by the cast and/or director ("The way Tammy has cut this scene doesn't make sense").[36] A further set of notes from Willson after a run-through on September 13 is much briefer and tends to focus on smaller points (e.g., "Much too much moaning in life boat"), but there was clearly a lot of tension in the air.

This was reflected in the mixed reviews the show received when it opened in its five-week pre-Broadway run at Philadelphia's Shubert Theatre on September 26. *Variety*'s reviewer commented that "It is not a show that can be taken for granted. Plenty of work remains to be done in sharpening, cutting and rearrangement." The review did, however, point out the major pluses too, namely a "superior score by Meredith Willson, an unexpectedly forceful, often off-beat book by Richard Morris, gorgeous scenic backgrounds by Oliver Smith and a magnetic and vibrant performance by Tammy Grimes."[37]

Daily Variety's reviewer concurred that it "looks like a probable candidate for success. It isn't any 'shoo-in' as might be said of 'Music Man' or 'Fair Lady,' but it has so much on the ball that there is no reason to believe that all the required corrections will not have been made before the musical leaves here. There had been plenty of word in advance here about Meredith Willson's superior score, and those were not idle statements, but oddly enough—and with all due credit to Willson's robust and rollicking tunes—'Molly Brown' impresses as a 'book' show—and an exceptionally good one."[38] This was high praise indeed for Morris's first outing as a musical comedy book writer. Philadelphia's *Evening Bulletin* added that the show was "extravagantly produced and enthusiastically performed" but ended a little more tersely: "There are, as it stands now, no really show-stopping numbers, and we certainly don't insist on them. But one would like to see a little more freshness and originality in the overall treatment."[39] Willson's friend Frank Loesser added in a letter: "I think you are very close to having a big one which will work," prefacing this with an acknowledgment that there were many "obvious repairs" to be made.[40]

Clearly, something had to be done. A report in the *Philadelphia Daily News* on September 29 revealed:

> The critical reception for his new musical at the Shubert was mixed. Willson's reaction was to get right to work. He has a Mason & Hamlin upright in his Warwick suite and when we visited him he was still in dressing gown, pounding away at the keyboard, making notations on music paper. He's a rarity among show people: Someone who reads reviews and if he thinks the criticism is just is grateful for it. There's a pretty ballad in "Molly Brown," called "I'll Never Say No," in which the tenor hero lets the leading lady know he'll never refuse any request she may make. "Did you like it?" [Willson] asked. It's a very appealing number and sets the mood for the lovers. "Well not a single reviewer mentioned it," Willson declared. "I'm very glad you appreciated it but I think the reason it got no attention was that it isn't merchandised properly. I'm giving it a new treatment now," he said and promptly played and sang the new version along with the added dialogue.[41]

Willson also found time to reply to an indignant letter from a Mrs. M. Warren Heiss complaining about "the profanity throughout the entire show."[42] Ironically,

Willson himself had made Morris remove dozens of swearwords from the L1 draft of the script that the composer had first read (i.e., L1),[43] but he was now firm in his rebuke: "We are involved twenty-four hours a day polishing 'Molly Brown' for Broadway so I am afraid I haven't the time to debate the degree to which 'hell' is considered profanity or the deficiencies of the score. The passing of time will throw further light on both of those questions."[44] And the show hit more trouble when both Grimes and Presnell came down with an infection and had to be replaced on September 29 and 30 by their understudies, Iva Withers and Jimmy Hurret.[45]

The Philadelphia production closed on October 25 ahead of its November 3 Broadway premiere at the Winter Garden. By the time of the New York opening, various changes had been made, ranging from deleting lines and changing arrangements to cutting "Colorado, My Home" (a curious choice since it had been reviewed positively in Philadelphia) and removing the lifeboat framing concept (just a brief scene on the lifeboat remained in Act 2). Among Dore Schary's papers at Wisconsin is a sixteen-page memo (delivered as an opening-night speech) dated November 3 in which he addressed "those concerned with THE UNSINKABLE MOLLY BROWN." It contains telling comments about the director's reflections on the process of bringing the show to Broadway. For example, he wrote: "Perhaps it is the same feeling that sponsors friendships during war; the experience of having been together when shot at by the enemy and having survived one attack, the breeding of a confidence that is shared when facing the final onslaught. Certainly you are entitled to your combat ribbons; we were shelled and machine-gunned, but you have stood up under the fire and are perfectly trained and equipped for the battle we should win in handsome style."[46] He went through the cast and crew one by one, including each member of the ensemble, praising specific aspects of their work and acknowledging that "many of you have performed with a wide assortment of miseries. It is of course a crazy, wild, insane tradition—but yet it always makes us thrill to see a trouper live up to the axiom, 'The show must go on.'" He added: "There have been bruises, and cuts and bloodshed—literally and figuratively."

It had not been an easy process, and to Schary's credit he was open about that, as well as paying tribute to the skill and patience of everyone involved. But when the show opened on Broadway, the reviews remained as divided as they had been in Philadelphia. John McClain's review in the *New York Journal-American* was headlined "Brass Bands, Tall Corn and a Smash Hit" and summarized: "'Molly Brown' is indigenous American musical comedy. It is the kind of thing we do better than anybody else in the world and when we do it well, as in this instance, it is a time for rejoicing." On the other end of the spectrum, Walter Kerr was faintly critical of most aspects of the show, for example: "But the score is also, let's say, similar. It is similar in some instances to Mr. Willson's 'The Music Man' (no doubt a good place to steal from), and it is similar to itself pretty often. That same old rhythm erupts like clockwork. Dore Schary's stage direction seems in as much trouble as the *Titanic* every now and then . . . and Peter Gennaro's production numbers, detonating as they are, frequently seem to be looking for another spot in the show." The other reviewers similarly found much to enjoy and much to criticize, with the *New York Times* calling it "a moderate measure of enjoyment."[47]

The one point on which all the reviewers were unanimous in their praise was Grimes's performance as Molly. Yet behind the scenes, there were frequent frustrations about her, as there had been in rehearsals. In response to a letter about her performance, Willson wrote on January 23, 1961, that "Tammy is a problem child all right though she does reflect the way she was directed. Of course, even with a bad director Ethel Merman always is completely understandable."[48] Indeed, this letter seems effectively to sum up Willson's feelings about the show's lack of success at the time: he blamed the wayward star and the lack of talent that he perceived in the director.

CONCLUSION: MOLLY GET YOUR GUN

When *The Unsinkable Molly Brown* opened in Philadelphia for its pre-Broadway tryouts, Richard A. Duprey commented in the *Catholic Standard and Times* that "Some may object to [Willson's] use again of the heavily-rhythmical patter songs that were so much a feature of [*The Music Man*]. One can, however, defend the use of this pleasing sort of business by suggesting that a good gambler . . . doesn't throw his dice away on a winning streak to switch to stud poker. Shakespeare and Moliere, for instance, knew how to stick to a pattern when they were ahead of the game."[49] This neatly encapsulates the challenge facing Willson in writing this show: if it seemed too similar to *The Music Man* he would be criticized and if he departed from its successful ingredients he would equally be criticized. The documentary sources suggest he felt it deserved a better director and more professional star, but the reception of his score was unrelated to these personnel: the reviews and public reaction reflected the fact that he was a victim of his own success.

The show went on a national tour with Grimes beginning in April 1962, two months after it closed on Broadway after a respectable 532 performances. Then in 1964 came a film version that departed from the stage show in numerous respects: Helen Deutsch wrote a new screenplay, Grimes was replaced by Debbie Reynolds, and of the Broadway songs only "Belly Up," "I Ain't Down Yet," "I'll Never Say No," and Johnny's Soliloquy were sung (a few others were used as underscoring), with "Colorado, My Home" put back in and a new song "He's My Friend" written specially for the screen version.[50] Only Presnell made the transition from the Broadway cast, along with the Broadway choreographer, Peter Gennaro.

Willson had tried quite hard to get Grimes cast as Molly and even wrote a letter to her on June 3, 1961, in which he expressed his "determination to see [her] as the star of the 'Molly Brown' movie," adding, "Tammy, it would be a sin for anyone but you to play Molly in the movie." But he went on to say that Hollywood producers such as the Mirisch brothers and Jack Warner had been put off the idea by her poor diction and stubbornness about directing her lines to the audience so they could be heard. "Insist on a full company rehearsal at the earliest moment to secure clarity," he added, "and please understand the sincerity of your most grateful composer."[51] But MGM decided to bank on a popular star, and Reynolds went on to make one of her most celebrated appearances in the movie. Upon seeing ninety minutes of the film in December 1963, Willson reported to his publisher Milton Kramer, "it looks like it could be a stunner. We have lost a few musical numbers but those that remain are really done up, down, through and sideways."[52]

Though offering some criticism, the New York Times called the film "big, brassy, bold and freewheeling . . . a cheerful and entertaining addition to the local screen scene."[53] So compelling was the pairing of Reynolds and Presnell in the film that in 1976, they appeared in a stage production of Annie Get Your Gun together, directed by Gower Champion. This was an interesting gesture that drew attention to Molly Brown's second reception problem (i.e., in addition to the pressure of the success of The Music Man): that it is fundamentally generic, albeit with excellent execution from book writer and composer-lyricist. The combination of the Cinderella/rags-to-riches story and the Wild West setting called to mind all too easily the world of Berlin's Annie Get Your Gun, and Molly Brown even replicated the same vocal types for the two lead characters. In drafts of the show's script, Molly pulls out her gun several times—on the lifeboat, to Johnny when she first meets him, to a passing group of tourists the morning after her disastrous Denver party is reported to the press in Act 2—and it is striking that only the third of these remained by the time the show made it to Broadway. While it would be too much to suggest the show could be retitled Molly Get Your Gun, the ease with which the stars of the Molly Brown movie could slot into the Annie roles underlines how much of the show is built on familiar tropes rather than fresh and original. Hamstrung by generic models and beholden to its predecessor in Willson's canon, Molly Brown lies in the shadow of a hit.

6

SINGING THROUGH EVIL TIMES

• • •

HERE'S LOVE, MIRACLE ON 34TH STREET, AND THE CHALLENGE OF THE MUSICAL ADAPTATION

INTRODUCTION

Writing in the souvenir program for the pre-Broadway tour of his third musical *Here's Love* in July 1963, Meredith Willson opined:

> Everybody knows that evil times have befallen the theater lately. Some lay the blame on the doorsteps of the critics; some on the recent strike of the New York linotype operators. I believe the responsibility lies with the writers. . . . What is evident, it seems to me, is that they are weary of trying to create plays that entertain audiences. So they create plays that do not entertain audiences. And the audiences stay home. . . . Isn't it self-evident that the kind of play most difficult to write would be one testing the author's abilities against those of his predecessors? On the same basic terms? I mean a play about comparatively normal people with comparatively normal loves, hates, and fears; a play told engrossingly, while the individual parts gather with brilliance and ingenuity into a satisfying whole for a completely rewarding curtain at the end of a thoroughly absorbing evening. By contrast, wouldn't it be easier, by far, to write a play about abnormal people whose lurid behavior provides an entirely new spectrum of colors, most of which have never before been considered suitable for the stage? With their own built-in climactics of sheer shock? Such a play certainly entails no obligation on the playwright's part to entertain or please; and it requires no ending at all—only a huge terrifying question mark. . . . I believe audiences go to the theatre to stick their heads in the sand for a few short hours hoping to hide from the ugly, sodden, inevitabilities, not to seek them out, praying for any sleight-of-hand theatricalism that will *opiate* the realities, not *magnify* them. Come home George M. Cohan, George Kelly and George Kaufman—Shaw, Shakespeare and Sherwood; all is forgiven.[1]

The Big Parade. Dominic McHugh, Oxford University Press. © Oxford University Press 2021.
DOI: 10.1093/oso/9780197554739.003.0007

Deriving from the pen of the same Meredith Willson who had advocated so passionately for disability rights when trying to create the character of Jim Paroo in early drafts of *The Music Man*, this reactionary essay—titled "Evil Times"— about the state of the American theater is a little surprising. In this moment, the writer of one of Broadway's biggest hits of the 1950s suddenly found himself at odds with the culture of his times.

When the article was reprinted in the *New York Herald-Tribune*, no less a figure than Stephen Sondheim wrote what he described as "an intemperate reply," calling Willson's attitude towards the theater "the senseless cry of a ruinously narrow mind." He continued:

> What is Mr. Willson's idea of normal? Normal as in "Hamlet" (incest, insanity, step-patricide)? Or "Richard III" (deformity, paranoia, infanticide)? Or "Macbeth" or "King Lear"? . . . I recommend that he read the writers he invokes. Is "Hamlet" an opiate? Or "King Lear"? Or even "Saint Joan"? . . . One thing that's wrong with the theatre is indeed the writers, writers like Mr. Willson who are boring audiences away by repeating their own formulas for success, formulas which worked because they *were* fresh— once. . . . Freshness and individuality, new styles and approaches, writers who are concerned with writing first and second-guessing second—these will, and in too small supply *are* revitalizing the theater. . . . Look at the statistics, Mr. Willson: freshness is even commercial. [Edward Albee's] "Who's Afraid of Virginia Woolf?" is bringing back the audiences that "The Unsinkable Molly Brown" drove out.[2]

Almost fifty years later, Sondheim would highlight "Rock Island" (from *The Music Man*) in his book *Look, I Made a Hat* for its originality and freshness,[3] so there is no doubt that the younger composer-lyricist admires the elder's best work; and if Sondheim's words seem aggressive, it is easy to sympathize not only with his frustration about Willson's apparent attitude toward creativity but also his incomprehension about the idea that Shaw and Shakespeare wrote only about the "normal."

More important for the purposes of this book, Willson's article does not do full justice to what he seems to have been trying to achieve with *Here's Love* as a project. For example, it was based on the popular movie *Miracle on 34th Street* (1947) and, as well as being his first theatrical adaptation of an existing source, was an early case of a Broadway musical being adapted from a non-musical film, long before this became a common phenomenon.[4]

The story of *Miracle on 34th Street* revolves around a sort of mystery plot, in which a man who claims to be Kris Kringle becomes the annual Santa Claus at Macy's department store but gets put on trial when his sanity is doubted, and a romantic plot, in which the cynical divorcee Doris Walker (who runs events at Macy's) is persuaded by attorney Fred Gayley[5] to believe in Santa Claus, using her precocious daughter Susan Walker to demonstrate how leaps of faith can be good for people. At the end of the story, Doris and Susan declare their belief in Kris, who is acquitted at a hearing when the judge observes the Post Office (a branch of government) delivering twenty-one sacks of letters to Kris, recognizing him to be the real Santa Claus; and Fred and Doris decide to get married.

The original film was released in May 1947—a surprising time of year at which to release a Christmas movie, apparently motivated by the head of the studio, Darryl F. Zanuck, feeling that more people go to the cinema in the summer than in the winter.[6] The risk paid off: it was nominated for Best Picture at the Academy Awards and won for Best Supporting Actor (Edmun Gwenn as Kris Kingle), Best Writing, Original Story (Valentine Davies), and Best Writing, Screenplay (George Seaton). It quickly became a family favorite and when Willson embarked on writing the musical version, *Miracle* had been seen on television several times in the years since its 1947 release, both in its Hollywood form and in two new made-for-television adaptations in 1955 and 1959.[7]

Willson was once more the book writer as well as the composer and lyricist on this project, demonstrating his ambitious approach and overarching vision. It was also his first set in the present day—he decided to update the 1940s story to the 1960s—and it dealt with powerful themes such as divorce, gambling, faith, and commercialism, showing that Willson's idea of "normal entertainment" did not exclude tackling several serious issues. In that sense, he *was* attuned to the changes in society and must have realized that the show could not simply rely on nostalgia. Nonetheless, in writing a musical about Christmas and a child's belief in Santa Claus, Willson was obviously going in the direction of a family musical, with all its saccharine perils, rather than the more mature subjects addressed in *Molly Brown*.

He had in fact announced the start of plans for a different musical called *The Understudy* in September 1961, just two months before *Here's Love* was first discussed in the press. In the *Los Angeles Examiner* Willson revealed that *The Understudy* required two big stars and that "In spite of its title . . . the story does not have a backstage setting."[8] The latter is difficult to reconcile with the only surviving evidence of this abandoned project in Willson's papers at Carmel, two draft synopses, the first of which is written in pencil and dated May 25, 1961:

> Rehearsal of a big B'way musical three days before the out-of-town opening night. Carol Star shines brightly in the full company closing number, after which George Victor, the director, gives his notes then calls for a ten-minute break. Carol, in marvellous spirits, tells Emory the vehicle is what she has been waiting for all her life—she knows that full star-recognition at last awaits her. They laugh together at Mary "Chump" Hendrix the understudy hovering, as usual, just out of ear-shot. Chump is the same costume size as Carol but considerably older—a pro—a vet. "And praying," says Carol, "for me to break my leg. Do you realize she's never more than three feet away from the time I arrive till I go home?" "Lucky to have such a conscientious understudy" comments Emory. "Stand-bys have the roughest job in showbusiness. Nobody tells 'em the action. Nobody knows they're alive till, God forbid, they have to go on— and *cold*, with no rehearsal." [etc.]⁹

Quite why Willson denied the theatrical setting of *The Understudy* to the press is unclear; nor do we really know why he set it aside. But the fact that he abruptly shelved it in favor of a musical version of *Miracle on 34th Street* is a sign of his commitment and attraction to the latter. In the end, Willson would be frustrated by *Here's Love*'s initial director Norman Jewison, who was replaced during rehearsals by the show's producer Stuart Ostrow, and was disappointed by how the production turned out. It had mixed reviews and a modest run on Broadway, though it has periodically been revived in stock, touring, and amateur productions. Yet how could a musical version by Meredith Willson of a beloved movie go wrong, especially one based on a movie where the *screenplay* specifically won accolades? This chapter considers the development of *Here's Love* as an adaptation, exploits archival materials that reveal the development of the show, and addresses its troubled reception.

DEVELOPING A MUSICAL *MIRACLE*

Here's Love was initially called *The Wonderful Plan*, showing that from the start Willson did not intend to make reference in the title to the movie on which it was based. In retrospect this seems like an odd decision commercially, now that it is conventional simply to add the words "The Musical" to a movie title when producing a stage adaptation: examples of this include *Ghost, Kinky Boots, Pretty Woman*, and *Billy Elliot*, among many others in the twenty-first century. (*Here's Love* has similarly been refitted in recent years with the title *Miracle on 34th Street: The Musical*, which is how it is now licensed by Music Theatre International.[10]) But in the early 1960s, it was conventional to do the opposite (i.e., create a new title), both with adaptations of non-musical films into stage musicals (e.g., *Ninotchka* became *Silk Stockings*) and with adaptations of non-musical plays into stage musicals (e.g., *Pygmalion* into *My Fair Lady*). The title *The Wonderful Plan* also indicated Willson's intention to recycle the song of the same name that had been cut from both *The Music Man* and *Molly Brown* (eventually it was dropped from *Here's Love* too).

When *Variety* announced the show on its front page on November 29, 1961, it reported that Twentieth Century Fox, which produced the screen *Miracle on 34th Street*, would have first refusal on the film rights to the new musical; this never came to pass but was a promising business scenario.[11] Stuart Ostrow, who had worked with Willson in various roles at Frank Music, was to make his Broadway debut as a producer with the piece, and the correspondence in Willson's papers at Carmel uncovers how actively Ostrow was involved in shaping the musical from every aspect.

For his part, Willson was already hard at work when the announcement was made in *Variety*. On November 28 he wrote a breakdown of the plot of the show into a numbered list of twenty-eight points, stopping at the hearing (trial) scene; it is not clear whether he was working from notes made on a screening of the movie, a copy of George Seaton's screenplay, or (less likely) Valentine Davies's novel that was published in tandem with the movie's release in 1947.[12] The following day, he wrote a more detailed synopsis of the final part of the story, heading the document "The Trial."[13]

Both parts of the synopsis draw attention to something Willson never had to deal with in his previous Broadway shows, namely the need to distill the essence of an existing, familiar story into a manageable form that could then be musicalized into a successful entity of its own. Indeed, at twenty-eight points plus three pages of prose description of the trial and denouement, the plot was arguably overcrowded with ideas from the start. Willson started to encounter the same kinds of problems as he faced in the *Silver Triangle* stages of *The Music Man*'s genesis—what was the show about and where should the songs come?—but this time, writing the book for a musical alone without a Franklin Lacey figure to support him formally, he struggled to clarify some of his structural ideas.

Although it is possible that further early drafts of the synopsis have not survived, it appears that Willson used only this initial loose description of the plot as the basis for writing much of the score (i.e., before a proper synopsis, scene structure, or script had been drafted). On January 2, 1962, four copies of Willson's demo recording of "I'd Like to Know Why" were cut by the Radio Recorders company in Hollywood (so it was probably written in December 1961),[14] and on February 3 he was invoiced by his copyist for producing copies of the sheet music for several further songs, namely "With Love," "Never Believe," "Give Me Brass," "We're On Park," "Look, Little Girl," and "Macy's Parade Special," with "The Tune Up" following on February 5 and "Push the Plastic Alligator" on February 18.[15] This apparent disconnect between the writing of the book and score may explain why the first four of these songs and "The Tune Up" did not make it into the show by the time it reached Broadway. The title of the musical remained in flux too: the above invoices are all marked *The Wonderful Plan*, but a letter from Willson's secretary (and future third wife) Rosemary dated February 27 announced a change to *Wouldn't It Be Wonderful IF* [sic] and also referred to *Love, Love, Love* as a recently considered title.

Willson returned to the plot a few weeks later, spending April 3, 4, and 5 writing breakdowns of the four main characters (Fred, Doris, Susan, and Kris), a technique he had found useful when trying to hone the book of *The Music Man*, though this time the emphasis was on making a list of each role's important plot points rather than merely describing their personality traits. (The title of the show had reverted to *Love, Love, Love*.) One of Willson's problems with the story was not knowing quite where to place the emphasis—on the romance of Fred and Doris or the trial of Kris Kringle—and this is reflected in the April 1962 character notes. For example, the April 4 description of Kris's personal plotline reads:

KRIS

1. Existing introduction.
2. a. Kris' concern with today's materialists.
   b. The challenge of Susan and Doris.
3. He gives up and loses all determination to fight the cynics' accusations.
4. He regains his faith thru [sic] the help of Susan, Doris and Fred.

a. He wins Susan and Doris.
b. He puts cynics in their place.
c. He units [sic] Fred and Doris. (He's the catalyst?)
d. He leaves us still with the possibility that he could be Santa Claus.

Willson seems to be trying to figure out Kris's purpose in the story, the question mark against "He's the catalyst?" indicating his uncertainty at this stage of development.

Also revealing are two different descriptions of Fred's character. The first makes him out to be romantically reluctant:

> Fred Gaily is the original Rock of Gibraltar, unassailable, classic bachelor. No By God woman is going to get her By God halter around his neck. At the end of the play Doris makes good her revenge: Brings [sic] this unyielding man to his knees 100%, fighting and struggling all the way. He finally says it: "I love you." Doris now rolls up her sleeves, takes out her knife, and tries—tries—tries to stick it in him. At the last second she throws everything to the winds, realizing and confessing that she loves him. "Not only am I hopelessly helplessly in love with you but I also *believe in Santa Claus*."[16]

This is markedly different to the Fred of the film or novel. In the latter, his introductory paragraph reads: "Being neighbors, he and Susan had become great pals and out of this had grown a pleasant and casual friendship between Fred and Doris. It was far more casual than Fred would have liked."[17] Indeed, Willson seems to have considered at least partly reversing the roles played by Fred and Doris, with Fred apparently being the more resistant of the two to romance.

But a day later Willson wrote a new version, a little more aligned with the Fred of the movie and novel:

FRED GAILY
We like Fred Gaily. Fred Gaily is a brilliant highly successful lawyer whose only apparent problem seems to be his unsuccessful pursuit of Doris Walker, his attractive next door neighbor for whom he is on the make.

a) He strikes up an acquaintance with Doris's eight-year-old daughter Susan hoping ultimately to meet Doris.

b) He uses Susan to get Doris into his apartment where he runs into a brick wall. Nevertheless he sings a very sincere love song. He has no success, however.

c) A new opportunity presents itself when Doris appeals to him to defend Kris because of her regret at having acted hastily.

d) He successfully defends Kris in his own way.

e) He wins Doris.[18]

Even here, though, Fred seems to have a predatory streak, undermining the charm of the equivalent character played by John Payne[19] in the movie. Another fragment about Fred in Willson's papers reads: "He is an incurable romanticist, a complete sentimentalist and his ambition, even firmer than before, is to love all women individually but not permanently."[20]

These issues about the romantic plot would continue to create problems with *Here's Love* right to the end and the drastic fluctuations of emphasis in characterization further highlight the disjunction between the score and book. On the other hand, a prose outline of the first act dated April 6, 1962, indicates that Willson had been thinking about where the songs would be placed in the show. Each of the nine scenes in this version is described in a sentence or two, and at the end of each description Willson names one or more songs to appear in the scene. The song titles are represented in Table 6.1 and again it is noticeable that many of them are unfamiliar from the Broadway score (see Table 6.2 for the latter and Table 6.3 for a complete list of songs and sources, including deleted numbers).

Later in April 1962, Willson wrote a more detailed outline of Act 1, this time in fourteen scenes. A further song title is mentioned, "You Don't Have to Prove It If You Sing It," and more detail is given about the plot, including a crucial change that would remain throughout all subsequent versions: Fred would now be a

Table 6.1. Song titles listed in the incomplete synopsis of April 6, 1962, GASF. Asterisks indicate songs that did not make it into the Broadway version in any form.

Scene Number	Song Title(s)
1	The Tune-Up* The Big Calown Balloons Macy's Parade
2	The Big Calown Balloons (reprise) Give Me Brass*
3	The Rhythm Game* We Live on Park* Never Believe*
4	Plastic Alligators or Move It Or Paint It* or Too Much of Everything* Love, Love, Love
5	I'd Like My Room in the Country*
6	Look, Little Girl
7	Psychiatry* and/or The Muscular Co-ordination Test*
8	Look, Little Girl (reprise)
9	Does Macy's Tell Gimbels? Yes Indeed* Love, Love, Love (reprise) Does Macy's Tell Gimbels? Yes Indeed (reprise)*

Table 6.2. List of scenes and song cues, final Broadway version.

Act 1		Act 2	
Scene 1	A street in the West 70s of New York. Thanksgiving morning. Songs: "Opening Act 1" and "Big Calown Balloons" (Chorus).	Scene 1	The Chambers of Judge Martin Group. The following Thursday morning.
Scene 2	Behind scenes at the Macy's Thanksgiving Day Parade. Following.	Scene 2	An Isolation Room at Bellevue. In the meantime. Song: "Pine Cones and Holly Berries—Reprise" (Kris and Susan).
Scene 3	Along the Parade route. Immediately following. Musical numbers: "The Parade" (Dancers) and "Rain Balloons" (Chorus).	Scene 3	Fred's Apartment. That night. Song: "She Hadda Go Back" (Fred, Alvin, Whitey and Climber).
Scene 4	On top Macy's roof. Immediately following.	Scene 4	A corridor in a New York State Supreme Court. 8:30 next morning.
Scene 5	Doris's apartment. That evening. Songs: "Arm in Arm" (Doris and Susan) and "You Don't Know" (Doris).	Scene 5	The Courtroom. Immediately following. Songs: "That Man over There" (Macy and Chorus) and "My State, My Kansas" (Macy, Doris, Shellhammer, Tammany, Judge).
Scene 6	Doris's office at Macy's. The following morning. Songs: "The Plastic Alligator" (Shellhammer and Clerks) and "To Toy Department" (fragment; Chorus).	Scene 6	The corridor. 3 p.m., Tuesday December 24th. Song: "Nothing in Common" (Doris).

Continued

Table 6.2. Continued

Act 1		Act 2	
Scene 7	Macy's Toy Department. Immediately following. Songs: "Bugles" (Kris and Hendrika) and "Here's Love!" (Kris, Fred and Chorus).	Scene 7	The Courtroom. Immediately following. Songs: "That Man over There—Reprise" (All) and "Love, Come Take Me Again" (Doris). [The latter song was cut and reinstated after Broadway.]
Scene 8	Another part of Macy's. Immediately following. Song: "Here's Love!" continuation.	Scene 8	Macy's Model Living Room Display. Immediately following.
Scene 9	Another part of the store. Immediately following. Song: "Here's Love!" continuation.		
Scene 10	Herald Square, outside Macy's. Immediately following. Song: "Here's Love!" continuation.		
Scene 11	A Playground in Central Park. Later that day. Songs: "Here's Love—Tag" (Fred) and "My Wish" (Fred and Susan).		
Scene 12	Doris' Office. In the meantime. Song: "Pinecones and Hollyberries/It's Beginning to Look a Lot Like Christmas" (Kris, Doris, and Shellhammer).		
Scene 13	Fred's Apartment. Late afternoon the same day. Song: "Look, Little Girl" (Fred).		

Table 6.2. Continued

Act 1		Act 2
Scene 14	In the street outside. Immediately following. "Look, Little Girl—Reprise" (Doris).	
Scene 15	Mr Sawyer's office. The following Monday morning. Song: "Pine Cones and Holly Berries—Reprise" (Kris and Miss Crookshank).	
Scene 16	Macy's Toy Department. That night. Musical Numbers "Expect Things to Happen" (Kris and Susan) and "The Toy Ballet" (Dancers).	

newly retired marine who is a junior lawyer rather than an experienced one who quits a long-established firm to defend Kris.[21]

Willson spent some time working on the title song of the show in May[22] and there are a couple of fragments of script dated June 15, 1962,[23] but the absence of further documents over the ensuing three months suggests that he may have spent the summer drafting the script and/or on vacation. The paper trail resumes on September 12 with a list of five points of the plot that needed changing or enhancing. Again, Fred's predatory nature was the focus of one of them: "Fred asks Doris to marry him. Fred, as an overture to Doris, offers a better environment for Susan (a house with a backyard, etc.). Doris is equally irate at Fred's proposal and the fact that he is using Susan as a shill."[24] Willson's reasons for making Fred's character less appealing are unclear, though it seems that he wanted to expand the plot about the relationship between Fred and Doris and may therefore have wanted to initiate greater adversity by creating more of a journey for Fred.[25]

The second half of the year also brought collaboration into the equation as Willson started to get written feedback on the book from producer Stuart Ostrow, with additional input from Norman Jewison, who had been hired as director at some point over the summer (it was his first theater assignment). On October 15, Ostrow wrote six pages of comments on Willson's latest version of the book, dealing with both large and small issues. For example, he remarked: "Somehow the title 'Here's Love' now seems too general for this most specific story. I'm still at sea."[26] Willson's idea was that the show should promote a message of love to fight against the "evil times" alluded to at the beginning of this chapter, and for

Table 6.3. List of songs and sources.

Song title	Sources/Comments
Act 1	
The Big Calown Balloons	Typed lyric sheet dated January 8, 1962, Juilliard. Listed on an early synopsis at GASF, dated April 6, 1962. Holograph sketches and piano-vocal scores, Juilliard.
Arm in Arm	Holograph sketches and typed lyric sheet (dated July 22, 1963), Juilliard.
You Don't Know	Copyist piano-vocal score and holograph piano-vocal score at Juilliard.
The Plastic Alligator	Copyist piano-vocal score at Juilliard.
Bugles	Copyist and holograph piano-vocal scores at Juilliard.
Here's Love	Listed on an early synopsis at GASF, dated April 6, 1962. Draft lyrics titled "Love, Love, Love" (GASF). Copyist piano-vocal score at Juilliard.
My Wish	Copyist piano-vocal score at Juilliard.
Pine Cones and Holly Berries/It's Beginning to Look a Lot Like Christmas	Holograph and copyist piano-vocal scores at Juilliard.
Look, Little Girl	Listed on an early synopsis at GASF, dated April 6, 1962. Copyist's piano-vocal score, two versions (GASF and Juilliard, the latter a duet for Fred and Doris).
Expect Things to Happen	Copyist piano-vocal score at Juilliard.
Act 2	
She Hadda Go Back	Copyist piano-vocal score at Juilliard.
That Man over There	Copyist piano-vocal score at Juilliard, including reprise version.
My State, My Kansas	Copyist piano-vocal score at Juilliard, including television version.
Nothing in Common	Copyist piano-vocal score at Juilliard.
Love, Come Take Me Again	Copyist piano-vocal score at Juilliard. Cut and then reinstated.

Table 6.3. Continued

Song title	Sources/Comments
Cut and Unused Songs	
Dear Mr. Santa Claus/If Santa Claus Was Crazy	Cut during rehearsals. Lyrics included in L1 (page dated June 26, 1963). Draft lyrics (dated April 11, 1963) at GASF. Copyist piano-vocal score at Juilliard.
We Live on Park	Listed on an early synopsis at GASF, dated April 6, 1962. Cut during rehearsals. Lyrics included in L1. Copyist piano-vocal score at Juilliard, title corrected in ink from "We're on Park." Holograph piano-vocal score, Juilliard.
The Wonderful Plan	Cut before rehearsals. Recycled from *The Music Man* and *The Unsinkable Molly Brown*.
Goodbye, Dear Sergeant/Captain (+ reprise)	Copyist piano-vocal scores for several versions of the song at Juilliard.
Master Sergeant Gaily	Copyist piano-vocal score at Juilliard.
We Don't Believe	Copyist piano-vocal score at Juilliard.
With Love	Unused song for Fred. Listed on a billing sheet for a demo recording session dated February 3, 1962. Copyist piano-vocal score at Juilliard.
You Don't Have to Prove It	Copyist piano-vocal score at Juilliard.
Never Believe	Unused song for Doris. Listed on a billing sheet for a demo recording session dated February 3, 1962, and an early synopsis at GASF, dated April 6, 1962. Copyist piano-vocal score at Juilliard.
Give Me [the] Brass	Unused. Listed on a billing sheet for a demo recording session dated February 3, 1962, and an early synopsis at GASF, dated April 6, 1962. Copyist piano-vocal score at Juilliard.
A Man in Authority	Copyist piano-vocal score at Juilliard.
The Mirror in the Toy-Toy	Copyist piano-vocal score at Juilliard.
Twelve Year Old Scotch	Copyist piano-vocal score at Juilliard.

Continued

Table 6.3. Continued

Song title	Sources/Comments
I'd Like My Room in the Country	Solo for Susan. Listed on a billing sheet for a demo recording session dated February 6, 1962, and an early synopsis at GASF, dated April 6, 1962. Copyist piano-vocal score at Juilliard.
The Tune-Up	Duet for Fred and Susan (patter song). Listed on an early synopsis at GASF, dated April 6, 1962. Piano-vocal score at Juilliard.
The Rhythm Game	Listed on an early synopsis at GASF, dated April 6, 1962. Possibly uncomposed.
Move It or Paint It	Listed on an early synopsis at GASF, dated April 6, 1962. Possibly uncomposed.
Too Much of Everything	Listed on an early synopsis at GASF, dated April 6, 1962. Possibly uncomposed.
Psychiatry/The Muscular Co-ordination Test	Listed on an early synopsis at GASF, dated April 6, 1962. Possibly uncomposed.
Does Macy's Tell Gimbels? Yes Indeed	Listed on an early synopsis at GASF, dated April 6, 1962. Possibly uncomposed.

L1: June 1963 rehearsal script (GASF, box 23, folder 31).
L2: Broadway script (GASF, box 23, folder 33).

a while the show was going to contain a "here's love" sequence in which the title song was sung while love spread across the world. Despite Ostrow's misgivings, the peculiar title for the show stuck.

He also asked Willson to consider reinstating a song for Doris called "Never Believe" in which it becomes clear how badly affected she has been by the end of her marriage to Susan's father, and made suggestions for additions to the lyric of "We Live on Park," a duet between Doris and Susan about the trials and tribulations of living at a fashionable address; Ostrow had recently been through the process of finding a property on Park Avenue and knew all about it. He made over two dozen further proposals, including several for using dialogue or ideas from the movie screenplay, demonstrating how actively and forensically involved Ostrow was in the writing of the work, even though he was credited as producer;

and Norman Jewison's name is mentioned several times as being behind some of the ideas, confirming the nature of his input too.

However, few of them were actually adopted by Willson, and Ostrow wrote again on November 7 with another twenty-three pages of comments and suggestions, copied (as was the previous missive) to Jewison. Many of these were proposals about the placement of blackouts, descriptions in the script, or other smaller specific issues of polishing. For example, he was keen for a clarification in the script of Susan's first appearance in the show, when she is seen reading a newspaper ("Please indicate Susan's newspaper is as big as she is and what Fred and the audience first see is . . . a paper walking across the stage").[27]

There were bigger issues too. Ostrow began the letter by apologizing to Willson that if some of his comments "seem[ed] picayune it's your own damn fault for being so advanced at this stage of the game," but added: "My major concerns are, of course, more serious and reflect some long-time differences of opinion." He had numerous criticisms of Willson's first scene between Susan and Fred, where Willson planned for Fred to drag Susan onto the roof to watch the Macy's Parade. Ostrow pointed out that it would be impossible to see the parade on Central Park West from a brownstone on East 70th Street, and also felt it would be uncomfortable for the audience to see a forty-five-year-old man take a six-year-old child he has just met to the roof of a building. Ostrow spent two pages on this point and Willson was sufficiently motivated to change the scene.

Willson also created a document titled "HERE'S LOVE CALENDAR" at some point, outlining the exact days on which each scene of the show were supposed to take place, starting with the Thanksgiving Day parade on Thursday, November 26 and ending on Tuesday, December 24, in an attempt to clarify the events in the plot.[28]

While Willson, Jewison, and Ostrow were still wrestling with the book, they also started to turn their attention to the practicalities of staging the show, especially in terms of hiring personnel. For example, a telegram of August 10, 1962, had reported to Willson the vocal range of the actress Janis Paige ("B FLAT TO B NATURAL BELTING TOP. HEAD RANGE ROUGHLY F TO G BUT NEED TO USE TO STRENGTHEN AND EXTEND RANGE."), who was later hired to play the lead role of Doris, though others (including Shirley Jones and Michele Lee) were also considered; she is best remembered for her performances in the movie *Silk Stockings* (1957) and in the stage version of *The Pajama Game* (1954).[29] In October, Michael Kidd was vigorously pursued to be the show's choreographer, a position he had held on numerous celebrated productions and movies (e.g., *Guys and Dolls*, *The Band Wagon*, *Seven Brides for Seven Brothers*). Willson sent him a telegram on October 22, saying he had been "very excited" at the possibility of Kidd's participation, and indeed "could not think" of the show being complete without him.[30]

Further correspondence between Ostrow, Jewison, and Willson in November discussed the general consensus that George Rose was their combined first choice to play Kris Kringle, with Leo McKern, Barry Jones, and Eddie Foy Jr. as Ostrow's second choices.[31] British actor Laurence Naismith, who was eventually cast in the role, was scarcely under consideration in the initial correspondence and seems a curiously low-key, uncommercial choice, though the fact that a letter from the casting agent to Ostrow mentions that the producer had "wanted to get away from" actors with an "already-created public image"[32] suggests this was deliberate.

For the role of Fred they looked at big names including Jason Robards and Lloyd Bridges but ended up with Craig Stevens of the television show *Peter Gunn* (1958–1961). The names of actors under consideration for all the roles were numerous, showing that the team had been careful to survey the field and had chosen what they wanted. With the benefit of hindsight the choices do not seem exciting, but the team appears to have cast people who would bring out certain qualities in the characters rather than star power. With the production schedule outlined in January 1963 for a June rehearsal period and a July opening in Detroit, the show's fate was sealed.

CREATIVE APPROACHES AND MUSICAL DECISIONS

As previously noted, the adaptation of an existing drama—and a popular one at that—into a musical was a new challenge and format for Willson. But his processes, strengths, and weaknesses when creating *Here's Love* were not dissimilar from those of his previous stage works. Once more, he recycled songs from earlier projects and used a range of his musical trademarks such as marches, contrapuntal songs, and unpitched patter songs. Although the show's mixed reputation suggests a diminishment in his powers, creativity was not in reality a problem: he wrote more songs than he needed, including several very good numbers that were cut, and he embraced a liberal approach to adapting *Miracle on 34th Street*, adding, changing, and developing story lines to make the material his own rather than an imitation with songs.

However, he lacked the stimulation and structural assistance provided by Morton Da Costa and Franklin Lacey that helped to make *The Music Man* a hit, and encountered a problem that had also hindered *Molly Brown*: tension with the director. In directing his first Broadway musical Norman Jewison was not an especially obvious choice for the show, and although he went on to direct the successful movie version of *Fiddler on the Roof* (1971), his subsequent career as a major (mainly non-musical) film director, including three Academy Award nominations, indicates that this was not a good match of personnel to project. Producer Stuart Ostrow explains in his book *Present at the Creation*: "Rehearsals weren't going well—author/director problems—so at Meredith's urging I replaced Norman Jewison as director and with the help of Michael Kidd's dances and musical staging the show was a soft hit. (It recouped its investment.)"[33]

It may seem bewildering that Willson could not turn a genuine hit out of such a beloved romantic property as *Miracle on 34th Street*. But part of the problem was his evident determination that the musical would stand on its own two feet and not rely on its association with the movie, right down to changing the title. It must have been obvious to him from the start that the theme of the plot had the potential to become too sugary with the addition of the trappings of a Broadway musical, and he also commented in an interview on the eve of the first preview in Detroit that "with a musical you have to have something to sing about. This called for a strengthening of the love interest."[34] In another interview, he acknowledged that *Miracle* "was a great film but that does not guarantee a great theatrical success."[35]

One manifestation of this "strengthening" was a drastic change in the characterization of Fred. Whereas the movie Fred is a gentle, romantic lawyer, Willson's Fred introduces a military context by making him a newly retired marine; this brings the contemporary context of Cold War America into the center of the story and emphasizes the shift of setting to the (then) present day. Presumably Willson's decision to make Fred's defense of Kris at the trial more difficult to achieve because of his lack of experience in the law (he has studied via a correspondence course but is not the experienced lawyer of Seaton's movie) was intended to add dramatic tension, but in effect it makes the story particularly difficult to believe (ironically reflecting the attitudes of Doris and Susan in the plot).

In the musical, Fred begins as a cold misogynist who might be more at home singing Henry Higgins's "A Hymn to Him" than Leadville Johnny Brown's "I'll Never Say No." Evidently Willson wanted both Doris *and* Fred to go on a journey of transformation in the course of the show, but in the process he also removed their appeal. The most extreme example of this is the rhythmic patter song "She Hadda Go Back," which Fred sings to his flatmates while waiting for Doris to arrive to ask him to represent Kris at the trial (he knows she is coming but she doesn't know that he knows). In the number, he describes how women are often late because they procrastinate and forget things like their gloves, keys, and purse: exactly the terms in which Higgins sings of women in "A Hymn to Him," in fact. And like Higgins's number, the purpose of the song is to make fun of Fred's misogynistic attitude so that his journey to convert into a more respectful, romantic character is made longer and more difficult. Reflecting this dramatic intention, the song employs the musical semiotics or signifiers of the pre-enlightened Harold Hill in "Trouble" and "The Sadder but Wiser Girl," including the use of a lot of short words of one syllable at high speed without pitch (denoting an insincere "sales pitch" rather than sincere expression). It also features the same kind of orchestral vamp as "Trouble," echoes the latter's call-and-response structure (with the other men repeating Fred's "She had to go back" in harmony), and begins with a ticktock metronomic sound to depict the lyric musically.

Both Fred and Doris also come across badly in the number "Look, Little Girl," which he initially sings to her (Act 1, Scene 13) after she antagonistically tells him how the story of her divorce has taught her about the nature of (all) men, and then she reprises it on her own immediately after (Act 1, Scene 14). Willson risks both a more complex vocal setting, in the loose-form monologue style of "My White Knight" (*Music Man*) and "Johnny's Soliloquy" (*Unsinkable Molly Brown*), and a mild oath ("When it comes to dames, I wrote the book, little girl, / The whole bloody book, little girl"), the latter highly uncharacteristic of the Willson who wrote the "Evil Times" article cited at the start of this chapter.

Fig. 6.1. "Look, Little Girl," mm. 28–31.

Musically, the number is one of the most interesting and inventive in the score, featuring chromatic intervals that must have been awkward for the non-singer Craig Stevens to learn (see Fig. 6.1). But toward the end of the song, Willson has Fred implausibly grab Doris and kiss her, which she does not resist; at the very end he asks why she kissed him back, and after she has rushed off, she asks herself the same question. This moment highlights one of the show's fundamental problems: that Willson expects us to accept that Fred and Doris secretly love each other while also promoting their aloofness and anti-romantic attitudes. When the Fred of the musical is so shallow and Doris is resolutely cold (unlike their movie counterparts), how could they become appealing musical comedy lovers?

Fred's slight seediness also affects his relationship with Susan, in the movie one of the purest threads and the vehicle through which he most powerfully supports Doris out of her insecurities. Whereas Fred and Susan already know each other at the beginning of the film, and Doris's housekeeper knows where Susan is when she goes to watch the Parade in Fred's apartment, at the beginning of the musical they are strangers and Fred walks up to Susan on the street:

FRED (passing SUSAN)

Hi, kid. You waiting for the parade?

(No answer. HE starts to unlock door. Glances back. HE goes down to SUSAN)

Hi, kid . . .

(Still nothing from the CHILD. HE takes his cap off, addresses it)

Captain Gaily, we're not getting through to this lady.
(Replaces cap, speaks in altered voice)
Well, try again, Fred.
(Takes off cap, addresses it again)
Very well, Captain, I will.
(SUSAN puts [news]paper up to face)

One can hardly blame Susan for resisting the approach of this apparently rather creepy man. Fred is from the start self-involved, thinks he is wittier than he actually is, and is neither charming nor sincere, unlike his screen counterpart. Why would Susan or Doris be in any way touched or changed by him?

Willson's version of Doris in turn has little of the warmth brought to the equivalent character by Maureen O'Hara in the movie. Similar to his redrafting of Fred, Willson exaggerates Doris's overbearing upbringing of Susan to the extent that they both lose some of their appeal. In Act 1, Scene 5, when mother and daughter first appear in the same scene, Doris greets Susan with "Hi, Boss!" and Susan responds with "Hi, Slave" (a troublingly racialized exchange). They hug and Doris gives Susan a present of some new slippers, but although they are obviously affectionate toward each other, we sense from their greeting that the relationship is dysfunctional. This is reinforced a few seconds later by the friendship duet "Arm in Arm," a catchy if relaxed swing number in which the supposed equality between the two is expressed by referring to Susan as the "captain" and Doris as "the crew."

Yet when Doris tucks Susan into bed, she delivers a speech about how Fairy Godmothers and Prince Charmings are not real, "and filling a little girl full of fairy tales can cause her to grow up thinking of life as a fantasy, instead of a reality." This is followed up by the song "You Don't Know," whose punchline reads "You don't know what [a story-book world] is and as long as I live / I promise you, you never will." To an extent, the disturbing nature of this message is offset by Willson's incredibly tender musical setting, which suggests Doris may feel some regret or wistfulness about the way she has brought Susan up; but on the whole, Doris's controlling nature as a parent makes her difficult to relate to.

Thus by the end of the first five scenes of the show, only the opening Macy's Thanksgiving Parade number was appealing or landed well. By all accounts this was a true highlight, in which Michael Kidd's imaginative choreography brought the parade to life accompanied by a mixture of typical Willsonesque marches (including one based on "Adeste Fidelis") and a more contemporary-sounding, jaunty ensemble number, "The Big Calown Balloons," describing the clown-shaped balloons used in the parade (Willson adds an "a" to "clown" to make it two syllables and therefore fit two musical notes). Reviews of this number were uniformly positive and it seems that the temperature was almost raised too high from the start—the equivalent of "Seventy-Six Trombones" in style and impact but much earlier in the show (therefore leaving nothing in reserve). No wonder the introductory scenes about Doris, Fred, and Susan fall a little flat—and Kris

Kringle's mysterious presence as a possible Santa Claus gets buried in the middle of the spectacle of the parade and the cynicism of the other leads.

Using another of his favorite musical tools, Willson follows the "You Don't Know" scene with a number in the Briefing Room at Macy's the next morning, where Shellhammer (one of Doris's employees) delivers a non-pitched rhythmic patter (stylistically between "Rock Island" and "Trouble") to the new clerks, giving them instruction on how to behave. The number is called "The Plastic Alligator," a reference to the seven thousand plastic alligators that Shellhammer has ordered by accident. He has decided that the only way to sell them is to use a jingle, because advertising laws meant that "you can claim anything if you sing it"; this will allow him to use hyperbole to sell a useless item.

At this point, the rhythmic speech gives way to the short jingle itself, in which Shellhammer promises: "This famous plastic alligator's guaranteed for life. / It'll swim like a fish an' blow like a whale, / Pour you a beer or a ginger ale." Although it is inherently banal (which is no doubt why it does not appear on the original cast album), that is a deliberate gesture on Willson's part: he is critiquing the media's advertising industry, which was of course important to his own earlier career (when he invented and wrote material for The Talking People), and is also posing a question about the nature of art. When Macy objects that "You can't claim a plastic alligator will pour you a beer or a ginger ale," Shellhammer responds: "Mr. Macy, if you sing it, you can even claim chewing gum doubles your fun. Singing is an art form. That makes it legal." But despite the cleverness of this concept, it also makes for another number that does not have huge expressive impact—in drawing attention to the banality of advertisement music it cannot avoid being banal itself. (It will, however, have a bearing on an important and effective plot point later on, as we will see.)

A curiosity of adapting _Miracle on 34th Street_ into a musical is that music already played an important role in the movie, quite aside from Cyril Mockridge's brilliant score. While Willson did not retain Susan's piano playing vignette from the film (perhaps it was too redolent of Amaryllis in _The Music Man_), he did keep the use of a Dutch Christmas song in Act 1, Scene 7, when the children are visiting Kris at the Macy's Toy Department. A Dutch orphan speaks to him in her native tongue and in the movie he sings "Sinterklaas kapoentje," a traditional Dutch song about Santa Claus, in response. Willson provided a new one called "Bugles," which has a similar folk song style to the one used in the movie, and it retains its diegetic function as a "song" within the story that the characters know is being sung.

Following "Bugles," Willson recycles the moment from the film in which Fred brings Susan to meet Kris at the store; her cynicism about the existence of Santa Claus is slightly pricked when she witnesses Kris speaking in Dutch to the girl and again when she discovers that Kris's beard is real (she knows her mother has hired him and she assumes the beard will be fake, as it normally is with the Macy's Santa). He also retains the plot device whereby Kris recommends that customers go to Gimbels to buy something—a plastic alligator in the case of the musical.

This impresses the customers and encourages them to shop at Macy's as a caring store, but Willson omits the key piece of information whereby the item is out of stock at Macy's but actually available at the other store:

BEARDED GENTLEMAN:
Now, what do you want for Christmas?
SUSAN:
What do you think I should ask for?
BEARDED GENTLEMAN:
Well—how about a nice plastic alligator?
SUSAN:
I *thought* so.
BEARDED GENTLEMAN:
They are a bit writhy but they're a lot of fun and the best place to get one is Gimbels!
SUSAN:
GIMBELS!
FRED:
Ask for a plastic alligator at Macy's and he sends you to Gimbels!
MRS. FINFER:
I know! People are talking about it all over the store. I can't believe it.
BEARDED GENTLEMAN:
Why not? People should be kind and helpful at any time of the year. But when Christmas time rolls around we ought to go a step farther: make it a tradition, so to speak, to treat everyone with love. [. . .]
TROUBLED TYPE:
But you don't mean *Macy's* should love *Gimbels*?
BEARDED GENTLEMAN:
I do indeed.

The plot device is therefore fudged. In the movie, Kris takes it upon himself to advise customers on where to buy toys that Macy's does not sell, a scheme that unexpectedly turns out to be good business for Macy's even when he sends customers elsewhere because they appreciate the useful information and reward Macy's with their custom more generally. But in the musical Kris merely sends people to other shops to show the other businesses love; it simply does not make sense.[36] Previously, the joke of the show has been that nobody would want a plastic alligator, and it's not a children's toy, so why would Kris—who is resistant to simply selling things for the sake of it—*sincerely* suggest that Susan might want one for Christmas? Even more important, the charm and delicacy of Susan's curiosity about Kris's magic powers is overwhelmed by Willson's awkward drawing-out of the conversation to provide a setup for the title song, "Here's Love." Gone is the idea of making the children happy, as is the idea of Kris being fired for insanity and then reinstated because Mr. Macy has discovered the business benefits of Kris's idea of sending customers elsewhere. The focus is now simply on "love."

The song itself is overwhelming too, even if it is irresistibly catchy: it takes the equivalent of the "Seventy-Six Trombones" production number slot in the first act by starting with a group of characters indoors and then building into a powerful full-ensemble piece that ends outdoors (in Herald Square). Musically, it shares characteristics with "Seventy-Six Trombones" as well: it is a march in 6/8 time (with patriotic connotations going back to Willson's association with Sousa) and the shape of the melody is not dissimilar to its *Music Man* antecedent. Neither song has a verse and in both Willson cleverly exploits the dramatic benefits of going straight into the refrain without too much telegraphing of the production number that's about to happen.

Yet "Here's Love" is more interesting in some ways. The beginning of the refrain is fragmentary, with "Me to you" then "and you to me" chopped into short melodic statements, creating an improvisatory quality (see Fig. 6.2). As Kris warms to his idea, the melody becomes more extensive and developed, as well as more harmonically unusual (such as the unexpected A flat major chord on the words "Here's love!"; see Fig. 6.3). Yet the lyric is not strong enough, with incoherent imagery such as "From the car with the bumper / To the car that needs a shove / Here's love," and overall the powerful effect of the production number does a disservice to the needs of the book—indeed, the book is reduced to generalities in order to serve the title and message of the song.

Fig. 6.2. "Here's Love," refrain, excerpt 1.

Fig. 6.3. *"Here's Love," refrain, excerpt 2.*

PRACTICAL AND ADAPTIVE CHALLENGES

Another of Willson's problems in writing the show was having to compose for a series of actors of limited vocal ability. In the original Broadway cast, nobody sang superlatively well: Janis Paige was vocally past her best as Doris and neither Kris nor Fred was played by a singer. In Willson's previous shows, there had of course been a lead character played by an actor-star of more limited lyrical singing ability (Robert Preston and Tammy Grimes), but this was offset by an outstanding singer in the co-star role (Barbara Cook and Harve Presnell). In *Here's Love* that was not the case, which may be why so many of the numbers seem not to pack a punch. This in turn does not help justify having turned it into a musical.

For example, in the scene following the "Here's Love" production number, Fred has a song called "My Wish" (Susan joins in briefly for the last few lines). Presumably to accommodate someone of limited vocal capacity feeling his way through the melody, there are a lot of repeated notes in the song, though Willson does his best to create some interest by exploring chromatic chords in a couple of phrases. Rather like the title song, the lyric is weaker than the music: Fred has just been making misogynistic comments to Susan (for example, "In ten years you'll be a dame. And dames don't love anybody but themselves"), but upon discovering that Susan never celebrates her birthday because it falls at Christmas, he decides very sweetly to sing her a birthday song, full of clichés such as "May your hopes be as high—as high as the sky's highest star" and "May your heart know the meaning of love." This does not cohere with the comments Fred has just been making, and once more the score does not sit comfortably with the book. (It is a shame, in fact, that the Fred of this song is not typical of the Fred of the book.)

Willson introduces another series of changes from the movie in the next scene, which covers a plot point that is moved further into the story in the musical. In the film, Doris fires Kris for being mentally unstable, but Mr. Macy calls her into his office to commend her for the positive impact of Kris's policy of sending customers to other stores when Macy's doesn't have something in stock; Doris then goes and persuades Kris to return to work, which he does successfully. But in the musical, Mr. Macy berates Doris for allowing Kris to send all the customers to Gimbels; Macy's stands empty, but Doris explains that it is a great marketing ploy for Macy's to be the caring store (which does not make sense when they have lost "the proceeds of an entire day from [their] cash register" as a direct result of this message).

Implausibly, Macy is convinced by the idea, but Doris discovers that Shellhammer (Doris's junior executive) has fired Kris, so she has to rip up his dismissal form and persuade him that it was a mistake. In this example, perhaps Willson's intention was to strengthen Doris's agency in the story: she is now the brains behind making "Here's Love" a marketing strategy, rather than it being an accident. But it also seems possible that the score was again dictating the content of the book, because Kris makes a speech about Doris and Susan being a "test case" for him and declares that the faith she has put in him (which in reality is her faith in a cynical exploitation of him) has restored his faith in Christmas, which has started to wane.

This becomes a cue for one of Willson's counterpoint songs—the old favorite "It's Beginning to Look a Lot Like Christmas" recycled from the trunk, sung alongside a new tune, "Pine Cones and Holly Berries." With a tendency to harmonically consonant motion, the new song is less distinctive than the old one, and to go by the evidence of the cast album the vocal deficiencies of Paige and Naismith were particularly pronounced in a song with interwoven melodies (see Fig. 6.4), but the number is unquestionably cute, with Willson at his amiable best. It returns in Act 2, Scene 2, when Kris has been confined to Bellevue, having been dismissed from Macy's because of questions over his sanity. Susan comes to visit him in his despondence and, mirroring the song's previous appearance, restores his faith in himself.

What "Pine Cones" unquestionably injects into the show is some much-needed charm. Other attempts along the same lines are arguably weaker. For example, in Act 1, Scene 16, Susan and Kris are in Macy's Toy Department at night, where he lectures her on the need to have an imagination ("Well, you've heard of the French nation—the English nation—this is the Imagee-nation"). This leads to a number called "Expect Things to Happen (Like the People in the Fairy Tales Do)," whose lyric is again inexplicably uninspired (for instance, "You let your face tell you ev'ry day how necessary soap is, / Let your heart tell you how necessary hope is"), leading into "The Toy Ballet." This structure of having a song about

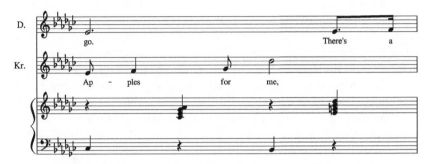

Fig. 6.4. "Pine Cones and Holly Berries," mm. 29–32.

dreams leading into a dream ballet shows how the *Oklahoma!* model (where "Out of Your Dreams" segues into "Laurey's Dream Ballet") was still exerting pressure on Broadway writers twenty years on.

In itself, depicting Susan's newly ignited imagination through dance is not a bad idea, and Kidd's choreography focused on the psychological dimension of her desire to have a house in the country and for Fred to become her father. The ballet also effectively sets up the conclusion of Act 1, where there is a sudden gulf between Doris, who still does not believe in Santa Claus, and Susan, who now does; Susan blames her mother when Kris is carried off by the police to Bellevue, and the curtain comes down. But the story is not really about Susan, and by devoting the show's only narrative ballet to her, Willson diverted attention unhelpfully from the two central plot arcs (Doris's belief in Kris, and the Doris-Fred romance).

Here's Love comes into focus in the middle of the second act, specifically in the lively and entertaining court hearing sequence (Scenes 4–7). It was noted earlier that Willson's first draft plot synopsis of the show was particularly detailed for this sequence—an extended prose description rather than the "list" approach he had taken for the rest of the story—and this may explain why it is somewhat more fluent and focused than much of the first act.

In the corridor outside the court room, Scene 4 briefly establishes that the District Attorney assumes it will be a quick, open-and-shut case, and Kris learns that this will be Fred's first-ever court appearance. The court scene itself is effective compared to much of the rest of the show, partly because much of the dialogue is lifted verbatim from the film; for example, when the D.A. asks Kris where he lives, Kris responds, "That's what this hearing will decide" and the Judge comments, "A very sound answer, Mr. Kringle." But the main reason it lands so well is that it arguably outdoes the film by using song to change the plot—thus, at last, justifying and benefiting from a musical adaptation.

The means for this are particularly amusing. When Mr. Macy is asked to take the stand and say whether he believes Kris is Santa Claus, he faces an impossible dilemma: support an absurd idea or be known by the public for dismissing the existence of Santa. Shellhammer and Doris come up with an ingenious solution. They subtly remind Macy of the law about jingles and he unexpectedly bursts into a diegetic song, "That Man over There (Is Santa Claus)" set to the music of Shellhammer's earlier "Plastic Alligator" jingle. This means Macy can bend the truth without perjuring himself, which in itself is highly amusing, and the song is taken up by the spectators in the court, leading to perhaps the catchiest number in the score. In the equivalent moment in the film, Macy simply says "Yes" when asked about Kris's identity and is then angry at being put in this situation; in the musical, he goes into extensive detail in the song lyric about how he knows Kris is Santa, using ridiculous logic ("I can tell by the krinkle on the bridge of his nose / The wink of his eye and the twinkle of his toes") that also supports the idea that this is a matter of faith rather than fact.

Later in the scene, Willson continues to use song to serve the drama effectively when Doris, Macy, Shellhammer, and Tammany (a political boss who wants to get the Judge re-elected and is worried that convicting Santa Claus could ruin the Judge's career) sing the number "My State, My Kansas" to persuade the Judge to be lenient. The song is a paean to the state of Kansas, which is where the Judge hails from, and the other characters imply that while it may be patriotic of him to uphold the law, it will be at the price of his popularity back home. (The song is another from the trunk: Willson had written it for a pageant called *The Kansas Story* that ran for a few weeks in Topeka and Wichita from June to July 1961.)[37] The over-the-top style of the number is ideal for it to act as a vehicle of persuasion in musical comedy terms, and it is a powerful conclusion to the scene as Macy bids farewell to the Judge as "Mister Group" rather than "Judge Group," bringing horror to his face.

The ensuing scene addresses how Kris's fate will be sealed: Fred sees a letter carrier delivering some mail to Kris as Santa Claus and realizes this may be the way to prove his case in law. While he rushes off to attend to the matter, Doris and Kris discuss Susan's Christmas present. Kris hints that Fred and Doris may be in love and she refutes the idea in "Nothing in Common"—a musical number where Doris delivers her lines unsung but with orchestral accompaniment (one chord per measure, a little like nineteenth-century melodrama). She outlines the many ways in which she and Fred are unlike and by the end of the number she breaks down in tears describing the time they kissed and how much it meant to her; music takes over as the curtain falls.

Willson again reproduces the action of the movie fairly faithfully in the penultimate scene of the show, in which the D.A.'s young son is brought in and testifies that his father has told him that Santa Claus exists—a damning admission for the attorney. Fred's trump card is then when he has the mail for Santa brought in by the letter carriers. He argues that since the Post Office is an official agency of the United States, and the Post Office has delivered the mail for Santa directly to Kris, the United States recognizes Kris as Santa Claus; therefore, the court should too. The Judge agrees and instantly issues his verdict, followed quickly by a short celebratory ensemble reprise of "That Man over There."

At this point, a crucial number was dropped before the show reached Broadway and then reinstated when it went to Los Angeles at the start of its post-Broadway tour: Doris was to sing "Love, Come Take Me Again," a traditional "eleven o'clock number" in which the lead character comes to a moment of self-recognition (an analogous example is Higgins's "I've Grown Accustomed to Her Face" from *My Fair Lady*). The number is an emotive waltz and packed a punch just when the show needed it, relating Doris's desire to let herself fall in love with Fred—but presumably to accommodate Paige's vocal limitations, it was removed during the tryout in Detroit. (Willson's official statement was: "I didn't want to lose that song . . . but it expresses much that already has been said.")[38] This meant the Broadway version of the show simply ends with a brief scene of dialogue in Macy's in which Doris declares to Fred, "Mr. Gaily, we do have something in common, we both believe in Santa Claus" and they embrace. But the lack of musical expression at this moment is symptomatic of a show in which the role and nature of music is not wholly coherent or consistently satisfying, despite its many fine and engaging points.

CONCLUSION: A LOT LIKE CHRISTMAS

Here's Love had an extensive pre-Broadway tour, starting with its world premiere at Detroit's Fisher Theatre on July 29, 1963, and moving for further runs in Washington, DC, and Philadelphia before hitting New York on October 3 (Fig. 6.5).

As noted earlier, the tensions between director Norman Jewison and writer Meredith Willson came to a head during the rehearsals and Jewison was replaced by producer Stuart Ostrow. In his autobiography, Jewison makes derogatory comments about Willson's "gigantic ego and manipulative wife" and draws parallels with Harold Hill—"A guy who arrives in a corny Midwest small-town square with a razor-sharp edge and an inflated opinion of his talent."[39] But it is hardly surprising that Jewison was resentful about being fired and presumably Willson—who was considerably more experienced and distinguished at this point—was equally convinced that the problems could be pinned on the inexperienced director. After all, the composer had the greatest faith in and respect for Morton Da Costa, director of *The Music Man*, which shows that it would be wrong to suggest that he was generally against directors or collaborators.

Fig. 6.5. Meredith Willson with Janis Paige and the young actresses playing Susan, during the troubled rehearsal period of Here's Love.

Nevertheless, there is no doubt that from the start of previews in Detroit there was a general perception that the show needed work. One telling document is a letter from Milton Kramer of Frank [Loesser] Music Corp., Willson's publisher, in which he makes numerous comments after seeing the performance on August 6, including: "I think more attention should be paid to how the drunk Santa is set up. It seems kind of muddy and sloppy off in the corner there," "Everything that has been done to Doris in the way of costume and make-up is awful," and, most amusingly, "Those aren't alligators; those are lizards."[40] There were more drastic criticisms too. Of the song "My Wish" Kramer noted, "I think the motivation for the song and dialogue is a little worked over. This coincidence of birthday and Christmas etc. is kind of a wordy complication. Also I think the set is completely wrong." He also critiqued the title song, saying it "will need some more funnies." Worst of all, he remarked: "I may be the only one that thinks so, but my suggestion about shortening the dream ballet is to start with the first note and cut from there to the finish. I think the whole thing is wrong."[41]

The press was much gentler but the earliest reviews already hinted at the key problems. An Associated Press report on July 20 called the show "a pleasant evening's entertainment," a lukewarm assessment that got to the heart of the problem: it was neither great nor terrible. The same review also touched on one of the book's main flaws: "There also is a so-so love affair between Janis Paige and Craig Stevens (of 'Peter Gunn' TV) which is resolved rather quickly, considering the two begin the play professing to detest the opposite sex."[42] Some of the other papers were more positive: the Detroit Free Press called the show "wonderful" and "a happy package," and referred admiringly to "Paige's big moment" in the song "Love, Come Take Me Again"—ironic, considering it was cut in Detroit, as was a song for the children at the top of Act 2, "Dear Mr. Santa Claus."[43]

By August 27, Ostrow and Willson had tightened things considerably and the production opened in Washington, DC, to a warm review in The Evening Star, albeit one with caveats: "It is so flagrantly all heart that only the heartless cad would cavil that its book is untidy, its pace errant, and its score a bit echoic."[44] The review particularly commented on how most of the songs "serve their purpose well" but "none to such triumphant effect as the courtroom numbers 'That Man over There' and 'My State.' These are the big joyous laugh numbers, the clincher sort of thing that permanently cements the bond between Mr. Willson and his congregation."

By Philadelphia, there was a similar balance in the reviews between praising the general effect of the show and acknowledging inherent flaws. For example, the review in the Philadelphia Daily News called it a "pretty Christmas package" and "a likely attraction for the family trade at any time of the year" but also admitted: "Less certain seems its drawing power for the expense account crowd and the people who like heavier seasoning with their song and dance fare." The reviewer also commented: "While there are no outstanding voices to give it maximum projection, it seems the Willson score for 'Here's Love' isn't in the same league with his previous Broadway efforts."[45]

On the whole, the New York critics erred on the side of the more critical of the tryout reviews in their assessments. There was similar half-hearted praise, for instance from Howard Taubman in the New York Times: "'Here's Love' is a model in which the family can ride in comfort. Shrewdly engineered, the model of an efficient musical." Particularly striking was Walter Kerr's review in the Herald-Tribune, which was excerpted by the producer in a publicity campaign as if it were positive but actually drew attention to the show's bombastic quality: "The title song sails across the pit as though it didn't need amplifiers, a nostalgic fragment called 'Pine Cones and Holly Berries' sounds perfectly comfortable under the oversize snowflakes splattered about the stage, and when, in the second act, the time has come to prove that there really is a Santa Claus, what sounds like a cast of two or three hundred get together to prove it with a walloping melody called 'That Man over There.' I mean, how can you fight it?"[46]

In her well-known Theory of Adaptation, Linda Hutcheon notes that "Whether it be in the form of a videogame or a musical, an adaptation is likely to be greeted as minor and subsidiary and certainly never as good as the 'original.'"[47] That has certainly been the case with Here's Love, a musical adaptation of a beloved film: it ran 334 performances on Broadway before a brief post-Broadway tour, it has never been filmed, and it has never had a major revival in New York or a major professional production in London, though there have been regional productions in the States and in the UK. From the start, there was a feeling that it never could live up to the original, and though the Broadway production and reviews were not embarrassing they were also unimpressive.

Another of Hutcheon's comments is also relevant: she argues that there is something "appealing about adaptations as *adaptations*" and notes that the phenomenon brings both repetition and variation at the same time, in other words "the comfort of ritual with the piquancy of surprise."[48] We have seen how Willson delivered exactly this in his adaptation: the use of a familiar story but with numerous variations (such as Macy's court appearance happening through song to allow him to declare that Kris is Santa Claus without perjuring himself). In this respect, he seems to have understood exactly what was required of a musical adaptation: invention and change rather than straight reproduction.

Yet perhaps Willson was a little too keen to deliver the antidote to the "evil times" discussed at the start of this chapter: a reactionary rather than creative position. And the show never recovered from the tension between the original property (the film) and the new one, something that producer Ostrow may have been acknowledging when the role of Fred was taken in the post-Broadway tour by John Payne, reprising the character he played on screen (a highly unusual move). The assassination of President John F. Kennedy on November 22, 1963 also caused a practical change to the show (a reference to him in the title song was removed the day after his death, as Peter Filichia reports)[49] and perhaps rendered its overall tone at odds with a time of national shock and mourning. Another specter cast its shadow over the musical too: from the band uniforms in the opening parade to the use of counterpoint numbers and patter songs, the show bears many of the hallmarks of the person behind *The Music Man* and Willson became a victim of his own success through negative comparison to the earlier work. Thus *Here's Love* was, as Willson puts it, a lot like Christmas: highly anticipated but swiftly over.

7

1491

• • •

THE FINAL VOYAGE

In an interview with the *Denver Post* on September 2, 1969, Meredith Willson disclosed that he believed his new show *1491*, which was due to open that night, would be his last. "Willson Convinced Columbus Is the End" read the headline. Although the article went on to hint that this was a regular feeling for the composer when overseeing the premiere of one of his musicals, there was a strong sense that this was likely to be his final voyage onto the stage: "Putting a musical together takes an enormous amount of creativity and Willson's latest musical about what Christopher Columbus was up to before he sailed has been in the making for five years."[1] Willson was sixty-seven years old when the show opened and he could look back on a varied and successful forty-year career in the music industry with enormous satisfaction. Though he considered at least three further musical projects in the 1970s, no wonder *1491*—which struggled through badly received tryouts on the West Coast and never transferred to Broadway—proved to be his last staged work.[2]

Curiously, there is a suggestion that Willson considered retiring much earlier. An extraordinary fifty-nine-page letter from Frank Loesser to Willson, undated but almost certainly written in 1964 anticipating the closure of *Here's Love* on Broadway, encouraged him against what he called "laurel resting" (i.e., resting on his laurels) and from simply spending his time making public appearances on television and in concerts, and strongly advocated adding to his body of works.[3] Loesser wrote that in his opinion this body of works "constitute[s] MEREDITH WILLSON—not the entertainer, not the travelling husband, not the giver of interviews or the philosophical friend of the military march or the leading citizen of Mason City but MEREDITH WILLSON who can do all those other things while his brilliant brain and electrically creative spirit are resting."

Loesser's words seem a little harsh when on the surface the sixty-two-year-old Willson had nothing to prove. Was he not entitled to enjoy himself making prestigious, nostalgic television specials such as the *Texaco Star Parade*, on which he appeared on June 30, 1964, alongside his wife Rini and special guest star Debbie Reynolds (promoting her performance in the then-new movie version of

The Big Parade. Dominic McHugh, Oxford University Press. © Oxford University Press 2021.
DOI: 10.1093/oso/9780197554739.003.0008

Molly Brown)? Willson's media career was long established, and he enjoyed being able to work in different capacities.

Yet Loesser had a point. Specifically comparing Willson's career to that of Harold Rome (composer-lyricist of *Pins and Needles, Wish You Were Here,* and *Fanny*), Loesser observed that although Willson was undoubtedly much more talented than Rome, people respected Rome as a writer because "he could quote a relatively formidable BODY OF WORKS." Loesser realized that in terms of career management, Willson needed to develop his catalogue as a writer for Broadway in order to join the canon. As Chapter 1 of this book showed, Willson could point to numerous achievements—including publishing a novel and several memoirs, being part of America's greatest orchestra and band, having a prolific career on radio, composing two symphonies, and writing the scores for two important films—yet most of this would be forgotten. Only *The Music Man* and to some extent *The Unsinkable Molly Brown* would count. Almost sixty years later, Loesser's prediction has been borne out by posterity.

Willson's reaction to his (younger!) mentor's observations is unrecorded, but by the beginning of 1965 he had started to work on *1491*. Indeed, Loesser may have been preaching unnecessarily to his friend because as early as April 1964 Willson had communicated with the source of inspiration for the new musical, the *Los Angeles Times* columnist Ed Ainsworth, albeit on another topic.[4] They had worked together on a pageant at the Hollywood Bowl in 1950 to celebrate the centennial of the state of California (*The California Story*) with Ainsworth co-writing the script, and they appear to have kept in touch from time to time in the intervening years.

On January 22, 1965, Ainsworth sent a memo to Willson outlining the thematic possibilities of *1491* (as it was named from the start), described under the headings "The Big Question" (regarding the size of the degree of the Earth's latitude, which affected the challenge for Europeans to sail to the Americas), "The Sea Fight" (Columbus's battle off Cape St. Vincent in 1476), "The Map" (Columbus's theft from the Portuguese of the Toscanelli map, which favorably misrepresented distances), "The Legendary Lures" (the myths surrounding foreign lands), "Palos de Frontera" (where Columbus made many of his plans), and "The Girl" (Columbus's lover Beatriz Enriquez de Harana of Cordoba). Ainsworth followed this up with a further four pages of historical detail on January 28.[5] After another two communications on March 1 and 4,[6] Willson must have been hooked because by the middle of March he had started to write: his last show was born.

1491 FROM 1965 TO 1966: OPPORTUNITIES, COLLABORATIONS, AND PROBLEMS

In fact, the earliest evidence of Willson working on the musical is a document marked "MW's notes from Morison's book," written in February 1965.[7] By this, Willson meant Samuel Eliot Morison's volume *Admiral of the Ocean Sea*.[8] He seems to have found this an inspiring read: for example he remarked on one point, "Columbus at thirty, the dangerous age which sometimes drains the fire from ardent youth. (a song?)" He followed this up on March 5 and 8 with extended character descriptions of the type he had used in developing his shows right from *The Music Man* onward, and after an incomplete rough five-page outline written on March 10 (marked "Paris"; the Willsons were on vacation), he produced what he labeled a "First draft of first outline," dated March 16.

Already, all of the key themes and situations that would engage Willson over the next four years of developing the show were in place, albeit not in anything like their final form: 1) the idea that many of the stories surrounding Columbus are myths and are often contradictory; 2) Columbus's selling of copies of his map to people in the town square (à la Harold Hill's "Trouble"); 3) the lack of a Spanish national (musical) instrument; 4) the rivalry between Columbus and Don José Esteban, advisor to Queen Isabella and a celebrated cartographer in his own right; 5) Esteban's romantic interest in Isabella, despite her marriage to King Ferdinand (a philanderer); 6) Columbus's charisma as the factor that persuades the love-struck Isabella to approve and fund his trip, despite her secretly knowing that he has lied about the details of his map and therefore the distance between Spain and the Americas; 7) Columbus's romantic relationship with Beatriz, who loves him but knows she cannot trust him to be faithful; 8) Columbus's close friendship with a character called Klunk (later Jacobini), who is a carpenter and who is working on inventing a new guitar; 9) Columbus's challenging experience with the Inquisition, which pursues him for his heretical opinions (i.e., prioritizing science over religion); and 10) Columbus's departure for the Americas at the final curtain.

Yet the outline also reveals the problems with race, colonialism, and imperialism that would cast a permanent shadow over the show and which probably explain why it has never been performed in New York or revived anywhere. There are four prongs to this issue. First, Willson attempted to engage positively with identity by showing how a Jewish immigrant character had to change his name (from Jacobs to Jacobini in the final version of the show) and suppress his background by assimilating into a reluctantly churchgoing Catholic. The intention here was unquestionably positive, and Willson was thinking about shedding light on anti-Semitism, and the role it played in the Spanish Inquisition and expulsion of the Jews, from the point of first making notes on Morison's book in February 1965. For example, one note reads: "All the Jews were expelled before Columbus sailed," and Willson comments that this may be why Columbus married Beatriz secretly.[9] But within this formulation is a sense of Jews representing the exotic other and in the version that made it to the stage in 1969, Jacobini is the stereotype of the Jewish comic sidekick, with his ethnicity (and its erasure) often the source of humor. To some extent, this problem was overcome by an explicit demonizing of the Inquisition's anti-Semitic comments, added to the book in the weeks leading up to rehearsal, but this caused another problem, namely that the other depictions of race in the show, outlined below, are not problematized in the same way.

Second, the political background to the story concerns the war between Spain and the Moors (the latter is a blanket, exoticising label invented by white Europeans that does not represent self-determined identity). At its most mild, this manifests itself early in the show in a racialized discussion (also imbued with misogyny) between Columbus and Klunk (Jacobini) about the need for a Spanish instrument: "No wonder the Moor has been unlodge-able [sic] from the sacred soil of Spain for over 700 years. Do not the Moors have their glorious lute, shaped like a Moorish woman? As wieldy, graceful, and patriotically thrilling to the Moorish heart in accompanying melody and chant as the Spanish 12 string atrocity is clumsy, awkward and uninspiring to the Spaniard?"[10] In the early outlines, and for several years' worth of further drafts, there is a sequence later in Act 1 in which Columbus describes to Beatriz his experiences visiting Africa as a boy. The March 1965 outline reads: "He and Beatriz exit on a wagon as he describes the horrible ritual dances which we now see involving males and females as naked as possible. They are greased; they wear outlandishly grotesque hairdos, amazingly like the big beehives and shaggy hairstyles of the girls and boys of today; the ritual dances are identical with the Watusi, the Jerk, the Surf, the Swim, the Frug, etc., complete with rear-end wobbles."[11]

As if the racialized description of the dance were not bad enough, Willson here makes a direct link between immigration and the youth culture of his own time, apparently suggesting that what he perceived as the decay in contemporary (white) North American culture was a result of the influence of Black African culture; he was explicitly out of synch with the civil rights movement. More generally, the siege of Granada, as a result of which "The Moors [are] expelled from Spain at long last," provides Columbus with the opportunity to ask Isabella for his ships; his argument is that now Spain has reclaimed its own land, it is time for it to go and claim someone else's. The heroic power of the lead character is based on the expulsion of Black people from Spain's shores. Whether he was at fault for absorbing history through an outdated book (Morison's) written long before or whether he was simply reactionary toward his times, Willson was certainly at odds with the important discussions about race happening in North America; this aspect of the text was considerably edited down by the time it opened in California, but the conflict between the Spanish and the Moors remained a latent presence in Act 1.

A third problem with the show is its exoticism of Spain and its people. The entire book and score are predicated on the appeal of othering a southern European country and culture, and from its Hispanic rhythms to its mysterious locale *1491* is barely more progressive than the depictions of Latin culture and countries in 1930s and 1940s Hollywood (e.g., the Astaire-Rogers *Flying Down to Rio* or the movie musicals of Carmen Miranda). Of course, Willson's Second Symphony ("The Missions of California," 1940) had already shown his interest in Latin music and history and with the popularity of the fairly recent movie version of *West Side Story* (1961) and the blockbuster *Man of La Mancha* (1965) just around the corner, this aspect of the show makes more commercial sense in context; but it is still problematic, with Beatriz representing the smart and sexy but uneducated

Spanish peasant, a foil to Columbus's "masculine" cleverness and aristocratic flair (representing whiteness).[12]

Fourth and lastly, the glorification of Columbus's "heroic" voyage to find the "New World," which is the topic of the show, even if the final scene only depicts his departure, erases its destructive outcome. The unspoken product of that voyage was the introduction of colonialization, leading, for example, to slavery and the genocide of the Taíno people of Hispaniola; Columbus's empowerment of Spain was at a significant cost to humanity.

When sending his first outline of 1491 to Milton Kramer of Frank Loesser Enterprises, Willson remarked: "If Yardo and Alooba are going to mean anything as a secondary love story, I will have to, with apologies to 'Bali Hai' [sic] and 'The King and I', have some threat to them also."[13] (Yardo and Alooba are a teenage Spanish boy and an African girl in the initial outlines, cut from later versions.) Willson's references to Rodgers and Hammerstein's South Pacific (1949) and The King and I (1951) remind us that at the time of his writing 1491, these two classic musicals were the benchmark for how to represent (characters from) non-Western cultures (as they were lumped together) on Broadway. More recently, these depictions have been problematized, as the following summary of reactions to the 2001 London revival of The King and I on the theater website Backstage broadly demonstrates: "It has an unprecedented advance sale of some $11 million (£7 million), and the opening night audience responded with an un-British standing ovation, but a few reviewers zeroed in on its political aspects. The Guardian said it was 'a political embarrassment that not even Richard Rodgers' seductive songs can redeem,' The Daily Telegraph said its 'whole attitude to the exotic East is faintly patronizing,' while The Times weighed in with a denunciation of 'the colonialist notion that exotic nations should ape the behaviour of western lands.'"[14] Today, critics and audiences rightly have mixed feelings about these issues, but in the early 1960s these Rodgers and Hammerstein works about white North American society's fascination with cultures other than its own were seen as models for other writers; no wonder Willson felt there was strong potential in a story about Spain, an explorer, the clash of cultures, and the power of creating colonies.

Despite these insurmountable problems, the next four years of writing improved the work immeasurably, and did address some of these problems. As always, Willson was fully committed to getting it right. A letter from Ainsworth dated December 27, 1965, begins, "My comments are all directed towards final polishing, which I know you will be doing right up through rehearsals," implying production might be expected in 1966.[15] But Willson must have known there was a long way to go. For one thing, he had sent the script to Richard Morris, his book writer on The Unsinkable Molly Brown, in September 1965 and received a four-page critique in which Morris complained of "too many short disconnected scenes," a lack of development of the female characters, and too much focus on the Spanish guitar (Willson's desire to make music a topic of the plot was a typical priority for him). He also expressed "great admiration."[16] Willson must have known that there was work still to be done and the fact he had involved Morris probably means he was ready for what was always an essential phase of collaboration for him.

For another thing, there was no producer or director yet attached to the project, so on a practical level there was much negotiation and planning to be done. Correspondence in the Carmel collection reveals that Willson approached his favourite producer, Kermit Bloomgarden of *The Music Man*, undoubtedly in a nostalgic attempt to recreate the magic of his first show. Willson sent him a draft of the script on September 16, 1965, just six months after starting the first outline, and the pair seem to have had three brief conversations about it. But Willson was unhappy with Bloomgarden's lack of engagement with him, which he put down to the producer's simultaneous work on a non-musical play about Columbus by Sidney Carroll (*Cristoforo*, which was intended for London but was apparently not produced).[17] "I have felt extremely handicapped this past year in not having had the producer, director counsel I enjoyed during the preparation of my other three musicals—particularly show No. 1," Willson wrote to Bloomgarden on May 20, 1966. "It was bad judgement on my part to have carried on for such a long time without [the] benefit of [a] producer."[18]

Another letter suggests Willson himself may have been dragging his feet. His mentor and publisher Frank Loesser wrote to him on June 21: "I thought by this time you would have sent me that script. Really, it will give me a much better concept of the whole thing—and a chance to form a possibly valuable opinion. . . . Of course, if you don't feel like [it] at the moment, then don't send it along. But I am trying to support your sense of urgency as well as offer my own two cents worth."[19] Loesser added that he had spoken to Cy Feuer and Ernie Martin (who had produced Loesser's *Guys and Dolls* among several other hits) about it and they felt the expense of the project was prohibitive. It seems Loesser's message did the trick because Willson responded a few days later, promising to send "a corrected carbon" of the script that day (June 27).[20] Loesser's participation was vital: not only did he arrange with Wilson to go through "a lengthy array of notes" on the script when they planned to meet on August 2, 3, and 4 ("Like it says in the song, we will 'pick a little, talk a little.' Or maybe a whole lot."), he also oversaw discussions between Willson and the producer of the show, Ed Lester of the Light Opera Company of Los Angeles.[21]

Over the next two months there was back and forth between Willson, his agency William Morris, Loesser and his company, and Lester's organization.[22] On August 5, Loesser took great care to caution Willson in making his agreement with Lester: "Your intention is to arrive on Broadway with '1491', and nothing by way of your contracts with Lester or anyone else should be allowed to impede the show's progress toward a successful Broadway opening and a long run there."[23] These concerns were described by one of Loesser's colleagues on August 15 and included the necessity to limit Lester's participation in royalties for the show beyond the Broadway company; giving Willson control over the cast album, scenery, and designer; and making sure that the cast and production team should be available for a Broadway run. Ominously, the memo ended: "What provisions have been made in the event Ed Lester wants to close [the] show[?]"[24]

Loesser offered a further six pages of comments about the agreement on September 13, including clauses allowing Willson's estate (rather than Lester) to control the choice of someone else to take over writing material in the case of Willson's death before the show's opening.[25] He also remarked that Willson's requirement that his company Rinimer be awarded 10 percent of the profits of the show on top of Willson's large advance of $25,000 "may put a serious dent in any effort Lacloa [sic][26] may make in asking another producing organization to join it—and such a circumstance might critically affect the possibility of this show's arrival on Broadway. 'Get the money and run for the train' is not always the wisest policy."[27] Broadway is business, and Loesser's moves to protect his friend in a commercial sphere are impressive.[28]

Willson was grateful to Loesser for his intervention ("contents happily noted") and agreed with him about the "comparative unimportance of the $25,000 advance," ending with a report on his (recently sick) wife's health and that of *1491*: "Rini shows steady improvement; and so I believe do the prospects of our Number Four child [i.e., the show] for a birthday in the not too distant future."[29] All parties must have agreed terms quickly, for on October 5 the following was announced to the press:

> Meredith ("The Music Man") Willson's newest musical play for Broadway, "1491," will be produced in the 1967–68 season.
>
> "1491" deals with Christopher Columbus' crucial year before his discovery of America. It is set against various Spanish locations, including the court of Ferdinand and Isabella.
>
> Willson wrote book, music and lyrics for "1491" after two years of research on pertinent original sources in Spain, Italy, the Library of Congress and the University of California at Los Angeles.[30]
>
> The pre-Broadway premiere of Willson's fourth Broadway musical will be presented in Los Angeles by the Civic Light Opera Association, it is announced today by Edwin Lester, general director. His New York co-producers will be announced on completion of negotiations.
>
> Ed Ainsworth, reporter-editor for the Los Angeles Times and an authority on early Spanish America, is credited by Willson with concept assistance on "1491."
>
> Willson's interest was awakened when he discovered primary sources which disclosed that the true life of Columbus was more exciting than the familiar but generally false textbook character drawn by Washington Irving and other accepted school-room biographies.[31]

THE VOYAGE CONTINUES: PRODUCTION AND BOOK TROUBLES, 1967–1969

These documents demonstrate how Lester as the producer was viewed by Willson and his advisors as a business *adversary* before an agreement to produce the show was signed. It was no comment on Lester's abilities: since founding the Civic Light

Opera, he had overseen a number of successes that had gone on to Broadway, including *Song of Norway* (1944), *Kismet* (1953), and *Peter Pan* (1954). And once the agreement had been signed, Lester and Willson started to collaborate: the contract was the passport to shared goals and interests. A particularly insightful example of this process is a letter from Lester to Willson written on November 17, roughly a month after the show had been announced to the press. Willson had given Lester a copy of the script and the producer remarked, "As I felt when you first performed the material for Eleanor and me, you have all the ingredients for a very exciting show—the title, the idea, the new kind of Meredith Willson score, the new interpretation of a great page in history, the characters, the colorfulness of the local, [sic] etc."[32]

But Lester also had criticisms about the book, while admitting it had "greatly improved" since he last saw it, "and my enthusiasm for the property is genuinely high."[33] He felt that the love triangle between Columbus, Beatriz, and Isabella was the basic point of the plot and that because of "the enormous amount of research" Willson had done, he was perhaps "trying to get too much" into the show. He thought that Isabella's decision to send Columbus to face the Inquisition when he rejects her romantically was "a very unusual angle" and a highlight"; by contrast, he thought the conquest of the Moors was "a side-track" (he would later reverse his view on this). Similarly, he thought the business with Jacobini was a distraction and was further critical of a subplot in which King Ferdinand goes out into society under the guise of a peasant character called Tio Paco. Lester's letter ends: "The casting of Columbus is of course the No. 1 objective." Willson's reply, if he wrote one, is not in the Carmel papers.

Lester's concerns about the book would never go away and ultimately became the cause of significant disagreement when the show opened in preview, but perhaps Willson was initially convinced of their force because there is little evidence that either party truly expected the show to be staged in 1967. Instead, the main focus of that year was on the practical questions of casting and choice of director, which gave Willson plenty of time to do more work. In February 1967, Lester wired Willson to advise him to "see Julia Migenes . . . Enormously talented girl. Might be a possible Beatriz. May still be in 'Fiddler' where she played the daughter who goes to Siberia. Beautiful voice, excellent performer, not pretty but engaging."[34] Willson was on a trip to New York and a handwritten list at the bottom of the page mentions "Bob Preston"; the composer was interested in having the original Harold Hill play Columbus (strengthening the parallels between the characters as written by Willson).

John Raitt (original star of *Carousel* and *The Pajama Game*) was also mentioned. Raitt was a strong choice artistically but was rendered impossible according to Lester because "he has been spoiled by his summer stock salaries which he is naturally not worth to us in proscenium either in California or in New York."[35] A further possibility for Columbus was singer and actor Sergio Franchi, who seems to have turned Willson down in March 1969 after a couple of years of back and forth but was the favorite choice of the composer ("I'm still not giving up hope in writing a musical for you when you're 'rich and tired of Vegas,'" he wrote, addressing Franchi as "Dear 'Columbus'" in a letter).[36]

For Queen Isabella, Willson was especially keen on Elizabeth Allen (star of *Do I Hear a Waltz?* on Broadway, opposite Franchi) after seeing her in the play *Cactus Flower* on its post-Broadway tour in Chicago, with other possibilities including opera star Roberta Peters, Joan Diener (Aldonza in the original *Man of La Mancha*), and Patricia Morison (Lilli in the original Broadway *Kiss Me, Kate*). In the end, the role of Columbus went to John Cullum, familiar to the Broadway stage for his appearance as the lead in *On a Clear Day You Can See Forever* (1965), with Chita Rivera (Anita in the original *West Side Story*) as Beatriz and soprano Jean Fenn as Isabella. That Lester both sought and secured Broadway veterans for two of the lead roles shows he was seriously committed to the production's success.

Even more impressive was his pursuit of several distinguished directors. In a letter of September 12, 1967, on a different topic, Lester referred in passing to Rouben Mamoulian as the director as if he had been signed.[37] This must have been an exciting possibility indeed: Mamoulian's extraordinary career spanned major Broadway productions (the original stagings of *Porgy and Bess*, *Oklahoma!*, *Carousel*, and *Lost in the Stars*) and movie musicals (*Love Me Tonight*, *Summer Holiday*, and *Silk Stockings*). His work on culturally sensitive topics may have been seen as invaluable in navigating *1491*'s more problematic elements, and he seems like an obvious choice. But within days he must have been dropped or withdrawn, for the sources show Willson was being asked to consider Charles Walters as director just nine days later on September 21. Although Walters had a couple of stage credits to his name (Vernon Duke's *Banjo Eyes* and Cole Porter's *Let's Face It*), his profile was mainly as a major director at MGM: his formidable list of over a dozen musicals includes the classics *Easter Parade*, *Good News*, *The Barkleys of Broadway*, and *High Society*.

But what Willson really wanted was to work again with Morton Da Costa. As with his abortive attempts to interest Kermit Bloomgarden in producing the show, Willson felt a nostalgic pull toward the director of *The Music Man*: after painful experiences with the directors of both *Molly Brown* and *Here's Love*, he wanted someone he could trust at the helm. He was so keen, in fact, that even after Da Costa had turned the project down, Willson went back to him in October and asked him to reconsider (again without success).[38] The hunt went on for some time.

Meanwhile, Willson continued to work on the book for another year: in his papers at Carmel, there are further drafts dated December 10, 1967, and September 1968, with some pages dated April and May 1968. In this period, the title page of the script now included the credit: "Written for and with Rini Willson." Willson's second wife had died on December 6, 1966, following the illness mentioned in a previously cited letter. He married his secretary Rosemary Sullivan in February 1968 but for the time being continued to honor Rini in *1491*'s development. Similarly, inside the script, Ed Ainsworth continued to be credited with "concept assistance."[39] Collaboration was vital to Willson and it must have been both a personal and professional blow to him when Ainsworth too died unexpectedly on June 15, 1968, at the age of sixty-six.[40]

By the fall of 1968, it was clear that the book problems of *1491* needed support and yet another collaborator was brought in. A new version, titled "Revised First Draft," was dated December 5, 1968, and marked "Book by Meredith Willson and Ira Barmak." (Rini Willson and Ainsworth were no longer mentioned.) Presumably the intention was for Barmak to play an equivalent role to Franklin Lacey's support with the book of *The Music Man* late in its development, which had worked well for that show. The new draft is indeed markedly different, starting with the introduction of a framing device where a modern father and son in present-day New York take down a book about Columbus and discuss the mysteries surrounding his legacy; this sets up the mythical atmosphere of the show more explicitly. The racist aspects are considerably toned down, with just a brief mention of the Spanish attack at Granada, and there is now much more flow to the show from scene to scene (a transformation not dissimilar to that of Lacey's work on *The Music Man*). Barmak's previous work had mainly been as an actor in small parts in Hollywood films and he would later go on to write and direct movies, plays, and television shows, but he had little profile at the point of working on *1491*. Nevertheless, his work on the script seems effective.

His presence on the musical did little to ease the growing tensions between Lester and Willson. For example, there was a distinct tone in a letter of November 21 when Lester wrote: "While our telephone conversation of this morning is fresh in my mind, I do want to re-state my opinion on the Finale of Act I. I cannot understand why you are so enamored of what you had."[41] He also commented, "I hope we can soon find a director in whom we all have confidence since the overall styling becomes a directorial responsibility," highlighting how the lack of someone in that role was hindering progress. He ended with a sharp request for Willson to send a copy of Barmak's next draft: "The sooner the better for all of us." Clearly the producer and composer-librettist did not see eye to eye.

The tensions continued on November 22 when Willson wrote to Lester to disagree with him on the alleged weakness of the action immediately preceding the curtain at intermission (Willson had Columbus kiss Isabella, signaling that he had gained his way with her to obtain his ships; Barmak had the act end by Isabella revealing that she has set the Inquisition on Columbus in order to keep him in the palace). "I used the exact [same] breaking of the ice between Harold Hill and Marian the Librarian in the act curtain of THE MUSIC MAN, if you recall," Willson ended. Lester replied, "I think your analogy of Harold Hill and Marian the Librarian is not quite pertinent," pointing out that everyone enters the theater knowing the history of Columbus and Isabella.[42]

Lester wrote again at length on December 13, offering seven pages of thoughts on Barmak's version (the "Revised First Draft"). While some of these were persuasive—he was quite right to praise the "unvulgarizing" of Beatriz (which made her less exoticized)—others were wide of the mark, such as his view, "I have always felt that the Spain-Moor controversy should not be dropped" (which directly contradicts what he had previously said on this topic).[43] In fact, Barmak had done the show a huge service by almost completely removing reference to this topic and it is difficult to sympathize with Lester's opinion.

As the process drew out even longer, by January 1969 they had at least settled on a director with whom Willson was satisfied. It was noted earlier that Richard Morris, the book writer of *Molly Brown*, had previously been consulted about an early version of the script for *1491*, and a fragmentary document titled "A Look at Staging and Revision of Scenes and Characters in Meredith Willson's '1491'" (dated January 20, 1969) shows he was keen to bring more simplicity to the narrative thrust.[44] Indeed, it was agreed that Morris would not only direct the show but also revise the script, using Willson's material as the basis. Morris's co-authorship was credited in the playbill[45] and the extent of his contribution is confirmed by numerous other documents. These include: a letter of February 26 in which Willson refers to "Dick's writing pre-occupation";[46] a page of notes on phone conversations related to *1491* from May, including reference to "Dick's present draft" and "a big improvement in this draft compared to Dick's original";[47] and a letter of July 5 from Morris to Willson, in which he agrees "we all have been working apart to [*sic*] much of the time" and remarks, "Ed set up a meeting for me to go over these pink pages on Sat. . . . They need a lot of cutting but I always over write."[48] Morris was now the primary force on the musical; it was his version of the book that was used in rehearsal and he was the director.

Morris's presence was explicitly Willson's idea: if he couldn't have the producer or director of *The Music Man*, perhaps the book writer of *Molly Brown* was the next best thing. But even this did not calm relations between him and Lester. The latter wrote a frank letter to him on May 6, 1969, beginning: "I am genuinely disturbed by your feeling of dissatisfaction with Dick Morris' book revision as you have indicated it to me in recent conversations."[49] From Lester's point of view, Willson was being stubborn in his desire to stick to his original ideas about the show and the producer said he was frustrated because "I engaged Dick at your behest." Yet it was too late for recriminations. Rehearsals were due to begin on July 21 at the Dorothy Chandler Pavilion in Los Angeles and move to the Pasadena Civic Auditorium in the second week of August ahead of *1491*'s opening at the Los Angeles Music Center on September 2.

MUSIC FOR AN OCEAN VOYAGE

When Edwin Lester listed what he saw as the assets of *1491* in his letter of November 17, 1966, after first signing on as producer, he referred to a "new kind of Meredith Willson score"[50] (albeit without elaborating on what that meant). Just under three years later, when the show had opened in Pasadena and was struggling, Lester wrote the following to the composer: "There is still room for improvement in 'Sail On', particularly since this has now become the theme song of the show and should be as typically Meredith Willson as a march can be."[51] Having originally praised its novelty, Lester now wanted the score to be more conventional; this tension was familiar from reactions to Willson's previous two musicals and must have frustrated him. But in the case of *1491* it is evident from hearing the piece that he had tried to write something distinctive, and while there are moments where his musical hallmarks are audible, most of the score represents a fresh approach to a fresh topic.

Admittedly, as already noted, some of this novelty is at the service of exoticizing the locale and characters, but arguably to no greater extent than the score of *West Side Story*. Indeed, in the dance music to "Tio Paco," the number in Act 1 during which King Ferdinand goes out into society in the disguise of a mythical peasant, the huapango style of one passage (Fig. 7.1) almost seems like a direct reference to Bernstein's "America." From the start of the Overture, Willson signals the setting of the show through a distinct musical tinta consisting of syncopated rhythms, triplet figures, series of consecutive major triads, and repetitions of figures with chromatic alterations. We are supposed to be in another place at another time, and even allowing for a critique of this as a process of othering, Willson's score is arguably a more richly beautiful attempt at using Hispanic markers than, say, Mitch Leigh's much more popularly successful score for *Man of La Mancha*. Ironically, Willson himself claimed that none of the music was particularly Spanish—"I figure Bizet wrote Spanish music to end all Spanish music. I'm not about to take those rhythms on."[52]—but that is not really supported by the score, which frequently uses such rhythms.

One of the defining features of the score is a freedom of melodic form that seems an attempt to suggest spontaneity—Willson's contribution to the development of how song and drama go together in music theater writing. He had previously explored this in specific examples such as "My White Knight" (*The Music Man*) and "Johnny's Soliloquy" (*The Unsinkable Molly Brown*), but rather than isolated episodes in the previous shows, here Willson makes it part of the fabric of the musical. Even out of context, the three snippets of three numbers in Fig. 7.2a–c give a clear indication of how Willson was setting words to music in a more fluid, operatic way, rather than relying on 32-bar commercial song models (or variations of them). This complements the richness of the harmonic language and vocal demands, particularly on the actors playing Isabella and Columbus. Jean Fenn (who played Isabella), of course, was an opera singer; Sergio Franchi, whom Willson wanted for Columbus, trained as a tenor and appeared in several operatic productions, so although the character was in the end played by the less

Fig. 7.1. *"Tio Paco," dance break, mm. 194–197.*

(a)

Fig. 7.2a. *"I'll Never Say I Love You,"* opening.

(b)

Fig. 7.2b. *"The Trastamara Rose,"* mm. 21–24.

(c)

Fig. 7.2c. *"The Queen and the Sailor,"* mm. 104–109.

vocally accomplished John Cullum, it is obvious that Willson's ambitions were for the score to be more "highbrow" than his previous musicals. He wanted to show what he could do and perhaps to write against the rock/pop grain of the times (e.g., *Hair* and Burt Bacharach's *Promises, Promises*). No doubt this is what Lester meant as a new kind of Meredith Willson score.

On the other hand, *1491* by no means presents as an opera and the operatic flavor of numbers such as Isabella's "Now I Know" and "Birthday" is countered by the Broadway flair of several of the numbers for Columbus and Beatriz, both individually and in duet. There is no doubt that Columbus requires a more legitimate vocal ability than Harold Hill (hence Willson thought of Franchi), but he conveys a similar personality in Willson's rendering. This is communicated through musical gesture too. His opening number "Get a Map" is a patter song incredibly similar to "Ya Got Trouble" in intent—a fast-paced salesman's pitch—but with a wide melodic range, going up to a high G. It is a terrific opening number that offers the people in the town square the opportunity to get away from their humdrum lives if they buy Columbus's map (Fig. 7.3).

Continuing the structural analogy to *The Music Man*, Columbus has a second number later in the first act that begins with a patter section and also acts as a selling tool in music, but this time in the form of a march—just as Willson had done with "Seventy-Six Trombones" in the same spot in *The Music Man*. Oddly,

Fig. 7.3. "Get a Map," mm. 7–14.

"For My Glory Land" also sounds like a patriotic American march in its opening section, rather too "Fourth of July" for the context (in which Columbus is trying to persuade the Spanish monarchs to invest in his ships), but then employs a dotted-quarter-note motif to suggest a Spanish rhythm. Perhaps Willson was under pressure from Lester to make reference to his *Music Man* score for commercial reasons, but whatever the motivation, it does not always contribute to a coherent whole (even though it is rousing).

The casting of Chita Rivera must have been an exciting opportunity for Willson, knowing that she could deliver a truly dramatic performance. The most obvious vehicle for her talents was a song from Act 2 called "Why Not?" in which Beatriz considers moving on from Columbus after having been faithful to him for years. "And if anyone's thinking of offering me any advice on how to be conscience free," she declares, "Just forget it—it has to be my turn now." Matching this strong sense of empowerment, the music is in fast cut common time and modulates several times in order to convey Beatriz's growing feeling of strength;

Willson also uses orchestral tacets (silences) to allow Beatriz's (Rivera's) voice to be heard boldly on important lines (e.g., "it has to be my turn now").

Beatriz's main number in Act 1, "What Does a Queen Have?," offers a different kind of theatrical experience. She asks what a queen has that she doesn't have and the musical setting is in a courtly 6/8; she tries to inhabit a regal musical setting while singing about how class blocks her from being royal. Cleverly, the analogue to this number is a solo of Isabella's, "Woman," a haunting ballad in which she talks about the woman underneath the regal garments: the opposite of Beatriz's predicament but an idea that unifies their situations.

During the course of the three-month run on the West Coast, the score changed regularly—so much so that it is unclear from the sources what the exact song list was at any point. The Carmel collection contains the bones of a piano-conductor score but it is loose and has had numbers added, edited, annotated numerous times, and moved to new positions. There is also a complete live recording in the Carmel collection of an undated performance, in which the applause is enthusiastic after almost every number as well as at the first unveiling of Oliver Smith's lavish set for the palace (the *My Fair Lady* designer's work was one of the production's strengths); this recording contains a number of changes compared to the Carmel piano-conductor score. Table 7.1 reflects the song list on the recording, but the confrontational correspondence between Lester and Willson after the opening reveals that new material was going in and out all the time—so much so that at one point, the musical director Julian Stein wrote a few lines of a new verse to "Get a Map" in Willson's absence, at Lester's request. This directly contravened the contractual agreement that Loesser had been at pains to put in place more than three years earlier.

But Willson's great mentor had died suddenly at the end of July 1969, a third major bereavement during the course of bringing *1491* to the stage, and although Willson objected to the use of Stein's material (indeed, he heard a rumor that Stein's wife had actually written the lines and Willson raised this with Lester), he did not much resist it beyond continuing to disagree with the producer's views on how to improve the show. At a certain point, with Richard Morris coming down with gout and Willson suffering from a throat infection, all involved must have realized that *1491* was a sinking ship. There was one small grace, however: Willson finally saw "The Wonderful Plan," a trunk song from *The Music Man* that he had tried to use in *Molly Brown* and *Here's Love*, appear on the stage. Challenged by the Inquisition to explain his view of the universe, Columbus responded with a revamped version of this favorite piece of Willson's, which had been repurposed to bring out its lyrical quality and almost entirely erase its rhythmic bounce.

SETTING SAIL

The *Daily News* reported on September 4, 1969, that *1491* had opened two nights earlier "to cheers from the audience and some reservations from the critics," also

Table 7.1. List of Musical Numbers according to live recording of the show, GASF.

Act 1	Notes	Act 2	Notes
Overture (orchestra)		Entr'acte (orchestra)	
Opening: Villetta (orchestra)	In some versions, the show opened with "Sail On" (Columbus).	The Wonderful Plan (Columbus, Esteban and Ensemble)	
I'll Never Say I Love You (Columbus)	Originally, "Pretty Girls" (Columbus) was heard here.	Genius (Esteban, Columbus and ensemble)	
Get a Map (Christopher)		Now I Know (Columbus)	Not in the show on opening night.
What Does a Queen Have? (Beatriz)	A piano-vocal score at Juilliard has "Woman" here.	Why Not? (Beatriz)	A piano-conductor score at Juilliard has "Lady" here.
Birthday (Isabella)	Originally, "Silken Song" (Isabella) appeared here.	Near but Never Too Near (Beatriz and Columbus)	
The Rose of Trastamara (Esteban)		Reprise: Where There's a River (Beatriz and girls)	
Court March (Orchestra)		Finale: Lash the Wheel (Columbus and men)	
I Did Steal the D'Amico Map/ For My Glory Land (Columbus and men)			
Where There's a River (Beatriz and Girls)			

Continued

Table 7.1. Continued

Act 1	Notes	Act 2	Notes
Woman (Isabella)			
Reprise: I'll Never Say I Love You (Columbus)			
Tio Paco (Ferdinand)			
The Queen and the Sailor (Columbus and Isabella)	A piano-conductor score at Juilliard has "Sail On" (reprise) here.		

noting that the production had cost $600,000.[53] Unfortunately, it was an understatement to say that the critics had "some reservations." In truth, the responses were mainly savage, despite some acknowledgment of the ability of the people involved.

Charles Faber's review for the *Hollywood Citizen-News* included the following: "Meredith Willson may find as little ultimate satisfaction in his 'discovery' of Columbus as the Admiral of the Ocean Sea found in the trials and tribulations he endured subsequent to putting most of the New World in Spain's pocket. . . . Mr. Willson's multiple talents and his dedication to entertainment above today's generally sordid level, cannot but leave the initially hopeful spectator with a sense of deep regret that the musical, striking as it now and again is, falls so far short of the original inspiration. The Los Angeles Civic Light Opera's production is almost too striking for the musical's own good, although it should be noted that Tuesday's opening night audience at the Pavilion, demonstrating the Los Angeles hang-up on elaborate scenery, was completely entranced as Oliver Smith's settings kept separating and reassembling themselves like one gorgeous arabesque of a giant jig-saw puzzle."[54] More bluntly, Dan Sullivan remarked in the *Los Angeles Times*: "Meredith Willson's new musical about Columbus doesn't work. Not because it is hokum (hokum can be fun), but because it is dull hokum," adding that "it is made of lead."[55] One line in his review reads: "What, one may legitimately ask, the hell???"

No better was the review from the *Los Angeles Herald-Examiner*, headed "Desperate Situation in '1491'" and calling it "desperately sincere, desperately self-important, and desperately inept."[56] More sympathetic in tone was Donald Freeman's review for the *San Diego Union*. If his overall assessment of the show came down to the same point—"great talent doesn't always necessarily create great works"[57]—he was more nuanced in his appraisal: "'1491' is [not] the disaster you may have heard. Less than first-rate Willson all the way, yes, but it's not all that woeful. Overall, Willson's music snaps at the ear with his characteristic strength and subtlety and the kind of solidarity of form and content that is rare in musicals."

Freeman's praise for Willson's score continued: "His speak-songs (which must be heard to be effective and they aren't always [heard]) have a crackling ginger, particularly one called 'Get a Map,' which was originally to have opened the show and would have helped beyond measure in that spot. One of his duets, 'The Queen and the Sailor,' has wit and verve. His love songs breathe a typically sweet, deceptive simplicity." Intriguingly, he ended: "What next for '1491'? If Mr. Willson can once again see Columbus plain as he saw him first, if he can remember how it was before the project grew muddy and complicated with other voices, if he can listen only to his own singular vision, then, perhaps, it will still work. Perhaps."

By this, the reviewer seems to imply that 1491 went awry when Willson started to collaborate with others—a view that he himself, in the unusual triple role of composer-lyricist-[co-]book writer, might well agree with. The friction between him and Lester had now become greater than ever. For example, on September 10 Lester admonished Willson for referring to Los Angeles as "New Haven" in an interview with the press—that is, implying that the production was a pre-Broadway tryout before transferring to New York—because "Anything we can do to get people coming to the show with an open mind is going to be enormously helpful. Apologies would serve to increase audience resentment. We have not trained our subscription audience to be guinea pigs for New York."[58]

During the next week, Morris, Willson, and Lester started to agree to make some changes. On September 19, Lester wrote a five-page outline of modifications they had discussed, including: a new opening to the first palace scene; cutting the length of the second scene extensively, most notably the song "Pretty Girls"; moving "I'll Never Say I Love You" to a different scene; the addition of an explanatory verse to "Get a Map"; and numerous cuts to dialogue throughout, as well as requests for several new numbers from Willson. More positively, Lester believed there to be genuine assets to the show, including "a good measure of surprise and theatrical magic" in the flow from one scene to the next, a strong cast, and good songs.[59]

That letter gives the first hint of something that would be a problem throughout the next two (final) months: collaboration was happening via letter but this was being used as a method to *avoid* rather than facilitate interaction. Five days later, Lester wrote again, claiming not to have "had any response . . . except [Willson's] complaint that the last scene isn't the same as [he] wrote it five years ago."[60] As before, Lester went on to outline changes and demands, concluding: "Since you have the biggest stake in '1491', your contribution is of course the main one." He also revealed that he was "holding off some New York Theatre men from coming out to see the show until we have gone further in cleaning it up."

Tensions escalated in October. A series of notes from telephone conversations between Willson's secretary and the production team show Willson had left Los Angeles for a few days in Arizona "to get rid of [a] throat condition" and Lester kept phoning to find out where he was ("E.L. says lot of work to be done on show").[61] Willson then sat through the matinee on October 18 and made extensive notes,

many of them scathing: "Dialogue in first scene very strange, completely unnat-
ural, self-consciously expositional"; "can't recognize dialogue at all, don't believe
it"; "so dull and unbecoming this historic moment"; and so on. Ironically, after
Willson had made lots of suggestions and re-engaged with the show's problems,
Lester responded: "Because we are trying to get the show in as good condition
as we can for the San Francisco opening and because Dick [Morris] has been out
sick so far this week, an extra burden of checking shows has fallen largely on me.
Consequently, as I wrote you, I do not have the time to answer both your letter
of October 21 and now the one of October 22 in the detail that they deserve."[62]
No doubt Willson felt he could never make the producer happy; and in his turn,
Lester must have been desperately looking at his investment and realizing that
1491 was sinking (he reported that "We have the poorest advance sale [in San
Francisco] in the entire history of our operation").

Nonetheless, when the show closed in Los Angeles on October 25 (marking
the end of the Civic Light Opera season), the *Los Angeles Times* noted that *1491*
had played to an unusually large capacity of 250,000 audience members over its
six-week run; the same paper's scathing review had not prevented people from
coming to see the world premiere of the *Music Man* writer's new work.[63] It next
moved to the Curran Theater in San Francisco. There is no further correspondence in the Carmel collection about the show and only one review from the brief
San Francisco run, in the *San Francisco Chronicle*: "It is a resolutely old-fashioned
musical, written by Meredith Willson with an assist from Richard Morris who
directed it. . . . But however grandly mounted, life, wit, and the delight of theatrical surprise are not to be found in '1491.'"[64]

THE FINAL DECADE

With the closure of *1491* out of town, Willson's career in the musical theater was
over. Yet as Henry Moore famously remarked, "There's no retirement for an artist,
it's your way of living so there's no end to it." To create would always be an important impulse for Willson and over the next few years he considered several ideas
for new projects. In 1971, for example, he explored Irving Stone's fictionalized
biography *Jack London: Sailor on Horseback* (1938), as the possible basis for a musical adaptation. Quite why Willson thought the life of a novelist (*White Fang*, *The
Call of the Wild*) would make a convincing musical is unclear but perhaps he was
attracted by Stone's heavily embroidered account of a passionate artist in pursuit
of his personal vision. All that seems to remain of the attempt is two pages of
handwritten notes, which have been transcribed into typewritten form, dated
October 15, 1971.[65] Since they consist of just a few lines of text, it is difficult to
make much sense of them.[66]

Another fragment of an aborted project is a two-page outline of a show called
Katrina. Willson biographer Bill Oates suggests the composer spent time on it in
1964 (just before he started work on *1491*)[67] and he may be right since the outline

is undated; it is also possible that he resumed work on the idea after the closure of *1491*, since the paper and typeface are more typical of his later correspondence. The titular heroine is based on his second wife Rini (born Ralina) and her exploits as an operatic soprano. The outline is incredibly thin in content: in the first scene Katrina fights with the conductor, who is called Richard but is obviously based on Willson; the rest of the first act is a flashback recounting Richard's ascent from radio conductor to Broadway composer; and Act 2 relates the bumpy road to putting on a musical about his hometown, Maple Hill.

While this may seem so absurdly autobiographical that it cannot be sincere, we should also note that Willson started writing his fourth memoir in the early 1970s, *More Eggs I Have Laid*, drafts of which (dated 1972–1974) reside in the Carmel collection. After the failure of his ambitious and novel *1491*, he reverted to this nostalgic project about his past glories; although substantial in length, it is unpublished.

There were two other musical projects on the horizon too. In August 1973, he met with writers Jerome Lawrence and Robert E. Lee to discuss a possible adaptation of their play of the previous year, *Jabberwock*, inspired by the childhood of author and cartoonist James Thurber.[68] There is a transcription of the meeting in which they talked about the possibilities; it was at least the second time Willson had discussed writing a musical with them, following on from their brief involvement with *The Music Man* in 1955. The model of the project also followed on logically from Lawrence and Lee's previous work: they had adapted their play *Auntie Mame* (1958) into the musical *Mame* (1966) with great success and must have hoped for a similar trajectory with *Jabberwock*.

They saw Mary Martin as a likely star for the role of Mary Agnes and suggested Kermit Bloomgarden as producer and Morton Da Costa as director. The last two figures played into Willson's nostalgic mood to reassemble the main team behind *The Music Man* and it is no wonder he was tempted by Lawrence and Lee's suggestions. But once more, the idea seems to have gone no further; perhaps the stress of *1491* cast too long a shadow.

Through all of this, one last idea kept cropping up for Willson's consideration, and by this he seemed seriously tempted. On Saturday November 13, 1971, the *Los Angeles Times* published its regular Dennis the Menace cartoon. It showed Dennis at a library desk with a pair of scissors and the caption read: "Where are the picture books?" The librarian's name card read "Miss Marion" [*sic*] in an homage to Willson by the cartoonist Hank Ketcham. Willson was so delighted by it that he wrote to Ketcham: "Thanks for the 'Marian the Librarian' plug. Our breakfast is always thin rye toast, banana-and-bacon, coffee and Ketcham."[69]

This began a series of exchanges in which Ketcham pursued a collaboration on a *Dennis the Menace* musical.[70] They met in January 1972 to talk about it[71] and there were further discussions via letter over the next year or so. Willson was keen but did not feel he could commit without seeing an outline: this time there was no question of him writing the book.[72] In his turn, Ketcham struggled to work out how to make a children's comic strip effective on the stage; notwithstanding models such as *You're a Good Man, Charlie Brown* (1967) and later *Snoopy*

(1975), it was not a straightforward venture. By December 1972, Ketcham's solution was: "Perhaps we SHOULD [sic] put it on film and call it THE MUSIC KID."[73] Once more, the focus was on an allusion to Willson's past success.

A gap in the correspondence suggests there was a three-year hiatus in the process. There then appears a new cartoon strip dated October 10, 1976, based on an outline titled *The Music Kid* by Bob Saylor, Ketcham's chief comic-strip writer.[74] The story is about Dennis's plans to be a music man when he grows up, inspired by his trombone; but he is told that it is actually a toy trumpet. The last caption reads: "Never mind, Dennis. All Meredith Willson had was a piccolo."[75] The strip seems to have been a deliberate ploy to re-engage Willson's attention, for he wrote in delight to thank Ketcham,[76] who then replied with a new suggestion that Willson should write the songs for a new TV series based on Dennis: "Perhaps my day dreaming is getting out of hand but what could be more representative of middle America than Mason City and DENNIS THE MENACE."[77] But apart from a further approach from Ketcham in 1979 in relation to a possible *Dennis* stage musical, the project fizzled out—and with it, Willson's activities in musical theater came to a quiet end.

CONCLUSION: *THE MUSIC MAN*'S MEREDITH WILLSON

In an interview from 1977, Willson told the journalist Charlie Huisking of the *Herald-Tribune* that "It was easy to come up with the idea for 'The Music Man' because it really happened. . . . A fellow came to my home town—Mason City, Iowa—selling band instruments. He was having trouble selling them, so he promised he'd teach the kids to play. There were salesmen like that travelling all over the Middle West in my youth. . . . This was a little more daring than most though. He actually set up a rehearsal in the gym. Well, of course he didn't know a bass drum from a pipe organ, so he started telling jokes. When that wore a little thin, he just sneaked out the door and ran out of town."[78] The title of the article was "Writer Says 'The Music Man' Is a True Story.'"

This revision of the genesis of *The Music Man* from late in his career typifies an inexorable trend that Willson could not resist. His life had been spectacular, embracing the highest levels of the entertainment industry; he had accumulated wealth, knowledge, and respect. Yet the problem identified by Frank Loesser in the letter quoted earlier in this chapter had started to overwhelm him by the end: because he didn't have a substantial body of works, his legacy was limited. The result was that instead of Meredith Willson's *The Music Man* simply being his most successful musical, Willson almost started to embody *The Music Man*—not the character of Harold Hill but the show as a whole. The interview above is a good example of this process: twenty years after the show's premiere on Broadway, Willson was telling new stories about its writing that made it seem more than ever like the plot simply emanated naturally from his biography. Yet we know from Chapters 2 and 3 that the direct process of transferring his life to the musical stage that he describes here is simply not true; it even sounds like a yarn.

Such was the dominance of this musical on his career that the show had started to shape the way he told stories about his life. That is not to say that it was unusual for traveling salesmen to visit homes in the Midwest at the time of Willson's childhood—far from it—but the way he says "it really happened" in this interview is symptomatic of a reframing of his career in the final decade of his life. It was a long time since he had enjoyed significant success, so Meredith Willson had started to become what he is today, little more than the figure behind *The Music Man*. Therefore, he found value in putting himself in the show when asked about his life, as if to say "I am *The Music Man*": now he wanted people to read his life through his work, but only through this one *specific* work.

This is, of course, a mythologization of an often-brilliant career, but perhaps it was inevitable, given how diffuse Willson's activities were. It is not easy to find coherence in the idea that the same man played Stravinsky premieres under the auspices of the New York Philharmonic, became a radio personality on *The Burns and Allen Show*, and wrote a chocolate-box musical based on *Miracle on 34th Street*. Willson had what we would call today a portfolio career, and its separate parts, from the army to the San Francisco Symphony Orchestra, from radio to Broadway, and from *The Great Dictator* to the Sousa band, do not add up to a conventional whole that can easily be packaged and understood. Even Bernstein, who had a similarly diverse career, is easier to engage with because he spent most of his time playing, conducting, writing, broadcasting about, or teaching classical music: we know what that means. Willson's career lacks that kind of hook, which is perhaps why his indisputable hit *The Music Man* came to be more personal to him over time—a label he could be proud of and which could give him status even if it meant diminishing the rest.

But we have seen that *The Music Man* is much more interesting in the context of his overall contribution to musical theater and that his pre-Broadway activities provide the richest way to understand that work. All four musicals engage with North American myths, whether about the small town, the Wild West, Santa Claus, or Columbus's voyage to the Americas. And the scores of all four are products of his rich life as a versatile musician. Willson's Broadway legacy may never transcend *The Music Man*, but with that universally appealing work due to return to Broadway in 2022 we can at least acknowledge the wider career and achievements of the man behind it.

NOTES

• • •

CHAPTER 1: SEEKING THE ROOTS OF *THE MUSIC MAN*

1. Meredith Willson, *And There I Stood with My Piccolo* (Minneapolis and London: University of Minnesota Press, 2009), 11–12.
2. Willson, *Piccolo*, 13–14.
3. Ibid., 16.
4. Ibid., 19.
5. Ibid., 16 and 18. In Helen Ristau's pamphlet on Willson's time in River City, based on recollections of his friends and acquaintances, his classmate Ralph Shepherd confirms that "His number one ambition was to play in the famous John Philip Sousa's marching band." See Helen Ristau, *Meredith Willson: River City's Music Man* (Mason City, Iowa: Larson Printing, 1995), v.
6. Willson, *Piccolo*, 19.
7. Meredith Willson, quoted in *Time* magazine, December 30, 1957.
8. For a useful analysis of Willson's relationship to Mason City, see Anna Thompson Hajdik's "'Right Here in Mason City': Meredith Willson and Musical Memory in the American Midwest," in Seth C. Bruggeman (ed.), *Born in the USA: Birth, Commemoration, and American Public Memory* (Amherst and Boston: University of Massachusetts Press, 2012), 175-193.
9. Most has explored the impact of Jewish immigrants on American culture at length, especially in two monographs: *Making Americans: Jews and the Broadway Musical* (Cambridge, MA: Harvard University Press, 2004), and *Theatrical Liberalism: Jews and Popular Entertainment in America* (New York and London: New York University Press, 2013).
10. Charles Hamm's contributions to the literature in this area include his book *Irving Berlin: Songs from the Melting Pot, 1907–14* (New York and Oxford: Oxford University Press, 1997).
11. The song can be heard on the Decca Broadway release of the cast album of the show, originally recorded on May 31, 1964, now available on CD (Decca 000021502). "Lila Tremaine" is track 9.
12. Alisa Solomon, *Wonder of Wonders: A Cultural History of "Fiddler on the Roof"* (New York: Picador, 2014).
13. Meredith Willson, *Eggs I Have Laid* (New York: Henry Holt and Company, 1955), 37.
14. Willson, *Eggs*, 41.
15. John C. Skipper, *Meredith Willson: The Unsinkable Music Man* (Mason City, IA: Savas Publishing Company, 2000), 4–5.
16. See correspondence between Dixie Willson and Allen Wallen, 1958–59 in the Willson papers at The Great American Songbook Foundation, Carmel, Indiana (hereafter GASF); this is discussed more specifically later.
17. See GASF, box 5, folder 32.

18. The complete letter is reproduced in Skipper, *Meredith Willson*, 40–45. A copy is found and was examined in GASF, box 42, folder 4.

19. Ibid.

20. Skipper quotes a 1970 interview in the *Washington Star* in which Willson states: "My mother and father already had a son and daughter, Cedric and Dixie. They were the apple of my father's eye. He was angry when my mother told him I was on the way. From that time on, my father never spoke directly to my mother by name and never in my lifetime did I hear my name pass through my father's lips." Quoted in Skipper, 46.

21. GASF, box 2, folder 27. Many thanks to Lisa Lobdell for the transcription of this letter.

22. Willson, *Piccolo*, 44–45.

23. Ibid., 64.

24. Ibid., 125.

25. Ibid., 19.

26. Ibid., 25.

27. Ibid., 72–73.

28. Ibid., 78.

29. Ibid., 78–79.

30. Ibid., 123.

31. Valerie A. Austin, *The Orchestral Works of Meredith Willson*, dissertation, University of Florida, 2008. Austin discusses Willson's early musical training at 48–51.

32. Willson, *Piccolo*, 18.

33. "Meredith Willson," biography, on reverse of piano arrangement of Meredith Willson, *O. O. McIntyre Suite* (New York: Robbins Music Corporation, 1934).

34. Ibid.

35. Austin, *Orchestral Works*, 52.

36. See ibid., 55–56.

37. Willson describes this experience in *Piccolo*, 30–31.

38. "Meredith Willson," biography, on reverse of piano arrangement of Willson, *O.O. McIntyre Suite*.

39. See https://www.law.cornell.edu/uscode/text/36/304 (accessed September 26, 2018).

40. *Piccolo*, 34–35.

41. See Bill Oates, *Meredith Willson—America's Music Man* (Bloomington, IN: AuthorHouse, 2005), 26.

42. Willson mentions a disastrous performance of *Sorcerer's Apprentice* in *Piccolo*, 41.

43. *Piccolo*, 42. More on Willson's time in Sousa's band is discussed in Ramon da Silva Moraes, "The Flutists of the John Philip Sousa's Band: A Study of the Flute Section and Soloists," doctoral dissertation, University of Southern Mississippi, May 2018 (ProQuest 10786479).

44. The New York Philharmonic's digital archives are rich with information about its history, including facsimiles of numerous concert programs. The archives can be accessed at https://archives.nyphil.org/.

45. The program can be viewed at https://archives.nyphil.org/index.php/artifact/dc7f1ea1-0074-4f40-a2a8-7a4964be50ae-0.1/fullview#page/1/mode/2up (accessed September 27, 2018).

46. The program is reproduced at https://archives.nyphil.org/index.php/artifact/7432c824-0677-4092-a7a7-3b5ec5a797b5-0.1/fullview#page/1/mode/2up (accessed September 26, 2018).

47. The concerts took place on January 22 and 23, 1925. Program at https://archives.nyphil.org/index.php/artifact/d421c690-50d6-4d40-8d64-4f31369e54a9-0.1/fullview#page/1/mode/2up (accessed September 26, 2018).

48. https://archives.nyphil.org/index.php/artifact/778360d3-6a8b-4a34-8852-de4978709d48-0.1/fullview#page/2/mode/2up (accessed September 26, 2018).

49. April 2 and 3, 1925. Program available at: https://archives.nyphil.org/index.php/artifact/76d32c80-f923-4bc2-a7f1-1b7d0ca41e5f-0.1/fullview#page/1/mode/2up (accessed September 26, 2018).

50. Oates, *Meredith Willson*, 35.

51. October 15 and 16, 1925: see https://archives.nyphil.org/index.php/artifact/46b34699-9846-47c0-bab8-e13de457a299-0.1/fullview#page/1/mode/2up (accessed September 26, 2018).

52. See the program at https://archives.nyphil.org/index.php/artifact/d9967766-2d07-4caf-a032-62d8115b5437-0.1/fullview#page/1/mode/2up (accessed September 26, 2018).

53. See the program at https://archives.nyphil.org/index.php/artifact/c1d2ae86-d0cf-4c95-8aa8-15db03a99d66-0.1/fullview#page/1/mode/2up (accessed September 26, 2018).

54. See the program at https://archives.nyphil.org/index.php/artifact/d558da22-e561-412a-819b-4a1cbe4650c1-0.1/fullview#page/1/mode/2up (accessed September 26, 2018).

55. See the program at https://archives.nyphil.org/index.php/artifact/6058f6f3-52e0-4a96-907c-ec038abb8244-0.1/fullview#page/1/mode/2up (accessed September 26, 2018).

56. See the program at https://archives.nyphil.org/index.php/artifact/48d8e4ac-26f8-4d01-825d-782ced816a28-0.1/fullview#page/1/mode/2up (accessed September 26, 2018).

57. See the program at https://archives.nyphil.org/index.php/artifact/7eac003d-e17a-4cc7-aeda-f52d4d123a03-0.1/fullview#page/1/mode/2up (accessed September 26, 2018).

58. See the programs at https://archives.nyphil.org/index.php/artifact/33b74135-e4b1-4ffe-9cb7-6a893836111a-0.1/fullview#page/1/mode/2up and https://archives.nyphil.org/index.php/artifact/d6ec5a7e-5bc0-4dc1-8509-c40db6318f3b-0.1/fullview#page/1/mode/2up (accessed September 26, 2018).

59. See the program at https://archives.nyphil.org/index.php/artifact/cdb18d98-502f-4a7b-9ee3-e6d3a9672917-0.1/fullview#page/1/mode/2up (accessed September 26, 2018).

60. See the program at https://archives.nyphil.org/index.php/artifact/77bad824-a7ae-420c-9df4-12bb9ed85ed4-0.1/fullview#page/1/mode/2up (accessed September 26, 2018).

61. See the program at https://archives.nyphil.org/index.php/artifact/37cddad4-e9d1-44bc-901b-269526555405-0.1/fullview#page/1/mode/2up (accessed September 26, 2018).

62. The program was performed with minor changes on January 26, 27, 29, 30, 31, and February 1; see https://archives.nyphil.org/index.php/artifact/9fbbb935-1afe-45ce-b6be-75b016cdf61f-0.1/fullview#page/34/mode/2up for the programs (accessed September 26, 2018).

63. See the program at https://archives.nyphil.org/index.php/artifact/bb0957c1-39f0-4d0a-b62f-dcd94cfa948b-0.1/fullview#page/1/mode/2up (accessed September 26, 2018).

64. See the program at https://archives.nyphil.org/index.php/artifact/1a65f079-a24c-44d9-acbd-65621430d3f7-0.1/fullview#page/1/mode/2up (accessed September 26, 2018).

65. See the program at https://archives.nyphil.org/index.php/artifact/2a7ff12e-19b5-4341-9c8b-a4bb236f5048-0.1/fullview#page/1/mode/2up (accessed September 26, 2018).

66. See the program at https://archives.nyphil.org/index.php/artifact/11c68780-e95a-48e9-9af5-4e4451d79566-0.1/fullview#page/1/mode/2up (accessed September 26, 2018).

67. See the program at https://archives.nyphil.org/index.php/artifact/11c68780-e95a-48e9-9af5-4e4451d79566-0.1/fullview#page/1/mode/2up (accessed on September 26, 2018).

68. See https://archives.nyphil.org/index.php/artifact/1ccf47cc-ded6-4f4c-b3db-303502c76151-0.1 (accessed on September 26, 2018).

69. See the program at https://archives.nyphil.org/index.php/artifact/dfa7e783-1510-4111-8ae8-d66d26f7854e-0.1/fullview#page/1/mode/2up (accessed on September 26, 2018).

70. *Piccolo*, 114.

71. See *Piccolo*, 117, Oates, 42, and Skipper, 52, for more information.

72. The column reads: "Christmas and New Year Greetings with Very Best Wishes from Meredith Willson, Concert Director." See http://www.sfmuseum.org/hist/willson2.html (accessed October 11, 2018).

73. *Piccolo*, 135.

74. Photographs of his NBC years can be seen at http://www.theradiohistorian.org/carnvl37.htm (accessed October 11, 2018).

75. Willson recounts a humorous story about him in *Piccolo*, 130–31.

76. See *Piccolo*, 139.

77. For more details, see Jim Cox, *Sold on Radio: Advertisers in the Golden Age of Broadcasting* (Jefferson, NC: McFarland, 2008), 255.

78. See https://www.oldtimeradiodownloads.com/variety/carefree-carnival to download the episode (accessed October 11, 2018).

79. Broadcast details from John Dunning, *On the Air*, 455.

80. An episode from 1938, featuring Mary Martin, Frank Morgan, and Fanny Brice, can be heard online: http://www.jimramsburg.com/uploads/1/0/7/4/10748369/good_news___6-16-38.mp3 (accessed October 12, 2018). Willson is heard speaking at several points.

81. The script can be viewed at USC's Cinematic Arts Library, in the MGM Radio Script Collection (box 1). My sincere thanks to Ned Comstock for drawing my attention to this wonderful source.
82. The broadcast can be heard on *The Wizard of Oz (75th Anniversary Anthology)*, released on Sepia Records 1246. See http://www.sepiarecords.com/1246.html (accessed October 11, 2018) for a track listing.
83. See Walter Frisch, *Over the Rainbow* (New York: Oxford University Press, 2017), 47–49.
84. *Piccolo*, 205–208. The broadcast is available at https://archive.org/details/CommandPerformance450215DickTracyInBFlat (accessed October 11, 2018).
85. The script can be viewed at USC's Cinematic Arts Library, in the George Burns and Gracie Allen Collection (script 598, box 29). My sincere thanks to Ned Comstock for drawing my attention to this source.
86. See https://songbook.historyit.com/detail-page.php?id=2021 (accessed October 11, 2018).
87. The first show can be heard online at https://www.youtube.com/watch?v=QdbPheEys4s (accessed October 12, 2018).
88. Recordings of several of the renditions of the song from the show (including the one from November 19, 1950, with Jimmy Durante and Perry Como) can be found in the digital collections of GASF. See https://purl.dlib.indiana.edu/iudl/media/r46q978051 (accessed October 12, 2018).
89. Smith's recording can be heard at https://www.youtube.com/watch?v=gVQVUTzh5K4 (accessed October 12, 2018).
90. This dialogue occurs around 51:30 at https://www.youtube.com/watch?v=QdbPheEys4s (accessed October 12, 2018).
91. The series of one-page handwritten manuscripts include "A Worm," which explicitly credits both Dixie and Meredith, and three others—"The Drummer," "Nightfaces," and "Politely"—in the same hand but without credit. Willson was still using the initial R at the start of his name, which suggests an early date of composition. Meredith Willson manuscripts, Juilliard, W008.
92. Willson, *Piccolo*, 196–200.
93. Juilliard, W008.
94. Ibid. John Bush Jones situates this song in a trend of American songwriters mocking Mussolini specifically at this stage of the war; see Bush Jones, *The Songs That Fought the War: Popular Music and the Home Front, 1939–1945*, 132.
95. Willson, *Piccolo*, 169.
96. Crosby's version can be heard at: https://www.youtube.com/watch?v=lQQuWXVLQBQ; Sinatra's more uptempo version is at: https://www.youtube.com/watch?v=xFKQJHNYth4 (both accessed October 12, 2018).
97. Bill Oates, *America's Music Man*, 65.
98. The broadcast—in which Crosby repeatedly struggles with the refrain and has to restart—can be heard at: https://www.youtube.com/watch?v=4uSbp5NHaHo (accessed on February 25, 2015).
99. Willson explains how he was inspired to write the song in *Eggs I Have Laid*, 141–42.
100. Ibid., 142.

101. Willson had hoped the song would have a featured role in the dramatic thrust of the movie, but the director, William Wyler, refused, hence the composer incorporated it over the end titles. See *Piccolo*, 177–79.

102. Anon, "His Score Won Race With Bridge," April 9, 1936: clipping from unknown publication, found on eBay.com (October 12, 2018).

103. Austin, *The Orchestral Works of Meredith Willson*, 152.

104. Austin, *Orchestral Works*, 172.

105. Austin analyses how the theme develops in ibid., 173–76.

106. Ibid., 195.

107. Austin quotes Willson's explanation of how the swallows "arrive year after year on St. Joseph's Day (19 March) and leave on St. John's Day (23 March). Since no one has a scientific explanation, perhaps there is a spiritual one. The swallow theme pervades the entire Scherzo." Quoted in ibid., 219.

108. Ibid., 226.

109. See *Piccolo*, 170–73.

110. Ibid., 59.

111. Quoted in John C. Skipper, *Meredith Willson: The Unsinkable Music Man* (Mason City, IA: Savas, 2000), 30–31.

112. *Piccolo*, 60.

113. Ibid., 129

114. Much of the film (though not the Technicolor sequence) can be viewed at https://www.youtube.com/watch?v=y6TlmQae09M (accessed October 5, 2018).

115. *Piccolo*, 129.

116. Oates, *Meredith Willson*, 43–44.

117. https://charliechaplinmusic.com/chaplins-music-man/ (accessed October 2, 2018).

118. Ibid.

119. *Piccolo*, 166.

120. Ibid., 166–67.

121. Ibid., 167–68. Willson describes how it "was all made before I ever came on the lot" and the music was added afterward.

122. Equally, as James L. Neibaur as observed, the physical similarity of Chaplin and Hitler is extended by their mutual enjoyment of Wagner's music, making the Wagnerian aspect of the film especially unusual. See https://web.archive.org/web/20120126114159/http://www.cineaste.com/articles/emthe-great-dictatorem (accessed October 2, 2018).

123. Steven Suskin incorrectly credits him with writing the music for the stage play too, but he did not participate in that incarnation of the work. See Suskin, *Show Tunes* (New York: Oxford University Press, 2010), 261.

124. *Piccolo*, 175 and 177.

125. See https://archive.org/details/pinkypupemptyele00will/page/n0 (accessed October 5, 2018).

126. Source: GASF, box 2, folder 11.

127. The first seven pages of the volume can be read on the GASF online archive at: https://songbook.historyit.com/detail-page.php?id=1649 (accessed October 5, 2018).

128. The album was released in 1959; in 2017 it was issued on CD by Stage Door Records.

129. Frank Colby, "What Is the Origin?," *Los Angeles Times*, March 17, 1949, A5.

130. John Webster Spargo, "Hilarious Bits in Meredith Willson Essays," *Chicago Daily Tribune*, October 3, 1948, e4.

131. Val Dams, "All in One Basket," *New York Times*, October 2, 1955, BR7.

132. Willson also appeared as part of a radio adaptation of *And There I Stood with My Piccolo* on March 10, 1949, as part of the *Hallmark Playhouse* program. The adaptation can be heard online at: https://www.oldtimeradiodownloads.com/drama/hallmark-playhouse/and-there-i-stood-with-my-picolo-1949-03-10 (accessed October 5, 2018).

133. Gilbert Millstein, "Mildly Baffling: Who Did What to Fedalia? By Meredith Willson," *New York Times*, February 10, 1952, 242.

134. Meredith Willson, *Who Did What to Fedalia?* (New York: Doubleday, 1952), 30 and 182.

135. Ibid, 141.

136. Ibid, 125–26 and 160–61. Willson also had a radio show of this name.

137. Ibid, 42.

138. See, for example, ibid., 58.

139. Meredith Willson, *But He Doesn't Know the Territory*, 15–16.

CHAPTER 2: FROM *THE SILVER TRIANGLE* TO *THE MUSIC MAN*

1. Willson, *But He Doesn't Know the Territory*, 15–16.

2. Ibid., 16.

3. A useful list of most of these can be found in Bill Oates, *Meredith Willson*, 185.

4. S1, 1-2-20.

5. Willson, *But He Doesn't Know the Territory*, 27.

6. Ibid., 38.

7. Ibid., 39.

8. Ibid., 51.

9. The Department of Energy report on the experiments and the conditions that the children were subjected to can be read at https://ehss.energy.gov/ohre/roadmap/achre/chap7_5.html (accessed November 1, 2018). The ethics and other contextual issues of the case are explored in James W. Trent's excellent *Inventing the Feeble Mind: A History of Intellectual Disability in the United States* (New York: Oxford University Press, 2017), esp. 275–77.

10. Willson, *But He Doesn't Know the Territory*, 28. The quotation refers specifically to the disability plot.

11. Letter of December 17, 1955, from Lawrence and Lee to Willson. GASF, box 14, folder 9.

12. Willson, *But He Doesn't Know the Territory*, 29.

13. Ibid, 36.

14. Sam Zolotow, "'Top Ten' Moved Up by Feuer, Martin," *New York Times*, February 10, 1956, 18.

15. Willson, *But He Doesn't Know the Territory*, 51.

16. Telegram from Kermit Bloomgarden to Meredith Willson, February 23, 1956. Kermit Bloomgarden Papers (henceforth *KBP*), box 7, folder 4.

17. Jesse L. Lasky to Kermit Bloomgarden, February 29, 1956, KBP, box 27, folder 1. Willson elaborates on this arrangement in *Territory*, explaining that Lasky was trying to interest a studio in a double feature: a documentary about brass bands and *The Music Man*. See *Territory*, 51–54. Copies of the screenplay for *The Big Brass Band* can be found at GASF, box 37, folders 6 (May 15, 1953, version) and 7 (February 15, 1955, version).

18. Lewis Funke, "Gossip of the Rialto," *New York Times*, January 13, 1957, X1.

19. Willson, *But He Doesn't Know the Territory*, 83–84.

20. Two-page report (anon. but possibly by M. E. Hart) inserted at the back of S4.

21. It is also surprising to read in several synopses of 1955 (e.g., SY2) Willson's comment: "How strong the odds seem against these two gentle people." This encapsulates the difference between Marian and Harold in these developmental versions and the Broadway version.

22. Lacey is a surprisingly obscure figure despite his participation in *The Music Man*. Willson reports that he met him while working on *The California Story* in San Diego in August 1956, but his name clearly appears on earlier drafts. In *Territory* Willson credits him warmly with helping him to shape the book of *The Music Man*, but there was later tension between them on two occasions. The first rift appears to have taken place in 1960, perhaps during the preparation for the London production of the show in 1961. A nine-page letter from Lacey to Willson dated February 1, 1964, offers an olive branch and implies that the disagreement was about the way Lacey's work on the show was referred to by Willson and that Lacey now understood it; a copy of Willson's one-page (positive) response also exists. (See GASF, box 3, folder 25.) Later, Lacey and Kermit Bloomgarden sued Willson for not sharing the royalties on the soundtrack of the 1962 movie version of the show; see *Variety*, November 9, 1970, 1 and 2.

23. Reproduced in Austin, *The Orchestral Works of Meredith Willson*, 260–68. Skipper, *Meredith Willson*, also engages with the issue; see 125–26.

24. The letters are housed in GASF, box 2, folder 28.

25. The royalties are in box 19 of GASF.

26. Willson, *Territory*, 43.

27. Although the sequence has not arisen during my examination of archival documents, it is vital to acknowledge the violence of Eulalie's leadership and participation in the Wa Tan Ye girls, the parody of Indigenous Americans during the July Fourth festivities.

28. Ethan Mordden, *Anything Goes* (New York: Oxford University Press, 2014), 314.

29. Willson's contemporaries Marc Blitzstein and Rick Besoyan also boasted these abilities but neither wrote anything of the prominent success of *The Music Man*. More recently, Lin-Manuel Miranda has also played all three creative roles, long after the golden age but his *Hamilton* is based on history and therefore an inherited structure, unlike Willson's *Music Man*.

30. See Dominic McHugh, *Loverly: The Life and Times of 'My Fair Lady'* (New York: Oxford University Press, 2012), chapters 1–2 for more information.

1. Willson, *But He Doesn't Know the Territory*, 43–44.
2. Ibid., 45. Roberta Freund Schwartz has noticed this too, in her fine article "Iowa Stubborn: Meredith Willson's musical characterization of his fellow Iowans," *Studies in Musical Theatre*, 3:1. See in particular p.33.
3. Scott Miller, *Deconstructing Harold Hill* (Portsmouth, NH: Heinemann, 2000), 82.
4. Marian is so hypnotized by the number in S9 that she sings a (solo) verse of the "Now in the moonlight" section.
5. Willson, *And There I Stood with My Piccolo*, 41.
6. Meredith Willson, "Selling Long-Hair," typescript of article headed "For Abel Green," GASF. Green was the editor of *Variety*.
7. Willson, *Territory*, 65.
8. Ibid., 61.
9. Ibid., 134. On the lyric sheet at GASF, Willson refers to them as "odd, though real, instruments."
10. Willson reveals these names in *Territory*, 78–79.
11. The drafts can be seen at GASF.
12. Willson's demo recording of the song can be heard on the CD release of the Original London Cast album of the show (CD code: Sepia 1173).
13. See Jody Rosen, "The American Revolutionary," *New York Times*, July 8, 2015. Accessed online at https://www.nytimes.com/interactive/2015/07/08/t-magazine/hamilton-lin-manuel-miranda-roots-sondheim.html on November 21, 2015.
14. He specifically remarks in *Territory* that the intention of the number was "to balance Harold's big first act song 'Trouble.'"
15. See for example: Ken Bloom, *American Song*, Volume 1 (New York: Schirmer, 1996), 770; and Ethan Mordden, *Open a New Window: The Broadway Musical in the 1960s* (New York: St. Martin's Press, 2001), 144. Geoffrey Block discusses the issue in his essay in George Rodosthenous, ed., *The Disney Musical on Stage and Screen* (London: Methuen, 2017), 89.
16. Willson, *Territory*, 175.
17. Admittedly, "Just Leave Everything to Me" opens with an adaptation of the "Call on Dolly" material from the stage version of *Hello, Dolly!*
18. Letter of October 2, 1957, from Herb Eiseman to Kermit Bloomgarden. Bloomgarden papers, Wisconsin Historical Society, box 77, folder 1.
19. Doris Day eventually recorded "Till There Was You" in 1966 and wrote to Willson that it "must be my favorite song in the whole world! I've just been singing it and I'm so filled with admiration that I had to drop you a note. Please don't think I'm nutty—This [*sic*] comes straight from the heart!" Copy at The Great American Songbook Foundation archives, Willson papers.
20. Letter of October 21, 1957, from Frank Loesser to Jule Styne. Bloomgarden papers, Wisconsin Historical Society, box 77, folder 1.
21. Willson, *Territory*, 171. The lyric is reproduced on 172–74.
22. Ibid., 174.
23. *Pace* Scott Miller, who claims "no one would've known" if the song had been cut. Miller, 88.

1. The reviews are collated in a scrapbook in the Willson papers at GASF. All the press quotes from this section are taken from this source.
2. The agreement is discussed in a letter of June 24, 1957, from Ernest Rubenstein (of Willson's legal representative's firm) to Max Allentuck (who was in charge of The Music Man Company). Bloomgarden papers, WHS, box 26, folder 14.
3. Letter of July 2, 1957, from Anne Gordon to Mrs. Douglas T. Warner, Bloomgarden papers, WHS, box 26, folder 14.
4. "*The Music Man* Estimated Production Budget," Bloomgarden papers, WHS, box 27, folder 8.
5. Barbara Cook contract, Bloomgarden papers, WHS, box 26, folder 13.
6. Robert Preston contract, Bloomgarden papers, WHS, box 26, folder 13.
7. "Contract notes," Bloomgarden papers, WHS, box 26, folder 13.
8. Drew Middleton, "West to Act Soon," *New York Times*, December 19, 1957, 1.
9. M. S. Handler, "Germans Voice Opposition to Taking U.S. Weapons," *New York Times*, December 19, 1957, 1.
10. Robert C. Doty, "U.S. Alters Stand," *New York Times*, December 19, 1957, 1.
11. Milton Bracker, "Army Fires a Jupiter Missile," *New York Times*, December 19, 1957, 1.
12. The reviews in this section are taken from Willson's scrapbook at GASF.
13. Of note, in the article Willson credits Morton Da Costa with inventing the "pitch pipe business" where Hill plays a note on his pipe to set off the barbershop quartet singing each time, distracting them from their mission to obtain his credentials. He also mentions that writer and comedian Goodman Ace was one of the people who urged him to write a musical in the first place. Frank Loesser is mentioned but Feuer and Martin are not, perhaps out of respect for Bloomgarden.
14. CD release of the original Broadway cast album of *The Music Man*, EMI/Angel Records, 1992. Information from liner notes/booklet, 6.
15. Letter of November 28, 1959, Preston to Bloomgarden, Bloomgarden Papers, WHS.
16. Arthur Gelb, "Music Man Talks about 'Music Man,'" *New York Times*, October 19, 1959, 36.
17. Famous entertainer Jack Carson was also considered for the role; he later played it in summer stock. See letter of December 16, 1959, from Max Allentuck to Meredith Willson, Bloomgarden Papers, box 27, folder 1.
18. Letter of April 12, 1958, from Morton Da Costa to Kermit Bloomgarden, Bloomgarden Papers, WHS, box 27, folder 1.
19. Letter of April 14, 1959, from Meredith Willson to Herbert Greene, Bloomgarden Papers, box 27, folder 1.
20. Louis Calta, "Woman Conducts 'Music Man' Today," *New York Times*, July 4, 1960, 8.
21. Unknown, "Music: Music Man's Lady," *TIME*, September 12, 1960. Accessed online at http://content.time.com/time/magazine/article/0,9171,897543,00.html on November 29, 2018.

22. The segment of the episode can be watched at https://www. youtube.com/watch?v=hJb-Q4oDFNs&fbclid=IwAR0c8E-7OPw2DwCBu2q2KjnrYJRRKolghoYeMiIoi-cw4Q2BHMW0Myw6noI, accessed on November 29, 2018.

23. The itinerary is discussed in a letter of September 29, 1958, from Betty Hart to Meredith Willson, Bloomgarden Papers, WHS, box 27, folder 4.

24. Letter of October 20, 1958, from Kermit Bloomgarden to Morton Da Costa, Bloomgarden Papers, WHS, box 32, folder 15.

25. Letter of June 3, 1958, from Sam Wanamaker to Harry Foster, Bloomgarden Papers, WHS, box 32, folder 15.

26. Letter of January 25, 1960, from Helen Harvey of the William Morris agency to Meredith Willson, GASF.

27. Letter of December 8, 1959, from Helen Harvey of the William Morris agency to Meredith Willson, GASF.

28. Letter of September 18, 1959, from Edward E. Robbins of the William Morris agency to Kermit Bloomgarden, GASF.

29. Anon., "Van Johnson Leaving The Music Man," *The Times*, February 17, 1962, 4. This run was a little disappointing compared to the success of *My Fair Lady*, *Oklahoma!*, and *The Sound of Music*, all of which ran for several years, but it was by no means a flop.

30. For example, there is a two-page letter from Willson to David Burns, telling him to emphasize or clarify several of his lines. Letter of June 7, 1958, from Willson to Burns, Bloomgarden Papers, WHS, box 32, folder 15.

31. Letter of March 21, 1961, from Meredith Willson to Harold Fielding. GASF.

32. "M.W.'s notes Oct. 18," Bloomgarden Papers, WHS, box 32, folder 15.

33. Letter of May 29, 1959, from Willson to Lefkowitz, GASF.

34. Letter of May 15, 1959, from Kermit Bloomgarden to Meredith Willson, GASF.

35. Letter of September 8, 1959, from Meredith Willson to Kermit Bloomgarden, Morton Da Costa, and Julius Kefkowitz, GASF.

36. Letter of September 10, 1959, from Kermit Bloomgarden to Meredith Willson, GASF.

37. Letter of September 18, 1959, from Ann Stein to Meredith Willson, GASF.

38. Copy of a telegram of December 15 from Warner Bros. (making reference to Jack Warner) to the William Morris Agency, GASF. The same page also contains a copy of a telegram from Columbia Pictures, dated December 16, who wanted to make a counteroffer, all too late.

39. An article by gossip columnist Hedda Hopper claimed that Willson called Hopper and was "madder than a mortician in the Promised Land" at the idea that Da Costa had brought about Preston's casting: "It was I—me, me, me, the Mason City country boy, with nobody's help and nobody's assistance who got Bob Preston in the picture!" Probably Hopper's account is unreliable. See Hedda Hopper, "Hedda Put in Middle on 'Music Man' Role," *Chicago Tribune*, May 25, 1962, B18.

40. In a brief letter written three days later, he adds the idea that the Buffalo Bills should record the soundtrack for the barbershop songs and actors should be hired to play their roles; this was not carried out in the film as the Bills both

sang and acted their Broadway parts. See letter of May 29 from Da Costa to Willson, GASF.

41. Letter of May 26, 1960, from Morton Da Costa to Meredith Willson, GASF.
42. Letter of May 31, 1960, from Meredith Willson to Morton Da Costa, GASF.
43. Letters of June 3 and 6, 1960, from Meredith Willson to Morton Da Costa, GASF.
44. Letter of August 1, 1960, from Mike Zimring to Meredith Willson, GASF.
45. Letter of July 11, 1960, from Morton Da Costa to Meredith Willson, GASF.
46. Undated note, "Steve Trilling," GASF.
47. Linda A. Robinson gives the dates for shooting and notes the ten-day saving, based on archival sources at the University of Southern California. However, an article of September 4, 1961, in the *Los Angeles Times* claimed shooting had wrapped twenty-two days early; this is also the source of the daily cost of shooting. Linda A. Robinson, "The Day They Stopped the Mail in Mason City," in Michael E. Connaughton and Suellen Rundquist, eds., *The American Village in a Global Setting*, 167. Joan Winchell, "'Music Man' Boss Sets a Fast Beat," *Los Angeles Times*, September 4, 1961, C7.
48. Anon., "'Music Man," *Los Angeles Times*, July 31, 1961, O9.
49. Larry Glenn, "'Music Man' Reprised," *New York Times*, August 6, 1961, X5.
50. *The Music Man*, DVD release, Warner Bros.
51. Hedda Hopper, "Mason City Goes All Out to Launch 'Music Man,'" *Chicago Daily Tribune*, B2. Hedda Hopper, "Meredith's Homecoming Was Rouser," *Washington Times*, B5.
52. Bosley Crowther, "Screen: Preston Stars in 'Music Man," *New York Times*, August 24, 1962, 14.
53. Philip K. Scheuer, " 'Music Man' Hits Key of G—Grand, Gaudy, Gorgeous," *Los Angeles Times*, July 8, 1962, M9.
54. Crowther, "Screen," 14.
55. Bosley Crowther, "A Fanciful Music Man," *New York Times*, September 2, 1962, 61.
56. *Variety* review, quoted in Robinson, "The Day They Stopped the Mail in Mason City," 149.
57. Bruce Weber, "TV Weekend: Bad Timing! Right Here in River City!" *New York Times*, February 14, 2003, E36.
58. Michele Willens, "The Music Man, Bringing Broadway to the Screen," *New York Times*, February 16, 2003, AR28.
59. Weber, "TV Weekend."
60. Edward Guthmann, "Broderick's Tepid Toot in 'Music Man,'" *San Francisco Chronicle*, February 14, 2003. Accessed online at https://www.sfgate.com/entertainment/article/Broderick-s-tepid-toot-in-Music-Man-2634696.php on December 6, 2018.
61. Geoffrey Block discusses this idea in his article on the Broadway canon. See Block, "The Broadway Canon from *Show Boat* to *West Side Story* and the European Operatic Ideal," *Journal of Musicology* 11, no. 4 (Autumn 1993): 525–44.
62. See Richard Christiansen, "Dick Van Dyke Leads the Big Musical Parade into Arie Crown," *Chicago Tribune*, May 11, 1980, d4.
63. Dan Sullivan, "Dick Van Dyke in 'Music Man' at Pantages," *Los Angeles Times*, January 1, 1980, F1.

64. Christiansen, "Dick Van Dyke Leads the Big Musical Parade into Arie Crown."

65. Walter Kerr, "'Music Man' Back with Van Dyke," *New York Times*, June 6, 1980, C3.

66. Stephen Holden, "City Opera: 'Music Man,'" *New York Times*, March 3, 1988, C28.

67. The quotations are taken from http://www.thisistheatre.com/londonshows/musicman.html, accessed December 6, 2018.

68. Peter Marks, "They've Got Memories Right Here in Mason City," *New York Times*, February 27, 2000, AR7.

69. Ben Brantley, "Rogue Is Free," *New York Times*, April 28, 2000, E1.

70. See https://www.broadway.com/buzz/191779/norm-lewis-to-star-in-the-music-man-at-the-kennedy-center-little-shop-tommy-also-on-deck/, accessed December 10, 2018.

71. https://www.playbill.com/article/african-american-concert-production-of-the-music-man-starring-isaiah-johnson-and-stephanie-umoh-begins-run-at-njpac-march-21-com-216247, accessed September 9, 2020.

72. See https://www.nytimes.com/1987/04/19/theater/trouble-in-river-city-right-here-in-beijing.html?scp=13&sq=Music%20Man%20Beijing%20opera&st=cse&pagewanted=1/, accessed December 10, 2018.

73. Reviews quoted from Nigel Simeone, *West Side Story* (Farnham, UK: Ashgate, 2009), 113ff.

74. Brantley, "Rogue Is Free."

75. Carol J. Oja, "*West Side Story* and *The Music Man*: Whiteness, Immigration, and Race in the US during the Late 1950s," *Studies in Musical Theatre* 3, no. 1 (2009): 13.

76. Ibid., 13.

77. Ibid., 27.

78. Warren Hoffman, *The Great White Way: Race and the Broadway Musical* (Rutgers University Press, 2014) [electronic version consulted, no page numbers].

79. See Simeone, Chapter 2, for a discussion of the early versions.

80. *Time* 72, no. 3, July 21, 1958.

81. Letter of July 21, 1958, from Meredith Willson to Betty Hart, Bloomgarden papers, box 27, folder 2.

82. Letter of October 20, 1958, from Betty Hart to Meredith Willson, Bloomgarden papers, box 46, folder 22, housed with synopsis of *Harold Hill III*.

CHAPTER 5: AFTER *THE MUSIC MAN*

1. Telegram from Morton Da Costa to Meredith Willson, May 24, 1959, GASF.

2. Harold Arlen and Johnny Mercer's *Saratoga Trunk* opened on December 7, 1959.

3. Letter of May 28, 1959, from Meredith Willson to Morton Da Costa, GASF.

4. Sam Zolotow, "Willson Working on Second Effort," *New York Times*, June 4, 1959, 27.

5. Ibid.

6. In an interview in the *New York Times* on October 30, 1960, Willson named *Saratoga Trunk* and *Take Me Along* as possibilities. See Lewis Nichols, "Willson at Bat Again," *New York Times*, October 30, 1960. Taken from *Molly Brown* Scrapbook, GASF.

7. Larry Tajiri, "Meredith Willson Writes Songs for 'Unsinkable Mrs. Brown,'" *Denver Post*, March 4, 1960, 34.

8. An article in the *Rocky Mountain News* announced: "Morris has changed the name to 'The Unsinkable Molly Brown,' on the theory that the word 'Mrs.' is negative in a title." Anon., "'Unsinkable Molly Brown' Opens Nov. 3," *Rocky Mountain News*, April 17, 1960 [page number unknown; taken from GASF scrapbook].

9. Sam Zolotow, "Schary Is Ousted as Chief at M-G-M," *New York Times*, November 29, 1956, 42.

10. Morris, *The Unsinkable Mrs. Brown*, undated script, third version, GASF, 2-8-57/2-9-58.

11. See GASF, box 21, folders 2, 3, and 4.

12. Aspects of the setting of the show also resemble Harold Rome's musical *Destry Rides Again*, which opened on Broadway in 1959 and would therefore have been familiar at the time of *Molly Brown*'s Broadway run.

13. So named because he was born on Christmas morning.

14. In the 1964 film version, Johnny is the one to slap Molly, an even more troubling version of the scene that makes her return to him at the conclusion harder to stomach.

15. Vera Brown, "Our Times," *Detroit Times*, October 22, 1959, 18.

16. Gene Sherman, "Meredith Willson Has a New Musical," *Los Angeles Times*, February 9, 1960, Part III, 5.

17. Joan Winchell, untitled article in regular column, *Los Angeles Times*, May 31, 1960, Part II, 3.

18. Jack Gaver, "'Music Man' Willson Prepares New Show," *Philadelphia Inquirer*, August 28, 1960,

19. Curiously, the copyist's version of the piano-vocal score used for rehearsal purposes starts the orchestra at the very beginning of the song, showing that Willson made the move into song even more seamless and gradual by removing accompaniment material that had initially been there.

20. All that remained of the effect was a moment in the Entr'acte (at rehearsal mark D in the published score) where the woodwind section played "Brass Bed" and the strings played "Never Say No," allowing the attentive audience member to notice what was going on and perhaps identify the dramatic consequences.

21. The song was also for a time discussed as Colorado's solution to Rodgers and Hammerstein's title song for *Oklahoma!* (1943). It "already is touted as another state anthem, being the likes of 'Oklahoma!'" according to one contemporaneous report. See Larry Tajiri, "Willson to Preview Colorado Songs from 'Molly Brown,'" *Denver Post*, April 2, 1960, 34.

22. See https://tunearch.org/wiki/Annotation:Kemo_Kimo for more information on the minstrel version and https://www.mamalisa.com/?t=es&p=1152&c=23 on "Frog Went A-Courtin'." Accessed January 21, 2019.

23. Memo from Willson and Morris to Dore Schary, September 1, 1960, GASF.

24. Letter of January 13, 1960, from Meredith Willson to Dore Schary. GASF.

25. Letters of January 13, 1960, from Meredith Willson to Kaye Ballard, GASF.

26. Letter of January 29, 1960, from Meredith Willson to Dore Schary. GASF.

27. Letters of January 13, 1960, from Meredith Willson to Shelley Winters, GASF.

28. Letters of February 3, 1960, from Meredith Willson to Dore Schary, GASF.

29. Newspaper coverage from the time claims that Mrs. Willson was behind the casting, having "discovered" him singing at the Hollywood Bowl. See GASF *Molly Brown* scrapbook, various clippings (including *New York Post*).

30. It is not clear which song Willson is referring to. Draft telegram of March 10, 1960, from Meredith Willson to Tammy Grimes, GASF. An annotation indicates it was actually sent on the 11th.

31. Anon., "Unsinkable Mrs. Brown," *New York Times*, March 8, 1960, 38.

32. Letter of July 6, 1960, from Peter Davis of the Theatre Guild to Meredith Willson; letter of July 13, 1960, from Willson to Davis. GASF.

33. According to a rehearsal schedule in GASF, the dancers' rehearsals began at New York's Ambassador Theatre on August 17, the singers' at the Golden Theatre on August 21, and the full company at the Fifty-Fourth Street Theatre from August 24. The production moved to Philadelphia for a week of technical rehearsals from September 17 to 25 ahead of the September 26 opening at the Shubert Theatre. See Rehearsal Schedule dated July 26, 1960, in GASF *Molly Brown* scrapbook. The start of rehearsals was reported in a *New York Herald Tribune* article on August 25; it also noted that the production was budgeted at $480,000. See Stuart Little, "'Unsinkable Molly Brown Rehearses with Full Cast," *New York Herald Tribune*, March 8, 1960, 12.

34. Memo from Willson to Morris and Schary, April 8, 1960, GASF.

35. Untitled six-page typed notes by Willson, GASF.

36. Memo from Willson and Morris to Schary, September 1, 1960, GASF.

37. Waters, "Shows Out of Town," *Variety*, September 28, 1960. Taken from GASF *Molly Brown* scrapbook.

38. Wate, "Legit Tryouts," *Daily Variety*, September 27, 1960, 1. Taken from GASF *Molly Brown* scrapbook. Note that *Variety* was a weekly publication while *Daily Variety* was published daily.

39. Ernie Schier, "'Unsinkable Molly Brown' Makes Musical Bow Here," *Evening Bulletin*, September 27, 1960, 67. Taken from GASF *Molly Brown* scrapbook. Wate, "Legit Tryouts," Daily Variety, September 27, 1960, 1.

40. Letter from Frank Loesser to Meredith Willson, September 27, 1960. Frank Loesser Enterprises' private collection.

41. Jerry Gaghan, "Refloating 'Molly Brown,'" *Philadelphia Daily News*, September 29, 1960, 43.

42. Letter from Mrs. M. Warren Heiss to Meredith Willson, October 14, 1960, GASF.

43. Willson describes his initial reaction to Morris's book in an interview in the *New York Times* with Lewis Nichols on October 30, 1960 titled "Willson at Bat Again": "I said, 'If you'll take the cussin' out of there and be mindful of beautifying the love story, I'm your boy.'"

44. Letter of October 19, 1960, from Meredith Willson to Mrs. Heiss, GASF.

45. Jerry Gaghan, "Subs Step In to Aid 'Molly,'" *Philadelphia Daily News*, October 3, 1960, 39.

46. Memo from Dore Schary to "Those concerned with THE UNSINKABLE MOLLY BROWN," dated November 3, 1960, Schary papers, Wisconsin Historical Society.

47. The reviews are all quoted from the *Molly Brown* Scrapbook at GASF.

48. Letter of January 23, 1961, from Meredith Willson to G. M. Loeb, GASF.

49. Richard A. Duprey, "Impish Tammy Grimes Captivates Audience in 'Molly Brown' Role," *Catholic Standard and Times*, September 30, 1960. Taken from GASF *Molly Brown* scrapbook.

50. Another song written for the film, "Dignity," was unused.

51. Letter of June 3, 1961, from Meredith Willson to Tammy Grimes, GASF.

52. Letter of December 9, 1963, to Milton Kramer of Frank Music Corp, GASF.

53. https://www.nytimes.com/1964/07/17/archives/screen-exploits-of-the-unsinkable-molly-brown-debbie-reynolds-stars.html. Accessed January 24, 2019.

CHAPTER 6: SINGING THROUGH EVIL TIMES

1. Meredith Willson, "Evil Times," program essay, *Here's Love*, Fisher Theatre, Detroit, July 1963. GASF.

2. Stephen Sondheim, "From the Reader: What's Entertainment?," *New York Herald-Tribune*, date unknown (c. August 1963). Copy accessed at GASF.

3. Stephen Sondheim, *Look, I Made a Hat* (New York: Virgin Books, 2011), 309. Sondheim remarks: " 'Rock Island,' the unique opening number, is surely one of the most startling and galvanic openings ever devised."

4. Of earlier examples directly adapted from film, only Cole Porter's *Silk Stockings* (1955) based on *Ninotchka* (1939) stands out as having endured to today to any extent (and that is mainly on the basis of the 1957 Fred Astaire movie adaptation of the musical).

5. This is the spelling in Davies's novel. Willson changed it to Gaily for *Here's Love*.

6. Among numerous sources to explain this strategy, the following website offers a focused discussion: https://gothamist.com/arts-entertainment/emmiracle-on-34th-streetem-was-actually-a-summer-movie (accessed November 26, 2019).

7. See for example Diane Werts, *Christmas on Television* (Westport CT: Praeger, 2006), 14.

8. Anon., "Willson Prepares New Musical, 'Understudy,'" *Los Angeles Examiner*, September 30, 1961 [page unknown]. GASF, *Here's Love* scrapbook.

9. The synopsis is in a notebook at GASF, box 34, folder 3.

10. See http://www.mtishows.co.uk/meredith-willsons-miracle-on-34th-street-the-musical (accessed March 31, 2019).

11. Anon., "Report 20th Has Inside Track on '34th St.' Willson is Tuning for B'way," *Variety*, November 29, 1961, 1.

12. Untitled typed synopsis (twenty-eight points), eight pages, dated November 28, 1961, GASF. Valentine Davies, *Miracle on 34th Street* (New York: Harcourt, Brace and Co., 1947). It is clear from Stuart Ostrow's letter to Willson of October 15, 1962, that they each had a copy of the screenplay to work from, so it may be that this was what Willson used from the start.

13. "The Trial," three-page typed synopsis, dated November 29, 1961, GASF.

14. Invoice dated January 2, 1962, from Radio Recorders to Meredith Willson, GASF. The demo has not been found in my research,

15. Invoices dated February 3, 5, and 18, 1962, from Norman Bartold to Meredith Willson, GASF.
16. Untitled character description of Fred Gaily, marked "LOVE, LOVE, LOVE" and dated 4 April 1962, GASF.
17. Davies, *Miracle on 34th Street*, 15.
18. Untitled character description of Fred Gaily, dated April 5, 1962, GASF.
19. Payne would eventually play the role of Fred in the national tour cast of *Here's Love*.
20. Typed fragment dated April 5, 1962, GASF.
21. Synopsis of "Love, Love, Love" dated April 23, 1962, GASF.
22. "Love, Love, Love," lyric sheets with holograph annotations, dated May 21, 1962, GASF.
23. Pages marked 1-9-41 and 1-9-42, dated June 15, 1962, GASF. These page numbers strongly imply that Willson must have written forty previous pages too, but these are currently lost.
24. Untitled list of notes dated September 12, 1962, GASF.
25. Of course, Harold Hill also displays unappealing characteristics in *The Music Man*; unlike Fred, he appears to face and overcome them.
26. Letter of October 15, 1962, from Stuart Ostrow to Meredith Willson, GASF.
27. Letter of November 7 from Stuart Ostrow to Meredith Willson, GASF.
28. Undated "HERE'S LOVE CALENDAR," GASF.
29. Telegram of August 10, 1962, from Janis Paige to Jules Sharr, copy held at GASF.
30. Telegram of October 22, 1962, from Meredith Willson to Michael Kidd, GASF.
31. Correspondence of November 12, 1962, between Ostrow, Willson, Jewison, and Michael Shurtleff (casting agent), GASF.
32. Shurtleff to Ostrow, GASF.
33. Stuart Ostrow, *Present at the Creation, Leaping in the Dark and Going against the Grain* (New York: Applause, 2006), 27.
34. "'Music Man' Willson Tells of 'Here's Love,'" *News Sentinel*, June 15, 1963. Copy in GASF scrapbook for *Here's Love*.
35. Ken Barnard, "I'm a Fellow Who Writes Marches," *Detroit Free Press*, July 14, 1963. Copy in GASF scrapbook for *Here's Love*.
36. The rehearsal version features an extra detail that was cut for Broadway: Gimbels "have some [crocodiles] this year that cry great big tears," so their crocodiles are better. This would have made a *little* more sense of the moment.
37. See Oates, *America's Music Man*, 152, for more information.
38. Armand Gebert, "Second Look at 'Here's Love,'" *Detroit News*, August 16, 1963, 22. Copy in scrapbook at GASF.
39. Norman Jewison, *This Terrible Business Has Been Good to Me* (New York: St Martin's Press, 2005), 59.
40. Letter from Milton Kramer to Meredith Willson, August 13, 1963, GASF.
41. Steven Suskin quotes a useful interview with dance arranger Peter Howard about the show: "When people are not together on their thinking, that's when you have problems." He also quotes orchestrator Don Walker: "I am not very happy with the orchestrations. They are a stylistic hodgepodge, opportunistic and often lacking in musical integrity. Part of the problem arises because we are

evoking no definite musical period, which often gives a score an overall style." Clearly, the musical aspect of the show struggled from a lack of coherence and purpose. See Suskin, *The Sound of Broadway Music* (New York: Oxford University Press, 2009), 424-425.

42. Anon, "Meredith Willson's New Music Lauded in Detroit," July 30, 1963, Associated Press report (publication unknown), GASF scrapbook.
43. Louis Cook, "Here's Love a Happy Package," *Detroit Free Press*, July 31, 1963, 4B and 7B.
44. Jay Carmody, "Willson-Santa Claus Merger a Natural," *The Evening Star*, August 28, 1963, B–14. Copy in GASF scrapbook.
45. Jerry Gaghan, "Jolly Yule Musical 'Here's Love' Now at Shubert," *Philadelphia Daily News*, September 18, 1963, 39.
46. Reviews from October 4, 1963, excerpted in a GASF scrapbook.
47. Linda Hutcheon, *A Theory of Adaptation* (New York: Routledge, 2006), xii.
48. Hutcheon, 4.
49. See https://www.playbill.com/article/stagestruck-by-peter-filichia-heres-love-com-78887 (accessed 15 January 2021).

CHAPTER 7: *1491*

1. Margaret Harford, "Willson Convinced Columbus Is the End," *Denver Post*, September 2, 1969, 10. Copy viewed in GASF scrapbook for *1491*.
2. Willson was not the first to consider a musical inspired by Columbus—or at least part of one. In 1945, Twentieth Century Fox released the movie *Where Do We Go from Here?* in which Kurt Weill and Ira Gershwin wrote a sequence involving Columbus's voyage.
3. Undated letter from Frank Loesser to Meredith Willson. Copy held at Frank Loesser Enterprises (location of original unknown). Enormous thanks to Joseph Weiss for providing access to this material.
4. Letter of April 1, 1964, from Meredith Willson to Ed Ainsworth, GASF.
5. January 22 and 28, 1965: Memo and story ideas from Ed Ainsworth to Willson, GASF.
6. March 1, 1965, from Ed Ainsworth to Willson: memo about Columbus. March 4, 1965: Memo from Ed Ainsworth to Willson about Isabella. Both housed at GASF.
7. "1491, MW's notes from Morison's book," February 23, 1965, GASF.
8. Morison, *Admiral of the Ocean Sea* (Boston: Little, Brown and Co., 1942). In a letter of October 22, 1969, to Lester, Willson refers to it by this title. There was a two-volume version published at the same time as the original (i.e., 1942) that included scholarly apparatus and one extra chapter. Willson seems to have read the one-volume version.
9. "Notes on Morison's book."
10. Outline, March 16, 1965, 3.
11. Ibid., 6–7.
12. On the mysteries surrounding Columbus's ethnicity, see, for example, https://blog.oup.com/2015/05/christopher-columbus-death-anniversary/ (accessed November 15, 2019). Of course, Willson was not party to this more recent

academic discussion, but the distinction between Columbus and Beatriz is explicit in the show, reflected in the casting of the white Cullum vs. the Latina Chita Rivera.

13. Letter of March 16, 1965, from Willson to Milton Kramer, GASF.
14. See https://www.backstage.com/magazine/article/brit-crits-hit-king-colonialism-charge-32700/ (accessed 15 January 2021).
15. Letter from Ed Ainsworth to Meredith Willson, December 27, 1965, GASF.
16. Letter from Richard Morris to Willson, October 6, 1965, GASF.
17. A copy of Carroll's playscript resides in Bloomgarden's papers at the Wisconsin Historical Society, Madison, Wisconsin, in box 43, folder 12; it is in the "unproduced projects" sequence of the collection. In his reply, which is also at GASF, Bloomgarden protested that Willson was being unfair and said that he had been waiting for Willson to finish a complete draft of the book and score.
18. Letter from Willson to Bloomgarden, May 20, 1966, GASF.
19. Letter from Frank Loesser to Meredith Willson, June 21, 1966, GASF.
20. Letter from Meredith Willson to Frank Loesser, June 27, 1966, GASF.
21. Letter from Frank Loesser to Meredith Willson, July 20, 1966, GASF.
22. See, for example, August 2, 1966, Memo from Frank Loesser Affiliates (Allen B Whitehead) to Frank Loesser, cc Milt Kramer—raises queries with the contract; letters of September 12 and 13, 1966—Allen Whitehead to Frank Loesser; Frank Loesser to Whitehead and Kramer—again about the contract. Both at GASF.
23. Letter from Frank Loesser to Meredith Willson, August 5, 1966, GASF.
24. Draft letter to Jerry Talbot from Frank Loesser associates, August 15, 1966, GASF. It is unclear what the response to this point was and there is no suggestion that Loesser Enterprises expected the show to close prematurely on the West Coast, but it is striking to see that the possibility of what eventually happened was considered by Loesser's company but was not initially part of the Lester-Willson contract.
25. Inter-office communication from Loesser to Allen Whitehead and Milton Kramer, September 13, 1966, GASF. He began: "With the greatest possible clarity Lacloa—after a glorious no-risk provincial run—can wash its hands of the project and continue no further."
26. It should be LACLOC—the Los Angeles Civic Light Opera Company.
27. Inter-office communication from Loesser to Allen Whitehead and Milton Kramer, September 13, 1966, 6.
28. One of Loesser's colleagues, Allen Whitehead, wrote further comments on the contract on September 12, 1966, noting that if Lester were to step aside as the New York producer of the show, the cast would have the legal right to withdraw from the show. He also requested an operating budget for the show if it were to go to New York, to help them to discover whether that "would make it impossible to find a theatre that takes a large enough gross to have any chance of running." GASF.
29. Letter from Meredith Willson to Frank Loesser, September 19, 1966, GASF.
30. There is little evidence at GASF of this research, though equally there is no reason to think Willson was inventing it. It does seem striking that the writer of this press release refers later to two years of research and being inspired by Willson's discovery of a primary source when Ed Ainsworth was almost certainly

behind the show's inspiration, but there is also no doubt that Willson himself
invested many months on getting his facts straight.

31. Press release, October 5 [n.d. but clearly 1966], Alex Evelove Publicity-Public
Relations, GASF.
32. Letter of November 17, 1966, from Lester to Willson, GASF.
33. Ibid.
34. Telegram from Lester to Willson, February 25, 1967, GASF.
35. Letter of September 12, 1967, from Lester to Eric Shepard of Ashley Famous
Agency, Inc., GASF.
36. Letter of March 4, 1969, from Willson to Sergio Franchi, GASF.
37. See letter of September 12, 1967, from Edwin Lester to Eric Schepard, GASF.
38. A letter from Willson's agent updated the composer: "TEC PRESENTLY
WORKING ON NOTES AS PROMISED AS HE TOLD MEREDITH HE
WILL NOT MAKE HIS DECISION UNTIL COMPLETION OF NOTES AND
RECONSIDERATION." Letter of October 9, 1967, from Abe Lastfogel to
Meredith Willson, GASF.
39. See scripts of December 1967 and September 1968, GASF.
40. The announcement of his death was front-page news in the *Los Angeles Times* on
June 17, 1968; copy at GASF.
41. Letter of November 21, 1968, from Lester to Willson, GASF.
42. Letter of November 22, 1968, from Willson to Lester; letter of November 25,
1968, from Lester to Willson. GASF.
43. Letter of December 13, 1968, from Lester to Willson, GASF.
44. Copy in GASF.
45. The playbill also reads: "With assistance from Ira Barmak," though it does not
appear that he was actively involved once Morris had taken over.
46. Letter of February 26, 1969, from Willson to Lester, GASF.
47. Notes on phone conversations with Ed Lester, May 18–23, 1969, GASF.
48. Letter marked "rec'd 7/5/69" from Morris to Willson, GASF.
49. Letter of May 6, 1969, from Lester to Willson, GASF.
50. Letter of November 17, 1966, GASF.
51. Letter of September 24, 1966, from Lester to Willson, GASF.
52. Harford, "Willson Convinced Columbus is the End."
53. Lee Silver, *Daily News*, September 4, 1969, 77, clipping from a scrapbook at GASF.
54. Charles Faber, "Willson's Spectacular '1491' Final Event of CLO Season,"
Hollywood Citizen-News, September 4, 1969. Contained in a scrapbook at GASF.
55. Dan Sullivan, "Columbus Musical '1491' Launched at the Pavilion," *Los Angeles
Times*, September 4, 1969, copy in GASF scrapbook.
56. Winfred Blevins, "Desperate Situation in '1491,'" *Los Angeles Herald-Examiner*,
July 4, 1969, D2.
57. Donald Freeman, "A Shaky Course for New Musical," *San Diego Union*, September
6, 1969, D4.
58. Letter of September 10, 1969, from Lester to Willson, GASF.
59. Letter of September 19, 1969, from Lester to Willson, GASF.
60. Letter of September 24, 1969, from Lester to Willson, GASF.
61. "Telephone notes," October 6–8, 1969, GASF.

62. Letter of October 22, 1969, from Lester to Willson, GASF.

63. Anon., "Stage Notes," *Los Angeles Times*, November 5, 1969, 12.

64. Paine Knickerbocker, "A Big Musical About Columbus," *San Francisco Chronicle*, October 30, 1969, 46. Copy in a GASF scrapbook.

65. Synopsis, *Jack London, Sailor on Horseback*, October 15, 1971, GASF.

66. He revisited the idea in January 1976 but again nothing much came of it. See GASF, box 33, folder 23, for 1976 work on the show.

67. Bill Oates, *Meredith Willson: America's Music Man* (Bloomington, IN: Authorhouse, 2005), 166–67.

68. A copy of the text of the play, dated January 1973, is at GASF, box 3, folder 9.

69. Letter of November 19, 1971, from Meredith Willson to Ketcham. Archive of the Music Man Museum, Mason City. Thanks to Gil McNaughton for his help in obtaining these letters, all of which (on this topic) come from the Music Man Museum.

70. See letter of December 15, 1971, from Ketcham to Willson and Willson's reply of December 23, 1971.

71. See letter of February 18, 1972, from Ketcham to Willson reporting that he was at work on the project.

72. See for example the letter of February 5, 1973, from Willson to Ketcham: "Shouldn't we start with some kind of a narrowing-down outline (from your fist)?"

73. Letter of December 31, 1972, from Ketcham to Willson.

74. Outline by Bob Saylor, THE MUSIC KID, received October 10, 1976; written March 15, 1976.

75. Copy of the comic strip in the Music Man Museum's archive.

76. Letter of October 11, 1976, from Willson to Ketcham.

77. Letter of October 27, 1976, from Ketcham to Willson.

78. Charlie Huisking, "Writer Says 'The Music Man' Is a True Story," *Herald-Tribune Reporter*, u.d. [but Willson is referred to as seventy-seven years old]. Copy in GASF.

BIBLIOGRAPHY

* * *

Archival Sources

The Music Man

Production documents, scripts, and correspondence

Great American Songbook Foundation: Meredith Willson Papers

February 2, 1954: Complete draft script, 120 pp.

June 7, 1955: Synopsis.

June 15, 1955: Synopsis.

June 24, 1955: Fragments of script from both acts, 29 pp.

June 25–30, 1955: Synopsis

July 5–7, 1955: Script fragments, Act 1, Scene 1 ("Gramma Bird" scene). 3 versions.

July 11, 1955: Script fragment, "Bushkins," 4 pp.

Undated, c. July 1955: Synopsis.

Undated, c. July 1955: One-page synopsis

Undated, c. July 1955: Two-page synopsis

Undated, c. July/August 1955: Synopsis ("The Love Story of Harold and Marian, which we will call The Music Man")

September 17, 1955: Synopsis fragments, Act 1, Scenes 1, 2, and 4.

November 15, 1955: Script fragments, Act 1, Scene 2 ("Holy, Holy").

November 15–29, 1955: Script, Act 1 draft, 59 pp.

December 13, 1955: Script, complete, 93 pp., "Draft 3."

December 20, 1955: Synopsis.

April 2, 1956: Script, complete draft in three acts, 99 pp.

April 13, 1956: Synopsis, two versions (one undated), 4 pp. + 4 pp.

April 18, 1956: Synopsis, two versions, Act 2, 4 pp. + 4 pp.

May 26, 1956: Script fragment, pp. 12–26.

October 1956: Script (first four pages missing), labeled by Willson "Early Draft of Music Man, approx Oct '56."

May 15, 1959: Letter from Kermit Bloomgarden to Meredith Willson

May 29, 1959: Letter from Willson to Julius Lefkowitz

September 10, 1959: Letter from Kermit Bloomgarden to Meredith Willson

September 18, 1959: Letter from Ann Stein to Meredith Willson

December 15, 1958: Telegram from Warner Bros. to the William Morris Agency

March 21, 1961: Letter from Willson to Harold Fielding

February 1, 1964: Letter from Franklin Lacey to Willson and its [u.d.] reply, box 3, folder 25.

u.d., Meredith Willson, "Selling Long-Hair," typescript of article headed "For Abel Green."

Wisconsin Historical Society: Kermit Bloomgarden Papers

February 29, 1956: Letter from Jesse L. Lasky to Kermit Bloomgarden, box 27, folder 1.

pre-June 1956: Complete Script ("Original Script and Notes"), labelled pre-June 1956, 102 pp. + misc. inserts, box 28, folder 12.

June 1956: Complete "First Mimeo Script," June 1956, 102 pp. + 3 pp. corrections dated April 5, 1957, box 28, folder 13.

November 27, 1956: Complete script, "FM Rev."

December 9, 1956–October 4, 1957: Script with multiple inserts ("Assembled Version"), WHS. [Contains scenes from different versions but no new material other than the lyrics to Shinn's version of "Trouble," dated December 9, 1956.]

January 19, 1957: Revised Master Script, 119 pp.

April 5, 1957: Complete Script, 108 pp.

Letter of June 24, 1957, from Ernest Rubenstein to Max Allentuck, box 26, folder 14.

Letter of July 2, 1957, from Anne Gordon to Mrs. Douglas T. Warner, Bloomgarden papers, box 26, folder 14.

July 17, 1957: Complete Script, 108 pp.

August 5, 1957: Barbara Cook contract, box 26, folder 13.

August 5, 1957: Robert Preston contract, box 26, folder 13.

September 10, 1957: Complete Script, 119 pp.

September 23, 1957: Complete Script, 110 pp.

October 21, 1957: Letter from Frank Loesser to Jule Styne, box 77, folder 1.

u.d., "*The Music Man* Estimated Production Budget," box 27, folder 8.

April 12, 1958: Letter from Morton Da Costa to Kermit Bloomgarden

April 14, 1959: Letter from Meredith Willson to Herbert Greene

June 3, 1958: Letter from Sam Wanamaker to Harry Foster

June 7, 1958: Letter from Willson to David Burns

July 21, 1958: Letter from Meredith Willson to Betty Hart

October 20, 1958: Letter from Betty Hart to Meredith Willson

September 18, 1959: Letter from Edward E. Robbins to Kermit Bloomgarden

September 29, 1958: Letter from Betty Hart to Meredith Willson

October 20, 1958: Letter from Kermit Bloomgarden to Morton Da Costa

November 28, 1959: Letter from Robert Preston to Kermit Bloomgarden

December 8, 1959: Letter from Helen Harvey of the William Morris agency to Meredith Willson

December 16, 1959: Letter from Max Allentuck to Meredith Willson

January 25, 1960: Letter from Helen Harvey to Meredith Willson

May 26, 1960: Letter from Morton Da Costa to Meredith Willson

May 29, 1960: Letter from Morton Da Costa to Willson

May 31, 1960: Letter from Willson to Morton Da Costa

June 3, 1960: Letter from Meredith Willson to Morton Da Costa

June 6, 1960: Letter from Meredith Willson to Morton Da Costa

July 11, 1960: Letter from Morton Da Costa to Meredith Willson

August 1, 1960: Letter from Mike Zimring to Meredith Willson

Music Sources
Juilliard School of Music
"Being in Love," lyric drafts (W181).
"Blessings," holograph score and typed lyric sheet (W078).

"Blow," holograph sketches and copyist's score (W079); holograph score and sketches (W110).

"The Blue Ridge Mountains are in No'th Car'lina," holograph score and sketches (W079).

"Don't Put Bananas on Bananas," lyric sheet with annotations, holograph sketches, copyist score with annotations (W079).

"Een-teen," copyist's score (W227); holograph sketch and score (W078).

"Fireworks," copyist score (W228).

"Goodnight, My Someone," holograph score and typed lyric sheet (W078).

"I Found a Horse-Shoe," holograph sketch (W078).

"I-o-wuh (The Iowa Indian Song)," copyist score (W686).

"I Want to Go to Chicago," holograph sketches (W079).

"Just Becuz," holograph sketch (W079).

"Lida Rose/Will I Ever Tell You?," holograph score and annotated copyist's scores, solo version (W266); holograph score (including counterpoint) (W145).

"Marian the Librarian," holograph score (W078); holograph fair copy score (W267); annotated lyric sheet (W079); holograph sketch (W267).

"Mother Darlin'," holograph score (W079).

"My White Knight" (solo version) annotated lyric sheets, holograph and copyist scores of extended soliloquy version (W232); four sections of extended version, holograph score (W267).

"My White Knight/The Sadder but Wiser Girl" (duet version), Copyist score (W233); holograph fair copy and annotated typed lyric sheet (duet); holograph sketches (two versions of the "White Knight" parts only) (W078).

"Piano Lesson/ If You Don't Mind My Saying So," Holograph sketches (score and lyrics) (W267).

"Rasmussen's Law," Copyist's scores (W303).

"River City, Go!," "Mason City, Go" version, holograph sketch and copyist score (W079).

"Rock Island," holograph sketches and copyist score (dated August–September 1957) (W305); holograph fair copy with piano accompaniment (W078).

"The Sadder but Wiser Girl," holograph sketch (W306); holograph melodic sketch, annotated typed lyric sheet, and holograph fair copy with extra lyrics (W078).

"Seventy-Six Trombones," holograph sketch with unfamiliar counterpoint and holograph score (W079); lyric sheets (W308).

"Shipoopi," holograph sketch and holograph score (W079); holograph sketch (six measures) (W008).

"Sincere" (W310).

"This Is It," score material (W686).

"Tomorrow," holograph score (W331).

"Too Soon Old," holograph score (W079).

"Trouble," holograph fair copy (W078).

"The Wells Fargo Wagon," holograph score (W079).

"The Wonderful Plan," holograph sketch (W110).

"You Don't Have to Kiss Me Goodnight," lyric sketch, holograph sketches, and alternative version (W079); holograph sketch (alternative) and holograph fair copy (W342); sketch (W008).

Great American Songbook Foundation
The Think System, holograph piano-vocal score.

The Unsinkable Molly Brown
Production documents, scripts, and correspondence
Great American Songbook Foundation:
May 24, 1959: Telegram from Morton Da Costa to Meredith Willson.
May 28, 1959: Letter from Meredith Willson to Morton Da Costa.
January 13, 1960: Letter from Meredith Willson to Dore Schary.
January 13, 1960: Letter from Meredith Willson to Kaye Ballard.
January 13, 1960: Letter from Meredith Willson to Shelley Winters.
January 29, 1960: Letter from Meredith Willson to Dore Schary.
February 3, 1960: Letter from Meredith Willson to Dore Schary.
March 10, 1960: Draft telegram from Meredith Willson to Tammy Grimes.
April 8, 1960: Memo from Willson to Morris and Schary.
July 6, 1960: Letter of from Peter Davis of the Theatre Guild to Meredith Willson.
July 13, 1960: Letter from Willson to Peter Davis.
September 1, 1960: Memo from Willson and Morris to Schary.
January 23, 1961: Letter from Meredith Willson to G. M. Loeb.
June 3, 1961: Letter from Meredith Willson to Tammy Grimes.
December 9, 1963: Letter from Milton Kramer of Frank Music Corp to Willson.
Morris, *The Unsinkable Mrs. Brown*, undated script, "third version," dated 2-8-57 to 2-9-58, box 21, folder 1. (L1)
Morris, *The Unsinkable Mrs. Brown*, undated script, second draft, undated, box 21, folder 2. (L2)
Morris, *The Unsinkable Mrs. Brown*, undated script, second draft, undated, box 21, folder 3. (L2)
Morris, *The Unsinkable Mrs. Brown*, undated script, second draft, undated, box 21, folder 4. (L2)
The Unsinkable Mrs. Brown, draft piano-vocal score (copyist's).

Wisconsin Historical Society: Dore Schary Papers
Memo from Dore Schary to "Those concerned with THE UNSINKABLE MOLLY BROWN," dated November 3, 1960.

Music Sources
Juilliard School of Music
"Belly Up to the Bar, Boys," copyist's piano-vocal score.
"I've A'ready Started In," copyist's piano-vocal score; typed lyric sheet dated December 8, 1959, with holograph annotations.
"I'll Never Say No," holograph piano-vocal score; copyist's piano-vocal score.
"My Big Brass Bed," copyist's piano-vocal scores (two versions), titled "The Big Brass Bed"; typed lyric sheet with holograph annotations (originally dated December 17, 1959, marked "correct" as of October 25, 1960).

"The Denver Police," copyist's piano-vocal score.

"Beautiful People of Denver," holograph piano-vocal score; holograph lyric sheets.

"Are You Sure?", copyist's vocal scores (three versions).

"Happy Birthday, Mrs. J. J. Brown," copyist's vocal scores (two versions).

"Bon Jour," two holograph piano-vocal scores; two copyist's piano-vocal scores.

"Chick-a-Pen," holograph piano-vocal score; copyist's piano-vocal score.

"Leadville Johnny Brown (Soliloquy)", copyist's score for earlier version (trunk song?) titled "I Could Never Say 'Good-Bye' to You Again."

"Colorado, My Home," holograph piano-vocal score; holograph piano-vocal score for "Reprise Finale" version; typed lyric sheet with holograph annotations, dated October 17, 1960.

"He's My Friend," holograph piano-vocal score; copyist's piano-vocal scores (two copies); published song sheet (piano-vocal).

"Tomorrow," piano-vocal holographs, two versions (one a duet); copyist's score for Prince DeLong's tango version.

"Dignity," holograph piano-vocal score; copyist's piano-vocal score.

Great American Songbook Foundation

"I Ain't Down Yet," copyist score marked "Final Revision" and dated November 11, 1959; copyist score for Finale Act 1 duet version for Molly/Johnny (marked "one town down") with holograph annotations and an added counterpoint for Johnny; holograph rhythmic sketch; holograph trio/piano-vocal arrangement; holograph lyric sketches and piano-vocal sketches for initial version titled "Tuckered."

"Belly Up to the Bar, Boys," holograph piano-vocal score; typed lyric sheet dated November 27, 1959, with holograph annotations.

"I've A'ready Started In," holograph piano-vocal scores (three versions, one titled "My Baby"); copyist's piano-vocal score.

"I'll Never Say No," holograph piano-vocal score for "extension" section; copyist score for duet version with "Brass Bed;" holograph sketch/fragment.

"My Big Brass Bed," holograph piano-vocal score; copyist scores for solo version and duet version with "I'll Never Say No"; typed lyric sheet dated December 16, 1959 ("The Big Brass Bed") with holograph annotations.

"The Denver Police," holograph piano-vocal score.

"Beautiful People of Denver," copyist's piano-vocal score dated October 3, 1960; copyist's piano-vocal score, "Device and Trickery" version sung by Doc Myerbeer.

"Are You Sure?," copyist's vocal scores (three versions).

"Bon Jour," copyist score marked "36" with holograph annotations; holograph piano-vocal score.

"If I Knew," holograph piano-vocal scores, two versions; holograph piano-vocal for cut reprise titled "Then I'd Know"; holograph barbershop quartet arrangement for The Buffalo Bills, originally written for *The Music Man*.

"Chick-a-Pen," holograph piano-vocal score of brief reprise/bridge into Act 2 Denver party scene with vocal for Molly.

"Keep-A-Hoppin'," holograph piano-vocal score titled "Hop-a-long Peter"; holograph piano-vocal score for "new intro"' holograph piano score for "After Radio Barrell," underscoring based on this melody, marked "New 15A: Replaced old 15A Robber Music I, II, III) with this."

"Leadville Johnny Brown (Soliloquy)," holograph piano-vocal score.

"Colorado, My Home," five holograph piano-vocal scores plus reprise.

"The Wonderful Plan," copyist's piano-vocal scores for solo (Shamus) and duet (Shamus/Molly) *Molly Brown* versions of song.

"One Day at a Time," holograph piano-vocal score and holograph sketch; copyist's piano-vocal score for Molly's version, two copies (one dated August 16, 1960, the other undated) with holograph annotations; typed lyric sheet dated January 22, 1960, with holograph annotations; copyist's piano-vocal score for Johnny's reprise.

"Another Big Strike/Extra—Extra," copyist's piano-vocal score with holograph annotations; alternative copyist's score headed "Extra-Extra (New)" dated October 24, 1960; alternative titled "Read the Label on the Bottle/Get Away Boys, You Bother Me," copyist's piano-vocal score with extensive holograph amendments.

"The Ambassador's Polka," holograph piano-vocal scores (two versions); copyist's piano-vocal score.

Here's Love
Production documents, scripts, and correspondence
Great American Songbook Foundation:

November 28, 1961: Untitled typed synopsis (twenty-eight points), eight pages.

November 29, 1961: "The Trial," three-page typed synopsis.

January 2, 1962: Invoice from Radio Recorders to Meredith Willson.

February 3, 5, and 18, 1962: Invoices from Norman Bartold to Meredith Willson.

April 4, 1962: Untitled character description of Fred Gaily, marked "LOVE, LOVE, LOVE."

April 5, 1962: Untitled character description of Fred Gaily.

April 5, 1962: Typed fragment (relates to Fred Gaily), untitled.

April 23, 1962: Synopsis of "Love, Love, Love."

May 21, 1962: "Love, Love, Love," lyric sheets with holograph annotations.

June 15, 1962: Script fragments: pages marked 1-9-41 and 1-9-42.

August 10, 1962: Telegram from Janis Paige to Jules Sharr.

September 12, 1962: Untitled list of notes.

October 15, 1962: Letter from Stuart Ostrow to Meredith Willson.

October 22, 1962: Telegram from Meredith Willson to Michael Kidd.

November 7, 1962: Letter of from Stuart Ostrow to Meredith Willson.

November 12, 1962: Correspondence between Ostrow, Willson, Jewison, and Michael Shurtleff (casting agent).

August 13, 1963: Letter from Milton Kramer to Meredith Willson.

1491
Production documents, scripts, and correspondence
Great American Songbook Foundation:

March 5 and 8, 1965: list of characters

March 8, 1965: Willson's draft Shakespearean Prologue (discarded)

March 10, 1965: Willson's 5-page outline

March 16, 1965: Letter from Willson to Milton Kramer; includes cast of characters and the text of the prologue (March 8, 1965)

October 6, 1965: Letter from Richard Morris to Willson

December 27, 1965: Letter from Ed Ainsworth to Willson

April 19, 1966: Draft outline and script excerpt by Willson

May 20, 1966: Letter from Willson to Kermit Bloomgarden

May 27, 1966: Letter from Kermit Bloomgarden to Willson

June 6, 1966: Letter from Willson to Kermit Bloomgarden

June 21, 1966: Letter from Frank Loesser to Willson

June 27, 1966: Letter from Meredith Willson to Frank Loesser

June 30, 1966: Letter from Willson's secretary to Kermit Bloomgarden

July 20, 1966: Letter from Frank Loesser to Willson

August 2, 1966: Memo from Frank Loesser Affiliates (Allen B Whitehead) to Frank Loesser

August 5, 1966: Letter from Frank Loesser to Willson

August 15, 1966: Draft letter to Jerry Talbot from Frank Loesser Associates

August 29, 1966: Handwritten letter from Ed Ainsworth to Willson

September 12, 1966: Letter from Allen Whitehead to Frank Loesser

September 13, 1966: Letter from Frank Loesser to Allen Whitehead and Milton Kramer

September 14, 1966: Letter from Frank Loesser to Meredith Willson

September 19, 1966: Letter from Willson to Frank Loesser

October 5, 1966: Press release announcing *1491* for 67–68 season

November 17, 1966: Letter from Ed Lester to Willson

February 25, 1967: Telegram from Ed Lester to Willson

April 9, 1967: Letter from Ed Lester to Meredith Willson

June 23, 1967: Handwritten letter from Ed Ainsworth to Willson

July 8, 1967: Handwritten letter from Ed Ainsworth to Willson

July 23, 1967: Telegram from Willson to Katie Ainsworth

August 21, 1967: Handwritten letter from Ed Ainsworth to Willson

September 11, 1967: Letter from Eric Shepard to Ed Lester

September 12, 1967: Letter from Ed Lester to Shepard

September 21, 1967: Letter from William Morris Agency to Abe Lastfogel

October 9, 1967: Letter from Abe Folger to Willson

October 24, 1967: Memo from Abe Fogel to Willson

January 5, 1968: Letter from Ainsworth to Willson

March 8, 1968: List of musical numbers from a script (no script!)

April 30, 1968: Script excerpt

c. May 1968: undated document, possibly by Ed Lester or Richard Morris, of "Arresting Moments" from *1491*

June 17, 1968: Obituary of Ed Ainsworth from the *Los Angeles Times*

June 24, 1968: Letter from Katie Ainsworth to the Willsons

July 1, 1968: Letter from Meredith Willson to Elizabeth Allen

July 17, 1968: Letter from Milton Kramer to Willson

October 28, 1968: Letter from Katie Ainsworth's lawyer to Willson

November 21, 1968: Letter from Ed Lester to Meredith Willson

November 22, 1968: Letter from Meredith Willson to Ed Lester

November 25, 1968: Letter from Ed Lester to Meredith Willson

December 13, 1968: Ed Lester's notes on "Revised First Script"

January 20, 1969: "A Look at Staging and Revision of Scenes and Characters in *1491*" by Richard Morris

January 28, 1969: Letter from Katie Ainsworth to Meredith Willson

February 3, 1969: Letter from Willson to Katie Ainsworth

February 26, 1969: Letter from Willson to Ed Lester

March 4, 1969: Handwritten letter from Willson to Sergio Franchi

March 17, 1969: Letter from Peg (Willson's secretary) to Richard Morris

April 4, 1969: Letter from Milton Kramer to Ed Lester

May 6, 1969: Letter from Ed Lester to Willson

May 10, 1969: Typed lyric for "Near But Never Too Near"

May 18, 1969: Notes of phone conversations between Willson and Richard Morris

June 25, 1969: Staff List and Rehearsal Schedule and "Old" list of Musical Numbers

July 5, 1969: Letter from Richard Morris to Willson

September 3, 1969: Statement from Lester to the *1491* company

September 10, 1969: Letter from Ed Lester to Willson

September 19, 1969: Letter from Lester to Willson

September 24, 1969: Letter from Ed Lester to Willson

October 18, 1969: Willson's notes on a matinee and separate notes sent to Lester about the music

October 21, 1969: Letter from Ed Lester to Willson

October 22, 1969: Letter from Ed Lester to Willson

October 22, 1969: Letter from Willson to Ed Lester; includes enclosure from a history book about Columbus

October 24, 1969: Letter from Lester to Willson

November 13, 1969: Willson's Final Notes on LA performance of *1491*

Music Sources

Great American Songbook Foundation

Complete piano-conductor score, heavily annotated

"Esteban's the Man You Have to Know," holograph (labeled "Send to Dick!")

First Act Finale: "The Queen and the Sailor," piano-conductor score

"Every Woman Is a Queen," holograph and piano-conductor score

"Ay, Would You Like to Buy an Island?"—Old Title of "Get a Map," sketch, onion skin, lyrics

"Get a Map," piano-conductor score

"1491," holograph sketch and piano-conductor score

"I For My Glory Land" Reprise (ann.) and "Glory Land Interlude," holograph and typed lyric sheet (ann. by Willson)

"Maybe It's Time," piano-conductor score

"It's Too Late," piano-conductor score

"Isabella Catholica," piano-conductor score

"I Did Steal The Map," piano-conductor score "Happy New Year," piano-conductor score

"First Footin'," holograph and sketches

"Silken Song," holograph sketches
"The Queen and the Sailor," piano-conductor score
"The Siege at Loha," piano-conductor score
"The Wonderful Plan," piano-conductor score
"Never Believe," piano-conductor score
"The Trastamara Rose," piano-conductor score
"Tio Paco," piano-conductor score
"What Does a Queen Have?," piano-conductor score
"Where There's a River," piano-conductor score
"Say It Over and Over," piano-conductor score "Why Not," holograph sketches and
    piano-conductor score
"Sail On"—Isabella Version, piano-conductor score
"Esteban's the Man You Have to Know," piano-vocal score
"Birthday (New 8/22)" and "Entrance of the Queen," piano-conductor score
"Genius," holograph sketches, typed lyrics with ann.
"Genius," Guitar solo + vocal line
"I'll Never Say I Love You," holograph score
"Please Don't Suggest That I Sing," piano-conductor score (ann.) and lyrics
"Lady," piano-conductor score
"Now I Know ('Old Copy')," piano-conductor score
"Please Don't You Stop," piano-conductor score
"Pretty Girl (two versions)," piano-conductor score

Other Projects
Great American Songbook Foundation
June 16, 1929: Letter from John Willson to Willson, box 2, folder 27
box 42, folder 4
October 15, 1971: *Jack London, Sailor on Horseback*—outline fragments
Undated: *Katarina*, outline/synopsis
Jabberwock, transcription of conversation with Lawrence and Lee, 1973
May 25, 1961: *The Understudy*, draft synopsis, box 34, folder 3.

The Music Man Museum, Mason City
November 19, 1971: Letter from Willson to Hank Ketcham.
December 15, 1971: Letter from Hank Ketcham to Willson
December 23, 1971: Letter from Willson to Hank Ketcham
February 18, 1972: Letter from Hank Ketcham to Willson
December 31, 1972: Letter from Hank Ketcham to Willson
February 5, 1973, from Willson to Hank Ketcham
March 15, 1976: Outline by Bob Saylor, *The Music Kid*.
October 11, 1976: Letter from Willson to Hank Ketcham
October 27, 1976: Letter from Hank Ketcham to Willson

Published Sources
Anon. "Meredith Willson," biography, on reverse of piano arrangement of Meredith
    Willson, *O.O. McIntyre Suite* (New York: Robbins Music Corporation, 1934).

Anon. "Meredith Willson's New Music Lauded in Detroit." Associated Press report, July 30, 1963 (publication unknown).

Anon. "Music: Music Man's Lady." *TIME*, September 12, 1960.

Anon. "'Music Man." *Los Angeles Times*, July 31, 1961, O9.

Anon. "'Music Man' Willson Tells of 'Here's Love.'" *News Sentinel*, June 15, 1963.

Anon. "Report 20th Has Inside Track on '34th St.' Willson is Tuning for B'way." *Variety*, November 29, 1961, 1.

Anon. "Stage Notes." *Los Angeles Times*, November 5, 1969, 12.

Anon. "'Unsinkable Molly Brown' Opens Nov. 3." *Rocky Mountain News*, April 17, 1960.

Anon. "Unsinkable Mrs. Brown." *New York Times*, March 8, 1960.

Anon. "Van Johnson Leaving The Music Man." *The Times*, February 17, 1962, 4.

Anon. "Willson Prepares New Musical, 'Understudy.'" *Los Angeles Examiner*, September 30, 1961.

Austin, Valerie A. *The Orchestral Works of Meredith Willson*. Diss, University of Florida, 2008.

Barnard, Ken. "I'm a Fellow Who Writes Marches." *Detroit Free Press*, July 14, 1963.

Blevins, Winfred. "Desperate Situation in '1491'." *Los Angeles Herald-Examiner*, September 4, 1969.

Block, Geoffrey. "The Broadway Canon from *Show Boat* to *West Side Story* and the European Operatic Ideal." *Journal of Musicology* 11, no. 4 (Autumn 1993): 525–44.

Block, Geoffrey. *Enchanted Evenings: The Broadway Musical from "Show Boat" to Sondheim and Lloyd Webber*. 2nd ed. New York: Oxford University Press, 2009.

Bloom, Ken. *American Song*, Vol. 1. New York: Schirmer, 1996.

Bracker, Milton. "Army Fires a Jupiter Missile." *New York Times*, December 19, 1957, 1.

Brantley, Ben. "Rogue Is Free." *New York Times*, April 28, 2000, E1.

Brown, Vera. "Our Times." *Detroit Times*, October 22, 1959.

Calta, Louis. "Woman Conducts 'Music Man' Today." *New York Times*, July 4, 1960, 8.

Carmody, Jay. "Willson–Santa Claus Merger a Natural." *The Evening Star*, August 28, 1963, B14.

Christiansen, Richard. "Dick Van Dyke Leads the Big Musical Parade into Arie Crown." *Chicago Tribune*, May 11, 1980, D4.

Colby, Frank. "What Is the Irigin?" *Los Angeles Times*, March 17, 1949, A5.

Cook, Louis. "Here's Love a Happy Package." *Detroit Free Press*, July 31, 1963, 4B and 7B.

Cox, Jim. *Sold On Radio: Advertisers in the Golden Age of Broadcasting*. Jefferson, NC: McFarland, 2008.

Crowther, Bosley. "A Fanciful Music Man." *New York Times*, September 2, 1962, 61.

Crowther, Bosley. "Screen: Preston Stars in 'Music Man." *New York Times*, August 24, 1962, 14.

Dams, Val. "All in One Basket." *New York Times*, October 2, 1955, BR7

da Silva Moraes, Ramon. "The Flutists of the John Philip Sousa's Band: A Study of the Flute Section and Soloists." Doctoral diss., University of Southern Mississippi, May 2018 (ProQuest 10786479).

Davies, Valentine. *Miracle on 34th Street*. New York: Harcourt, Brace and Co., 1947.

Doty, Robert C. "U.S. Alters Stand." *New York Times*, December 19, 1957, 1.

Duprey, Richard A. "Impish Tammy Grimes Captivates Audience in 'Molly Brown' Role." *Catholic Standard and Times*, September 30, 1960.

Faber, Charles. "Willson's Spectacular '1491' Final Event of CLO Season." *Hollywood Citizen-News*, September 4, 1969.

Freeman, Donald. "A Shaky Course for New Musical." *San Diego Union*, September 6, 1969, D4.

Frisch, Walter. *Over the Rainbow*. New York: Oxford University Press, 2017.

Funke, Lewis. "Gossip of the Rialto." *New York Times*, January 13, 1957, X1.

Gaghan, Jerry. "Jolly Yule Musical 'Here's Love' Now at Shubert." *Philadelphia Daily News*, September 18, 1963, 39.

Gaver, Jack. "'Music Man' Willson Prepares New Show." *Philadelphia Inquirer*, August 28, 1960.

Gebert, Armand. "Second Look at 'Here's Love.'" *Detroit News*, August 16, 1963, 22.

Gelb, Arthur. "Music Man Talks about 'Music Man.'" *New York Times*, October 19, 1959, 36.

Glenn, Larry. "'Music Man' Reprised." *New York Times*, August 6, 1961, X5.

Guthmann, Edward. "Broderick's Tepid Toot in 'Music Man.'" *San Francisco Chronicle*, February 14, 2003.

Hamm, Charles. *Irving Berlin: Songs from the Melting Pot, 1907–14*. New York and Oxford: Oxford University Press, 1997.

Handler, M. S. "Germans Voice Opposition to Taking U.S. Weapons." *New York Times*, December 19, 1957, 1.

Harford, Margaret. "Willson Convinced Columbus Is the End." *Denver Post*, September 2, 1969, 2.

Hoffman, Warren. *The Great White Way: Race and the Broadway Musical*. New Brunswick, NJ: Rutgers University Press, 2014.

Holden, Stephen. "City Opera: 'Music Man.'" *New York Times*, March 3, 1988, C28.

Hopper, Hedda. "Hedda Put in Middle on 'Music Man' Role." *Chicago Tribune*, May 25, 1962, B18.

Hopper, Hedda. "Mason City Goes All Out to Launch 'Music Man.'" *Chicago Daily Tribune*, B2.

Hopper, Hedda. "Meredith's Homecoming Was Rouser." *Washington Times*, B5.

Huisking, Charlie. "Writer Says 'The Music Man' Is a True Story." *Herald-Tribune Reporter*, u.d.

Hutcheon, Linda. *A Theory of Adaptation*. New York: Routledge, 2006.

Jewison, Norman. *This Terrible Business Has Been Good to Me*. New York: St. Martin's Press, 2005.

Jones, John Bush. *The Songs That Fought the War: Popular Music and the Home Front, 1939–1945*. Hanover, NH: University Press of New England, 2006.

Kerr, Walter. "'Music Man' Back with Van Dyke." *New York Times*, June 6, 1980, C3.

Knickerbocker, Paine. "A Big Musical about Columbus." *San Francisco Chronicle*, October 30, 1969, 46.

Little, Stuart. "'Unsinkable Molly Brown Rehearses with Full Cast." *New York Herald Tribune*, August 25, 1960.

Marks, Peter. "They've Got Memories Right Here in Mason City." *New York Times*, February 27, 2000, AR7.

McHugh, Dominic. *Loverly: The Life and Times of "My Fair Lady."* New York: Oxford University Press, 2012.

Middleton, Drew. "West to Act Soon." *New York Times*, December 19, 1957, 1.

Miller, Scott. *Deconstructing Harold Hill.* Portsmouth, NH: Heinemann, 2000.

Millstein, Gilbert. "Mildly Baffling: Who Did What to Fedalia? By Meredith Willson." *New York Times*, February 10, 1952, 242.

Mordden, Ethan. *Anything Goes.* New York: Oxford University Press, 2014.

Mordden, Ethan. *Open a New Window: The Broadway Musical in the 1960s.* New York: St. Martin's Press, 2001.

Most, Andrea. *Making Americans: Jews and the Broadway Musical.* Cambridge, MA: Harvard University Press, 2004.

Most, Andrea. *Theatrical Liberalism: Jews and Popular Entertainment in America.* New York and London: New York University Press, 2013.

Nichols, Lewis. "Willson at Bat Again." *New York Times*, October 30, 1960.

Oates, Bill. *Meredith Willson: America's Music Man.* Bloomington, IN: Authorhouse, 2005.

Oja, Carol J. "*West Side Story* and *The Music Man*: Whiteness, Immigration, and Race in the US during the Late 1950s." *Studies in Musical Theatre* 3, no. 1 (2009): 13–30.

Ostrow, Stuart. *Present at the Creation, Leaping in the Dark and Going against the Grain.* New York: Applause, 2006.

Ristau, Helen. *Meredith Willson: River City's Music Man.* Mason City, IA: Larson Printing, 1995.

Robinson, Linda A. "The Day They Stopped the Mail in Mason City." In *The American Village in a Global Setting*, eds. Michael E. Connaughton and Suellen Rundquist. Newcastle: Cambridge Scholars, 2007.

Rodosthenous, George, ed. *The Disney Musical on Stage and Screen.* London: Methuen, 2017.

Rosen, Jody. "The American Revolutionary." *New York Times*, July 8, 2015.

Scheuer, Philip K. "'Music Man' Hits Key of G—Grand, Gaudy, Gorgeous." *Los Angeles Times*, July 8, 1962, M9.

Sherman, Gene. "Meredith Willson Has a New Musical." *Los Angeles Times*, February 9, 1960, Part III, 5.

Schier, Ernie. "'Unsinkable Molly Brown' Makes Musical Bow Here." *Evening Bulletin*, September 27, 1960, 67.

Simeone, Nigel. *West Side Story.* Farnham, UK: Ashgate, 2009.

Skipper, John C. *Meredith Willson: The Unsinkable Music Man.* Mason City, IA: Savas Publishing Company, 2000.

Solomon, Alisa. *Wonder of Wonders: A Cultural History of "Fiddler on the Roof."* New York: Picador, 2014.

Sondheim, Stephen. "From the Reader: What's Entertainment?" *New York Herald-Tribune*, date unknown (c. August 1963).

Sondheim, Stephen. *Look, I Made a Hat.* New York: Virgin Books, 2011.

Spargo, John Webster. "Hilarious Bits in Meredith Willson Essays." *Chicago Daily Tribune*, October 3, 1948, e4.

Sullivan, Dan. "Columbus Musical '1491' Launched at the Pavilion." *Los Angeles Times*, September 4, 1969.

Sullivan, Dan. "Dick Van Dyke in 'Music Man' at Pantages." *Los Angeles Times*, January 1, 1980, F1.

Suskin, Steven. *Show Tunes*. New York: Oxford University Press, 2010.

Tajiri, Larry. "Meredith Willson Writes Songs for 'Unsinkable Mrs. Brown.'" *Denver Post*, March 4, 1960, 34.

Tajiri, Larry. "Willson to Preview Colorado Songs from 'Molly Brown.'" *Denver Post*, April 2, 1960, 34.

Trent, James W. *Inventing the Feeble Mind: A History of Intellectual Disability in the United States*. New York: Oxford University Press, 2017.

Wate. "Legit Tryouts." *Daily Variety*, September 27, 1960, 1.

Waters. "Shows out of Town." *Variety*, September 28, 1960, 70.

Weber, Bruce. "TV Weekend: Bad Timing! Right Here in River City!" *New York Times*, February 14, 2003, E36.

Willens, Michele. "The Music Man, Bringing Broadway to the Screen." *New York Times*, February 16, 2003, AR28.

Willson, Meredith. *And There I Stood with My Piccolo*. Minneapolis and London: University of Minnesota Press, 2009.

Willson, Meredith. *But He Doesn't Know the Territory*. Minneapolis and London: University of Minnesota Press, 2009.

Willson, Meredith. *Eggs I Have Laid*. New York: Henry Holt and Company, 1955.

Willson, Meredith. "Evil Times," program essay, *Here's Love*, Fisher Theatre, Detroit, July 1963.

Willson, Meredith. *Who Did What to Fedalia?* New York: Doubleday, 1952.

Winchell, Joan. Untitled article in regular column, *Los Angeles Times*, May 31, 1960.

Winchell, Joan. "'Music Man' Boss Sets a Fast Beat." *Los Angeles Times*, September 4, 1961, C7.

Zolotow, Sam. "'Top Ten' Moved Up by Feuer, Martin." *New York Times*, February 10, 1956, 18.

Zolotow, Sam. "Willson Working on Second Effort." *New York Times*, June 4, 1959, 27.

Zolotow, Sam. "Schary Is Ousted as Chief at M-G-M." *New York Times*, November 29, 1956, 42.

CREDITS

• • •

INDEX

• • •